Call Me Joe

Don Otey

ISBN: 1723281697
ISBN- 9781723281693

Dedication

This novel is dedicated to my long-time friend Jim Caddigan. In our working days we were a dynamite team. Jim, you appreciate a good read. I hope this effort holds your attention.

Other Novels by Don Otey

Minerva's Net

Guild of Deceit

Dread and Breakfast

Tank Hill

Terror's Mask

Kiss the Panther

The American Joes

Then The Stillness

Lightning Bolt

Terror's Return

Another Bolt of Lightning

Patience or Revenge?

ACKNOWLEDGEMENT

As with everything I do in this life, I must acknowledge the light of my life. My dear Jo Ellen, you tolerate my passion for writing and make it all possible. To my bride of sixty years, **thank you, love.**

Chapter 1

Joe Whitley emerged from the northern Virginia office building of JW Industries into a cool misty rain. His aide called out to him and Joe turned just as a sharp crack pierced the air.

The distinguished looking gentleman moaned and slumped. Raymond Crane, the aide holding out Whitley's hat to him, shielded Joe with his body and caught his fall. Three security guards rapidly formed a protective circle as a second audible report was followed by the thud of an impact with the ground. The bodyguards drew their handguns and scanned in all directions. One of them, a large hulk of a man, barked into his Bluetooth mike.

"The man is down! Send medical aid to the entrance now." A dark stain spread across the fallen gentleman's suit front. Crane placed the hat on Joe's head against the quickening rainfall.

Joe looked up at his aide through foggy gray eyes and said, "Feels like a speeding semi just ran over me, Ray. Tell those sign wavers I'll hear them out later." His eyes closed as the company medical team arrived.

On this drizzly fall morning in 2000, Joe Whitley, fifty-five-year-old self-made businessman, had fallen short of this intended peacemaking goal. He had looked out his office window at a group of protesters holding signs proclaiming 'Unfair to Labor'. Whitley was a billionaire business owner but he was also very much a scrappy individualist who never shied away from a challenge. If these employees were upset he wanted to find out why and correct any wrong done to them. He would offer a civil conversation inside out of the rain with their leaders. Then something dropped him in his tracks and abruptly changed his plan.

Ray Crane and one of his security men named Roberts followed the medics and Jonas's gurney into the elevator. Crane told Roberts, "He was about to get drenched. He insisted his appointment could wait till he talked to the protesters. I grabbed his favorite hat, caught up and was about to hand it to him when this happened."

We can't be sure yet," Roberts said, "but the medic thinks a bullet tore through his chest. I called his doctor as soon as we got him indoors. He's losing a lot of blood."

The medics continued to minister to the wounded Joe and apply pressure to his wound. He opened his eyes and appeared to be saying something in a ragged whisper. Before Ray could lean close enough to hear him the man's eyes closed and he emitted a loan groan. His long lean frame went still. The elevator doors opened and they lost no time wheeling him into the JW emergency room.

* * *

Joe lay bleeding inside the medical area with an IV drip in his right arm. Doctor Samuel Greenlee, his personal physician, had insisted he add this emergency room at the headquarters building three years ago, and at last it was finally paying off. Whitley lay on the crisp white cover of the room's medical platform. Medical technicians scurried about while he drifted in and out of consciousness.

"Did you reach my doctor?" he asked weakly as the strength drained from his body.

Raymond Crane loomed over Joe and answered, "Doctor should be here any minute."

The EMT gave him a reassuring smile and said, "You're doing fine, sir. Just relax."

Then Joe heard him whisper to his teammate, "I think the bleeding finally stopped."

Yeah, right, Joe thought. *I'm probably worse than*

they're letting on. The coppery smell of fresh blood concerned him, even more so now that he realized it was his own. He couldn't pinpoint the source of his anguish, but something had set his chest on fire. It hurt like some evil sadist was boring a hole in his front with a dull drill. Despite the EMT's words, this was one of the few times during his hectic fifty five years that Joe had been genuinely scared.

Whitley closed his eyes and tried to concentrate on anything but the sharp pain. *They're working on my upper chest. A heart attack wouldn't cause me to bleed. Was I stabbed? That close to my heart? Oh god, what's happening?* He tried to concentrate, to second guess what they weren't telling him. Then the room slipped away.

Joe stirred and opened his eyes sometime later. There was still a flurry of activity around him and Doc Sam's comforting voice issued instructions to whoever was assisting him. He dimly saw Doc's face but there was a look of concern. Joe asked, "What's going on, Sam? How bad is it? And don't try to smoke me."

The doctor answered, "If you follow my orders, Joe, you should be good as new in a few days. You have a clean through and through wound. I suspect it was a rifle shot from some distance. Everything is under control. Just save your energy and let me look after you."

"Shot? What?" He mulled that over and tried to fathom why anyone would want him dead. *I'm not a violent man*, he reasoned. *I can count my enemies on one hand, and they're business rivals I've bested fair and square.*

Whitley let his mind drift back. He'd been an orphan since the age of six, and his earliest memories were of the church-run children's home where he'd lived through his high school years. That was a strict upbringing involving regular chores and responsibilities, labor on the home's farm to earn his keep, and hard study to keep himself at the top of his class in school. Scholarships and after-hours work saw him through college with a business degree. Joe drove himself relentlessly to the top and now owned major shares in multiple companies in fields as diverse as retail merchandising, trucking and building construction. He had always tried to deal with people on the basis of the strong principles the orphans' home had drilled into him. That's the only way he knew to operate. Why would he be anyone's target?

Doctor Greenlee admonished, "You're not an easy patient to hold down, Joe. I'm checking you into Fairfax Hospital overnight. If you do well, we'll talk about releasing you tomorrow for some home rest. I don't want any arguments."

Few people called him Joe. The doctor who had tended to him for more than twenty years was one of them; the others were his best friends George Adams, Hiro Kato and Carlos Estrada. George's kids called him Uncle Joe. While he drifted in a painful half-awareness, Joe's mind turned to George and how he would react to this incident. Then he thought, *Someone, in a frightful instant, stripped me bare and reduced old Joe W. to a terrified youngster. There's so much more I want to do in this life, wonderful plans I've kept putting off thinking I was invulnerable. Now all that may never happen.*

Chapter 2

"The doctor ordered him to rest, gentlemen," the head nurse told the two visitors. "I know Mister Whitley insisted on seeing his friend now, but please keep the visit short."

Raymond Crane nodded and escorted George Adams past security into a private suite. George, hands down Joe's closest friend and most trusted confidant, dominated the room with his six-foot-two, 240-pound frame. They filed quietly into the room and hesitated, waiting for Joe to open his eyes and acknowledge them from across the room.

Joe finally realized they were there and chuckled. "Oh, come on, fellows. Don't look so serious. It'll take a lot more than this to do in old Joe W."

He was propped up in the hospital bed sporting a wide smile. He made a strange picture with his left shoulder bandaged and his favorite gray homburg perched atop his head. George Adams couldn't resist laughing Then he said, "We need to tawk, Joe. Sumpins scroowie here. Last time I checked de shirt went on before de hat. You anxious to leave?"

"Listen to you, George. Hell, you're more shook than I am about this. I can tell when you get riled and start givin' me your Noo Yawk tawk."

Adams laughed. "Best speech coaches available an' I forget when I get rattled."

"Just jerking your chain, pal. Don't need you getting all flustered. And yes, you're damned tootin' I'm ready to leave, but the doctor says I have to stay here under observation tonight. Thanks for coming."

"Anything for you, Joe. You know that."

Ray left and George settled into the chair at the side of the bed. Joe placed his hat on the nightstand, stroking it with his fingertips. "Little beauty saved my life a couple hours ago. If I hadn't turned to take this hat the first shot would have hit me square on. Next time you saw me I'd have been made up a lot better, but my toes would be pointed straight up."

Once again, Joe had turned to his best friend to put a measure of order into what had happened to him today. Their steadfast friendship was the strongest connection in the life of the owner of JW Industries. Joe, a bachelor, did not remember his parents. He had adopted as his siblings the kids at the orphanage where he spent most of his first eighteen years. Fifteen years ago, he and George met and instantly bonded like brothers. By then both of them were making waves in their chosen fields of business and becoming wealthy men.

George, three years junior to Joe, was the product of a family that had scrambled for a living in New York City. His size belied George's mild nature, but it helped keep him out of danger. His life transformed when he went off to college on scholarship and began an imminently successful and profitable career in the pharmaceuticals industry. Joe viewed him as the brother he'd always wanted and felt that George and Evaline Adams and their two children were as close as he would ever come to having a family. When, early on, Joe referred to George as African-American, Adams had quickly corrected him. *"Got no hyphen in my heritage, Joe. Last time I checked I was a hundred percent American, Noo Yawk born an' raised. Just happens I'm black and damn proud of it."*

Adams had ignored his crushing schedule today to rush in from his suburban Maryland office when Joe asked to see him. George insisted on knowing all about the injury before they went on.

"Tell me what's up here, Joe."

"Tell you what I know, Georgie. Somebody must have a big problem with me that he tried to solve with a bullet. If it had struck an inch or so lower I wouldn't be telling you about it. As it is, I'm facing time lying flat."

"Jeez, oh flip. How'd a lovable guy like you tick off somebody that bad? Any clue who did dis to you?"

"I have a strong hunch who *ordered* it done, George, but I can't tell anybody yet, not even you."

"You said there was a favor you wanted," George began. "Ax and it's done."

"A few hours ago, I was sailing along fat and sassy, George, and then the whole world nearly collapsed on me. For a while I was sure today was my last day on earth."

"Sassy maybe, but no way I'd call a scrawny six-three toothpick fat. As much soul food as I've fed you on de side, I still have a good seventy pounds on you."

"That's the other reason I wanted you here, pal. I'm not prone to depression, but for a while there I was pretty down. Needed a couple of your patented Adams wisecracks to bring me around."

"So? The favor?"

"I'll be out of here after lunch tomorrow. Can you get Hiro and Carlos here for a session at my place tomorrow? I know it's a lot to ask of you busy guys on such short notice, but . . ."

George interrupted with, "I already called them on the way down here. They'd be torqued if you didn't let 'em help."

"Thanks. The past few hours have been a life-changing experience for me. It made me think about all the things I want to do before I turn loose of this questionable life. Have you ever stopped to think, George, what are the most important challenges facing the country that's been so good to us? More to the point, have you ever thought about what four lucky rich guys like us could do about those problems if we joined forces? I've devised a plan, but before I say any more, I want you to tell me whether it makes sense."

"Hiro called me back. Said he'd be wheels up from LA on his jet by four in the morning. Carlos said tell you to hang tight and he'd see you tomorrow. I'll get 'em gathered up at your place by noon. How 'bout a clue what this is all about?"

"Give me overnight, George, to get it all sorted out in my mind. This is important to me, so I want to say it right the first time."

"That's good enough for me, Joe."

Chapter 3

Tuesday morning the newspapers heralded: "Billionaire Businessman Shot by Assassin." Stories released nationwide related how Joe Whitley, the power behind JW Industries and one of the country's richest men, was in the hospital hanging onto his life after a sniper's bullet felled him. Fortunately, the word had leaked out late in the day, so the stories appeared primarily back in the business pages. Joe detested cheap, overblown publicity. He read the dire pronouncements while he nibbled on breakfast in his hospital room, laughed out loud and issued a two-word assessment: "Horse manure. You and me, Mark Twain. They tried to write both of us off prematurely."

So, by now whoever ordered the hit on me—and I have a good idea who that was—thinks old Joe is dangling on the edge of oblivion. Good! That gives me time to prepare before the truth slips out. I'll outsmart my foes yet. But this whole episode is my wakeup call to make plans for my future, even if it turns out to be a short one.

Whitley thought about the verbal challenge he would pose to George and the others. He picked up a tablet and pencil and began to jot down what he viewed as America's most pressing problems. *That sniper did me a favor,* he thought. *He made me face the inevitable. Whether it happens at the hands of an assassin or I simply burn out from my frantic, overactive life, I'm closing in on my twilight years. What can I leave behind as evidence I was ever here?*

He was totally absorbed when his long-time friend Sam Greenlee stopped in to check on him. Sam also had been his personal physician for more than two decades.

“How’s your outlook on the world today, Mister Whitley?” Greenlee asked and began to check Joe’s charts and inspect his bandage.

Joe looked around as if searching for a third person in the room. Then he stared back at Doctor Greenlee and asked, “Oh, were you talking to me? Thought maybe somebody had finally found the daddy I looked for most of my life. Didn’t we agree a long time ago you and I were just Joe and Sam to each other?”

“Guess that answers my question. Didn’t take you long to get your spunky charm back, did it? A lot of folks only see you as a big, important man. I happen to know the largest part of you is a feisty, determined youngster. Ready to go home?”

“I thought you’d never ask, Sam. Got some important business on tap today.”

“Now, that could be a problem. The forensics folks tell me your security people recovered two slugs imbedded in the ground outside the front entrance of the JW Building. Looks like a professional sniper could have fired them from an upper floor of the building facing yours. Remember, one of those nasty projectiles has your DNA on it. You’re a lucky man, so don’t push the envelope. I’ll have you discharged after lunch. Promise me you’ll stay home till you regain some strength.”

“Okay, I understand. The hospital gets another day’s pay but tell them to keep my lunch. I’ll be sharing that at home with my friends. They’re coming for a get together, three of my closest pals to help me reset my thinking. No heavy work today, doc.”

“Just don’t crowd your luck. Give yourself a well-deserved vacation.”

Joe smiled and nodded. Both of them knew that his nature was to do what he damned well pleased, doctor’s orders or not.

An hour after noon Joe, his bandaged shoulder concealed by a fresh silk shirt and his gray homburg perched firmly astride his noggin, emerged from Fairfax Hospital. At Raymond Crane’s insistence, they were using a back entrance. Two of his security men whisked him quickly to a cream-colored sedan.

“Understand, Ray, I’m humoring you,” he said as he settled into the back seat. “Can’t let those SOBs get the idea they’re intimidating me. I expect to outlive most of them by a damn sight. Joe W’s too ornery to go away easy.”

He peered out the window at a day that looked world better than the rainy Monday that had nearly ruined his week. Skies were clear and the sun beamed down on a man happy to be alive. There was a new feeling of purpose in his bones, the desire to put his life in order and make long range plans.

Then the blazing sun hid briefly behind a big, puffy cloud and the blue sky darkened for a long moment. Joe felt an involuntary shudder pass through him as he understood that, not unlike the sudden occlusion of the sun, his charmed life could be snuffed out in an instant.

But his trusted friends were on their way. This was definitely a day for action.

Chapter 4

Three men arrived minutes apart at Joe Whitley's Loudoun County home in the early afternoon. A staff member greeted them and ushered each arrival into the understated elegance of the sitting room. Warm reunions took place amid hugs and back slaps. These were scions of industry, normally viewed in public on their best measured and sedate behavior. But today they were behaving unashamedly like long separated family members.

George Adams, whose alarming calls had summoned the others to the Watkins home, lowered his china coffee cup and posed a question, "How long has it been? Three months? Four?"

Hiroshi (Hiro) Kato answered, "Way too long. More like six months. I've really missed you fellows. Just wish this didn't have to happen to get us together." At 48, Hiro had grown up on the West Coast as a third generation American of Japanese descent. Kato, short in stature at five-eight on a 140-pound structure, spent considerable time staying fit. Beneath his polite, soft-spoken exterior lurked the hard body of a black belt martial artist. His mental acuity had carried him to success and a fortune during the electronics revolution. He was CEO and Chairman of the Board of the international electronics conglomerate K-Tronics. Hiro's flight from Los Angeles had landed thirty minutes ago at Dulles Airport.

Carlos Estrada agreed. "Tough way for us to be yanked up. We've all been up to our ears in bidness. This news downright kicked me in the britches. I been hyperventilatin' all the way here." Carlos, 47, brought to their group the dark Hispanic good looks of a man considerably younger. He'd flown in from Dallas this morning. Carlos, the product of immigrant parents, had built from scratch Carl's Foods, one of the largest grocery chains in the country.

George chuckled. "What's so funny, Adams?" Hiro asked.

"This whole episode scares the wits out of me. Sorry, guys. I'm not making light of what's happened. Hell, Joe Whitley is my bro. Just struck me funny how much money and influence is gathered up in this room. Old Joe's one of the few guys in the country that's made more bucks than we've each stumbled into, but we didn't think twice about showing up when he axed."

As they waited for Joe to appear from upstairs, George, Hiro and Carlos regarded each other impatiently.

Finally, George voiced what they were all no doubt thinking. "Don't know about youze guys, but I didn't sleep much last night. Joe's experience set me to pondering. I believe this shooting was an epiphany for him. Don't be surprised if he sounds down, maybe maudlin when we see him. Appreciate you guys rallying like this. I know you're both busier than one-armed fry cooks."

Had a short night myself," Hiro echoed. "Couldn't sleep a wink on the plane, but I wasn't about to miss seeing everybody. Wonder what it is Joe has on his mind?"

"Well," said Carlos, "whatever he's upset about, I learned a spell ago to listen up when he speaks. Let's let him git it said first. See, I think we're gittin' carried away."

George tried to explain. "I gather this near-death experience prompted him to think back over his life. Sounded like he has some unfinished business he wants to attend to."

He accepted a coffee refill and continued. "It was something he axed me that played on my mind; kept me bouncing around all night. His words made me think about the future and how good life has been to me. As I told both youze by phone last night, he wanted each of us to write down a list of what we consider America's biggest problems."

"What was it he ax … uh, said?" Hiro questioned.

"He reminded me we're powerful men and we've earned what we have honestly. Now the question is what we're willing to give back. As he put it, what's our legacy gonna be?"

"So that's why we're here?" Hiro asked.

"That and to help answer another heavy question he laid on me," George replied. "He asked what I thought were de woist problems de country faced. That made me wonder if he was playing with some grand plan, maybe pooling resources to take on problems that call for special attention. His plans, grand or otherwise, always get my attention. Joe has a special knack for success."

Just as he finished Joe greeted them from the sitting room entrance.

"My, my, gents. Look at those serious faces! You look like you're at a funeral. I'm the one that skirted the big sleep. As today's kids would put it, old Joe W. cheated the grim freakin' reaper, and this morning I feel like a new man. Loosen up. Let's have lunch and a few laughs. We can get down to business later."

"Fine by me, Joe," George answered, delighted at his pal's mood. "You look mighty bright and upright for a man the mornin' news sheets reported was knockin' on death's door."

Joe gave them a broad grin. "What's that old expression? I'm shickled titless just to be standing. One of my favorite philosophers, Woody Allen, once said, 'It's not that I'm afraid to die. I just don't want to be there when it happens.' I've asked my wonderful cook Molly to prepare something special for lunch today, and she never disappoints. Shall we?" He motioned in the direction of the verandah and led the way.

"Didja wanta tell Hiro and Carlos what happened?" George asked.

Joe sat down and grimaced uncomfortably. "If you insist. Took a slug in my shoulder is what happened. Doc tells me it should heal okay. It's what *didn't* take place that's important. I didn't end up face down as some pretty powerful interests hoped I would. What they don't know is that I'm onto them. Their time is coming. The main reason I asked you all here is I have a proposal to make. Your answers could affect the future of our country in a way that four poor but very lucky kids could not have imagined a couple decades ago."

Hiro scanned the faces of the others then looked back at Joe who wore a look of resolution. It was a look he knew well, the one Hiro called Whitley's bull dog face. He prompted Joe. "I heard there was a labor protest at your headquarters. Did one of those sign carriers try to do you in?"

Joe changed positions and winced with the pain in his shoulder. "Wasn't any of them. Doc says my security guys dug a couple of slugs out of the ground. They looked to be from a sniper rifle. One of those beauties went through me. Somebody fired it from a distance, probably an upper floor of a nearby building. My folks are all over looking for clues."

"I just assumed" … Kato said, but Joe cut him short.

"Hiro, you know me and these labor types. I'm not against my employees organizing. Just don't like some of the leeches that run the unions. A few of my workers have asked for union, but most of them figured out sooner or later they'd rather deal with my managers direct and rejected unionizing. Nobody understands better than I do how to take care of them."

Estrada spoke up. "So kin yew surmise who done this dirty deed?"

"Pretty sure who *hired* it done, Carlos. It may not be my last brush with sudden death, either. That's one of the reasons we had to talk. Fellows, I came too close to buying it yesterday. I watched the doctor work on me and, for the first time in my life, realized how fragile my own mortality is. Scared me out of my drawers. It's time I made plans for the legacy I want to leave when I move on, and I want to give my three best friends a chance to buy into that dream."

"Anythin' you say is worth listenin' to, Joe. Lay it out."

Chapter 5

A stone-faced nurse came in to check on Joe. She swept the assembled group with her stern stare. "Mister Whitley, I hope you don't plan on working *here* today. Remember what the doctor said about resting."

She drew closer and made eye contact with each of the visitors. Behind her, Joe formed a sour smirk. George had a hard time stifling a laugh.

"Okay," Joe replied reluctantly. "We'll make it short, but only because you said 'please,' kind lady." She turned and exited with the beginning of a smile.

"Maybe we *should* do this in stages," Joe admitted. "That bullet took all the starch out of me. I feel downright wrung out. Let's have a bite of lunch, get a start on our brainstorming, enjoy a leisurely dinner together, and set a time to continue tomorrow. If you fellows can manage to stay over, I have rooms ready for you. Can I ask for one more day of your valuable time?"

All three nodded their assent.

They proceeded to the airy porch and sat around a shaded table with a starched white table cloth. China and crystal sparkled and the wait staff stood poised for action. Joe motioned to a waiter who delivered a round of everyone's favorite beverages precisely according to the boss's instructions.

Then he proposed a toast. "To my best and most steadfast friends. May you all live long and continue to prosper, and may we always be as close as we are today." He paused then added, "Considering I almost wasn't around to enjoy this beautiful day, I appreciate your friendship all the more."

Their chatter and laughter belied the gravity of what had happened to Joneonly a day ago. To the casual observer, this wouldn't look like a gathering of four of the country's wealthiest and most innovative businessmen. Disregarding the plush surroundings, it seemed more like a bunch of good old boys kicking back. What was about to take place, however, could have lasting implications for the future of their country for generations to come.

After a heartily shared lunch, Joe gave their server the nod to break out his private stash of smokes. Whitley had kicked the cigar habit years ago, but he knew how much his friends appreciated a quality smoke. His supply of fine Havanas was kept locked away exclusively for the men who now shared his table. They lit up and continued their spirited banter.

Joe waited until they were relaxed and mellow, scanned the faces around him and lightly tapped his glass with a spoon. The clear, bell-like ring of crystal marshaled their attention as he rose to speak. A small bird landed on the porch railing and began chirping. Joe motioned toward him and laughed.

"Guess he had his say. Now it's my turn. Here we are nearly a year into the next decade. As we've talked about before, our nation looks to be hell-bent on its own destruction before we reach the next. I asked George to have each of you jot down what you consider the country's gravest problems. Who wants to start our discussion?"

George was first to respond. He drew a sheet of paper from his shirt pocket and ticked off his list. "Here's my thoughts: threat o' global war, rampant crime, and equal opportunity. You know how I feel about the shape we've got ourselves into. Somebody has to chase the wolves away from our door or they're gonna eat us whole."

Joe watched Hiro and Carlos reach for their notepads. "I see you did your homework. "Let's look at our suggestions then kick them around. Hiro?"

Kato took his turn. "You and I have talked about this before, Joe. The country's downslide scares me. The Cold War threw a shadow over the whole world. Reagan ratcheted down that threat. But there's always a new enemy to take the place of the Soviet Union—like one of the Middle East countries. That problem may be beyond the reach of us four. Health is an issue we *can* work on, illegal drugs and diseases like this AIDS virus. Then there's education, building the skills of young folks, especially in the sciences. For all the progress we've made, we're just not keeping pace with the rest of the world in scientific education and research."

"Good points, Hiro. How about you, Carlos?"

Estrada considered his answer. "Shoot! Sounds to me like we're agonizin' over problems a lot bigger'n us. We got a bottom line in here somewheres or are we just havin' a hissy fit to git it off our chests?"

Joe chuckled listening to his pal's Texas twang. *I give Georgie a hard time about the Big Apple twist George's 'handlers' couldn't seem to get out of his delivery. Sometimes, though, it sounds as if Carlos is speaking a foreign language. But as the Tex Mex often says, 'people gotta take me like I am. Got no room for change in me'.*

"Fair question," Joe answered. "Remember I said I wanted to leave a legacy? This is about what four lucky men can do to leave something important behind to work on national problems."

Carlos nodded and began, "Okay, then, I say national defense is a whole nuther thing we oughta let the President and our military handle. We don't do near 'nuff to fight hunger. In this land of plenty seems to me we oughta be able to feed ever'body. Health, education, the chance for every dude to get ahead, less crime interferin' with our lives—they're all important."

"Right on." Joe perused his summary list. "You all know my background is economics. The U.S. from the beginning has been based on the free exercise of capitalism. We've strayed from that. We keep on electing officials that blindly pursue the same paths that set us back again and again. So I want to add one item to our problems list—partisan politics. It critically affects every one of the threats you've named."

"Howzat?" George asked.

"The Constitution mandates a representative republic. It's not a perfect document, but it's hard to recognize after the way our Congress and courts have bent and twisted it. The founding fathers saw the 'public good' as uppermost. I contend most of our lawmakers only care about being reelected. Where are our *citizen* lawmakers? All I see are in-bred career politicians."

"But experience counts for something," Kato argued. "We can't have a bunch of learners trying to run the government."

Why not," Joe countered. "Seems to me the first batch of new guys did a great job building the best framework the world has ever witnessed. Beats the hell out of a bunch of old fogies their aides spoon feed and prop up long enough to vote. At least temporary politicians would be in tune with the folks back home and not be consumed by the goal to spend a career on Capitol Hill. Buying votes might actually go out of style."

"You ain't goin' party man on us, are you, Joe?" Carlos asked.

"No way," he snapped. "I say a pox on the Democrats *and* the Republicans! Both major parties are rotten. What we need is more independent thinkers in Washington. I'm damned tired of people applying labels to their opponents. Left, right, center, they're all obsolete terms. And who knows what makes a liberal or a conservative these days? For that matter, for cripes sake, just what the hell is a moderate anymore? What I want to see is some folks with the guts to insist we govern by the Constitution or change it properly by popular vote."

"Wow!" George blurted. "Gwan, man. You *are* some sorta stoked. Sure you're telling us everything?"

Joe let out a long sigh and seemed to come to grips with something gnawing at his gut. "Fellows, I'm not ready yet to make any by-name accusations. But I'm convinced getting shot yesterday was just the culmination of something that's been coming on for a long time. There are folks out there who are hell bent on remaking our country in their own warped image. I sounded off one time too many and nearly got myself killed. Before they succeed, I'm determined to put into motion a long-term solution for their misbegotten efforts. The biggest problem America has is internal. It's wrong-headed politicians determined to win at any cost. We can correct that."

His friends took note of Joe's dead serious expression and the discussion heated up. The question he had put to them took on the form of a business challenge. These were clever men. Once turned on to a problem, any problem, Whitley, Adams, Kato, and Estrada became tigers intent on stalking out workable solutions. They dug in now with that same intensity, whittling each of the items on the list down to its manageable elements. All attention was turned to 'What can *we* do?'

Joe laid his answer on the table. "You fellows know I'm a devoted student of the Constitution. Four of the founding fathers—Washington, Madison, Wilson and Pinckney—understood the dangers of straying from its mandates. They proposed setting up a national university to train leaders; selecting the cream of American youth and instilling in them a love of country and a desire to serve. I believe it's still the answer and it's what I propose as our legacy.

You didn't see a bunch of lawyers trying to form a new government back then either. What we really need is high performers from all professions. Let a parliamentarian or two worry about the fine points of law. I want businessmen, farmers, engineers and housewives saying what's good for us.

The American people have always had the ability to control their government. They can do it every four years at the ballot box. It's complacency that prevents them from throwing out the rascals among our legislators. All I want to do is give them some examples of what they can accomplish in numbers then let the Joes and Marys take charge."

The group fell silent. Joe watched his friends wrestle with his words, stare down at their legal pads then off into space. Finally, George Adams penetrated the wall of quiet.

"In the language of my checkered youth, 'damn straight, Joe'. Let's rock an' roll!"

Hours later, just before the group adjourned for dinner, Joe summed up their progress. "Our plan is coming together. Let me tell you where I stand. Whatever we decide I'm committed. I have no heirs, and I respect *your* judgment above all others. The country needs to make a sharp turn to recover its destiny. I pledge my energy and my fortune to that purpose. Stand with me. That is our legacy, friends."

With handshakes all around, the four men embarked on their search for answers. Two hours and three visits from Joe's nurse later, he summarized.

"We've identified the biggest problems facing the country. As influential men, we have the power to make a down payment on earning some of the grace that's been granted to us. I plan to make good on that pay back. We can build a plan to salvage our nation before apathy and creeping socialism devour us.

Let's take some down time to celebrate our reunion."

The four friends spent a relaxing evening together. They shut out the stresses of the everyday world of business and basked in their unique fellowship. Joe Whitley's brush with death never reentered the conversation.

After what had been an especially long day for all four men, they set a baseline for action. Tomorrow would be a new beginning for these men who had adopted long-term improvement of their country's structure and well-being as their personal responsibility.

Chapter 6

Wednesday morning dawned bright and clear. Joe Whitley had a sunny feeling that matched the new day. He was stiff and sore from the wound and all that bed rest, but the EMTs and Doctor Sam had done a masterful job of repairing the injury near his shoulder. Doc Sam was right. He was a very lucky man to be standing upright this morning. Beginning here and now, he would start paying back the grace granted to him.

The four men were steered out onto the verandah where the skilled cook had laid out a sumptuous breakfast. George looked up from his heaped plate when Joe appeared. "Didjah forget about breakfast, Joe? Lord knows you can use the calories."

"Enough with the skinny jokes, George," Joe answered. "You fellows find everything you want, or can I have Molly whip up something special?"

Carlos answered, "Looks to me like we're ridin' high in some larrupin' good vittles. I see all four legal spices, too—salt, pepper, ketchup and Tabasco. Maybe a roasted porker with an apple in his chops?"

"That could be arranged," Joe fired back. Carlos snorted and dug into his food.

After the meal they all took a break while the staff set up their meeting area on the sunny porch. Each man arrived with his own annotated list of where they had left off the previous night. A focused, business-like discussion carried them through the morning.

"We'd better start winding down and let my folks get this place ready for lunch, fellows. It's been a productive exchange. Allow me to recap."

George, Carlos and Hiro sat back and sipped their Kona coffee as Joe took over and continued. “First I want to say I’m impressed anew how you three took on this weighty dilemma and sorted it out. No mystery to me why you’re successful business leaders. It’s in your blood.”

George, never one to take praise well, issued his usual self-deprecating come back. “Yeah, we’re real swell guys. What exciting ideas did we invent?”

Joe grinned. “We decided to attack the problems of crime, hunger, health and education. I got agreement from you to add two more long-term issues, energy sources, which we all see as a future problem, and partisan politics, moving back toward respect for the Constitution and away from partisanship. Sounds a bit ponderous, but I never knew anybody in this group to back down from a challenge. The consensus is that our best approach is to find and sponsor the country’s brightest and best young men and women. They’ll be our protégés to start a revolution in the biological and agricultural sciences, engineering, education, medicine and law.”

“It makes sense,” Hiro said. “once the voters see what they can do when they join forces, we’re on the way to making this truly government *by the people.”*

“Well put, Hiro,” Whitley answered. “We accept that our project may take a decade or longer to reap significant changes. That means we can hope to make a big difference by 2010 or later. The sooner we launch our efforts, the quicker that will come about. It beats the alternative, which is watching the US rot from within.”

So far Joe was getting positive head nods from his friends, so he moved on.

“Okay. We established four basic ground rules. First, only the brightest and most promising young people will be selected as our protégés. Second, our candidates must each affirm their faith in the Constitution and an absence of involvement in partisan politics. Some would call that a litmus test, but we concurred it’s the only way we’ll survive as a nation. We agreed to provide funds as needed to educate and support the efforts of these young men and women.

But that will be done in ways that will keep our names from being associated with the effort. Our reward will be seeing the US return to the values that matter. We all pledged to see that our selectees never have to worry about employment and financing of their ideas. Does that sum up our decisions?"

Again, assent around the table. Then Hiro spoke up. "I understand we don't want credit or publicity, but we should have a name for our project, a way the four of us can refer to it."

Carlos scribbled something on his pad. He raised a hand and called out, "How 'bout this idea? Since we're fixin' to help people wake up to problems that put the country's future at risk, why don't we call it Project WAKE?" He let that thought seep in for a moment then added, "Whitley Adams Kato Estrada. WAKE, sorta like 'wake up America'. Nobody but us will know those letters are our initials. It can be our own code name."

Faces lit up around the table. "All in favor of our ground rules and the project name?" Joe called out to a chorus of ayes. He picked up his spoon and struck his water glass, which rendered a sustained bell-like peal.

"The next decision to make is staffing," Joe said. "We'll need a dedicated staff to handle the money and provide legal advice to carry out our wishes. I can assure you that my personal lawyer, if he's acceptable to you, can be counted on to exercise the utmost discretion. There are powerful people that won't understand or trust what we're doing. A worse threat is special interests that will do anything necessary to stop us. We must remain anonymous and appear uninvolved in the efforts we're setting in motion. If you agree, I'll have documents drawn up for the legal and administrative structure for your approval. We can settle on a chief of operations and swear him to secrecy."

"Call for a vote and let's hear that gong again, Joe," Carlos said.

"All in favor?" Hands went up and Jonas tapped the glass once more.

"Last, but certainly not least," Joe said, "there's funding. We need to select a target number for the staffing and for financing the initial class of candidates. I pledge a million dollars as my part of the startup and money as required in the years to follow. I know all of you have families to provide for, so pledge whatever you feel is right."

"I'll chuck in another million," George answered.

"When WAKE gets up a head of steam, I'm in for a mil a year."

"Count me in for the same," Hiro said. "Can't think of a better way to return what this country's done for me."

Carlos chimed in. "Ditto. Put me down for a million and annual updates."

Joe looked at a page of calculations he had worked on before coming to breakfast. He jotted down new figures and studied the results before announcing, "Subtracting the staffing and legal costs, I estimate that will allow us to select an initial candidate class of about twenty individuals in the 2000 class. Do we agree that Project WAKE begins as soon as we all sign the papers?"

A round of hearty ayes went up. This time Joe tapped out a lively rhythm on his goblet.

"I think what we've done here today," their leader said, "could well be a strong force for salvaging America. With so many incompetent, greedy folks trying to run the country and botching the effort, this is a first step in the right direction. We'll grow our own crop of patriots and let them secure the future."

George Adams, normally the calm and steady member of the group, showed he'd grasped both the enormity and the energy of their undertaking. "Youze guys understand, I hope, that we're taking on some powerful people. Not only are we challenging half the folks on Capitol Hill. I see all manner of bad guys gunnin' for us when we sic our smart youngsters on them an' their monopolies. "Big oil, big medicine, big lobbies. It's a list longer'n yer arm. But I welcome the challenge."

"You got it, Georgie," Joe replied. "If it was anybody else, I'd say we might not survive it. But we're achievers and we can do this."

Chapter 7

A week later Joe Whitley swiveled away from his large desk and gazed out at the first snowfall of the season. Big white flakes floated down, coating the now bare tree limbs, playing themselves out as rivulets of water coursing down the plate glass windows. That was where he sat, riveted to the scene, when Raymond Crane interrupted his daydream.

"Have news for you, sir …" Ray's words jarred him back to the present.

"I was just sitting here thinking, Ray. That window the private investigators identified as the sniper's vantage point is directly across the lawn from this office. He didn't have to wait for me to come outside; could have gunned me down sitting right here at my desk any time he chose. Scary as hell. Is there any more from the private eye?"

"That's what I was about to tell you. I took the investigator's call a few minutes ago. He identified the shooter; said the rest is up to us." Ray passed him a sheet of paper with a name, Carl Thomas, and an address.

Joe took the note. His hand quivered with anger for an instant, but he collected himself. This had to be done right. Temper wouldn't help.

"I want to see this man today. Have our security pick him up and bring him here."

Ray stared at him and saw those steel-gray eyes stare at the name of his would-be assassin. What was the boss planning?

"Why not let somebody on the security detail question him, Mr. W?"

"Don't worry, Ray. I'm not looking for revenge against *him*. He's just a hired hand. I want him to confirm who arranged the hit."

* * *

When Joe returned from lunch there were three people waiting in his office. Raymond Crane was there along with Jim Bledsoe, the chief of his security detail. The third man was a lanky, dark-haired individual with oversized brown eyes. He stared at Joe with a half sneer.

"I assume you're Carl Thomas," Whitley began and walked over to stand directly in front of where the man sat. "I'm the man you shot last week; the same guy who's about to make you a one-time deal. Give me the name of the person that hired you, admit you shot at me, and I won't turn you in for attempted murder. That should save you at least twenty- five years in prison."

You got nothing on me, old man," Thomas spat at him. "Go find somebody else you can bluff."

Joe bent down so close to Thomas he could smell the man's foul breath. He put his right hand to Carl's throat and began to squeeze. Thomas emitted a gurgle and tried to stand. Joe increased the pressure and issued a warning. "If that's the way you want it, I can crush your Adam's apple now and call it even, Carl." The man's brown eyes watered and he struggled to speak. Joe eased up.

"The name, please."

Jim Bledsoe marveled at Joe's controlled rage. He knew his boss had spent a tour with the Army special forces before he went into business. Joe was also a devotee of the martial arts, including several of the oriental disciplines, but Jim had never seen him use his skills outside the dojo. There was more to this mild-mannered tycoon than any of those around him realized.

Thomas rubbed his throat and forced a raspy cough. He started to say something, then took note of Whitley poised over him and thought better of it. He mumbled a name.

Joe prompted, "Louder, please." When he repeated the name, Joe turned and asked, "You get that, Jim?" Bledsoe confirmed.

"Okay, here's the deal, Mister Thomas. You sign a written confession and I have my personal secretary notarize it along with my two witnesses. We make an audio tape so your voice is heard making the same confession. You go on your merry way and we forget this ever happened. If anything untoward happens to me, an envelope is opened and your butt goes up the river."

When the confessions were finished, Thomas stood and asked, "Are we through here? I have places to go." Bledsoe went to stand toe to toe with him and whispered in his ear, "Not quite, you ferret. I want you to clearly understand something. There's no statute of limitations as far as I'm concerned. If Mister W is ever mysteriously injured or meets an untimely death, I'll find you and personally make sure you pay. Now get out of here."

Thomas slunk away.

Joe turned to Bledsoe, held up the sheet of paper where he'd written a name and ordered, "Find this Mel Jarvis character for me, Jim. I want a one-on-one with him."

Chapter 8

Two weeks after Joe and his friends agreed to launch Project WAKE, he visited the George Adams family at their home in Maryland. This was a favorite getaway spot for Joe. The peaceful Catoctin Mountain setting offered a welcome respite from his demanding schedule, and he considered the Adamses family.

Christmas would soon be here. Evaline and the children had filled the house with decorations including two massive Christmas trees. Whitley sat in the large living room immersed in conversation with Carson, the Adams' handsome 19-year-old, and his pretty 17-year-old sister, Jenetta.

"Uncle Joe, are you coming for Christmas Day?" Jenetta asked.

"Haven't missed for ten years, have I? Wouldn't be Christmas for me without you two and one of your mom's dinners," he replied. "Besides, this year there's a very special present I want to watch you open, Jenny."

She brightened. "And I'm looking forward to hearing another one of your stories about the little orphan boy. You never run out of tales about your youth. I'm so glad to have you for an uncle." Carson looked at their guest's nearly empty cup of egg nog and asked, "Can I refill that, Uncle Joe?"

"Freshen it up, Car. I swear your mom puts a secret ingredient in this nog. Best I ever tasted." Joe offered his cup for a refill.

George Adams waved his goblet and put in his order as well. "Here's mine, Car. Filliduppagin. Bring 'em to the den. Joe and I have some tawkin' to do before dinner."

The men walked toward the den. Joe said, "What's on your mind, George?"

"Thought you might give me an update on the project and what that private eye found out about your shooter."

They cradled the fresh nogs Carson delivered and sat on the big brown leather couch in George's elegant library/den. Joe's eyes took in the mahogany furnishings, the rich wine-colored drapes and shiny brass fixtures. Feeling completely at home, he sank back into the cushions and surveyed the extensive bookshelves. George collected the classics and he read extensively. But his most prized possessions were treatises and papers on chemistry, medicines and diseases.

As a teenager George had developed a keen interest in a range of ailments and their treatment. In particular, he had nurtured a burning ambition to make a difference in the fight against diabetes. This goal steered him into a career as a biochemist and success in the production of pharmaceuticals. His parents, both diabetics, had eventually succumbed to the disease's ravages. Even with Evaline's heroic efforts to keep George on track, his own inherited diabetic tendency and a compulsive appetite presented a continuing challenge.

"How's the WAKE setup going, Joe?"

"The draft documents are nearly complete," Joe replied. "Everything will be ready for us to meet with Carlos and Hiro and finalize arrangements soon after the holidays. Then we can focus on selecting the first group of candidates."

George sipped his eggnog and smiled. "Sounds great. Hell of an idea you had. Seems all of us were thinking this way but we couldn't bring it together. I'm ready when you are, Joe." He hesitated and took on a serious expression.

"And what did your snoopers find out about that weasel sniper?"

Joe recapped his experience after the shooter was identified. He drew a laugh from George with the details of his 'deal' with Carl Thomas. "But Thomas was just a hired man. I'm tracking this thing to the source for a showdown."

George waited for him to continue. When he didn't, Adams nudged him for more. "And you still don't know who sent him?"

"Oh. I'm ninety percent sure I know, but my guys have some more snooping to do before I confront the guilty party. When I take him on, I want to have enough proof to bury the scoudrel. His political career will be shot."

Adams immediately picked up on the word 'political'. "Some *elected* SOB set you up?"

"Do me a favor and forget you heard that, George. You know I'm about as non-political as they come; in fact, that's one of our guiding principles for the project—promoting non-partisan action in favor of adherence to the Constitution. It's either that or we lose to the band of socialists in both parties who want to take over our lives and dictate to us. We need a bold move like WAKE and a hell of a lot of determination to foil those no-goods. You and I may not see the end results in our lifetime, but it has to start NOW."

"If one o' those political sleazes tried to have you killed, we can't let that go, Joe."

"Well, most of them give me pains, but there's one I particularly need to settle up with. When I close this matter, you won't have any doubt who hired my shooter."

Chapter 9

Joe Whitley answered his office phone and heard the voice of Jim Bledsoe, his security chief.

"I may have solved our mystery, Mister W. You have a few minutes to talk?"

"Come see me now, Jim." Joe advised his secretary, "Bledsoe's on his way up. Hold my calls."

When the two men were alone Whitley told Bledsoe, "I'm all ears."

Jim produced notes and began his report. "We finally figgered out why this Mel Jarvis, the man your shooter gave up, was so hard to find. He's been out of the country for the past ten days. Went to Nigeria and came back in country just yesterday."

"Nigeria? Who the devil is this guy? Did one of our African offices do something to hack him off?"

"Apparently got nothin' to do with *where* he was, boss. That's where he traveled with the man he works for. He's a Senatorial aide and this was some kind of political junket."

Joe had a private thought that lifted the corners of his mouth. Now they were at last getting somewhere. He had little doubt the name that would eventually surface would confirm the strong suspicion he'd had all along.

"Jarvis is on the staff of Senator Rand of the minority party," Bledsoe said. "They got back to Washington last night."

"And my old friend Blaine Rand was over in Africa spending some more of the taxpayers' money I take it."

"So you know the Senator?"

"I know him much too well," Joe said. "Have you been able to speak with Jarvis?"

"We had a cozy chat last night at his place—more like it was in the early hours of this mornin'. Mel wasn't thrilled about his wake up call, but he knew enough to give straight answers to my questions."

Joe didn't ask, and didn't want to know, what that meant.

"So?"

"Well, I made it plain to the man he had his skaggly butt in a sling. After a while he blabbed out he hired the shooter. The Senator ordered him to find somebody to throw a scare into you, and Jarvis hired Carl Thomas to do the dirty work. The shooter's instructions were to spook, not kill you, boss."

Bring Jarvis to me."

* * *

Twenty-four hours later Joe was eyeball to eyeball with the Senator's aide.

"We need to make a swap, Mel," he began. "I need something from you. In exchange I'll arrange an extended vacation for you."

Jarvis cast a sidelong glance at Jim Bledsoe, who was staring at him. Then he looked up at Joe, twisted nervously in his seat, and asked rather sheepishly, "What is it you want?"

"You gave the order to have me shot, but it came from somebody higher in the pecking order. I want that name."

"Don't know what you're talking about, Mister Whitley."

"Let's cut the bull and get down to cases, Jarvis. I know your boss, the Senator, put out the contract. I want your written and oral statements confirming that your boss ordered my shooting. We'll have Jim here and my secretary witness and notarize them."

"Say I did what you're asking," Jarvis challenged. "How long do you think I'd be around after I admitted it? There are men that can order me disposed of and never blink an eye."

"Not if we get you a new name," Whitley fired back, "and send you to a nice warm island for a lengthy paid vacation. We forget you were ever involved and the real instigators pay the price. Rand goes back to being a long-suffering private citizen by gentlemen's agreement. No trial. No uproar."

"Sure. But my career would be over," Jarvis said. "No way I'm cutting my own throat. There has to be an alternative."

Jim didn't need prompting. He walked over and stood next to where Jarvis was sitting. "Sure, there's another way, but it's not somethin' you wanta hear, Mel," Jim said. "I hope you know a good deal when you're starin' at it."

Jim handed Jarvis a note pad and a pen, and the startled man began to write.

Chapter 10

All the arrangements had been completed. Carl Thomas had admitted shooting at Joe. The Senator couldn't touch his aide, Mel Jarvis, who was now relaxing on a sunny beach in the Caribbean under an assumed name. Joe checked his phone index, picked up the receiver and placed a call.

"Joe! Good to hear your voice," Senator Blaine Rand gushed. "Sorry to hear about your injury, but happily I see you've recovered."

Whitley set his jaw and thought, *You hypocritical ass, butter wouldn't melt in your mouth.* With some difficulty he controlled his displeasure and replied.

"I thought you may find time, Senator, to have a drink, maybe dinner, with me."

"Wonderful. How about tomorrow night at my club, the Regency in Arlington? You know the place. Say seven o'clock?"

"Fine," Whitley said. He could almost see Rand drooling over the thought something had finally brought Joe to his senses. The Senator had been working on him for years trying to get his verbal and financial support. Joe had no intention of supporting Rand or, for that matter, any politician. Contrary to what Blaine may be thinking, this would not be the kind of meeting he was anticipating.

* * *

When Joe was announced to Senator Rand at the Regency, his host quickly appeared. Blaine Rand cut an imposing figure. He stood nearly as tall as Joe's six- three and had perfectly coiffed dark hair.

"Haven't seen you in a coon's age, Joe," the politico chirped, telegraphing an artificial smile and extending his hand.

It was true Joe hadn't interfaced with the senator in quite some time. He took a closer look and confirmed that the phony still clung to having his hair tinted. From the look of his unnaturally smooth skin, Rand must also be undergoing regular botox enhancements for his wrinkles.

Despite all the cosmetic efforts, Joe knew the martinet beneath as a glad-handing back-stabber financed by some of the most nefarious elements and special interests in society. Just shaking his hand was a disgusting experience. But he endured it for the satisfaction he looked forward to when their visit was over.

"Well, you know how it goes, Senator. Keeps a fellow busy humping to make money, bleeding taxes, and dodging bullets." Rand's expression showed discomfort for an instant, but he recovered.

"Come on in, friend, and share a drink before dinner. The barman here is an artist, and some of the finest beef this side of Nebraska awaits us."

The two men moved to the paneled tap room and took a table in a back corner. Tartans hung about the room and coats of arms embellished one entire wall. Rand gave a high sign to the bartender and received a head nod in return. A refill for the senator's scotch arrived along with a drink for Joe courtesy of a perky young miss in a short skirt and black stockings.

"To old friends," his host said and tapped glasses with him. Joe took a sip and reflected, *I have to give credit where it's due. He's the consummate politician. Old fakir even remembers my preference for Stoli martinis with big, plump cocktail onions.*

Rand unleashed a verbal diatribe and Joe soon managed to tune him out. Man was a veritable word factory. A picture of an organ grinder and monkey sprang into Joe's mind. The more Rand talked, the faster the grinder worked his arm and the harder the little monkey danced and screeched. Only this box wasn't pouring out music. It was spewing words. Somewhere in there, Joe caught bits of his pitch: 'energy for the future', 'my efforts on behalf of my constituents', 'for the common good'. There was a numbing sameness to his high-sounding claims. The senator was spreading the same verbal manure he did daily on the Hill.

Joe provided head nods at the appropriate places and let Rand's pitch go over his head. He was totally ignoring the actual words, instead thinking of how this one-sided conversation was about to come to a screeching halt.

Rand actually put his presentation on pause and stared quizzically at Whitley. "Are you with me, Joe?" the senator asked. "I wanted to know if you felt as strongly as I do about the energy bill I'm sponsoring. Wondered if you'd like to help us get the word out to the people."

He blanched at Rand's words. For years Joe hadn't allowed anyone other than Doc Sam and a few close friends to call him Joe. More importantly, he wasn't about to help 'get the word out', which Joe read as 'kick in big bucks', for anything this weasel was involved with. He sipped his second vodka martini and declared himself ready for the showdown. His fingers scrabbled in a pocket for a small item.

"Senator, do you know the term 'worthless as a plugged nickel'? That's what I'm holding. It's drilled and plugged with pot metal. Consider this my total lifetime contribution to your work." Joe flipped the nickel with his thumb and it landed on the table between them.

Rand's smile gave way to an expression of total shock. "What are you saying?" He spilled his drink.

"Let me put it this way, Blaine. For once in your life, shut the hell up and listen. It's my turn to do the talking."

Chapter 11

Senator Rand sat there with his mouth wide open. He tried to speak but, to Joe's amazement, no words came out. Maybe no one had ever told him to shut his yap. Once again, he made certain that only the senator could hear what he said next. This was a matter strictly between the two of them. "I've been trying to tell you for years, Blaine, that I don't back partisan efforts. Hell, I might as well pound my money down a gopher hole. You apparently are a bit of a hard sell. Forget greasing me for support. It's not gonna happen. Get some of your industrial buddies or union lobbies to kick in to finance your con game. I like the idea of alternative fuels developed with private money. But that's not what I came here tonight to talk about. I want to know what prompted you to hire Carl Thomas to shoot me."

Wha …wha … what?" Rand squawked. For a while, Joe thought his outburst had put Rand's mouth permanently out of order. But the senator finally had his voice back. "Why would you say such a terrible thing, Joe?"

"Oh, and I have a request, senator. No, it's a demand. Do not *ever again* call me Joe. Only my friends do that, and you are *definitely* not my friend."

Rand slammed his glass down and made a movement to stand. "I won't take this, Jonas Whitley! I'm a US Senator."

Joe stood up over him, took Rand's hand and bent it backward, urging him back into his seat. When he turned loose, Rand sat peering up at Joe with tears in his eyes and massaged his wrist.

"Oh, you'll listen to every last word I have to say,

Blaine. It won't take long. Your heinie's in the proverbial wringer. What I'm about to tell you may be the best advice you'll ever get." Whitley reached into his pocket and withdrew a folded paper. "Here. Read this for starters."

Senator Rand read the copy of the notarized statement from Mel Jarvis that Rand had ordered an assassin be hired to shoot Joe Whitley. His green eyes seemed to grow in both color and size. He reached out to return it to Joe and started to stammer, his face flushing a bright red. Joe returned to his seat and calmly continued.

"Let's discuss this like men, Senator. Keep that sheet as a reminder. I have the original. We also have your man Jarvis on tape spilling his story and both written and oral statements from the shooter, Carl Thomas. I'd say your senatorial hide is firmly nailed against the wall."

"What is this," Blaine asked, "political blackmail?"

"There's nothing political about it. I told you I don't play in that pigpen. This is about making sure you never pull a stunt like this again. Don't know what kind of false ideas you've been fed. I've never spoken a bad word about you. And I damn sure don't back your opponents because they're almost as bad as you are. But it's time you quit pretending you represent the voters of your state."

"It can't be for money," the senator protested. "Damn, man, you're insanely rich."

Jonas didn't say a word, just stared at Rand with a big grin lighting his face. The senator's green eyes fluttered and a serious frown wiped out a year's worth of botox injections. He seemed to tighten all over and reached up to mop his sweaty brow.

"What are you planning to do to me?"

"Oh, I don't expect to physically harm you, Blaine. That would be letting you off way too easy."

"Then what is it you hope to gain?" Rand tried to go on the offense. "You are aware I can ruin you and all of your businesses, Joe Whitley."

"Zip it, Blaine. All I want to hear from you is a public announcement. Your political career is over. One week from today, no later than 7 PM next Thursday, you will make a statement to the press. You're reluctantly stepping down from office. Make up a reason: health, family, personal problems, I don't care."

"And if I don't meet this ridiculous demand?" Rand gathered himself to stand. Joe grasped the senator's wrist again.

"Do we have to go through this all over again, Blaine? I'm trained to break every bone in a man's body with little effort. Don't make me demonstrate."

Rand winced and settled back into his seat. "Please, no."

"The originals of the statements from Jarvis and Thomas will be released at exactly this time next week unless you do as I say. All three of you will be taking nice long vacations at the government's expense. Let's see. Conspiracy in an armed murder attempt should earn you about twenty-five years. The choice is up to you, Blaine. It's the only offer I'll make."

Blaine Rand sat nursing his pained wrist and exuded hate but said nothing.

On the way out, Joe passed the cocktail waitress and told her, "The Senator appears to have a problem with his hand. See if he needs help."

*   *   *

Six days after his meeting with Rand, Joe took a call from George Adams.

"Hey, George, how's business?"

"Sweet, Joe. It's like I had a license to print my own money."

"You do have the knack, my friend, What's on your mind?"

"I have a question about what a certain senator said today."

"You mean the retirement announcement? The answer to your question is yes. I said you'd know when it happened. The less said the better. I consider the books balanced."

Joe talked briefly with his friend then signed off and peered out the window. *One down and one hell of a bunch to go,* he thought. *With Rand's murky contacts, I could be blindsided anytime. Can't prove it, but I believe the oil sheiks have their hooks into him. Could be why he put the finger on me in the first place. I've been pushing for domestic drilling and developing alternative energy sources. Wish WAKE could move faster.*

Patience, Joe.

Chapter 12

The sponsors of the WAKE project gathered in the media room at Carlos Estrada's home outside Dallas in late 2003. Three years ago they had made their decision to launch the project and set about choosing their first candidate class. Since then, four meetings, most of them at remote locations, had provided the four men updated progress briefings from the small, dedicated project staff. In another year the US electorate would select a new president, and the outcome was looking more and more in doubt. They were anxious to see their proteges offer hope for the future.

Hiro Kato admired the shine on the new boots peeking out from under his jean bottoms. He swiped a handkerchief across one shoe tip. "Great idea, Carlos, these cowboy boots for everybody. The tooling is great and they're much more comfortable than I would have guessed. It did seem a shame, though, getting them dirty on our tour of the ranch."

"I thought you'd like the change, Hiro. Told you I'd get you big operators in down-home gear one of these days. Does a man's soul a world o' good hangin' out in casual duds and clearin' his mind. And a little horse manure never ruined a good boot. By the way, you make one hell of a ninja cowboy, Hiro."

George chipped in with, "Great boots. But if you 'spect us to dance in these things, I got just one thing to say. Fuhgeddaboutit!"

"Never entered my mind, podner. You're the first feller of your, er, persuasion I ever knew that don't show a particle o' rhythm."

They took their places. Four pairs of boots settled on the foot rests extending from their leather movie seats. Raymond Crane, now the project's chief of operations, walked to the podium, and a staffer handed each man a gilt edged notebook marked Progress Report.

"Good morning, gentlemen," Raymond said. "I have good news to convey in my periodic report to you. Your project is moving along ahead of expectations."

Noting they were thumbing through the notebooks, Crane prompted, "The visuals I'll show are replicated in your folders. As you know, since the legal papers were executed by the four of you, early last year, three classes of 20 candidates each have been selected for the project."

The first screen image displayed a breakdown of their protégés by career area and geographic location. They covered all of the fields originally envisioned: agriculture, chemistry, engineering, physics, education, law and a few others as well. Candidates were from all over the country. They were attending the very best schools for each of their chosen fields.

"The first three classes each consisted of 20 bright youngsters finishing their senior year in high school," Ray said. "Profiles of some of these individuals are provided in your written reports for your convenience. We sought out candidates through numerous unrelated channels. As agreed in the basic ground rules, all participants were given a demanding intelligence and aptitude test. We did extensive background checks and gave a lot of weight to their demonstrated morals and life styles. They were also asked questions about the Constitution and their view of the major political parties. Each candidate was asked to specifically respond to their opinion of the principles espoused by the founding fathers.

As of this past summer we are holding week-long seminars on in-depth study of the origin and content of the Constitution. The proteges have enthusiastically welcomed that program addition.

From time to time, discussions have been held with them to assess their continued belief in those principles. In concert with your directions, we recently offered each member of the initial class an option. He or she could opt out of the program and its strong Constitutional creed and accept full tuition to complete college studies. Or they could remain under sponsorship as committed proponents of the Constitution and continue to receive support beyond college. The one other stipulation is that they remain unaligned with a political party."

George shifted around and issued a cough, perhaps a sign of his impatience to get to the bottom line.

Ray continued. "This slide shows the choices made by the 60 individuals in the first three classes. Forty-eight of them chose to continue as committed members of the program. Only 12 opted to sever ties and receive the remainder of their college expenses with their anonymous sponsor's thanks. That's a phenomenal 80 percent retention rate. It seems, gentlemen, that we selected our candidates well. The same choice will be given to future classes. As you saw on the first slide, that means we have a solid group of proteges dedicated to Constitutional adherence and excellence in their respective fields of endeavor. Something you may want to note in your books is the unusual degree of success many of our young folks have already enjoyed at their tender age. We have a high number of science fair winners, people working on innovative concepts we could all benefit from in the future, even two youths with patents pending."

All in all, the progress report convinced the four donors that their money was being well spent. They adjourned to the den after the formal update to discuss how to ensure continued success for WAKE. Hiro Kato kicked off their bull session.

"Three years into our effort and, if anything, I'm inclined to expand it. You've had the best opportunity to go over the figures with the staff, Joe. What would another million dollars do?"

Whitley did some quick calculations. "From what Ray and the legal folks tell me, with our overhead already covered, if we each added a million dollars per year we could finance another ten candidates, protégés I call them, annually. We'd be looking at 30 new potential super stars each year."

George Adams quickly interjected, "Then mark down another mil from me, too." Carlos Estrada raised his hand and called out, "And me. I can't wait to see what all this raw talent brings off. We need a big turnaround. Hell, we might actually put a solid citizen in the White House. That Bubba from Arkansaw turned out to be a real scootch. In cowboy language, that's a pain in the ass. The same old problems just keep gettin' worse and nobody shows the smarts to find sensible fixes. Don't look like we got a lotta prime prospects for replacin' him when he runs out his string either."

Joe made the count unanimous. "Okay, we'll add another four million per year to the budget. Understand, though, these youngsters, as impressive as they may be, are still budding talents. It may be another twenty years before they reach their potential. We have to be patient. There's an old proverb that says *slow but sure wins the race.* We're growing a whole new crop of superstars, so it won't happen overnight."

Carlos asked, "And how 'bout the guarantee to insulate the four of us from WAKE? A lot of folks might be suspicious if they realize we're in cahoots."

"As Ray explained, the paths we use for distributing funds are incredibly complex and widely separated. The four of us are unlikely suspects as their benefactors. Remember that only we four even use the word WAKE. To everyone else, including the staff, the benefactors are employees of small businesses with names like Acme, Futuro, and Tactics."

"Still, we can't be too keerful," Carlos said. "I worked my butt off for what I've put together, and there are folks that hate success. I worry that the things we agreed to for security may not be enough. Look how that Senator went after you, Joe."

"Remember," Joe replied, "that we also agreed to jump on the slightest indications of danger to ourselves or WAKE and protect each other. I can only say be patient."

"Well," said Hiro, "I can be as easy-going as the next guy, but the anticipation is killing me. You're a genius at hatching good ideas, Joe and this one tops them all. God willing, we'll live to enjoy the results."

"Well put, my friend," Joe replied. "Only God knows the outcome. All we can do is keep pressing ahead and hoping for the best. I think we need to be aware of one glaring fact, though. This will eventually come down to choosing whether 535 elected officials continue to go their own way in running the country or three hundred million citizens insist they do what we demand. It won't be pretty, but a revolution of sorts is the only way we'll ever get our country back. The four of us, in everything we do, must remember this has to be a peaceful, lawful revolution and we can never seek any personal gain other than the satisfaction of seeing a return of power to the people."

Chapter 13

In November, 2005, on the fifth anniversary of their decision to launch WAKE, the four founders assembled in southern California at Hiro Kato's palatial residence. Their periodic contacts by telephone and occasional one-on-one encounters kept them apprised of how the project was moving along. Now they would receive another full disclosure briefing.

Joe Whitley, now sixty years young, arrived feeling unusually weary. In recent months his usually abundant energy seemed to have diminished greatly. He'd cut back on the martial arts sessions, delegated less important events to his staff, and occasionally sat alone staring out the office window. He would ask Doc Sam for another complete checkup after this trip, but for now, seeing his best friends and reviewing WAKE took precedence.

The report rendered by Raymond Crane and his helpers was, again, encouraging. Of the total of one hundred forty WAKE candidates selected so far, one hundred twenty had chosen to remain for the duration. The current class was made up of 30 outstanding proteges. Time would tell, but it seemed, from sample stories of their achievements, that the protégés were well on their way to becoming stars of the future. Not only were they excelling in their formal education. Most of them were well along toward launching, well-versed and determined to help ensure government as foreseen by the Constitution.

The men adjourned to Hiro's dining room and shared a full- course Japanese meal called a 'kaiseki' by their host, accompanied by warm sake rice wine. Two lovely young Oriental women entertained them by alternately playing instruments that looked like a small lute and a long zither. "Let me offer a bit of my ancestors' culture," Kato explained. "Kumiko is playing a four-string biwa lute and Sachiko's instrument is the many-stringed koto zither. The music is heaven-sent for my digestion. The kimonos we're wearing are designed for formal occasions. Our zori sandals and tabi socks, likewise, are formal wear.

George, ever the comedian, just had to slide in his nickel's worth. He held up one size thirteen foot and wiggled his toes. "My big toes thank you, Hiro. They haven't been this liberated in years. Split toed socks, huh?"

"You look preoccupied, Joe," the host remarked. "Are you feeling well?"

Whitley snapped out of his stupor and reassured him. "Just trying to figure out how I'll top cowboy gear and Japanese attire when we meet at my place. Maybe bib overalls, clod hoppers and straw hats?" That drew a chuckle from the others.

When they had finished the meal, Hiro led them through a small garden filled with running water, ponds, and a gently flowing waterfall. Lily pads and bonsai trees covered the grounds and koi swam about. They proceeded to what turned out to be a very special room. Hiro asked them to remove their sandals before entering.

"This, dear friends, is a traditional Japanese tea room. It's a new addition to my home since you last visited. It is my retreat. May I ask that we now observe silence as Kumiko and Sachiko honor my guests?"

The room was plain and open, adorned only with tatami floor mats and a simple flower arrangement. A charcoal fire built in a floor recess heated water in a submerged pot.

Whitley, Adams, Kato and Estrada sat down on straw mats clad in their ornate Japanese kimonos and tabi socks. The two women knelt nearby. Joe touched one of the dragons embellishing his kimono and silently thought, *The clothes and the soft music do kind of put me at ease. I can see why Hiro loves this place.*

"I have asked the young ladies to honor us with the traditional tea ceremony," Hiro said. He nodded and the music stopped. The two women cleansed each utensil in a pre-determined order with precise movements. Hiro placed green tea powder in a bowl and added hot water. He whisked the tea as if measuring and counting his moves then passed the bowl to Joe. When Joe had bowed and sipped from his bowl, George, Carlos and Hiro followed suit.

Joe viewed the contented faces around him and marveled at how the ceremony had eased his tension. He remembered the question from Carlos at their last meeting about the security of WAKE. As far as he could determine, the careful efforts of the founders to remain anonymous had succeeded so far. He felt no danger from outside their group, but Carlos had clearly been worried. In Joe's case, though, there could be a matter of much more immediate concern. His fatigue and recurring onsets of grinding pain were cause for concern. The particularly sharp jolt that hit him now reinforced his decision to schedule a visit with Doc Sam before the week was over.

Chapter 14

Joe Whitley and Raymond Crane sat closeted in Ray's office at Paramount Public Relations with Jim Bledsoe in the next room. PPR, a small business, provided cover to handle funds distribution to Project WAKE candidates.

By this time in mid-2007 the project had been active for seven years. The backers of WAKE entrusted Joe to keep a close watch on how their money was being spent, and Joe insisted he could never be visibly associated with PPR. Jim Bledsoe had, as usual, delivered him through a rear entrance directly to Ray's private enclave.

"So," Joe said, "my partners want an update, Ray. How are we doing?"

Ray answered, "I'm confident our report to them later this year will be most encouraging. The original class of protégés has finished college and many of them are now in graduate school. The summer apprenticeships of all our candidates in their chosen fields are progressing well. These are special people. They'll be well seasoned and ready to make significant contributions to society soon."

Joe smiled but his attention was divided. His mind had drifted far away.

Crane stopped and registered a look of concern. "What is it, Mister Whitley?"

Crooking his finger and waving it at him, Joe issued an admonishment. Given Ray's importance to WAKE and their confidential dealings, such formality had disappeared from their relationship. He had asked Ray to call him Joe.

"Sorry, Joe," Ray corrected himself. "That was a strange look. Are you concerned about something?"

Joe snapped back to the moment. He had been preoccupied with the recurring weariness and pain that seemed to hang over him like a cloud. Doc Sam reassured him that tests showed no abnormalities, but Joe increasingly felt older than his 62 years. He brought his attention back to Ray's question.

"I'm just wondering if we're keeping the names of my friends properly insulated. They insist on remaining anonymous. Beyond you and Jim Bledsoe, no one should ever be able to connect us with this project."

"Every possible precaution has been taken, Joe. We've been meticulous in clearing our funds outlays through multiple channels before they reach the final organizations that publicly support our candidates. My guiding principle has been that no credit is asked or desired by the men who gave birth to the project. As far as we can tell, no one has penetrated our wall of secrecy."

"Good. Let's keep it that way, my friend."

A rap sounded at the inside door. Joe called out, "Come in, Jim."

Bledsoe walked into the room and announced, "I just took an urgent call from your secretary. Consuela Estrada wants you to call her at Carlos's office. There is an emergency. She said you'd know the way to reach her."

Joe thought for a long moment then went to the desk and picked up his briefcase. He and his three partners in WAKE were careful to use scrambled transmissions over satellite phones for securing all of their important conversations. Joe kept his briefcase-mounted instrument with him at all times. He quickly calculated that if Connie was in her husband's office, Carlos must have left his sat phone there. Not a good sign.

"Wait here, fellows," Joe said and carried his briefcase to the small adjoining room. He opened the case, picked up the receiver, and punched in Estrada's coded sequence in Dallas. Connie answered immediately.

"Carlos is in danger," she told him and squeaked out a panicked wail.

Joe waited and let her sob. Then he spoke softly. "Connie, I can help. Please collect yourself and tell me everything."

"He left work, Joe, to see a man he called an old friend from college—his code phrase. His secretary knew to call me. That's all I know. Please find him."

Each of the four sponsors behind WAKE recognized their vulnerability as wealthy men. There were crazies and greedy people out there who might wish them harm. Joe, George, Hiro and Carlos all had code phrases to use when they were under duress. The code words were known only to their wives and, in Joe's case, to his security chief Jim Bledsoe. Carlos had instructed his secretary that if he ever referred to someone as an 'old college friend' she was to immediately contact Connie. In fact, Estrada had never attended college, but had made his way up the hard way from the beginning—with sweat and his own inherent intelligence.

"Listen, Connie," Joe said softly with resolve. "I'll be on the next thing that flies to Dallas. Wait at the office for my call. Do not allow anyone to remove anything from his office. My security man and I will meet you there and get our work started. I promise you, Connie, we'll find him."

Joe closed the briefcase and called his personal secretary at JW Industries by land line. "Marla, I need flight reservations for Jim Bledsoe and me to Dallas. No, it has to be commercial. No time to prepare and file a flight plan for the company jet. Get us booked on the next bird going to DFW and reserve a car at the airport. Call me on my cell phone. We'll be on our way to Dulles Airport."

He returned to Ray's office and filled in Jim and Ray. "Jim and I are off to Dallas. Somebody's snatched Carlos Estrada and we're going to get him back."

As Jim led the way to their car, Joe held up the briefcase and chuckled. "Guess this carry-on is all we have. Scivvies and toothbrushes we can buy. I won't let anybody hurt my friend. Carlos refuses to hire a security detail, so you're about to do double duty. Call for whatever backup you want. I'll cover it."

Jim Bledsoe, a former unconventional forces man and FBI special agent, had been Joe's head of security for three years. Joe knew him well enough to see he was already planning on the fly. The wheels were grinding and there was a spark of anticipation in his eyes. Joe began to feel the surge himself. This was like his old Army days when he had been trained to put everything out of his mind and concentrate on the mission.

"Got it, boss," Jim confirmed. "I have lots of sources to draw from. Say the word and we start taking names and kicking behinds."

Chapter 15

Joe made his sat phone call to George Adams as he and Jim sped toward the airport.

"Whaddya mean he's been snatched?" George blurted. "Took a lotta noive to pull a stunt like dat. Do we have any clue who grabbed Carlos and why?"

"Not yet, George. Jim and I will be at Carlos's Dallas office by no later than three o'clock. Marla has us booked on a flight we're busting our humps to make. You'll know what's happening as soon as I do. I have to call Hiro now."

When Hiro answered, Joe's message was the same: "*Carlos is in trouble. We're on our way. Will call when I know more.*" Hiro replied, "Good luck, Joe. And call me down there if you need *anything*."

He updated Connie Estrada by cell as they rushed through the Dulles terminal. Told her what time they expected to meet her at Carlos's office. They barely made the gate time, boarded and found their seats in first class. By now Joe's pulse was pounding. He looked down at his boots, a gift from Estrada that had become his favorite footwear. If they had to go physical to get Carlos back, Joe looked forward to putting a boot up somebody's backside.

"May I bring you something, gents?" The flight attendant hovered over them with a painted on smile.

Joe ordered vodka and settled in. It wasn't Stoli and onions, but it would pass. He took a generous sip and sank back into the head rest. A sharp stitch of pain knotted his right side and drew his hand tighter around the glass. *Damn!* Joe thought. *I don't need this right now.* He squeezed his eyelids shut and willed the pain to go away.

* * *

Bledsoe wheeled the rental car into a reserved space in front of the Carl's Foods building in Dallas. Joe walked ahead of him as they homed in on Carlos Estrada's office suite. Consuela, who was sitting with the secretary in the reception area, literally threw down her coffee cup and ran to Joe when he entered.

"Oh, Joe, I'm so scared. Why would anybody want to hurt Carlos?"

"Hang in, Connie. Let us scope this out. I brought Jim Bledsoe with me. You've met Jim, my security chief. He and his friends are the best in the business at these situations. Now tell me how long he's been gone and what's been done to try to reach him."

His words seemed to help her get organized. She filled them in, agreed to let Jim Bledsoe and Joe explore the office for clues and watched their painstaking search.

Bledsoe was first to discover a possible lead. "Listen to this," he said. "One of the entries on the message recorder is a voicemail from somebody named Miguel. Listen and tell me what you think, boss."

He played the message for Joe and observed the frown that crept over his face. "I see you picked up on it, too," Jim said.

"You mean the implication of what this Miguel *didn't* say? The caller sounded like someone issuing a threat more than just asking for a face-to-face meeting."

"Exactly," Bledsoe answered. "Had the air of a smooth operator deliverin' a warnin' without incriminatin' himself. Mrs. Estrada, I know it's a common Hispanic name, but does the moniker Miguel ring any bells?"

Connie thought for a long time, giving the appearance of someone scanning her memory banks very carefully. "There is one person that comes to mind. Carlos recently introduced me to a Miguel Sanchez at a charity event. I didn't particularly like his manner."

Joe looked up from Carlos's computer. Connie had used the password for Carlos's personal files to access them for him. "I found a cryptic comment in one of his files," he said and scrolled back to the entry. "He wrote 'I fear my acquaintance with Miguel El Pecoso may come to no good. He frightens me.' That caught my eye."

Connie grinned and told him, “El Pecoso is a nickname that means the freckled one.

When I met Sanchez I was surprised by his freckles. Poor man had a terribly pock marked face, too. Carlos must have been referring to him.”

“Jim . . .” Joe began.

The security man was already dialing the phone. “Done, boss. Got contacts out there that can tell us all about this Sanchez character, prob’ly even what he had for lunch.”

Jim turned his attention back to the telephone and said, “Tom, this is Jim Bledsoe. I need some information.”

* * *

Joe convinced Connie to go home and trust them to find Carlos for her. He and Jim continued a thorough inspection of everything in the office and waited for Jim’s call to be returned. They turned the place inside out, but there didn’t appear to be any other leads until Joe looked at a note pad on the desk and did a double take. There was an impression he couldn’t quite make out.

“What does this say?” he asked Bledsoe. Jim squinted at the pad then picked up a pencil and began to rub the lead across its surface. Words appeared.

“Looks like it says “Sanchez, Woodhaven, 9:30,” he read.

Joe went to the door and asked the secretary. “Is there a place called Woodhaven around here?”

She answered, “Country club and golf course north of town. Carlos sometimes meets business clients there.”

“Tell me how to find it.”

She wrote down directions and handed them to Joe. Then she reached for the ringing telephone, listened and said, “Just a minute.” Placed her hand over the receiver and told Joe, “The caller wants to speak with Mister Bledsoe. I’m transferring him to Mister Estrada’s line.” When the phone on the desk rang, Joe signaled Jim to pick up.

Minutes later Jim said, “Got the low down on the freckled one, boss.”

“Tell me later. We’re on our way to the Woodhaven.”

* * *

They left the city behind them and drove down a long lane skirted by green fairways on both sides. The Woodhaven proved to be an impressive layout. It was quite a departure for a plain-spoken good old boy like Carlos. A uniformed valet greeted them and took care of the car. Joe and Jim walked across the wide porch into a richly appointed foyer and homed on the sounds of people dining.

The maitre d’ greeted them at the dining room and was most helpful. Joe introduced himself as a close friend of Carlos who was in town briefly and wanted to see him. The waiter indicated Mister Estrada had met for a late breakfast with another Hispanic gentleman, who said he was expected. When Joe inquired about a name, the waiter didn’t have one, but the mention of freckles drew a smile and a head nod.

“Sounds like the other man,” he confirmed. That convinced Joe that Miguel Sanchez was their target.

Back in the car, Joe asked, “So what did your source have to say about this guy, Jim?”

“He identified seven men by that name, but only one described as having freckles and facial pock marks. The bad news is he’s a known drug dealer operatin’ outta Mexico. Sounds like your friend’s vibes about him were right on.”

“You think someone among your many contacts might have an idea where Sanchez hangs his hat in Mexico?”

“Not a problem, sir. Give me awhile and we’ll peg this mystery man.”

“While you’re at it, Jim, call in a few of your best assault troops. We’re about to set up an ops center here and plan a little trip to the sunny south.”

Chapter 16

Joe was impressed by how quickly Jim Bledsoe assembled his attack force. Bill Garmin, also of the JW security detail, flew in. Four of the hardest looking individuals Joe had seen since his Army Ranger days were with him. Bledsoe, a native Texan, was also a former soldier and later a federal agent. Jim had been a wise choice to head the JW security detail. If they pulled off this rescue it could be time to arrange a handsome pay raise for him. Joe asked Connie to make arrangements with Estrada's people, and before the night passed Jim had a command post activated in the offices of Carl's Foods. The rescue plan started to come together.

Bledsoe's latest contact—seemed he knew just about everybody—provided a detailed dossier on Miguel Sanchez. Clearly the authorities knew he peddled drugs, and they had an extensive data file on him. They just had not been able to pin specific charges on him. He traveled back and forth between Mexico and the U.S., nearly always under surveillance, and flaunted his contempt for law enforcement. Sanchez had put a burr under the saddle of many a police officer in Texas as well as a number of other places.

Joe got into the rush of the first unfolding black operation he'd been a part of fornerly forty years. "Got a line on where we might find Mister Freckles, Jim?"

"Miguel has a big estate in Monterrey, Mexico, but he spends a lot of time in Nuevo Laredo at his truckin' outfit. Story is he likely runs a coyote operation smugglin' aliens across the border. Guess it's a sideline to back up his drug trade."

"El Pecoso is a busy boy," Joe said. "Time we threw some stink in his game."

"Don't take this wrong, boss, but I think you should stay here while we make our foray. Things could get antsy, and it's my job to see to your welfare. Garmin will be here. The two of you can keep your fingers on how we're doin' and bail us out if we need it."

Joe understood Jim's tactful hint. This is a young man's business. Joe, well beyond that stage, moved a step or more too slow to keep up with these fellows. Besides, those troublesome pains might come back at the wrong time. "Whatever you say, Jim. You're the expert here. Maybe I should be calling you boss."

Bledsoe ignored his poke. "Thanks, Mister W. Now here's our plan. My sources tell me Sanchez is in Nuevo Laredo. He's been there for the past several days 'cept for a one-day trip up here to Dallas. If he has Carlos, that's where they'll be, unless he's stashed your buddy at the mansion in Monterrey. I'll take my team into the Laredo airport. My contacts will help with the short trip from there. As far as you're concerned, I went on a huntin' trip. If I need help, I'll ring your sat phone."

That was fine with Joe. The less detail he had on their plans, the better, in case anyone tried to track the operation back to him. He called Connie to reassure her.

"Connie, I'm going to be in Dallas until Carlos gets home."

"Then stay here at our place, Joe. Please."

"One of my men is here. We'll bunk at the Carl's Foods building and take turns watching over my sat phone."

"At least you can have dinner here tonight. Bring your man and the phone along. Mi casa su casa, Joe. This way I'll know as soon as Carlos is freed. And thank you for all you're doing."

"Hush, Connie. Carlos would do the same for me. Bill Garmin and I will be looking forward to dinner. We'll be at your place by seven."

Chapter 17

Joe Whitley and Bill Garmin had dinner with Connie Estrada with the sat phone nearby. Bledsoe would report back from his identical terminal. Then they returned to the command post at Carl's Foods, where they took turns standing watch over the instrument. Bill had just wakened Joe for his next stint. Joe stared at his watch in the semi-darkness and noted the time—well past midnight. When would Bledsoe check in and let him know how the operation was going?

The hot, strong coffee kept him awake. He sat in the subdued glimmer of the room and puzzled over what this episode was all about. Why would Carlos even associate with a criminal like Sanchez, much less host him at the Woodhaven? And the biggest question: what could Sanchez possibly have against Carlos that would justify kidnapping him? As far as Joe knew, his pal never slighted anybody in his life. Just isn't in his nature. Carlos is almost too honest and caring to have made it to the top in the backbiting world of business.

* * *

Jim Bledsoe and his band of assault troops, having arrived at Laredo Airport and crossed the border in three small rugged terrain two-man dune buggies, neared the target complex in Nuevo Laredo, Mexico. Jim had called in a favor from a friend with the civilian Sentinel Corps that patrolled the border nightly looking for illegal aliens crossing. Jim reserved the empty seat on his vehicle for the man they were there to rescue. The two-man buggies navigated the rough country expertly, working around and through the scrub and cactus, their tightly muffled engines nearly silent in the humid night air. When they approached a row of three wood and tin high roofed structures, Jim throttled back and signaled for the others to stop.

"Okay men," he said just above a whisper. "This is the place accordin' to my sources. We each take one o' those structures and commence our search. Stash your rides outta sight and fan out to cover the last two buildings. I'll take the closest one. First team to spot activity signals us with his beam light. Remember, surprise is the key. We're not here to terminate anybody—unless they leave us no choice. The mission is to find Estrada, secure him and head for the border. Understood?"

Hands up confirmed their understanding. Each two-man team took a building and commenced a well-rehearsed stealth process. Minutes later a flashing signal appeared from the exterior of the second building, and the others swept in to join forces.

Bledsoe donned his mask; his men followed suit. All face gear was in place and adjusted as their thumbs up high signs indicated. Jim reached down and lifted a small canister from his buggy, cracked open the warehouse door and began spraying.

A rush of sound came from inside. Sleep-laden voices sprang to life and, amid the swearing and heavy footsteps, occupants bounced off walls and furnishings in their haste to exit. Curses filled the air. In the dim light Bledsoe could make out dark figures scurrying, stumbling, and falling to the floor. He ducked and heard the whistle of their gunshots pass over his head. Then there was an eerie calm.

He motioned for the team members to enter and police up the scene inside. They secured three sedated men with strap ties and moved them to the area where their bunks stood. Jim checked every corner of the main room then began to force doors. In a side room he leveled his light beam on a bound, reclining figure on a mattress.

Jim smashed the single window with his gun butt to let out the fumes, returned to the mattress and did a quick visual check against the photo in his pocket. He removed his mask and knelt to cut away the man's bindings. "Mister Estrada?"

"That's me," the cowering man answered apprehensively. He looked and sounded confused. The gas fumes began to diffuse.

"I'm Jim Bledsoe, Mister Estrada. Joe Whitley says howdy. We're here to get you outta this pig pen and take you home."

* * *

"Yes, this is Whitley," Joe replied to the voice over his sat phone. "That you, Jim?"

"Give a listen, boss."

The next voice Joe heard turned his long day around.

"Joe, my friend, bless you," Carlos said.

"Are you all right?" Joe asked. "If those mugs hurt you …"

"I'll be fine, Joe. Those boys tossed me in a room blacker'n midnight under a skillet an' tried to starve me. But your folks did a great job."

A sudden loud jumble of background noise rattled and Bledsoe came on the line again. "We have a small problem here, boss. I'll ring you back." The phone went dead.

Chapter 18

"Quick! Stow those guards," Jim Bledsoe directed.

His team members put the bound and gagged men behind obstructions out of sight and took up secure positions around the room. From the engine rumbling outside, Bledsoe suspected an eighteen-wheel truck had drawn up in front of the warehouse. Voices, laughter and rapid-fire Spanish filled the air. He covered Carlos Estrada with his body and moved with him to a far corner of the warehouse. The voices came closer. All five assault team members trained their weapons on the front door.

The first head through the door was that of a large, mustachioed and muscled Hispanic man. He took a long look around the room, called out, "Jose … Diego … Cesar?" and hit all the light switches. Two other men followed him in, one a short fellow carrying an automatic weapon at his side and a slightly older looking guy in a suit, tie and dress hat. They both looked perplexed, their eyes searching. The warehouse flooded with light but must appear totally empty to the visitors.

The lead Mexican brandished a handgun, turned around to his companions and said, "Tenga cuidado, jefe."

Jim knew enough Spanish to understand the man with the mustache had cautioned his 'leader' to watch out. The big guy pointed his gun at the ceiling and fired a warning shot. A second shot slammed into the wall near Bledsoe's head. Jim took aim and brought down the hulking Chicano with a single bullet to his knee. The big man's companions drew their weapons and fired wildly around the room. Jim and his team hugged the floor as the small man emptied his automatic weapon in a wide swing around the warehouse.

Then 'jefe' yanked the smaller man toward the door. They didn't give the wounded bruiser wallowing in pain a second look, just turned tail and bailed out.

The assault team waited for Jim's order then pursued them outside. An eighteen-wheeler rolled away. Jim's men rushed to their dune buggies, mounted them and pursued. Jim Bledsoe and Carlos Estrada followed on their buggy.

"Lights off and keep your distance," Bledsoe barked. He was calculating on the fly. Since the big guy had addressed one of the other men as 'leader' that could mean Miguel Sanchez was with them. The one clear glimpse he'd had of the last man in seemed to confirm it—lots of freckles.

Their mission was already a success, but Jim had to put the squeeze on Sanchez for what he'd done to Carlos.

He clicked on his radio and directed the others. "They're heading south. Could be crossing the Rio Grande well below the Laredo bridge. That truck could be hauling some interesting cargo. Hang back, maintain silence and be ready to break contact on my call."

The ruck turned onto Mexico 85 with the three dune buggies in pursuit. Several miles down the road the truck veered off onto another paved road and pointed due east.

Bledsoe took the lead to stay in contact but didn't press. He punched in a series of numbers and lifted the radio. "Hello, Sentinel. This is Desert Rat. Estimate we're ten miles south of Nuevo eastbound over secondary road, trailing a possible coyote cargo."

The answer came back, "Copy, Desert Rat. I know where they're headed. We'll alert the feds. Don't get your feet wet."

Minutes later Jim spotted activity and throttled back. The terrain vehicles idled off the road as the truck halted briefly then rolled through thecheck point they'd found—an illegal crossing, Jim surmised. As soon as the truck had crossed, he motioned.

"Fun time, chaps. Pedal to the metal. We're bustin' through."

The dune buggies bore down on a pair of khaki clad men at the crossing as they worked to retract the crossing bridge. One of them stumbled into the road and shouted something while his pal retrieved a rifle from their jeep and pointed it at Bledsoe. Jim ducked down behind the wheel; he urged Carlos onto the floor. He gunned the buggy to its limit, aimed and sent a round into the jeep's front tire. A rifle shot through the buggy's windshield whistled over his head. The man in the road jumped into a roadside ditch.

The buggies roared by and across the makeshift bridge back into the US. "Now we melt into the night," Jim told Carlos, "and let the feds do their job. We don't need any publicity for the stunt we just pulled; couldn't stand the paperwork."

Carlos smiled back at him. For the first time, Bledsoe noted a large bruise on his passenger's jaw that was turning puffy and dark.

The vehicles pulled behind some scrub brush and shut down. "The drill now," he told Carlos, "is to lie low here on the US side of the river till the hubbub settles down." They watched from a distance as the eighteen-wheeler was hemmed in by multiple vehicles and halted. US agents converged on the truck with weapons drawn. They pulled three men from the cab. One of the three Mexicans mouthed something and an agent slammed him hard against a truck fender for his effort. Jim hoped it was el jefe himself.

A check of the truck's big trailer produced a flow of human cargo. Jim stopped counting at eight but there were more. In minutes both the truck and its occupants were in custody. The area returned to its normal state of dusty stillness. Jim turned to Carlos to explain.

"Now we sit here long enough to be sure everybody is gone. I imagine you're pretty hungry by now. Sorry, Mister Estrada. All I can offer is breakfast out of a can."

"Anything would taste like a feast, Jim. If not, we can put hot sauce on it. My hosts weren't exactly generous with the rations."

"Want to tell me about that nasty bruise on your cheek, sir?"

"I think you can call me Carlos by now, Jim. You just saved my hide." He touched the bulging dark spot and winced. "Miguel has a short fuse. He used me for a punching bag while his goons laughed. Seems the freckled one is mad because I won't hire his illegals with phony papers. Then one o' his boys, a Chicano big enough to hunt bear with a switch, lit into me. Hurt like a sumbitch." Jim pictured the big goon with a shattered knee back in the warehouse. He hoped that was the brute Carlos was talking about.

They shared their rations cold, hunkering down as a chilly wind blew across the desert. Jim put a leather coat around Estrada's shoulders, looked down at his watch and said, "Ten more minutes then we haul ass out of here back to the Laredo Airport." He gave the men on the other buggies the ten-finger high sign to stay put.

Bledsoe's phone rang. He listened, broke out in a broad grin and said, "Many thanks, Sentinel. Your little horsies served us well. They're dirty and runnin' dry. We'll meet you at the airport north lot. Happy huntin', Sentinel."

Jim explained the message he'd been given. "Even better than we hoped, Carlos. The feds have Miguel Sanchez in custody. They nailed him with cocaine in his satchel and fourteen illegals in the trailer. I don't think El Pecoso's gonna be runnin' back an' forth across the river for a spell."

Jim punched numbers into his phone. "Joe," he announced, "sorry I left you hangin'. Sanchez and his mob showed up. Shots fired but only one casualty, a big plug-ugly Chicano. He's gonna need a new knee. We tailed them back into Texas. I had to keep silence on our end. The authorities were waitin' for Miguel and his boys when they crossed over. My contact tells me Sanchez is lookin' at multiple charges. Your friend is with me. He's tired but fine. We'll be home on the first flight." He handed the phone to Carlos.

"You've told me I need to hire a security detail. I'm convinced. We got a tradition down here.
Anybody drivin' a pickup waves at the other truck drivers. After this, I'm liable to start wavin' and duckin'."

"Have a good trip home, Carlos. I'll tell Connie you're on your way."

Chapter 19

The late afternoon flight from Laredo back to Dallas was nearly empty except for Bledsoe, Estrada, Garmin and the four assault team members. Carlos looked somewhat better but had visible bangs and bruises. Bledsoe's men lounged tapped out after the hectic twenty four hours that took them from the east coast to Dallas then down to Mexico and back. To a man they slept and snored loudly. Jim felt too stoked to rest. Carlos wrote at breakneck speed in a spiral composition book he'd bought in the air terminal.

"Don't let me keep you awake, Mister E," Jim said. "I pretty much run on nervous energy, but after what they put you through, I imagine you're bushed."

Carlos looked up from his writing, slugged down a long swallow of bottled water, and answered. "I didn't get where I am by shirkin'. Those bums cost me a full day's work I need to catch up on. I'm not the world's smartest grunt, Jim, just the hardest working slob you'll ever meet. Life goes on and Carl's Foods needs managin'. Pass me another one of those bottled warters. I'm plumb dry as yesterday's toast."

He went back to writing feverishly. When he finally closed the spiral book, Carlos stared out the side window at the darkening sky. Jim took the opportunity to ask the question that had been nagging at him.

"Mind talkin' about yesterday, Carlos? There could be more to this kidnappin' than we think. Maybe I'll pick up some clues."

Estrada looked him in the eye and asked, "What else is there to tell? I wouldn't hire his illegal aliens with their forged documents. That was a big nuh-uh to Freckles."

"Humor me. There has to be something that would make him reckless enough to grab you. I'd like to hear everything that happened after he showed up at your office."

By the time they were preparing to land at DFW, Jim had the full account of Estrada's harrowing day. As he and Miguel walked away from the Woodhaven club house, a couple of Sanchez's Mex-muscles had tossed Carlos into the back seat of a car. They'd boarded a private plane at the airport. Miguel began slapping him around as soon as they were airborne. All the time Carlos served as a punching bag, Sanchez continued to berate him for turning away his fellow Chicanos who needed work.

"I told him flat out," Carlos related, "that his illegals aren't my fellow anything. I'm US born, and where I come from, we obey the law. That got me this sore jaw before we came anywhere near Nuevo. I think he's more hassled, though, that I know too much about his shady dealin's."

"Now we're getting somewhere," Jim said. "Tell me what that means."

"Well," Carlos continued, "I had my doubts about ol' Freckles. Put some fellers to snoopin' through his background. That man is a drug dealer and, as I figgered, he's runnin' a coyote operation bringin' illegals into the country."

"Do you have solid evidence?" Jim asked.

"My people got eyewitness accounts and gathered up physical evidence of what he was messin' around with. El Pecoso has reason to be worried. I was about to hand over the info to a federal agent friend o' mine."

"Did the subject of ransom come up, Carlos?"

"Not straight up, but I heard my guards talkin'. I think Sanchez was gonna hold up my family for big money to get me back. But why would he turn me loose with what I had on him?"

Bledsoe hesitated then reluctantly answered his question. "He wouldn't. That money would have been wasted. Sanchez had to get rid of you since you had him by the short hairs."

"You clean out saved my life, Jim. I owe you."

"No, Mister E, it's part of my job. Thank Joe Whitley. He refused to let this sorry el Pecoso character get away with snatchin' his friend. As us good old boys from Texas used to say, Joe put his foot down and said, 'no way, Jose.' Uh … sorry 'bout that, Carlos."

Estrada laughed out loud. "No offense taken. You're the one that pulled my tacos out of a hot spot."

Bledsoe recovered from his embarrassment and asked, "Any idea why Miguel came back to the warehouse?"

"Guess he got a kick out of working me over and wanted another go at it. Thirty years ago, back when I was a scrappy ghetto kid, I coulda put a whuppin' on a guy like him one on one. But now he's got youth and a vicious attitude on his side." Carlos leaned back and closed his eyes.

Jim had a strong feeling there was more Carlos wasn't telling him.

Chapter 20

They barely reached the gate at Dallas when Connie Estrada raced to Carlos and threw her arms around him. Seeing their reunion made the whole assault operation worthwhile to Joe and a much better memory for Jim Bledsoe.

Joe Whitley and Bill Garmin stood off to one side with Jim and his midnight marauders. Whitley shook their hands and thanked them for their work. "Rooms are booked for all of you at the best hotel in town. Bill will drive you there. I've given him an unlimited expense account, so have a ball. You deserve it. There are first class seats back to D.C. tomorrow afternoon. It's the least I can do."

Carlos came over and gave Joe a big hug. He whispered, "For a while there I thought I wasn't gonna see home again. I'll never be able to thank you for what you did."

"What are friends for?" Joe answered. "If I'm ever in a pickle, it'll be comforting to know you and my other pals are out there. As long as we stick together there's not much we can't work out. George and Hiro will be here late tonight. We're staying over in town. Hope you're up to a pow wow tomorrow."

"For you fellers, any time." Carlos shook his hand then latched onto Connie.

* * *

The four founders of Project WAKE sat in the media room of Carlos Estrada's house. Joe had summoned George and Hiro after Estrada's rescue and they arrived within hours. Two years ago, they had received an encouraging report of the project's resounding success in this room. Now they were just happy to be together with Carlos safe at home.

After a warm reunion Joe Whitley stood and addressed the group. "I don't have to tell you how traumatic yesterday was for all of us. Won't be the last time somebody tries to make life tough for one of us. Gents, we were vulnerable enough before we undertook WAKE. Things won't get any easier along the way. There's no reason to believe the experience Carlos had was in any way tied to the project, but we must all double our efforts to stay under the radar. The payoff by WAKE to our country is too great for any of us to screw it up."

Carlos waved his hand for attention. He looked around the table and began, "I owe all of you a big 'scuse me for upsettin' your schedules. After what I learned about Miguel Sanchez, it was dumber'n dirt to meet with him again. My snoops told me what a low down crook he is but I didn't have the smarts to back off. Thank God, Joe and his folks hopped on it and yanked my cohones off a hot griddle. It won't happen again. Once burnt is plenty."

Hiro Kato spoke up. "Hey, you did what any of us would have done—make sure you could nail the weasel. I don't think we've drawn undue attention to ourselves outside our little circle here. I carefully consider my actions every day to stay low key and not attract attention. What else can we do?"

"I hear you," Joe replied. "But look what happened to me. Senator Rand thought of me as a threat, and I guess I was. Now I find out he'd actually thrown in with the Middle East oil folks. Four flusher was sabotaging domestic efforts to exploit our own oil supply and to develop nuclear, natural gas and other energy sources. When I defied his backhanded slaps at our own economy, it must have put too much heat on him. Damn near got myself killed. We know how hard we've all worked to get where we are, but there are people that hate us for our success. What I want to propose is that we hold all our future get-togethers at neutral sites to avoid being identified as close friends. We should avoid any actions that could identify us as opposing people who are in positions to strike back. Our WAKE protégés will, in due time, take care of cleaning up the messes we detest."

"May be hard for you and me to pull off that idear, Joe," George said. "Everybody knows we're close. Hell, we even live close to each other."

"So we accept that and go on as before, George. But we protect our roles in WAKE and forego any form of activism. Our first priority now has to be to ensure WAKE proceeds and fulfills its promise."

` Carlos chipped in. "Sounds good to me. I do have one worry, though. In lookin' into Miguel Sanchez I uncovered something unsettlin'. A former friend o' mine, an appellate court judge, is tangled up in Miguel's drug dealin'. Dug deeper and found out he's also in the pocket of Middle East oil; been stiflin' efforts to build an oil processin' plant out in west Texas. Fellers, I got to turn that ol' boy in to the Rangers."

"As we've discussed before, Carlos," Joe reminded him, "one of the long-term objectives of WAKE is to see the right kinds of people lawfully elected and appointed to positions of authority. That includes the judiciary, a group it will take considerably longer to clean up. Matter of fact, if they suspected you'd found him out, that judge could have been the main reason you were kidnapped in the first place. Give all your info to the feds and make it clear you want no further role in the fall out."

Carlos nodded and dug into the fruit basket. He tossed a Rio Grande Valley citrus over to George and said, "Have a ornje, big guy."

George chuckled. "That's an ahh-ringe, partner. So where's our next get together, Joe? We're due for a project update from Ray Crane."

"I'll be in touch with you soon over our sat phones," Joe said. "Ray is putting the finishing touches on his report, and I'm checking out a meeting place. I think you'll be pleased. Stay safe, friends. Keep the faith. Better times are coming."

Chapter 21

Joe and Jim rode home on George Adams's company jet. They had left Virginia yesterday in a big hurry, literally with what they had on their backs and little else. Bill Garmin had brought along extra clothes for Jim, and Joe had made a quick trip to WalMart, a far cry from his normal apparel shopping. Not only was this ride a lot more comfortable than the commercial flight; George made sure they had Stoli and fat cocktail onions for Joe's favorite martinis. Bledsoe took a seat in the rear of the passenger cabin while Joe and George kept up a steady conversation most of the way back to Virginia.

When Jim got up and went to the latrine, Adams asked, "What's de problem, Joe? I'm worried. Fahcrissake level wit' me."

Joe did a double take. "Did I lay it on a little thick at our meeting? You know how adamant I am about helping people retake control of how the government regulates their lives."

"No arguing with that," George replied. "You know we agree. It's de way you look that scares me."

"I've always been ugly, George. It's no big deal."

"Don't try to make light of it. I've known you how long, fifteen years? We don't BS each other, not ever. You're holding something back. I can see it in your eyes. Your hands shake when you think nobody's lookin'. Damn it, Joe, smatta witcha?"

Whitney set down his glass, his hand suddenly trembling so violently he nearly spilled his drink. He looked at George with an expression that struck Adams as downcast and resigned. *Oh, god, I wish I hadn't asked*, George thought.

"Doc Greenlee says I have a problem. Been putting up with shakes and recurring pain off and on for months. He's sent me to specialists, the best people available, but they can't seem to find what's causing it. I'm way too young to feel this crappy, George."

"I don't like what you're not sayin'. Joe, you're the best friend I ever had. Don't go cavin' in on me. Carson and Jenetta need their favorite uncle."

"Last time I looked I was their *only* uncle—and an honorary one at that."

"A title well earned."

Jim returned to the cabin so they felt uneasy continuing their conversation. For the remainder of the flight they went silent, but both of them wrestled with agonizing private thoughts. Adams struggled with what he could do to perk up his pal, and he worried about how serious Joe's ailments may be. Joe wondered how much longer it would be before he had to stand aside and pass the WAKE project baton to George.

Just before they parted at Dulles airport, George threw out a reminder. "Evaline said to tell you she's saving a turkey leg for you on Thanksgiving. Car and Jenny will be looking for you, too."

Joe nodded and turned away. He stared at the fluffy clouds far below and tried to concentrate on anything but his discomfort. He inhaled deeply, held his breath and winced as a sharp pain knifed through his side. *For as much progress as Project Wake has made, we have miles to go. I thought I was in danger with one mean politician on my case. With what we're planning, the whole sorry lot of them will be after us to protect their interests. Now Carlos and I have both set off the Arab oil leaders. Looks like it could be a tossup which kills me first, some pissed off power merchant or this gnawing pain that's deviling me. Thank God, George is around to back me up. He won't let our plans die.*

Chapter 22

In the early summer of 2008 all four of the WAKE members, as influential businessmen, were invited to an awards ceremony in St Louis for the brightest and most promising new college graduates from around the country. They gathered, along with other prominent members of the business and academic communities, to honor this year's crop of scholars with special recognition.

Whitley, Adams, Kato and Estrada mingled with the crowd carefully avoiding any outward show of interfacing with each other. Their primary purpose for attending this gathering centered on a close up look at the WAKE protégés among the honorees. Those young folks had already begun to make their marks on society. None of the protégés, by design, knew that the four men had been responsible for their generous scholarships. That fact would remain carefully hidden until some undetermined future time. The founders had plans to see to their future employment and continued sponsorship.

George Adams met for the first time the brilliant young biochemistry grad he'd been hearing about. Joe Amos finished at the top of his class and would embark on graduate work when the fall semester began. This engaging young man was already being identified as a future star in his field.

"I'm honored to meet you, Mister Adams," Joe Amos said. "Your reputation in pharmaceuticals is legendary."

"And I have to say you're making *yourself* known, young man. Did you pick a focus for your grad studies?"

"Actually, sir, I'm a bit conflicted on that matter. I want to make a difference in the development of new medicines, but I also have an intense interest in new energy sources."

"No reason you can't do good in both areas, son. I wish you the best. When you're ready for some practical experience, I'd like to see your resume. We have lots o' room for young men like you—summer, part time, full time, whatever fits your needs." George handed him a personal business card, and they plunged into a discussion of biochemical trends.

Meanwhile, Hiro Kato was getting to know JoAnne Donovan, a young lady who had distinguished herself as an electrical engineer. JoAnne currently held a patent on a state of the art electronic device. She presented an unusual combination of beauty, personality and brains.

Hiro asked JoAnne, "Are you pursuing a graduate degree?"

"Yes, sir," the lovely blonde told him. "I'm going into a master's program in electrical engineering on a scholarship in the fall. My focus will be in nanotechnology, studying the applications of nanometer sized electronic devices." Hiro already knew her plans. He had arranged the grant for her continued education using WAKE funds.

"Do you need a position this summer? My company has intern openings."

She thought for a moment and answered, "I have an obligation for a week of training later this month in Los Angeles. It's a continuing part of my undergraduate scholarship commitment to learn about the underlying principles of government and the Constitution."

"That's a worthwhile endeavor, JoAnne. We can accommodate your taking a break to attend. You could start at either my California nanotech operation or in our Maryland division immediately after the training. We can offer you a handsome salary."

Kato also knew about her recurring training classes in constitutional law, since WAKE conducted them under other auspices. He steered JoAnne to a seat and began filling her in on the advantages of establishing a corporate connection early.

Carlos Estrada and Joe Whitley sought out specific attendees and held one-on-one discussions with them as interested businessmen. Carlos cornered Terrell Jenkins, a very promising agriculture grad with a desire to find better ways to feed the world's hungry. They talked about this passion, and Carlos broached the possibility of Terrell's spending some time abroad working first hand with the people Carlos liked to call his 'hunger missionaries'. They worked on hybrid crops bred for short, dry growing seasons. Carlos also got acquainted with Ryan Bolger, a business grad who wanted a future in food distribution who knew and admired the reputation of Carl's Foods.

Joe Whitley started with Ken Parker, who would enter law school in the next term. Ken had been a devoted student during the latest Constitutional law session presented at a West Virginia resort. Joe considered him a model for the type of citizen politician he envisioned would help revolutionize politics. Carrie Zeitler, another law student, bent Joe's ear with her passionate plea for truly representative government.

* * *

After a long and encouraging day with these young people, the founders left in their private planes. They individually found their way to a secluded retreat in rural Alabama and convened a session the following day with Raymond Crane, their WAKE operations chief.

George Adams looked down the rustic lodge's long conference table and spoke to his associates. "I think all of us had an eye-opening day with the young folks. I couldn't be happier with the way they've taken hold and become people to be reckoned with. We still have a long wait ahead, but de day will come when our protégés help remold dis country back into the shinin' example it was meant to be."

"Well put," Joe Whitley seconded and rose to chair their meeting. "Ray's report that WAKE has produced a whole slew of solid citizens about to appear on the scene is fantastic. Yes, the time isn't here yet, but it's coming, thanks to your generosity."

Carlos Estrada chimed in. "What impresses me most is every one of the young people I talked to are lightin' out to serve on two fronts—their chosen field and a real contribution in an elected position. These candidates appreciate the message of Constitutional law and they're ready to work for its return."

"Amen," Hiro Kato pronounced and pounded his fist on the table. "Not only have we established a baseline for real progress on national issues, we're producing leaders. They understand it's time to end the back-stabbing politics and work for the people, not the party."

"All in all, friends," Joe interjected, "I'd say our money has been well spent. As of today I am increasing my pledge to three million dollars per year."

* * *

When the others had left for home, George lingered with Joe at the lodge.

"Now I want a progress report from *you*, Joe. You're looking fitter'n I've seen you in a while, but I want it directly from, 'scuse the expression, the horse's mouth. How's your health?"

"George, I couldn't be better. Doc watches over me like a mother hen, and he tells me all is well. I'm bound and determined to make it through till 'stand up day' when we see these young folks announce to the world a new day has arrived."

Adams gave him a firm handshake, let out a long sigh of relief, and encircled Joe in a bear hug. He was pleased. But Joe hadn't been a hundred percent honest.

Chapter 23

Joe Whitley sat alone in his office thinking about the future. Spread before him on his oak desk was an array of written accounts prepared by Ray Crane on the WAKE protégés' achievements. Those reports buoyed his spirits.

This is what I dreamed could happen," he said, as if the young people were there with him. "I always knew we had the power to turn things around if we invested in you youngsters."

The glowing accounts continued to pile up on the academic successes reached by the early classes of WAKE participants. Watkins smiled, knowing that the superstars weren't even aware yet of the promise they represented. The time would come when the story of the WAKE project would be disclosed to these chosen candidates. Then the project would advance into its second stage, a period of mutual, concerted actions among the protégés to reverse the country's decline.

Joe Amos, a brilliant biochemist, appeared to be well on his way to breakthroughs in new medical compounds. His undergraduate work and progress as a summer employee at George Adams's GMed were gratifying. Young Lori Wong, an education major, had just finished her master's thesis on rescuing textbooks from their revisionist approach to American history. Terrell Jenkins worked in Africa making great strides in increasing crop production in arid regions.

JoAnne Donovan, the engineering student who had so

impressed Hiro Kato, had applied for a patent on a process for manufacturing nanometer machines, the minute devices that held promise in so many disciplines, including disease detection and targeted treatment through the human blood stream.

The two law students Joe had spent time with at the awards ceremony last year were making their own marks as members of law reviews and proponents of adherence to Constitutional law.

He gathered up the reports and returned them to his private vault where he kept WAKE documentation secured. Only he and Jim Bledsoe, his security chief, knew what lay in that vault.

Joe looked at his watch. Eleven AM. He picked up the telephone and dialed. “This is Joe Whitley, Amy,” he said to Doctor Sam Greenlee’s nurse/receptionist. “I have your message that Doc Sam asked me to call. Is he available?”

“Hold on please, Mister Whitley. I’ll ring him,” she replied.

A wait of several minutes followed. Joe began to fidget with the items on his desk. He stared out the window at an overcast day and began to feel closed in by his surroundings. Drumming a finger on the desktop he mused, anticipating the purpose of Sam’s earlier message. In fact, Joe had received the note when he arrived, but purposely delayed returning Doc’s call for fear of what he may be facing. Important news was overdue.

“Joe, I’m sorry. I had a patient,” Greenlee said. “I have the reports back from the last two specialists you saw. Can you come over and discuss the results with me?”

“Wanta give me a hint, Sam. I’m a big boy.”

A noticeable pause ensued before the doctor answered. “It’s not what you wanted to hear. I think we need to talk today. Can you be here before noon?”

Whitley caught his breath and exhaled a long sigh. He managed to say, “I’m on my way, Sam.”

Chapter 24

Deep in the back woods of Vermont, the WAKE staff and its four benefactors met for their annual assembly in 2009. The trees glowed in shades of gold and red and a chill filled the air. Raymond Crane had found a secluded camp with both adequate facilities and privacy. The four principals quietly gravitated toward the site by diverse and intricate routes. They were anxious to hear Crane's progress report now that five classes of WAKE protégés were busy on academic and business campuses around the country.

"Welcome, gentlemen." Crane stood before the group in a small conference room carefully secured by Jim Bledsoe and his detail. "There is exciting news. The project has reached a new milestone with more than five hundred active participants. We have participants currently in graduate studies in the physical and biological sciences, medicine and law. Members of the two initial classes are already on their own and demonstrating superb performance. There are twenty patents held by our young associates. Fifty of our people have been recognized by their respective professional societies for achievements of the highest caliber. Among their numbers are dozens of young men and women living their commitment to Constitutional government by holding positions from town council to state legislature, even as they excel in their chosen fields. We will, during the course of our presentation, highlight these achievements. A more complete description is provided in your notebooks."

Whitley, Adams, Kato and Estrada rapidly warmed to the tone of Crane's introduction. They were thumbing through the leather volumes that would, after this meeting, be secured in their individual private vaults at home.

Three hours later the four founders finished their special session and shared a sumptuous catered lunch served at their protected retreat. Joe took this opportunity to voice words of caution to his friends.

"Fellows, we've set something very important in motion here. Just don't ever forget that a lot of the people holding the reins of power won't step aside easy. It may not be apparent yet, but I see another push coming by the scoundrels I call revisionists. This time the revisionism is firmly imbedded in both major parties. They're bound and determined to take power from the common folk and invest it more and more in themselves. Seems they're convinced the rest of us are too dumb to know what's good for us."

"That's a new word to me, Joe," George said. "

Whatcha mean by revisionist?"

I'm talking about the proponents of big, centralized government, over-control of our lives. Worst of all they push unlawful changes in the system and force policies that flat out violate the Constitution. We have perfect examples in Teddy Roosevelt's progressives, Woodrow Wilson's ruthless rule, and Franklin Roosevelt's power grabs with no regard for their Constitutionality. I see dangerous signs of the same attitude in both the current Dems and the GOP. Any improvements our young protégés can bring about could be stifled by greedy politicians gathering power at the federal level. We can't forget those are our biggest foes."

After lunch Hiroshi Kato stood with George Adams on the patio outside the conference room as they puffed on a couple of Joe's quality stogies. They felt the effects of the brisk mid-day winds that whipped fallen leaves and whirled them about their feet. "Bit on the fresh side out here for a California boy, huh, Hiro?" George asked.

"A few hours ago, I was basking in eighty degrees, George. But I wouldn't have missed this for a month at the beach. Were you as blown away by Crane's report as I was?"

Adams grinned. "Hell of a brainstorm old Joe had," George told him. "I'm beginnin' to believe we can pull this off. As Joe told us at the outset, it was always a matter of showin' bright youngsters the unvarnished truth and lettin' them take it from there. God willin', I'll live long enough to see some of our people sit on the Supreme Court and occupy state governor mansions."

"Don't stop there," Hiro retorted. "After reading the histories of our young associates, I can see a WAKE member settling down at 1600 Pennsylvania Avenue someday. Now wouldn't that be a shot in the arm for promoting citizen politics? And with what just happened to us—a community organizer, of all things, sitting in in the White house—anywhere is up. Last time I checked, the oceans were still rising and 'Hope and Change' was an empty promise."

Carlos Estrada appeared on the outdoor terrace and cautioned his friends, "You two better take those smokes inside by a warm fireplace. It's colder'n a witch's patootie out here. I have better things to do than sit by your hospital beds." He held one hand into the buffeting wind and proclaimed, "Feels like a genuine blue norther to me, folks."

Hiro shivered and agreed. George, even in shirtsleeves, had the edge on his companions. The bulk of his two hundred big frame was a great insulator. "You warm weather dudes haven't seen true cold weather. I remember a winter in the big apple when even went on strike . . ."

His tall tale was interrupted by Carlos. "Joe asked me to tell you he wants to see you in his room, George. Sounded important. By the way, did you notice how restless and uncomfortable Joe was durin' our meetin'? That little lecture he gave us after lunch had a worrisome note about it. I don't think he's well."

Adams gave a quick head nod in answer and took a long last draw on the Havana. He carefully snipped away the smoldering ash and pocketed the prized smoke for later. "Thanks, Carlos. See you two at dinner." He hurried off to find Joe.

* * *

George rapped on Joe's door and waited. He knocked again and wondered what was keeping him. After a third try, he finally heard the safety latch being thrown and the door opened slowly. A sallow, tired-looking Joe Whitley, using the door for support, managed to stammer, "Help me, George."

He led Joe to the bed and helped him lie down. All manner of nightmare scenarios raced through George's head. Stroke? Heart attack? Poison?

"Talk to me, Joe. What can I do for you?"

"Just let me rest awhile. Stay here, Georgie. I need to tell you something."

Adams did all the things that sprang to mind: checked Joe's pulse rate, felt for a fever, put a cold cloth on his forehead, looked for obvious signs of trauma and clues in his eyes. He was reaching for the telephone to summon medical aid when Joe's hand squeezed his forearm.

"They can't help, George. Give me a minute to get myself together and this will pass."

His recovery was agonizingly slow, but Joe finally began to show some color and his eyes cleared and brightened. "Damn, man, you scared me out of my droopy drawers. What's going on, Joe?"

Joe's mouth trembled. He forced the words past his lips. "I'm dying, George."

Adams sat in total shock, fumbling for words that wouldn't come. All he could do was grasp the hand of the man who was, after his family, the most important influence in his life. The declaration Joe had uttered was the last thing George wanted to hear from him. But it was a moment he had feared ever since Joe began to have his recurring pains.

Whitley slowly continued his explanation. "I told Doc Greenlee I'd been feeling better for months. He knew I wasn't being straight with him. Doc tried one more specialist two weeks ago. This one did a new test they hadn't run before." He swallowed hard and held back, as if not saying the words would change the outcome. Then he gave in.

"I have a rare blood disease, George. It's begun attacking my vital organs."

"My god, Joe! How …?" George couldn't finish. "How long?"

Joe completed his question. "They told me there were unproven procedures they could apply, heroic measures that might prolong my life as much as two years." The effort was still plainly uncomfortable for Joe, but he pressed on. "That would involve constant hospital care and completely take over my life. But that's not my style, Georgie."

Joe's voice faltered. George reluctantly asked, "And what's the alternative?"

"Less than a year," Joe muttered. "One damned year to pack a lifetime into." For the first time since they met, George held Joe and they both sobbed.

Chapter 25

In the autumn of 2010 three men came together in Loudoun County, Virginia. They shared a heavy personal load.

George Adams, Hiro Kato and Carlos Estrada embraced and shook hands in the parlor of Goose Creek Chase, the home of Joe Whitley. This was the day they had dreaded for the past year, ever since that blustery day at the retreat in Vermont. On that day George had called Hiro and Carlos to his room as they were preparing to depart for home. His news about Joe's declining health was devastating. Over the ensuing months each of them made visits to Joe, being especially careful to avoid any mention of his problem. But they sensed that Joe knew they were well aware of the unavoidable deadline he faced.

Now that call had come, the final summons from the acknowledged leader of their group by way of Jim Bledsoe, his security chief. Joe was teetering on death's edge. Without hesitation, all other commitments immediately shelved, they hurried to his side. George, Hiro and Carlos prepared themselves for the inevitable.

Bledsoe escorted Joe's three co-founders to the bedroom, exited and closed the door. An anteroom off the bedroom held a computer, written records and a safe. Those documents represented their leader's accumulated knowledge of the cherished Project WAKE.

Joe sat propped up in bed with his boyish smile fighting its way past the pain that was conspicuous. On his head sat the favorite gray homburg perched at a jaunty angle.

"Hope I didn't interrupt anything important." Joe began to laugh, a gesture that too soon gave way to a rattling, almost fitful, cough.

"Can I get you sumpin', Joe?" George asked.

"What more could I possibly want, Georgie? Hell, I got my three best friends, a comfy bed and my favorite top hat. You could clip me one of the Cohibas in that humidor and offer one to Hiro and Carlos. When I quit over twenty years ago, I swore I wouldn't touch another smoke till my dying day. Time and circumstance finally caught up with me. Light my last stogie, George."

Adams prepared two Havanas for himself and Joe as their companions lovingly coaxed their prized smokes to life. Joe Watkins lifted a trembling hand to the cigar George placed in his mouth and inhaled. "Brings back memories of a misguided youth," he told them.

"Well, here's my story in a nutshell, fellows. I've been living with this devilish intruder in my blood far longer than I've let on. It's finally whipped me, poisoned all my vital organs. But I can't complain. Old Joe W. has lived a charmed life, and my best pals have helped me put my biggest dream on the road to reality. I have no doubt you'll see it through. I've asked George to steer it to the finish. All I ask is that you three keep WAKE squeaky clean and lawful in every respect. None of us are in this for personal gain. We only want what's right for our country."

Joe began to cough again. Adams took the cigar from his lips and placed it on a china plate on the nightstand. "Save your energy, Joe," he said. "We're not goin' anywhere."

Whitley finally caught his breath and looked at George with a mischievous twinkle in his eye. "I'm on a roll. Besides, there's not much time left to say it all."

Hiro and Carlos looked at each other and paled.

"When we began WAKE I told you it could take at least twenty years to mature," Joe said. "I may a bit off but I firmly believe it's coming. I predict that by 2020 you'll see this country on the brink of an historic recovery. The destiny our Constitution's framers foresaw will once again be within reach. I'm leaving all my possessions to George Adams through an assortment of business entities. He is my sole heir with a single stipulation— that he use whatever assets are required to make WAKE the success we all want. Jim Bledsoe has instructions to help George retrieve any and all information on the project from the next room, destroy the computer, permanently empty that space and do what George orders with it. Raymond Crane and my lawyer will help with the transfer of documents and funds."

Joe reached down and pressed the call button by his side. Jim Bledsoe appeared at the door carrying a mahogany case about two feet across. He set it on the bed.

"Thank you, Jim," Joe said and waited for him to quietly leave them.

"George, open it for us." Adams swung open the lid revealing the container's blue velvet interior. The box held a bottle and four goblets.

"Gents, that's a bottle of the finest cognac known to exist, a Very Old Luxury. I ask you to share a final toast with me to our friendship and to the success of WAKE. My hope is my fortune can be put to good use bringing WAKE to completion. I know you three can do it."

He nodded to George, who poured for each man, handed Joe his goblet last, and raised high his own glass. Joe tipped his homburg and said, "To friendship and WAKE."

The other three repeated his words and drank. Joe's face lit with a smile that would have pleased the little orphan boy he'd been so very long ago. Then his hand dropped and the empty glass slipped from his fingers.

The torch had been passed.

PART TWO

Joe Amos

"Joe Number Two"

Chapter 26

Joe Amos thought about what lay in front of him as his last semester began in 2011. At age twenty-four he would soon earn his doctorate in biochemistry, his thesis on chemical compounds and treatment of diseases was ready to present to the faculty advisor. Jordan had finished his undergraduate work in three years and gone directly to postgraduate study. Soon he would be the youngest person tapped as a PhD by his grad school.

Amos was in several ways a remarkable young man. He was intelligent as well as athletic and possessed of good looks. Somewhat shy at times, he tended to meld into his surroundings until asked to perform for an exam or in the laboratory. Then Jo\e excelled and showed unusual insight into the intricacies of biochemical processes. Already he had uncovered and studied human enzymes that were proving to be significantt finds for medical research.

His athletic good looks and outgoing nature made him a magnet for friends. Lean and an inch over six feet, he excelled at the middle and long-distance track events. Wavy brown locks and soft gray eyes attracted the ladies, but Joe had allowed himself little time to pursue them. Above all, he was a serious and devoted scientist. The future was bright if he could measure up. Still there remained one knotty question as he sat by the fireplace in his small off-campus apartment.

Why do I feel as if I have been programmed to meet some pre-planned goal?" he asked his roommate bill. "Ever since I began my charmed academic life six years ago, there's been this nagging thought that I may not be captain of my own destiny. If there's anything I insist on, it's that I have control of my own life and bear responsibility for who I become."

"I have no doubts about that, Joe. You're about the most self-assured and determined guy i ever met. Way too hardheaded, but you always know where you're pointed."

"No, what I mean is, how could those folks choose me out of thousands who are probably smarter than I am and give me the chance to earn a PhD? My family didn't have money or influence, and I didn't actively pursue the scholarships I was given. The foundations that financed my education contacted me, and they remain a mystery to me.

All I am really sure of is that one of them believes in strict adherence to the constitution. I wrote an essay and stated my own beliefs. The summer training sessions I went to told me I was already well aligned with what they were teaching us, application of constitutional law and non-career politics. But there must have been others with better credentials than mine."

"You know what they say about looking a gift horse in the mouth, Joe. It was their money to spend and you've worked hard. Go with the flow, man."

"*Maybe I am a bit paranoid about my sponsors, Joe mused. Guess I made all their gates and lucked into a fantastic deal. Still, every time I try to single out somebody to thank, nobody admits to being in charge. The Federalist Foundation and America Foremost remain mysteries. Is somebody pulling strings while I dance for them?*

Joe went off talking to himself. He sat alone with his knee bobbing at a furious pace. The involuntary movement was a sure sign he was working his way into a dither worrying.

Knock it off, Amos. It should be enough I'll soon earn my doctorate, go off into the real world and start making a difference. His part time employment at GMed between school terms gave him a leg up on his career. George Adams, the owner, had shown personal interest in him since they met at the awards ceremony in Saint Louis. Joe worked in a first-class lab environment with state-of-the-art tools. Adams had asked if he would take the lead in developing a new diabetes medicine when he finished school. The salary was impressive. George even committed to provide a project staff picked by the young biochemist.

Yes, life was good. Joe wanted to take the plunge. But would he really call the shots? If he committed to GMed, would some shadow figure emerge and demand pay back he couldn't make? Joe was convinced of one fact: whatever he accomplished as a scientist had to be because it was what he wanted, not to satisfy someone else's goals or prepaid claim on him.

Chapter 27

Today would be a new start for Joe Amos. Standing in front of his bathroom mirror, the freshly minted PhD looked at his reflection and marveled at how far he had come. The gray eyes stared back at him with a mixture of resolve and trepidation. There was so much Joe wanted to do. Could he measure up? He ran a comb through his wavy brown hair and smiled. Hadn't he met all the tests so far?

Amos regarded his hard body, the six-one frame and long stride that carried him to track victories on so many days. Joe was not a bulky man but rather a strong, lean and youthful specimen well aware that a healthy body and a quick mind must operate in concert.

He noted the time and hurried to dress for work. A sleek red convertible, the one luxury he had permitted himself to date, waited under a custom cover in the garage space behind his modest apartment. The short drive over western Maryland roads to GMed near Frederick would leave him time to settle in at his workplace before his appointment with the board chairman.

* * *

George Adams put his telephone call on hold and greeted his new employee. "Morning, Doctor Amos. Grab a cuppa cawfee an' a seat. Be right with you." Must be a busy day for him, Joe thought. He'd noted his boss lapsed into his New York speech pattern when he was in a hurry or up tight.

Adams brought the call to a conclusion and turned his attention back Joe. "How's your lab look to you? As you can see, all the folks you asked for are there full time."

"Impressive, sir. Couldn't hope for a better team. I know every one of them well from my summers here. They're capable people."

"Didn't want to slow you down. This diabetes research you're to do is personal with me, Joe. You can count on all the help i can give to find the treatment that improves my own life. By the way didjuh eatchet?"

Joe couldn't stop the laugh that came on.

"Wasamatta?" George asked.

"Sorry, sir. It's your New York accent. Be patient with me. I'll learn."

George chuckled. "they've been working on me for years with speech coaches. I do fine till i start moving too fast and get flustered. Then the old city lingo seems to take over. Let – me – try – again. Did – you – eat - yet. doctor?" Joe shook his head. "Not yet. And may I ask a favor of you, Mister Adams? My friends have always called me Joe."

A smile lit George Adams's face. "Then Joe it is. And I'd like for you to call me George if you would. I'm looking forward to our working together. I'll order some breakfast delivered and we can talk awhile before you dive into the lab." Adams pointed to the sitting area with a burgundy leather sofa, two armchairs and a massive coffee table. Joe took a seat and waited.

Georg frowned. "Now we're past the slang barrier and on a first name basis, there seems to be something else that's distracting you. I hope we can be open and honest with each other. What is it?"

Joe decided the time had come to dispense with the issue that clouds his start at GMed. Maybe he was far afield here, he thought, but he had to know.

"This may sound odd to you, George. I keep getting the feeling my future has been preprogrammed, that I've been on the outside looking in. I suspect you may have been in on that planning."

Adams settled back in his big chair and took a deep breath. His smile told Joe the question he'd asked had struck a nerve. George pulled at his right ear lobe with two fingers, rubbed it slowly as if debating a decision, then continued. When he leaned toward Joe and began his answer in almost a whisper, a wall between them began to crumble.

What I'm about to tell you," George started, "Is something I have waited years to say. Please hear me out before you make a judgment."

Joe heard the noticeable change in tone and measure in his boss's voice. He puzzled over what revelation could follow the serious introduction Adams had just made.

"Your path these past eight years has been closely monitored, Joe. Everything you've accomplished is totally through your own effort and ability, but interested people stood ready to help steer you if you needed it."

"Wait! I have to ask, sir. You mean our first meeting in Saint Louis was planned? That you'd been watching me before that?"

"Yes to both questions, and there's much more. I want to tell you about another man named Joe. Joe Whitley was my best friend."

The two talked through the morning. Joe was anxious to get down to work, but the story now unfolding pushed all other considerations to the dim background. George described how Joe Whitley rallied a group of his friends to create an initiative aimed at recapturing the promise their country held for the world. He explained that these men knew from the outset the undertaking would involve mentoring young people with extraordinary aptitudes and talents; that it would be a long process that others may deem as a threat bordering on illegal. But, Adams assured him, their intent was honorable and their methods consistently within the bounds of law and decency. Joe Whitley had passed on, but the surviving members carried on the work they believed in so strongly.

So the foundations that sponsored my education are organizations you and your associates are involved with?" Joe asked with a strong note of disbelief.

"Assawayigoze, as we used to say in the big apple. Formed, staffed and controlled," Adams replied, "Just as we did with a number of other entities we set up to sponsor hundreds of young people. But you need to understand, Joe, that's the only way we could operate in the face of our natural adversaries. Powerful forces, made even more formidable by public apathy, hold sway at all levels of government and industry. They're career politicians and ruthless businessmen who manipulate us and have spent the country into near bankruptcy. These potato heads care about nothing other than advancing their own causes and fortunes with total disregard for the public welfare."

"And where, sir, do you stand in the political spectrum? Are you liberal, moderate or conservative?"
"I'd have to be listed as 'none of the above' by current definitions. My partners in this effort are just as non-political as I am. I truly want to believe I am *for the people*, for representative government from the bottom up. We have so many shades of progressives, socialists, and fascists scampering around you can't even sort 'em out wit' a scorecard. There are way too many revisionists, as Joe Whitley called them, who want to change the rules as they go on a whim. Political parties, to me, are a good idea gone wrong; a lot like unions that began of necessity but forgot their roots to push unreasonable demands, greed and corruption."

"Now I think I understand the purpose of my training `sessions on constitutional law, boss. As much as I enjoyed it, I kept wondering what it had to do with me as a biochemist." "

Yes, Joe. We wanted you to appreciate the *why* of your work as much as the *how*. We humans are capable of so much with hard work and the minds granted to us at birth. But to be truly successful, we have to apply our decisions in humane, ethical ways. You can make badly needed breakthroughs to combat disease. How those findings are put to work for the most good, however, is too often a matter of governance. We want to work to elect citizens whounderstand the people's needs and will work to fill them."

A light seemed to go on in Joe Amos's eyes. "I remember hearing in my summer training sessions about the plan offered by James Madison, George Washington and others. They wanted to establish a national university to train leaders for the newly united states. Are you telling me those classes I attended were . . ."

"Our version of the national university? You got it, Joe."

Again, he rubbed his ear lobe and hesitated. “what my friends and I call project wake is exactly that. Washington and the others knew the confederation of states they were forming was way too vulnerable to be handed over to ambitious, greedy men. They wanted to train bright youth to be leaders instilled with a love of the nation and a desire to serve it. Project WAKE puts that idea into practice to school youngsters as experts in all the arts and sciences.”

`So the others who were in summer classes with me … were they all participants in this Project WAKE?”

“Yes. Each student was sponsored and watched over by one or more of the educational foundations we set up. And your group was only one of several that met in various parts of the country every summer.”

“Meaning there must be a small army of men and women trained under your auspices now filtering into the workplace.”

“In every nook and cranny of science, engineering, education, medicine, law … the cream of the next generation of achievers. There are over a hundred ‘Joe Amoses’ in the making and more added each year.”

“I’m overwhelmed,” Joe said.

“Don’t be. You deserve credit for everything you’ve done so far. We only watched and gave a little nudge now and then. Now the rest is up to you, Joe. Keep this strictly between us. I’ll do my best to not interfere, but I’m here any time you want to talk. Make me proud.”

Chapter 28

Joe Amos and George Adams remained closeted in George's office past noon. They had made a strong connection neither of them expected. Adams explained the intricate plan for the future he and his fellow WAKE founders had so carefully constructed. The impact of what Joe learned about WAKE and their sponsorship of his education began to sink in.

He said, "I suspected there was more to my selection than I knew, George. Why didn't you tell us students earlier about the project?"

"We couldn't take de risk," George answered. He reached up with his big fingers and pulled at his ear lobe. Joe cataloged that gesture, thinking to himself, *George doesn't realize he's telegraphing when he reveals confidential information. Good thing I'm not a competitor of GMed.*

Adams continued. "We gave each young WAKER every opportunity to opt out. The least any of youze would get out of it was a college education paid for in full. But you weren't ready to hear the big picture yet. Besides, too many outsiders would fight what we were tryin' to do—break their tight-fisted control."

"I can see," Joe replied, "how some people could consider what you're doing a deep conspiracy. But the Constitutional training I've had convinces me that troubled times call for strong measures. Seems every other great society has imploded through neglect and corruption and I don't want that to happen to America. I need to think this through on my own, but it sounds credible to me."

"Joe, you're exactly what we hoped for when we started this project. You understand what underpins our republic. You know we have to stay on guard to keep our federal government system from bein' driven by ambitious, greedy men. We had a one-word expression where I grew up: 'Chips.' It meant 'you break it, you buy it'. We're looking to call chips on some old boys been running things into the ground. If they're gonna screw things up, they have to take the heat for doing it. I hope my friend Joe Whitley is watching and smiling. With folks like you we're bound to win this battle."

Joe shifted in his seat. He felt a new sense of personal relief about his past. There remained, however, lingering doubts about *his* role with regard to the WAKE grand plan. For Joe there was a lot to be sorted out. George watched his young protégé's expression and Joe's knee bob, a sure sign of nerves and uncertainty.

"I know this is a challenge to accept, Joe," George told him. "We'll hit it off just fine between us. I can feel your honesty and resolve. G'head and question our motives. I respect that. Please believe that my friends and I would much rather be open and upfront with what we're doing. But the people we want to unseat, greedy businessmen and career politicians, have other ideas. Our protégés, young folks like you, are a serious challenge to their control. We had to work undercover."

"Believe me," Joe said, "I know you're being honest with me. I just need time to absorb what you've told me."

"Set your own pace, son. We have time. But remember, every day these power brokers get stronger. My best friend Joe Whitley nearly had his life shortened by a greedy politician and that man's corrupt dealings with the Arab oil interests. Another of the co-founders of WAKE had a close call because he bucked the drugs boys *and* the oil peddlers and was a threat to another crooked politician. There are a lot more influence peddlers just as capable of visitin' revenge on us. Our edge is stayin' undetected till it's time to pounce on the bad guys and expose 'em once and for all." "Oh, I don't question there are those who'll fight you and work against fairness and a sense of the public good in our leaders. This whole WAKE proposition is just a bit hard to comprehend without some soul-searching. I want to be a good soldier, but it may take time."

“Time we have, Joe. We have to do dis right de foist time. Too much depends on it. But determination and patience are our bywords. Think about it, son. My door is always open. I want you to be more than a good soldier. What’s most important is to believe in what we’re pursuing and genuinely want it to happen.”

"I’m a biochemist, boss, not a politician.”

“True, but all our proteges can do their share of public service while they also serve in technical fields. Keep believing in a federalist form of government. Work in your chosen field but try to make time to be a citizen lawmaker at some level. We can suggest governmental actions we believe in, but the decisions about how to apply them will be up to the young people. A new peaceful national revolution is getting underway and you’re a part of it, Doctor Amos . . . uh, Joe.”

Chapter 29

His early days at GMed were even more fulfilling than Joe anticipated. He had full authority to do everything necessary to find a new treatment regimen for diabetes. The people and company facilities were the very definition of excellence. George Adams, despite his own demanding schedule, somehow found time to check in regularly on the progress of Joe's team.

Within a few whirlwind weeks, Amos and his cohorts set about brainstorming paths to developing a new medication and charged ahead down multiple investigative paths. Joe knew that the answer to effective treatment lay in finding a way to control blood glucose on a continuing basis until the diabetic's body reacted as if it were being fueled by naturally produced insulin. He personally believed the key may lie in manipulating human enzymes.

The young biochemist and his mentor sat in the new laboratory at GMed on a spring night. George had appeared late in the work day armed with an impromptu meal for the two of them and asked him to stay and chat.

"Hope you like soul food, Joe," he told his protégé. "Nothing like fine Southern barbecue, collard greens, potato salad and cornbread to get the juices flowing. Got us a special treat to finish up with, too—pecan pie." I love them all, George. It surprises me, though, that somebody who grew up in a big northern city would appreciate them."

"Spent most summers with my granny down in South Carolina, Joe. Two things that woman could do. She cooked like an angel and she knew how to fan a smart-mouthed kid's britches. Between well-deserved whippings, she got me hooked on soul food."

"Sorry to break the news to you, boss, but you aren't exactly equipped to handle a calorie overload like this. We're going to have to get you on a better diet."

"You sound like my dear wife, Evaline," Adams chuckled. "God bless her, she works hard to keep me in line, but a fellow has to have a little leeway now and then." He dug into the juicy pork ribs and smacked his lips. "Umm – better than the finest steak."

"Boss, I always heard that loyalty is a two-way street. I've signed on to put everything I can muster into finding a better way to treat the disease that plagues you. Can you meet me half way and promise you'll stick to a reasonable diet till we perfect our solution?"

George looked up from his feast and hesitated. His eyes began to water. Reluctantly, he stared at the succulent rib swimming in sauce and slowly returned it to the box.

"I'll take that challenge! Matter of fact, let me propose something. We both know the initial tests for any new medicine have to be done exclusively on animals. Then I want to volunteer to be your first *human* test subject."

Joe shook his head vigorously. "Too risky, George. We couldn't …"

"Listen up, Joe Amos. You're a bright young man. You understand how much dreams mean. This work you're starting is my best chance to leave something important behind when I go. Let me be an active part of it. I can convince my doctor that I'll be in good hands as your 'lab rat'. We'll push the envelope together."

"I can't let you do it. You're too important to too many people to take the risk."

George waved his hand. "End of discussion, Joe. Sign me up. Between you and ol' Doc Jeffers, I'll be in good hands. Now let's talk about that break you said you need to meet some commitment.

"Oh, the summer session. You know I've been going to WAKE's summer training courses on Constitutional government. The next one is scheduled for mid-July over in West Virginia. I can cancel out if it's necessary."

George frowned. "You'd stop going now?"

"I gain new insight every time I attend. Puts a whole different face on the big picture. But our project here is so important I should concentrate on that for now.

Adams thought to himself, *Fine testimonial to Joe W's dream of a national leadership university. He'd be proud it's producing people like Joe Amos.*

"Don't ever stop learning about the foundations of our country, Joe. By all means, take the time off and go," George said emphatically.

Chapter 30

Before Joe realized how fast time was passing, the days of summer heat pressed in on the western Maryland hills. His team's work forged ahead, but he was practical enough to admit that their road to a new diabetes regimen would be long and arduous. For the next week, however, his thoughts would be on Constitutional government as befitted his commitment to the sponsors who had seen to his education. He laid out a full and challenging week of tasks for his people and set out for the West Virginia hills on Sunday. That would give him a quiet evening before classes began. Putting the top down on the red convertible, Joe drove away with the wind blowing through his brown hair.

*   *   *

The college campus sat on the outskirts of the town of Glenville. It seemed an idyllic setting for the mental reset Joe looked forward to experiencing. Fresh mountain air and the beauty of nature in full bloom would be a welcome change from his sterile and often confining laboratory. The campus even boasted a track where he could be alone with his thoughts and enjoy the exhilaration of physical exertion. He checked into the men's dormitory, learned he was one of the first arrivals, changed and headed directly to the track.

Joe warmed up to begin a leisurely run. He soon picked up the pace as the sheer pleasure of running overtook him. He was back to days of track meets and all-out effort, of breaking the pain barrier and running for the blissful high of speed and motion. Then it happened. A leg cramp seized and sent him tumbling onto the infield grass, crumpling and grasping his thigh muscle. He lay face down writhing in pain, the smell of wet turf and freshly mowed grass in his nostrils. Then a subtler aroma, a perfume, drifted down to him.

"Are you okay?" a pleasantly female voice asked over his shoulder. He rolled onto his back and looked up to see a stunningly attractive blue-eyed blonde wearing a red track outfit. "You were really moving out there. But I think you overdid it."

"Got carried away," Joe replied. "Thought for a minute I was back in my glory days as a jock. Guess age and inertia caught up with me. I'm Joe Amos," he managed to say. "You live around here?"

"Don't you think you ought to move around on that leg and work out the cramp," she asked, but Joe just lay there transfixed. Her fresh beauty and warm smile had thrown him totally off guard.

He let her help him to his feet and they began walking back and forth across the infield. The cramp started to ease. Or had she just made him forget it? "You didn't answer my question," he pressed. "Are you a student or maybe faculty here?"

"Neither," she said and stopped, as if purposely holding back.

Joe filled the awkward silence. "I'm here for a special one-week summer session that starts tomorrow."

"Me, too," she said and gave him a broad grin that made him feel warm all over. "I'm JoAnne Donovan, and we may be attending the same course. Comparative Government?"

That was the name being used this summer for their gathering. Joe was aware from George Adams's revelations about WAKE that a number of like sessions would be conducted throughout the summer at various facilities around the country. George had further revealed that these seminars were designed by Project WAKE to train protégés for their roles in rescuing the country. But Joe dare not use the word WAKE since George had sworn him to secrecy about the project and its long term plan.

"That's the one, JoAnne. Guess we'll be spending a lot of time together this week."

"I look forward to it," she said, beamed her disarming smile, and let him speculate as to any implications in her statement.

* * *

The next few hours made his trip a resounding success even before the first classroom session convened. Joe's time this year had been totally dedicated to finishing school and getting started on his first real job. Since the initial day at GMed he'd found himself absorbed in an around the clock foot race to cement his research team and launch their important project. There simply was no time for female companionship on *his* killer schedule. That may change.

"Tell me about Joe Amos," JoAnne probed as they sat in the town soda shop. It appeared to be one of the few gathering spots for summer students. "You said you're a biochemist?"

"Well, that's what my sheepskin says. Finished my PhD in May and went to work at GMed Pharmaceuticals. We're exploring a new regimen for treating diabetics."

"Big company with a solid reputation," she said. "I understand they're an industry leader. And I take it you ran track in your college days."

"A lot better than I did today," Joe answered and massaged his sore thigh muscle. "Okay, now it's your turn. Just who is JoAnne Donovan?"

"Let's see," she mused. "Where do I begin? Grew up in Georgia, took a few laps around the track myself doing the 440 and running legs in the relays. Earned my electrical engineering degree then went off to MIT for grad work. I'll have my doctorate a year and a half from now. Want to specialize in the new field of nanoelectronics."

"Nano? … Oh, if I remember correctly, that's the science of extremely small electronic circuits, right?"

"Correct, Doctor Amos," she said and made an imaginary check mark in the air. "Us EE's refer to it as the world of the teensy weensy." She gestured with her fingers and said, "Itsy bitsy. Nano has potential implications in multiple fields including diagnosis and treatment of disease with nanometer sized electronic devices. Our goal is to inject them directly into the patient's blood stream."

"That's an interesting field for a lady—a blonde Irish lady at that."

"Oh, that's from my mother who's a native Minnesota Swede. She gave me my height, too. We're both five nine."

Joe spent the balance of the day reveling in his good fortune. By the time he escorted her to her dorm and said good night, all other concerns faded and he could think only of the tall, shapely Irish/Nordic beauty who had totally captured his imagination.

Chapter 31

The second day of classes continued with the fifteen eager young students Joe Amos had met yesterday. He scanned around the room and took inventory. They had carried on a lively first day session and returned today preloaded with questions. There appeared to be the usual mixture of first-timers and veterans like him. He flashed back to when he sat in his first summer class. Back then he had wondered aloud to some of his fellow attendees whether this was a productive use of their time. As the subsequent sessions unfolded, they not only earned his full attention but made him a staunch believer in the Constitution and its principles.

Joe recognized a few of the students. JoAnne Donovan was obviously an old timer, so to speak, and well founded in the course, but they'd never been in the same group before. That told him that George Adams and his associates intentionally rotated the students among the groups.

The scholarly gentleman leading the class reached a peak in his enthusiasm for the subject of the day. He explained events of the year after the Constitution was drafted.

"So you see the careful thought that went into improving upon what had been a grand but somewhat incomplete attempt with the Articles of Confederation. The Continental Congress had made an important, if imperfect, start. What remained was to frame a Constitution that would ensure the long-term vigor of the new United States of America. Hamilton, Madison and Jay wrote their Federalist Papers after the Constitutional Convention of 1787. Those essays made the case for New York to welcome and ratify the newly drawn Constitution."

He paused and shuffled his notes before looking up over his half-lens reading glasses. "Can anyone tell me the most important contributions the Federalist Papers made?"

JoAnne raised her hand. "They revealed, for the first time outside the convention, the thought process the founding fathers used in drafting the Constitution, framed the arguments for and against specific articles in the document, and showed the rationale behind its final language."

"Very good, JoAnne. Now this question is for those of you assigned to read and analyze essays 23 through 36. What does number 23 tell us about the goals and limitations set on the federal government?"

Silence followed as students pored over their notes. Finally, a young man, perhaps a first timer, spoke up. "The states ceded to the new federal government that part of their own sovereignty necessary to promote the common defense, maintain public peace, regulate commerce with other nations and between the several states, and oversee foreign relations."

"Good. This next one is a toss up. What does the Constitution tell us about the sovereignty of the thirteen original states?"

A hand went up. "Sovereignty remained with the states," a fresh-faced woman answered. "That's the primary principle of American government. King George recognized the independence of thirteen states who then decided to join together for their common good."

"Excellent," said the prof, punching the air with a forefinger. "And what guarantees the states retain their powers and protects them from an oppressive federal government?"

A male student answered, "The Tenth Amendment to the Constitution says, *'The powers not delegated to the United States by the Constitution, nor prohibited by it to the States, are reserved to the States respectively, or to the people."*

So it went through the week. Joe Amos, even after his previous time in yearly sessions, continued to marvel at the wisdom with which the founders honed and constructed that wonderful document, the Constitution. He emerged from the week's discussions more convinced than ever that his future should include a turn at public service as a citizen politician. He kept replaying what the last instructor said as his parting comments.

"Ladies and gentlemen, the founding fathers gave us a new concept they called federalism. The Constitution incorporated the genius of that concept. Forrest McDonald published a book in 1985 entitled *Novus Ordo Seclorum*. I recommend it to your reading."

He held up a green paperback with the great seal of the United States on its cover. "In this book McDonald says that when the founders drafted the Constitution they created a *novus ordo seclorum.* For those of you not up on your Latin that translates to 'a new order of the ages."

He paused and a hush filled the room. "A grand experiment, a radically new order," the professor emphasized. "We must hold that light on high and never let it waver.

Joe agreed. Another resolution also had become important to him. He promised himself that the young lady who had captured his attention must be part of his life. JoAnne Donovan had affected him like no other woman he'd ever met. His head spun just thinking about her. They both had heavy commitments, he to his medical research and she to finishing her education. But after that, who could say?

Chapter 32

Joe Amos immersed himself in perfecting his diabetes treatment. His team at GMed made bold advances in understanding the causes, effects and treatment of the insidious disease. Revelations unfolded regarding the chemical composition and organic interactions in nature's most fantastic mechanism, the human body.

The team assembled on a hot Maryland summer day in their small conference room at the call of Doctor Amos. He looked around and made eye contact with each associate.

"I wanted to bring everybody together and take a break from the grinding routine you're going through. We've worked hard, faced a lot of setbacks and frustrations. But our successes are monumental. We've learned lessons about human enzymes and trace body chemicals that will be used over and over to improve medical technology. You've uncovered important new findings about how the body reacts to both internal and external stimuli. We've formulated regimens for treating diabetes that were unknown until we tested and verified them here. I want you to know how much everyone at GMed appreciates your efforts. We still have much work to do, but I'm confident we'll reach our goal of producing the best ever diabetes treatment."

* * *

Later Joe sat with GMed's owner George Adams in the lab. He had been spending considerable time revisiting what George told him about Project WAKE — that it was four men's initiative to salvage a declining country, to establish a national leadership university as envisioned by the founding fathers. George and his friends built on that idea by creating an open school populated with bright young scholars in all the major disciplines. Joe's initial fear that he'd been part of a conspiracy was gone. He saw the achievements he and other WAKE protégés had been prodded to produce by the patient hand of the WAKE founders.

"Howgozit, Joe?" George asked. "Your folks are sure proving they can do wonders for my health."

"I still feel bad about your insisting on being our primary test subject, George. You're much too important to GMed and the country to be taking these risks."

"Wouldn't have it any other way, Joe. It would be absoid, to use a New York expression, to ask others to believe in what we're doing if I don't do my own part. Besides, I feel like a new man." George patted his much leaner front and smiled. "Lost thirty ugly pounds, found new energy, and Evaline says I act twenty years younger." His familiar ear tug told Joe that last item was a bit of inside information George considered confidential.

"Boss, the work from here on out will be a lot slower," Joe said.

"I'm well aware of that, son. No doubt in my mind, though. We're well on the way to marketing a product that'll revolutionize the control of diabetes, providing we can survive the damnable bureaucracy."

"Exactly, George. Soon the good old federal government will take over and apply its tangled approval process. We both know that moves slower than the earth's tectonic plates. We have a great new medicine well on the way to being ready for patients worldwide. Now a whole army of officious meddlers have to have their say while millions of sufferers wait."

“Don’t go negative on me now, Joe. That’s an attitude reserved for us *old* geezers. Your team has done wonders. Remember, damn near every achievement American science has made for the past century has been delayed and frustrated by de good intentions of government lackeys that put more stock in dottin’ I’s than in implementing proven science.”

Joe fidgeted with the items cluttering his desk, patted his foot nervously, stood and reseated himself twice.

“Okay,” George finally said. “Out with it, Amos. You look like you’re wrestling with a shirt full of ants. What’s got you so hyper?

Joe leaned back in his chair and began slowly. “What you said is right on, boss. The hard work is done and my team is fully capable of bringing our new medicine to the market, but we can’t speed up the regulators and foot draggers. Maybe I could be more productive by moving on to another effort.”

“What’s that mean? You want to leave GMed?” George sounded crushed.

“No, no. You’re a great mentor, George. I would never turn my back on you after all you’ve done. It’s just that I’ve wanted for years to do something significant to find reliable new alternative energy sources. My dream back in college was to find a way to unlock the energy stored in biomass products to generate electrical energy. Our work on the new medicine has unlocked interesting possibilities. We’ve discovered human enzymes we didn’t know existed. I think proteins like those could be the catalyst for extracting biomass energy. The time may have come for me to change my focus.”

George thought about that for a long time. He rubbed the fuzzy gray stubble covering his scalp. Joe watched and agonized that he must have sounded ungrateful to the man who helped make him a success. He tried to read George’s eyes, get an indication of his reaction. It was a tense wait.

Finally, Adams smiled. "You're pure right, Joe. I know about dreams. This company was my dream. I wouldn't axe you to forego your goal for the woild. You'd need to pick your successor on the meds project and promise to be around if they need you. Show me a written proposal. Convince me and I'll gladly spin off a startup and give you a stake in it. New energy sources will be critical in the future. Let's attack that problem before it gets any worse."

Joe felt the world start to spiral around him. George was a man who not only had the money to face new challenges; he also had the guts to take risks. His quick acceptance of this undertaking stunned Joe. He managed to stand on his second try and extended a hand across the desk to Adams.

"Thank you for understanding."

"I look forward to seeing your proposal," George said, shook his hand and stood to leave. Joe dropped back into his seat and took a long break to ponder what had just happened. *How dumb lucky can a fellow be? I was plucked out of the amorphous mass of eager youth by anonymous sponsors and guided through my education. Then George Adams gave me the chance to excel as a new biochemist. I'm on the verge of making life better for millions of diabetes sufferers. Now he's backing me to launch my dream of searching for viable renewable energy sources.*

Joe looked out the window and made a solemn pledge. *I* will *succeed and repay what's been given to me. The medical and biomass projects are as much for my own fulfillment as for others. Then I'll pay back WAKE by taking my turn as a citizen politician.*

He said aloud as the boss left, "Thank you, George. I won't let you down."

Chapter 33

Soon, a modest startup began for Doctor Joe Amos and his small staff. George Adams and Joe located a large vacant farm house with a sturdy cinderblock outbuilding far out in rural Loudoun County. There they quietly launched a new company they named EnzAm.

What sounded like a medical group was actually Joe's dream of a concerted effort to cleanly and efficiently manufacture electrical energy from biomass products. In the style of GTE, which no longer stood for General Telephone and Electronics, the company would be simply EnzAm to everyone except George and Joe. They would refer to it as Energize America. Joe went about recruiting a supporting staff of the brightest biochemists available.

He and one of his prospective associates, Doctor Fred Vinson, sat in the dining room of the Hillsboro Inn on a warm spring day. The quaint, out of the way tea room smacked of tradition and custom, a far cry from the revolutionary work the EnzAm team was pursuing.

"Let me understand, Doctor Amos. You want my commitment but can't say specifically what I'll be working on?" Fred Vinson asked, barely concealing a smirk.

"I know that sounds strange," Joe replied. "The nature of our project and its potential impact on powerful interests forces us to maintain secrecy for now. I can assure you this is one of the major biochemical challenges of our generation. It involves the use of enzymatic proteins. Beyond that I ask that you respect our need to remain below the radar of those who could wreak havoc on our work."

"Well, the salary and benefits you've offered are certainly inviting, Joe. I know your reputation as a researcher and believe you share my goal of making a contribution. Our tour of the facility this morning tells me you've spared no expense in building a first-class research lab. But this cloud of secrecy is a bit hard to accept."

"I ask your patience on that point, Fred, but I won't apologize for the need to be cautious. An integral part of our employment contract with you will be that you are free to terminate after six months and receive the full first year's salary. If you exercise that option, we'll ask that you sign a non-disclosure agreement to never reveal what you've learned at EnzAm."

* * *

The two young scientists were in contact by telephone five days later.

"Joe, this is Fred. I've thought about your offer. I have to say the shroud you wrapped around your end goal had me worried and gave me some long nights. Oddly, the element of uncertainty is an exciting plus. I can live with the requirement for non-disclosure if our arrangement doesn't work out. I accept your offer."

"Believe me, Fred, once you see what we're going after, you'll be as enthusiastic as I am. Your contract is ready and so is your work area."

One by one, Joe selected his team and set to work on energizing America with a new alternative source of power. For years researchers had been attempting to derive from various organic products, wood, corn, even garbage, a yield of energy that would justify using existing sources to extract that yield. Joe had worked on the idea and hypothesized ways to make the process work. Now George

Adams and GMed had brought him hope that his theories were closer to realizing. Joe's average work day expanded to sixteen hours and more, which left him time only for quick meals and a short night's rest. Each night he stumbled upstairs in the converted mansion to renew his strength for another grueling day. Even in his state of near exhaustion, he had never felt so motivated.

* * *

A heavy December winter sky hung over the Virginia countryside as Fred Vinson prepared to leave EnzAm for the day. He and Joe Amos were the last two in the lab.

"Time I got on the road, Joe, before this snow starts." Fred stared across the desk at him and said, "You're looking a bit worn down. Too many late-night sessions or are you moonlighting with Miss Right?"

"The way we've been pressing, Fred, I haven't even had time to *find* a Miss Right or even a reasonable facsimile. What we're doing is too important to risk being distracted from my singular purpose."

"What actually got you started in the biomass arena?" Fred asked. "Seven months of watching you work like a slave has rubbed off on all of us in the project, but I worry about your health. I get the feeling there's something almost obsessive driving you."

Joe took a deep breath and exhaled slowly. He considered his words with extreme care: *Of all the workers involved,* he thought, *Fred can best relate to the truth about the source of EnzAm. But It's not my call. He knows I worked at GMed on medical research before starting EnzAm; but George Adams wants no connection between the two companies. My meetings with the boss are always concealed and on neutral ground. And I can't mention WAKE to Fred.*

Before Joe could frame his answer, Fred continued. "Seven months ago I had my doubts. Now I've caught the bug and I'm passionate about biomass energy conversion. It's just a matter of time before we succeed. You know I'm with you till we produce an efficient energy release. Then we'll knock a big hole in the fossil fuel problem."

"I know that, Fred, and I owe you an answer. My motivation is bigger than EnzAm. This effort involves others who are dedicated patriots. They understand the long-term threat fossil fuels, particularly foreign oil, present to the U.S. They want to put us on a self-sufficient basis using alternative fuels. I'm sworn to secrecy on the larger picture they've entrusted me with."

"With all due respect, Joe, if these 'benefactors' are such patriots, why all the secrecy? Average Americans have a way of promoting the right movements from the grass roots up if they're made aware of all the facts."

"That's true," Joe replied. "We also know that firmly imbedded special interests will stop at nothing to keep their power and control. Unfortunately, they're well equipped to run roughshod over the public will. In fact, dare I say it, some of them are people we've elected to much more authority than they ever deserved."

"Then we could be targets because of what we're doing? These people might use deadly force against us?"

"Yes. But the goal, Fred, is worth the personal risk.

Chapter 34

Joe received a summons from George Adams for a private meeting. He left the EnzAm lab earlier than usual and drove to the picturesque little village of Middleburg. George waited in a quiet back corner at the Red Fox Inn.

"What's it been," George asked, "five weeks since we had a sit down?"

"At least," Joe answered. "*You're* looking great, boss. Trimming down. Guess my old crew is taking good care of you."

The waiter took their drink orders. He turned to leave, but George stopped him and insisted they wanted to order dinner right away. "I get one night a week off my diet regimen and tonight's the night."

When the drinks arrived, Adams lifted his soda and clinked it against Joe's martini glass. The glow of health and noticeable twinkle in his mentor's eyes gave the best testimonial Joe could want for the success of the diabetes project. George doubled as their one and only human subject to date and he looked healthy as a plow horse.

"I can't wait to get our new med fully developed and through the approval process," George told him. "Got a new outlook on life t'anks to your team's work. No doubt in my mind we're about to revolutionize diabetes treatment."

"It's not my team now, boss. Tom Frantz is doing a great job leading them. It's good to get a break in my killer work schedule at EnzAm, particularly since it's a chance to see you. I sensed there was also a note of urgency in your invitation."

"We'll get to that, Joe. First, tell me how things are goin' at EnzAm. Any hard spots?"

"It's a long road but we're off and running. I'm more convinced than ever that artificial enzymes are the answer. We plan to make chemical copies of natural enzymes and use them to break down the cellular structure of municipal solid waste to extract its stored energy. I'd like nothing better than to revise the old saying to read 'garbage in, *energy* out'."

"So EnzAm was a good move," George said. "I see great t'ings ahead. For now, though, it's the diabetes work that concerns me, Joe."

"I spoke with Tom about three weeks ago," Joe replied. "He tells me their research is progressing and the results are very encouraging."

"And I believe him. He's a good man. You trained him well. I just need your word we're gonna bring this off. Give me your honest opinion, son. How long before we put a drug on the market?"

"Tom and his team are totally devoted to their work and certainly competent. I won't second guess them, but I'll give you my take on where I think they are as of now."

"That's all I ax."

Joe said, "Could take a while to explain, and I seem to have an onion deficiency." He laughed and held up his glass.

"You're the second Joe I knew that was hooked on those pickled onyerns," George told him and gave the waiter a signal. "Used to tell Joe Whitley he ought to just spear the little devils from the jar in place of wading t'rough all that alcohol to chase 'em down."

Joe smiled and leaned over the table to continue. "I've told you that at least three of the enzymes we uncovered in the diabetes lab are potential catalysts for transforming and controlling blood glucose. The team uses one of them as the medium to treat you. But you, of all people, know biochemical research is a minefield. For every small breakthrough there are multiple false starts and disappointments."

Joe went on with a lengthy explanation that would have sounded like double talk to anyone else, but he and George were accustomed to the intricacies of biochemical terms. When he finished, he sat back and waited for George's reaction.

"Impressive, Joe. Now distill it down for me. Are we two years from government approval, five years, longer?"

"To cut to the chase, George, what those hard-working folks have so far is a sound theory that one of three enzyme proteins could be the solution for glucose control. Now they have to narrow that down to the best option and do extensive testing with laboratory animals. After that they simulate the natural protein with a lab product in oral or injectable form. Then they face the biggest test of all, convincing the FDA the product is safe for human testing. And that's only the beginning of the approval cycle."

George set his glass down with a thump and furrowed his brow. "Damn it, Joe, I've been through all that too many times. Hoped you'd soften your answer. Sometimes an old guy like me needs to be lied to just a little."

"Sorry, that's my optimistic assessment."

"Makes me wish I had something stronger than Coke in this glass," Adams said and took a swallow. "But Evaline would kick my formerly fat butt." He rubbed at his ear.

"You want specifics. I'll give you a straight answer, George. Figure another five years for synthesis and purification, animal testing, and institutional review boards. After that they submit their Investigational New Drug paperwork."

"The old IND rat race." George shook his head. "Been yanked down that dark tunnel by the buzzards at FDA. Clinical studies till we drop, then we still have to make a New Drug Application. De NDA could take years to approve."

"So no matter how we try to wish away the review and paperwork tangles, the answer isn't rosy, boss. If Tom and his folks hit all the stops on time, GMed may be another eight or nine years getting the medicine to market. Given a few upsets and a stubborn bureaucrat or two, I predict ten years from now will marke the first year of general use. But the outcome will make every long day and sleepless night worthwhile. Millions will benefit."

"Gives me a reason to hang around, though," George said. "I'm determined to see us make life easier for diabetics like me. Now—new subject—can you spare two or tree days away from work? I have a friend I want you to meet."
Joe gave him a puzzled look. "Is that why you sounded edgy when you called?"

"Partly," George said. "We're picking up vibes your work at EnzAm is drawing attention in some dangerous circles. This friend may be able to help us avoid outside complications. He can meet with you over the weekend. You can take the company jet."

"Then I'll clear my calendar from Friday through Sunday. Where am I going?"

"Big D. Dallas," George answered with a broad smile.

* * *

On his drive home George reflected on the future he envisioned for EnzAm. *Joe Amos just might pull off his energy conversion scheme after all. Reminds me of myself when I was startin' out. Young man's got a fire in his gut and the stubbornness to stick to it. And he's a hell of a lot smarter than ol' George A ever professed to be. Didn't want to alarm him, but he's got to understand there's some rotten folks out there that can't afford for him to succeed. If biomass energy turns out to be commercially feasible, big oil is in trouble, and Joe's gonna have a big old bulls-eye on his back.*

"Suck it up, George," Adams admonished as he crossed the bridge into Maryland. "Amos knows what he's doin', I've clued him in on our intel reports. But I can hook him up with the most common-sense cowboy I know and let them thrash out a solution. Then we'll take on all comers."

Chapter 35

Four days later the GMed company jet departed for Dallas with a single passenger, Doctor Joe Amos. Finally, he could enjoy the first real break from work since arriving fresh out of school. At least when he worked at the GMed lab he could get away at night. Now that he lived in the big house where EnzAm bustled, he often went back downstairs to revisit the day's activities. Even the weekends seemed to be a blur.

Joe found the flight to Texas a welcome respite, an opportunity to think about something besides organic compounds, enzymatic proteins and intricate chemical processes. He settled back into the soft leather seat and thought ahead to what may lie in wait in Dallas. George Adams remained circumspect in identifying the friend Joe would meet there. So far Amos only knew he was a close friend of George's and that he may hold the key to countering some undefined danger George felt outsiders posed to EnzAm.

As the jet taxied into a parking slot outside a satellite terminal at DFW airport, a long black limo appeared at its side. Moments after the exit door opened, a young man about Joe's age appeared in the cabin.

"Howdy, Doctor. I'm Ryan Bolger. Mister Estrada asked me to bring you to lunch at his club. He's in a board meeting that should be breaking up in another thirty minutes or so."

Joe stuck out his hand. "Joe, please." As they shook he did a double take. Something about Bolger was familiar. "Have we met? I have this strange feeling I know you, Ryan."

Don't think so. I'm from Kansas. Went to Stanford business school and been with Carl's Foods for a while. That's Mister Estrada's company, the one he built from the ground up." Something about the way Ryan averted his eyes bothered Joe.

As they rode east along Route 35, Joe racked his brain trying to remember where he may have seen Bolger. JoAnne Donovan popped into his mind, too, as she often did these days. Since their time at the summer seminar in West Virginia, they had kept in touch by mail and telephone. She now had her doctorate and was working at K-Tronics in California. He had gone to Boston twice to see her at school. Since her graduation, Joe flew to California twice and she made one trip to see him in Maryland. These infrequent visits were bolstered by letters and telephone conversations that renewed and confirmed a growing bond. Joe kept thinking, *If only she could be closer ...*

He peered over at Ryan Bolger and a switch turned on in his memory banks. St. Louis! The first time he saw both JoAnne and Ryan was at the ceremony where he and George Adams also carried on their first conversation.

"We *have* met, Ryan. In Saint Louis. You and I received awards and we participated in a panel discussion."

"Jordan Amos!" Bolger said and nodded. "Small world or what?" Something told Joe that Ryan's reaction wasn't exactly a first blush recollection.

* * *

The limo rolled up to the front entrance of the Woodhaven Country Club. Ryan steered him to a small private dining room where they ordered cocktails and waited for Joe's host to arrive. They launched into stories of experiences since their first meeting and how both of their careers had taken off, thanks to the special interest of men like Adams and Estrada.

A darkly handsome Hispanic man surged into the room. Joe pegged him as being perhaps in his fifties. Appearing to catch his breath, the new arrival extended a hand to Joe and said, "Sorry 'bout the wait, Doc. My meetin' ran a little long. I'm Estrada. Call me Carlos. George Adams has told me all about you. Thanks for comin' down to Dallas."

Joe, Carlos and Ryan sat down for lunch and talked about the weather, the economy, everything but what Joe thought he was coming to Dallas to discuss. He was beginning to feel conflicted at this point. There was too much to be done at the lab to waste time on travel just to socialize. Maybe Carlos was being careful with Ryan listening,

"Pardon me for being brusque, sir," Joe finally interjected. "I understood there was a matter of some urgency you wanted to discuss, and I know your time is valuable."

Carlos and Ryan looked at each other and exchanged an unspoken communication. Joe felt momentarily isolated. Then Carlos chuckled out loud.

"You're 'zackly what George advertised. *Amos is all bidness*, he said. *Always cuts right to the core of things*. Joe, I've watched the ups and downs of biomass research for a long spell now. From what little I could get out of George, I b'lieve you're onto somethin' big. I'd like for Ryan here to be the Carl's Foods rep to help out with your energy work."

"We were just renewing our acquaintance," Joe remarked. "I met Ryan when we were both finishing undergrad studies."

"Good. Here's where I'm comin' from. I have an intense interest in attempts to make usable energy from waste. My stores cover eight states and an after-product of what we do is more tons of waste food and packagin' than you can shake a stick at. That makes us polluters, not by choice but as a natural result of our operations. Convertin' biomass could knock a hole in a large problem we're helpin' to create. We'd be clearin' waste and producin' energy in the bargain."

"Right on, Carlos," Joe said. "It's my hope that we can drastically reduce the number and size of commercial waste dump sites all over the country. You wouldn't believe how many wrongheaded decisions, including court rulings, have frustrated efforts to transform waste into energy. One long-standing court decision, reversed after years of infighting, ruled that biomass processors were not entitled to the right to have a city's waste delivered to their site for conversion. What kind of nonsense is that? Consumers retain the rights to the use of their disposed waste? Unbelievable."

"Oh, I know about the hoops researchers have had to jump through," Carlos said. "That's a big reason your work caught my attention when George let it slip he was dabblin' in the energy field. Took a lotta pumpin' to get him to tell me what was goin' on, but he finally opened up and clued me in on EnzAm."

"Carlos, the boss left me with the impression there could be immediate danger to our research. Said it was trouble you could help us avoid."

Estrada motioned toward the double door entrance. "Recheck those doors, Ryan. We don't need uninvited listeners."

When Ryan had flipped the door latch and returned to his seat, Carlos lowered his voice. "That's why Bolger's here. George and I first met both you young men at that awards ceremony for graduating college seniors. Adams tells me he's brought you up to speed on Project WAKE."

"Uh … well …" Joe's mouth froze up when he heard that closely guarded word again. Then it began to come together when Carlos nodded. They'd made a very special connection.

"That's right, Joe," Estrada continued. "George and I helped start the project. You and Ryan are both members of the first WAKE class. Before this plan is spilled to the public, you'll meet a whole slew of people from that first class. Now let's talk about the danger George and I both sense."

Joe felt a sudden electricity in the room.

Chapter 36

"I know what you're doin' is real technical, Joe," Carlos said. "Think you can dumb it down for a Texas boy?" Joe liked this self-made billionaire. There wasn't a pretentious bone in his body, and he was clearly smarter than he professed to be. Carlos sounded a lot like a certain North Carolina Senator who used to tell people *'I'm just a country lawyer'.*

Joe looked around the large meeting room with its paneled walls and wildlife murals. He discovered that someone had recently held a briefing here; they'd left behind a blank flip chart and several color markers. He dragged the easel over and began to draw. When his sketch was finished, he started stepping through the process EnzAm was attempting to make work.

"This is an oversimplification and we're far from making it functional," Joe explained. "Biomass, as you no doubt know, contains stored energy in a reusable but not readily accessible form. We seek to go beyond squawking about landfills and contamination and make them a viable source of commercial, distributable energy."

Ryan raised his hand and asked, "Where it says input, does that include all forms of MSW?"

"I see you've been brushing up on the terminology," Joe said. "And the answer is yes. All municipal solid waste—that is, food spoilage, household throwaways, paper products, all have latent energy content. That includes plastic. The old saw that plastics last forever in a landfill will no longer be true. Landfills and garbage composts, even hardened sludge from sewage plants, all can be turned into usable energy. We'll use them as inputs here at this entry point." Joe made a check mark on the right side of his drawing.

"And the overflow from food markets could be a steady input source," Carlos offered.

"Yes. Then the source materials go through a reduction phase in this first chamber."

"Reduction?" Ryan queried.

"The waste is decomposed, its cells literally reassembled," Joe explained. "We discovered in searching for a diabetes cure that certain human enzymes, basically proteins, break down and reorganize material at the cell level. We're working to isolate the most efficient enzyme and use it to decompose waste material. The cellular structure will be reduced to a densely packed mass containing the same residual energy."

"But won't that take loads of this enzyme?" Carlos asked.

Good question. That's why we have to first achieve the reaction with a small amount of the real protein then fabricate a lab-made substitute in large quantities. A spray of artificial protein and water melts down the waste into its individual cells. We apply heat and pressure in the reforming chamber to harden the sludge into a dense solid cake form. Then we transport slices of the cake to this combustion section. Concentrated pressure shatters the cake to release energy to fuel a power turbine."

"Well, you're the only scientist in the room, but it sounds logical to me," Carlos said. "Now let's talk about the reason for your trip. Some way the word is leaking out about what you folks are doin', maybe from a source on your staff. Oil interests and others in high places see EnzAm as a threat to their influence. You oughta be workin' under more secure cover. These are people that can apply whatever force they choose to stop you. Worst part is, they'll do it so slick the first clue you have may be way too late—when bad guys show up to put you out of bidness permanently. That's where I can help. Together we can set up online testin' in a remote part of Texas. George is okay with that if you are, Joe."

"You really think it's that serious? Until George mentioned something amiss it never occurred to me we could be a terrorist target." Just saying the word terrorist sent a shiver down Joe's spine.

"If I was you," Carlos cautioned, "I'd be suspectin' everybody around me. Until you can move the lab, you need to tighten down on every phase of your operation. I can provide a secure location for your team to work down here in Texas— and all the garbage you can process. The world's best security man works for me. His name is Jim Bledsoe, and I've known him since he worked for Joe Whitley, another of Wake's founders. Jim saved my life six years back. He can tell us how to keep EnzAm secure till you relocate. After that you can work in an underground site."

"If that's what it takes to make our project safe, let's get started," Joe said.

"Fine. Jim will ride back with you and scope out your setup. You'll meet him at dinner tonight at my place. We're gonna make a great team, Joe." He stood and shook hands.

Joe Amos just wanted to be left alone to perfect the science that could help millions of people by breaking the back of the oil monopoly. Now he was being told he had to worry about every member of his staff and who might be spilling information to dangerous outsiders.

And Joe thought his work had been exciting before!

Chapter 37

Progress at EnzAm was slow but steady. Joe and his team continued under the watchful eye of Jim Bledsoe and his security experts with each and every team member quietly under surveillance. Records of tests conducted and findings derived stayed under lock and key and no papers or storage media left the lab.

Joe repeatedly voiced his concern to Bledsoe. "Jim, it's hard for these folks to devote themselves to their work under so many security restrictions. They feel pressured. Makes them think we don't trust them."

"That's one of the hazards of working on the edge of technology," Jim answered. "I respect the way these people throw themselves into what they're doing. But as my grandma used to say, *'It only takes one rotten apple to spoil the pie.'* Keep reassurin' them it's in everybody's interest that you all keep your findings in house. Blame it on the threat of industrial espionage, not the bad guys we suspect. Meanwhile my folks will work to shut off information leaks."

"Who do you suspect?" Joe asked.

"Sorry, doc, I can't tell even you yet. Trust us."

The team was well along toward breaking down the cellular structure of waste products. They sensed they were one reaction away from a breakthrough, a single energy-releasing burst away from revolutionizing alternative fuels technology. And the key was an artificial enzyme they had named Adamslase in honor of the boss.

* * *

Joe Amos now shared the secure satellite phone network with Carlos Estrada, George Adams and Hiro Kato. From his terminal he could stay updated on the construction of the clandestine solar-powered site in west Texas where George and Carlos were building an underground test bed for the biomass project. An update proceeded by phone in Joe's upstairs EnzAm quarters.

"Sounds encouraging, Carlos," George said, and Estrada's voice beamed back over the speakerphone. "Not a speedy build out here, George, but it's damn sure secure. Bledsoe's folks will keep that Virginia site buttoned down for us while we finish this place off first class."

George boomed, "The sooner the better. My snoops tell me there's a lot of chatter bouncing around about a place in horse country Virginia doing some strange experiments. Jim's security guys have physical security nailed, and they're staying low key watching individual employees. They won't even confide in Joe."

Carlos assured them, "Best I can tell, 'less something goes catty wumpus on us, we should finish work out at Site Green six to eight months from now. Hang in and let Jim's boys handle things up your way."

"Easy for you to say," Joe answered. "I have this picture of a bunch of pajama-wearing Arabs overrunning the farm with guns blazing."

George vented his frustration. "Worst part is, the chatter leads us to believe a big part of the threat to EnzAm is home grown. It may even involve folks on the DC side of the Potomac. You know, on that hill at the end of Pennsylvania Avenue."

"Damn," was the simultaneous exclamation from Joe and Carlos.

Chapter 38

On the morning of September 11, 2001, a watershed event had occurred over the skyline of New York. Two hijacked airliners exploded into the twin towers and awakened America. For the first time Americans realized they were vulnerable to foreign attack.

Now more than13 years later, another tragedy was about to unfold in the quiet countryside of Loudoun County, Virginia. No public record of the event appeared and no outcry arose. The few who were privy to the details thought it best to spare the citizenry the pain of hearing about a second terror assault on home soil. And it remained to be determined whether this was the act of foreign or domestic sources.

A blazing sun rose peacefully over the Blue Ridge Mountains on Tuesday, October 9. 2014, Joe Amos's careful orchestration of the transition to Texas Site Green pointed toward the following January. Only Joe and Fred Vinson knew when the move would happen and where they would relocate. Team members all indicated their willingness to continue at the new place. They were assured that family needs would be honored and the company would cover one-time expenses. Joe, for security, misled them to believe that the new EnzAm home would be in the hills of either West Virginia or Pennsylvania. Joe and Fred carefully avoided any mention of Texas.

Jim Bledsoe and Joe Amos closeted themselves upstairs in Joe's living quarters. "We know the source of the leaks," Jim announced. "With your agreement we'll take care of that problem today."

Joe stared at him and weighed his words. What did *take care of* mean? Bledsoe's detail was not exactly prone to less than all-out action. They were capable and professional, but woe be unto those who thought they could cross them. "You want my sanction to do *what,* Jim?"

The security man took one look at Joe's expression and laughed out loud. "Don't worry. We don't expect to spill any blood. This person will be quietly isolated, pumped, and dismissed. We want to know exactly what's been leaked. Charges won't be leveled, but the mole will never work in the biochemistry field, maybe anywhere in the country, again. Say the word and the take down commences."

"Aren't the spy's actions treason or something?" Joe asked.

"Worst charge we could make stick right now would be industrial sabotage. The publicity wouldn't be worth the effort. It would only tip off the heavies that are conspirin' to torpedo your operation. I doubt their spy is of any use to them once out of EnzAm, but we'll send her to some place hard to find. No physical harm, the mole just disappears for your safety."

"Her? Did you say her?" Joe's mind raced. He had five female staff members, two researchers and three administrative people.

"Damn. Stupid slip on my part, Joe. Yes, I said her. If you give us the go, your records entry clerk will be gone by the end of the day."

"Jane? How do you know?"

"You really don't want to know the details. Let that be my worry. She's the one who's been funnelin' info to the bad guys. Just tell me yes or no."

"Do it, Jim."

"I need to tell you this may not be the end of our problems," Jim told him. "If they have eyes on us we may not get away clean with removing her from the site. Worse, she's probably passed the word there's a relocation in the works. They could decide it's their last chance to capture your records."

"What are you saying? Would they try to steal our data?"

"I'm sayin' if they figger out their game is over, they may pull a frontal assault. This could turn into a shootin' war."

Joe came unglued. "Why would we sit here and let ourselves be attacked? How could we defend against an all-out assault? I can't let my people be put in that kind of danger, Jim."

Bledsoe showed one of those sly smiles Joe had come to regard as saying *I've got your back.* "Not a lot of choice. If it's gonna happen, we just have to be ready. EnzAm is about to get some emergency help—telephone service and a power line check. Only the guys in the back of those trucks aren't from Virginia Telephone or Potomac Power. They're my people. If an attack comes, we'll be ready for them."

Joe thought about the steamroller that could be revving up to run him over and felt the bile rise in his throat. He needed no more convincing that this could turn into a wild day here on the farm.

Chapter 39

True to his word, Jim cornered Jane Walters, showed her they had her pegged as the mole, and explained her short list of options. She chose relocation far away. Jim had her discreetly escorted out the back door of EnzAm. The 'maintenance crews' finished their tasks while Jim's backup force slipped quietly, one at a time, into the lab warehouse. Dusk began to settle over the ridges just beyond the farmhouse. All seemed well in a calmly executed reduction to the project staff.

However, on wooded hilltops west and south of the property, two observers swept the farmhouse with powerful surveillance scopes. The observer to the west called his cohort.

"Looks like the maintenance men are leaving. What has it been, three hours since you saw the woman being taken away?"

"Just about," the watcher on the south side confirmed. "The other workers seem to have drifted away. Easy target, Ari. The probe team will be here any minute. A helicopter dropped them off half a mile from here fifteen minutes ago."

"Good. When they arrive I'll give you a call. We can leave these cold woods and have a cup of hot coffee while the attack proceeds."

Joe Amos and Jim Bledsoe locked away all the lab records in the secure vault and did a thorough sweep of the entire building just in case. "You really think this is going to happen, Jim?" Joe asked. "I thought your man whisked Jane away without anybody noticing."

"We can't take any chances," was Jim's answer. "I know what I'd be doin' if it was me out there on surveillance. Fact is, we know watchers have eyes on us. From now till you pull up roots for other parts, we're gonna have to be constantly on guard. The folks we've upset won't pull any punches. Sorry to be ordering you around, Joe, but I want you upstairs till I say different. Your car and mine have been out of sight in the garage all day. My men are positioned and ready. Keep your lights off upstairs. I want them to think nobody's left inside."

Joe nodded, locked the front door and stepped on the first stair tread. It squeaked. "Gotta fix that," he told Jim.

"I'll come for you when it's safe down here, Joe."

The wait in his second floor apartment wasn't easy. Joe played out scenarios in his head with dark clad assassins swarming all over EnzAm, laying waste to equipment, blasting into the vault to carry off data. Somehow the movie in his mind always ended with his sitting room door flying open amid a hail of gun fire.

* * *

Bledsoe set up inside the house in a vantage point overlooking the front door of the cinderblock lab structure. The moment a stranger poked his head inside that building he was prepared to tighten the noose. A defense force of ten men toting automatic weapons and side arms waited. Once the main attack force, if it came, was trapped, Jim would serve as the stop gap against anyone finding Joe upstairs. He had enough rapid-fire ammo to stand off a sizable squad of intruders.

Strict radio silence was the ironclad order to his men. He and each defense team member carried a hand held remote that would pass all the non-verbal directions they needed by means of low-intensity colored light sequences. Jim alternated his attention between scanning the outdoors with infrared goggles and checking his remote for signals. This was the part he hated most about his work, the seemingly endless wait to get a well-planned operation underway. And it may be something he had to bear for untold nights ahead as long as the EnzAm location was known and under observation.

Jim thought back to when he first met his current employer, Carlos Estrada. That little swing into Mexico to thwart Estrada's kidnapping involved a drug dealer and a small force of thugs. After Joe Whitley died, Carlos insisted Jim come to work for him. Now he felt it deep down in his gut that George Adams's spin off company was about to be overrun. He worried, *The price of poker, as they say down home, just went up. No telling how many trained gun wielders we may face before the night's over. If I've planned properly, none of my men will be hurt.*

He heard a sound upstairs and winced. *Tone it down up there, Joe,* he mumbled under his breath. *I got enough to handle without you drawing their attention.* Turning his focus back outside the window, he thought he detected movement. Jim focused in on the forty-foot span between him and the lab's front door. If anything moved, his goggles would find it. Nothing. Nerves?

You are way the hell too young to be getting skittish, Bledsoe. Keep it together and concentrate. As the point man, it's all up to you.

A single, short low beep sounded, and he locked his eyes on his palm. A sequence of light signals flickered, paused, and repeated. *Heads up! Something or somebody has been sighted on the grounds.*

Jim stuck his face against the cold window pane and homed in. There it was again, a subtle flicker of movement followed by the unmistakable infrared heat imaging of a human presence, two, now three. He watched patiently as six figures approached the lab building and saw two of them circle opposite sides of the block structure to cover the rear.

He hit the signal button on his remote and tapped out a light sequence that let his men know the unwanted visitors were at the entrance. Now his plan could play out as designed. One of his men stationed behind the lab would take care of any intruders at the back door with a tranquilizer gun. Two men were positioned to cover stragglers or second wave marauders outside. The other seven hid inside to cope with whoever breached the lab. Jim passed the signal and received confirmation.

Then he heard soft sounds at the front door of the house. Someone was picking the lock.

Chapter 40

Bledsoe turned away from the window and swung his M-16 automatic toward the front door. *The action in the lab is up to my team now. I'm on my own. Slow and steady, Bledsoe. If a whole army of these bad boys storms the house, you have to keep Joe Amos safe.*

Given the choice he would withhold his fire, take people down quietly with tranquilizers, and let his men set their trap at the lab. The last thing he needed now was noise to alert the attack force that they were about to get a big welcome at the lab.

Come to me, little flies, said the spider. Come into my web. Just don't make me use this shredder. The little bullet hose he held could burp a steady hail of slugs capable of stopping a determined penetration. He fingered the trigger guard of the 16 and worked his way across the living room; slid down against the wall. The front door inched open. Two men in black coveralls appeared. They both had wicked looking AK-47's slung over their shoulders. The men cautiously surveyed the front hallway.

Jim calculated the odds and saw he had the advantage. Only one man had a drawn handgun, and he could drop both of them before they knew he was there. But he hesitated to press the issue for two critical reasons—distracting the takedown in the lab and, above all, keeping this a bloodless event if at all possible, The public simply wasn't ready to read headlines that screamed *Terrorist Attack On Suburban Virginia.* He hugged the wall and took the tranquilizer gun from the holster under his arm.

He popped a dart onto the end of the barrel. The two intruders would make his decision. If they came toward the living room he had no choice but to spray the foyer with the M-16 and cut them apart.

"Upstairs," the first man in said barely above a whisper. "That's where the head man lives."

Bledsoe heard the bottom stair tread squeak under a heavy foot then creak again. He counted to three, took a cautious look around the corner of the wall, and saw the intruders both climbing the stairs with their backs to him. He aimed the tranquilizer and hit the back of the second man's neck with a dart. His target slapped his neck, slumped with a groan and smacked the stairs face first, his handgun doing a cartwheel back to the floor below. Bledsoe popped another dart onto the gun.

The lead attacker saw his companion fall and scrambled to the top of the stairs. By the time Jim could react, he had vanished.

"Well, now you've screwed the duck, Bledsoe," he chastised. He leveled the semi and pointed its laser spot upward. There was no way he could get to Joe Amos before that scuzz ball broke into his quarters. He dashed up the stairway, his assault weapon leading the way.

When Jim rolled into the hallway on the second floor he saw no one. The door to Joe's apartment stood wide open and the lights had been turned on. That left no option. He had to take his chances on a face-to-face with the intruder and hope Joe wasn't caught in the cross fire.

"Toss in your weapon. Then come in slow and easy," a voice from inside ordered, "or your friend is dead." Jim clicked on the M-16's safety, lowered the gun to the floor, gave it a shove through the door and answered, "Just stay cool. No need for anybody to get hurt." He checked his hand gun in the holster at his back and raised both hands.

"I'll say this just once," his adversary barked. "Face down on the floor."

Jim slowly sank to his knees, put one hand behind him, and looked into Joe Amos's startled eyes. The man behind Joe had a forearm around his neck and was squeezing. His right hand held what looked like a Glock nine aimed point blank at Jim.

Joe's mind seethed with rapid fire thoughts, all of them negative. But as he watched Jim, his best hope for rescue, being subdued, he acted on instinct. *I can't let this bum ruin everything,* he decided. In simultaneous moves he rammed an elbow backward into the gunman's ribs and stomped down on his right foot.

The unwelcome guest loosened his hold and yelped in pain. Joe made a dive to his left and curled into a ball. He heard a single gunshot and was sure he'd just managed to get himself killed, but no pain came. There was a grunt and then silence.

Joe uncurled and searched the room cautiously. Jim was prone on the floor with a gun in his hand. The prowler lay face down holding his unfired Glock. "Ballsy move, my man," Jim said as he got to his feet. "Where'd you learn that?"

"Strictly adrenaline and fear," Joe answered. "Are you all right?"

"I'm a damn sight better than I was a minute ago, thanks to you."

Jim went to the front foyer and tied up the sedated man lying there. Chances were 'Charlie' wouldn't come around for the better part of an hour, but Jim was trained to practice safety in depth. Charlie's pal upstairs was beyond help.

"Will you be okay in here, Joe?"

Amos nodded and replied, "Looks—what's your term?—looks secure, Jim."

"Here," Bledsoe said and handed the Glock to Joe. "Anybody else comes up here, aim and shoot. We'll sort it out later. And use two hands. It kicks like an angry mule."

Joe stared at the handgun and started to say something, but Jim cut him short. "You'll be fine, Doc. I have to go to the lab and see how my troops are handlin' the rest of this scroungy group. Stay put till I get back. We oughta have a van full of these bad boys to hand over to the authorities in a bit. I'll call the friend I alerted at the Bureau.

The FBI would take over from there. Bledsoe scooted away to join the action next door. As he hustled out the back door he heard noises coming from the block building.

He held his weapon at ready position and plunged ahead thinking, *Hope I haven't over-advertised. Either my guys have things under control or I'm in for one doozie of a shock.*

Chapter 41

Bledsoe swept the scene—'put his head on a swivel' was the operative term. If anything was amiss he had some serious one-man work ahead of him. Clearing constantly in all directions, he entered the lab building. Shuffling and banging noises came to him and there were voices shouting orders, but he couldn't be sure whether they were his own men or the prowlers.

He crouched in the dark and passed the threshold into the admin area. This was where he and Joe had secured records in a closet size vault. Just as he entered the room someone hit a light switch and overhead light flooded the space. Jim hit the floor hard and aimed his weapon.

"No sweat, boss," Harry Jenkins called out. "The friendlies are in charge."

When Jim followed Harry into the main lab, his first sight was a neatly trussed trespasser with one of his security men standing over him. Jim lowered his M-16 and scanned the room. Six interlopers in black garments were laid out across the floor. He counted nine of his men, some standing guard, others gathering and piling up an impressive array of weapons.

"These dudes were armed to the teeth," Harry said. "Good thing we had it planned by the numbers. Man, you wouldn't believe the look on their faces when I hollered 'surprise'. They had the vault door halfway rigged to blow away and most of their weapons set aside out of the way while they worked. Caught 'em flat footed."

Jim did a recount and blanched. He said, "You're one man short, Harry. Where's Tommy? Don't tell me . . ."

"Everybody's accounted for," Jenkins answered. "I think Tommy's back there taking a whiz. The smack down went like clockwork in here, boss."

A team of three FBI agents appeared on site half an hour later. They rounded up the eight prowlers, three of whom were just now beginning to recover from the tranquilizer darts. Two of them had been darted where they were covering the rear entrance, and the one Jim had put down inside the house spat insults at him until he stuffed a gag in his mouth.

"You give me a headache," Jim said. "Be a good little snoop and behave for the nice agents."

In the weeks that followed, the Bureau charged the intruders with armed robbery and domestic terrorism. They intensively grilled their prisoners to determine who was behind their actions. The story of what had happened in the normally quiet Virginia countryside remained untold in the media, but Jim's feedback indicated the search for blame found its way into the back alleys and byways of Washington, perhaps even up Capitol Hill.

* * *

When the dust had settled at EnzAm, Jim Bledsoe asked for an emergency meeting with George Adams, Carlos Estrada and Joe Amos. The subject was the immediate future of the biomass energy project. The men traveled individually to a secluded spot in the Arkansas Ozarks in mid-October for their gathering. They met in a rustic cabin southwest of Little Rock.

Jim Bledsoe finished his detailed briefing to the other three men on the likelihood of replays of the attack they had recently weathered. His conclusion was that as long as the location of the revolutionary biomass energy research was known and accessible, there would be no single day normal activities could proceed at the laboratory. A cloud of imminent threat, maybe even loss of life, would constantly hang over the Loudoun farm.

"Not an encouragin' outlook, gents," George stated. He had listened patiently and with no outward signs of emotion until Jim voiced the words 'loss of life'. At that instant, the pencil he was tapping the table top with bore down hard and the lead broke. "Sounds to me like we have a big decision to make."

"Exactly why I wanted all the players here," Jim emphasized. "We're at least two months away from activating Site Green according to your estimate, Carlos. I see that period as an extremely dangerous time."

Carlos thought about that and straightened up in his seat. He'd been scribbling notations on a tablet and studying them closely as Jim laid out the security dilemma.

"I think we can make this happen sooner," he declared. "As soon as you told me what had happened at EnzAm, I pressed my lead contractor for answers and gave him added incentive. He put his guys to workin' harder'n gnats in a hail storm. Way I figger, we can commence limited operations at Site Green within two weeks and put the staff in temporary housin' on site. We can settle in later. The families' household goods can be moved to the houses we've found in a couple of towns within fifty miles of Site Green."

"Works for me," George agreed. "If any team members can't meet that schedule, I'll take them back on at GMed and we can find replacements. Can you adjust to that, Joe?"

"Given the threat to my people if we stay here, I'd much prefer we make the move, even if we have to slow down our work for a few weeks. Yes, I say let's do it." He looked at a big smile breaking out on Jim Bledsoe's face and inquired, "What's that about, Jim?"

"Just occurred to me where that leaves our harassers. We've been planning this move for months. Got so many dead ends and false steps mapped out, our foes are gonna be chasin' all over the West Virginia mountains and half of Pennsylvania looking for destinations that don't exist. Even have forwarding addresses for staff members dummied up. Give me a few days and I'll have everything arranged."

Chapter 42

In early November 2015 Joe and his team made their move to the new Site Green facility. The ultramodern complex was literally carved out of the mountainside in west Texas. A self-sufficient solar plant generated its power. Even that critical feature of Site Green could be easily concealed from view with retractable covers built to resemble rough terrain. Adjustments were made to the final construction phase to meet the early move in date.

Team members reported to the underground facility and took up residence in on-site quarters. Their trails were carefully covered. Even their mail was trans-shipped from previous home addresses by one of George Adams's shell companies. The Loudoun site shut down and, by all outward indications, the EnzAm staff suddenly vanished. The workers and their families, in fact, were reestablished in two remote west Texas towns in the shadow of the mile-high Davis Mountains. EnzAm's married team members made regular trips down the mountain for time with their families.

Joe Amos, fresh in from the frosty outdoors, asked his assistant, Fred Vinson, "What's your assessment of the move? Is the team taking their change of venue in stride?"

"Once our families settled in nearby," Fred assured him, "it's been work as usual. The wide open spaces do promote a feeling of isolation at times, and the cold weather takes getting used to. But, hey, given our long hours and the security, none of us are outside much, anyway."

"I'd say things are going well, Fred. We may be closer to a breakthrough than we thought. And after the calamities we suffered last year, this time around has to be better."

* * *

Three weeks later Joe sat in his newly purchased home in the town of Alpine on a two-day break. As much as he was absorbed in matters at Site Green, there was an important void in his life. Nearly four years had gone by since that life-changing encounter with JoAnne Donovan at the summer conference. They had managed infrequent visits back and forth and kept each other up to date on their activities, but there was a noticeable degree of holding back on the part of both of them for security reasons. Ironclad commitments to their respective companies forced them to avoid repeating the details of their projects. A recent revelation and a frank conversation with George Adams had put a new slant on all this uncertainty. One thing Joe *could* be sure of, though. After each short interlude with JoAnne he felt her absence more keenly than before. Joe checked the time. Seven PM. He picked up the telephone and dialed.

"Donovan here." her sweet voice chimed.

"Wondered how your weekend was going," he said. "Been making lots of little nanos?"

"You make it sound like knitting baby booties, Joe. It's a little more complicated than that. Hard, slow work, like I imagine your research crawls along. Say, you're calling at a late hour back there. Are you still at work?"

"I have an admission," Joe replied with a note of embarrassment. "I'm not calling from the east coast. You and I are a bit closer in time zones than we were. Been trying to decide how to tell you we've moved."

"You're just brimming over with surprises, aren't you? Remember, I still don't even know what your hush hush project is all about. Now that you've moved, is there any reason you can't tell me where you are and what you're doing?"

"As I've said before, Jo Anne, there are good reasons why I've built a wall between us on this work. My boss has finally cleared me to read you in, and I'm anxious to rest. In fact, there's a lot I want to say to you. Can you find, say, three or four days to spend with me if I come to California? We can go somewhere and get away from our killer workloads."

"What are you suggesting, Joe?"

"I mean we could get away together and unfog our brains. Don't know about you, but it's been all work and no play for me and I ned to kick back. Go to the beach, see a show, hang out. I think both of us could use a break."

Her silence gave him pause to wonder how this must sound to her. "Uh, separate rooms, of course. I would never ask . . ." he wondered, *Why do I always get so flustered talking to her?*

"I just want to spend some quality time with you, JoAnne."

After a barely concealed snicker, she spoke up. "How can I say no? I can clear—let's see—four days starting a week from this Friday. That okay?"

"Great. I'll book rooms near the beach and pick you up at your place that morning. Give you a definite time soon as I have it worked out. I have much to tell you."

"Morning? How close are you to California?"

"Deep in the heart of li'l ole Tex – as, ma'am," he drawled.

* * *

Joe made the reservations, flew to LA and rented a classic blue Corvette convertible. He picked up JoAnne in style. When she came to the door in shorts and a halter top he finally admitted he was actually out of snow country. They locked up and took her bag to the car. She obviously was finding time to stay in condition as evidenced by her shapely legs and hard body. Joe dropped the convertible top to welcome in California sun, though he clearly didn't need the warmth after seeing her.

He found his way back to the Pacific Coast Highway and swung north toward Malibu. Their hotel was beachside, and they checked into adjoining rooms. His parting shot to her when she disappeared into her room was, "Okay, little miss track star. I challenge you to a race down the beach."

Amos changed quickly and went to the sand's edge to warm up in his trunks, track top and running shoes. JoAnne's appearance on the beach turned heads. Her golden hair was pinned up and those blue eyes had a look of determination. She wore a bright green bra and bikini and green running shoes. When JoAnne began her warm up routine, he couldn't help noticing activity came to a halt while the men observed her every move.

Before he realized what she was doing, she started toward the water and flung out her own challenge. "Last one to the end of the beach is an out of shape has been."

Joe reached his stride and labored to catch up. She looked over her shoulder and taunted him till he caught up and lifted her into his arms. Then he turned and ran into the water with her, dunking her thoroughly, shoes and all.

Their days together invigorated and inspired him. JoAnne provided the spark that was missing in his life, an energy that made him want to reach higher and be more than he had ever dreamed. The trip that had begun as a purposeful test of his feelings for this amazing woman was turning into a watershed that was about to give him new purpose.

Chapter 43

The night before Joe was due to return to Texas, he stood in his hotel room shower getting ready for dinner out with JoAnne. He had them booked at a spot with a spectacular view of the ocean. This place had a reputation for the seafood dishes JoAnne loved. Joe looked forward to what could be a life-changing evening.

As the water cascaded down over him, he thought about the way they had opened up to each other these past three days. His mind replayed their conversation the first night at the nearly empty outdoor café; the talk that had swept away the walls of secrecy maintained at the behest of their employers.

"You wanted to know more about what I'm doing in Texas," Joe had said. *"I sense you've* also *been holding back. What puzzled me most was that you and I have known for six years that we were part of a program of special leader training. Not being able to talk about the work we're dedicated to was hard to take. George Adams swore me to secrecy on an initiative he called Project WAKE and I never mentioned that word to you."*

Her blue eyes had flashed something when he said WAKE. "I recently learned that Hiroshi Kato owned K-Tronics and connected some dots," he'd told her.

"I already knew that Joe Whitley, George Adams and Carlos Estrada were principals in the group that started WAKE. It hit me what that name could stand for. So I had the W, A and E. Who could the K be? I asked George last week over our secure phones about Kato and he confirmed my suspicion."

At that point JoAnne had let out a long sigh and admitted, *"Yes, Joe, Hiro filled me in on their project. Exciting, isn't it?"*

"I told George about you, JoAnne, and how important it was for me to level with you. Told him I was sure you were a WAKE protégé, though we'd never talked about the project. He and Hiro talked and he told me it was time we were up front with each other. They trust us."

He remembered she beamed that perfect smile and said, *"I've been walking on eggs all weekend trying to decide how to broach the subject, Joe. Kato gave me the go ahead to share with you, as another of their WAKE students, the details of our ongoing research efforts. Said it may even pay dividends. It's time we both cleared our consciences."*

They went on that evening to purge the backlog of frustration at not being totally honest with each other. JoAnne explained that her nano experiments had reached a critical point and competitors would risk anything to catch up. Delivering nano medicines by introducing microscopic electronic devices into the blood stream could revolutionize medical treatment. He admitted that his work on diabetes was now out of his hands and he'd moved on. Joe revealed the landmark progress they'd achieved on biomass energy conversion. For the first time he shared with an 'outsider', as he had been forced to consider her, the fright of the October terrorist attack on EnzAm.

A new dimension was added to their relationship. Joe knew from the first moment at the college track that JoAnne was special, and their infrequent meetings had convinced him he was right. Now they shared knowledge about sciences so well guarded and exclusive it set them apart, made them partners in a grand revolution.

He had come to adore everything about this unique woman. She was beautiful, witty, and spontaneous. She made him laugh, and when they were together, there were only the two of them with all else distant and unimportant. JoAnne was probably the most intelligent woman he had ever met. She had a wide range of interests and he had yet to find a subject on which she was not instantly conversant. Where was his head? For years he'd avoided the obvious.

He turned off the water, stepped out of the shower and toweled off. He stared into the mirror deep into his own gray eyes and cemented a decision. Then he reached for his electric razor and chuckled under his breath.

"Good thing I brought this electric along. The way my hands are shaking, I might be dangerous with a blade."

"My dear Miss Donovan, I hope you're ready for a big night."

Chapter 44

Before dinner that evening Joe tried hard to make everything just right. A verandah table with a view overlooking the ocean awaited them. He went to her door decked out in the California casual garb he'd spent a king's ransom for on a quick swing into the city. Joe presented his lady a single perfect rose with a flourish and a sincere compliment: "You're gorgeous, JoAnne. See, even the rose is blushing."

She was a feast for the senses in her shimmering blue blouse and navy skirt, her sapphire pumps, wearing just a hint of a perfume that was new to him. They drove up the shore, parked in a hillside lot and climbed a tiki-torch lined staircase to the timber and glass structure perched atop a palm-dotted crest. JoAnne's strong legs put a jaunty bounce in her step. She took his hand and urged him along.

At dinner they dined on the freshest seafood prepared expertly. JoAnne, who grew up near Savannah and loved seafood, looked pleased with his choice of dining locations. Joe, on the other hand, could have been eating cardboard without noticing. His attention was riveted on the lovely woman across the table. He kept leaping ahead to an important moment that would come before the evening was over. Joe's mind planned and rehearsed his role in that moment with nerves ragged, heart pounding, and his resolve threatening to melt.

They finished the meal. JoAnne registered surprise. "I've been in LA all this time and never found this place. It'll definitely be on my list of regulars."

While they waited for the check, she broke his concentration with a question. "Joe, have you ever seriously thought about what you want out of life? I mean, we both have our current work, and at times it seems to be all that matters, but we know better. Where do you expect to be in five to ten years?"

He came out of his trance back to the present and managed, "Life? Oh, you mean the future. Been thinking about that a lot since I burrowed down in that west Texas gopher hole and drowned myself in the biomass pursuit. I've engaged in a lot of after-hours soul searching."

"And what did your soul tell you?"

"Told me to be selfish for a change, to think of what Joe Amos needs from life. I grew up in a loving family. Now I want one of my own, someone to *share* my future and make me look forward to each new day."

"But you're doing something that could benefit a lot of people," JoAnne reminded him. "That should be a source of great satisfaction to you."

He signed the check and downed the last of his wine. "Look at that sun dipping out there, JoAnne. Let's go outside and watch it set." Joe stood and offered his hand.

She nodded, put her hand in his and let him steer her into the warm night air. They walked along a foot path to the very top of the rise; turned toward the setting sun. Joe put his arms around her and nestled her back against his chest. They silently watched the Pacific surf crash against the rocks below as the sun cast its image along the horizon.

Joe kissed the back of her neck, put his lips next to her ear and whispered, "Why can't all my nights be this beautiful? I love you, lady."

She turned toward him and they clung to each other. He kissed her softly. Joe thought about the sheer drop to the ocean a few feet away. They were on another precipice as well, on the keen edge of a moment that could determine their future.

Please don't let me screw this up, he thought. *It's now or never.*

Joe looked into her sparkling blue eyes. "Hope I can do this right. It's not the sort of thing a fellow gets a chance to practice." He dropped to a knee.

She seemed to be holding his hand a little tighter, but her expression told him nothing. He began slowly, "JoAnne Donovan, you are my dream come true. You changed my life the moment we met. Life is so much more when you're near me. I love you with all my heart. Please say you'll marry me."

He waited for what seemed an eternity. Joe imagined what was going on in her head, the conflicting pros and cons that could be twisting and delaying her answer. She had obligations, important goals, questions he probably couldn't answer. The miles that separated them presented a huge roadblock. Still, all that really mattered to Joe was that they commit to a future together. The how was something they could work out in time.

JoAnne's lips slowly curled upward into a smile. Her answer was a single word, but it was all he asked. "Yes!"

He stood and kissed her. Fumbled in his pocket and brought out a shiny gold band with a pair of hands clasping a heart. "Wear this, JoAnne, till I can get you the most elegant diamond I can find."

She stared down at the ring and asked, "A cladagh? I love it, Joe. And I love you."

Chapter 45

"You haven't been the same since your trip to California, Joe," Fred Vinson said tentatively with a sheepish grin.

Joe Amos wasn't one to open up around the workplace, a setting he reserved for focused attention to the tasks at hand. He and Fred had become friends, though, since Vinson joined the team, and what Joe felt after JoAnne's commitment needed to be shared with someone. He struggled with that again, came to grips with it and motioned for Fred to come to his small office.

Once they were behind a closed door, Joe opened up. "Fred, that trip was more than a vacation. I went to see the woman who's changed my mind about life's priorities. Asked her to marry me and she said yes."

Fred's usual restrained exterior crumbled with the good news. His eyes bulged behind thick glasses and he stroked a stubbly dark beard. "And I thought you'd flipped out on me. You've been going at a dead run. I've had to scramble to keep up with you." He gave Joe a firm hand shake and said, "Good on you, man. When will I meet this mystery woman?"

"In time," Joe answered. "We have some details to work out."

* * *

Those important details and their solution surfaced even sooner than Joe anticipated. The next weekend he answered his home phone to hear JoAnne's voice.

"How's frontier life treating you, cowboy?"

"Almost like summertime, smart alec; twenty-nine degrees and biting wind. I won't ask you about your weather."

“Come on, let me crow a little, Joe. Took a jog down the beach this morning, and now I’m working on my tan. But that’s not why I called.”

Joe kicked the recliner back, put his feet up, and offered, “Make my day, pretty lady.”

JoAnne began haltingly. “Wanted to … Mister Kato and I … oh, hell. Can I come see you, Joe?”

“Absolutely any time your heart desires. On second thought,” he amended, “give me a day to clean up this place and ready a room for you. I don’t want you to get a bad impression of the house. It’s really a pretty neat hangout.”

“I was thinking about a weekend trip. We can make it sort of a St. Patty’s break with my special man. Have a couple of serious matters to talk over with you.”

“Not a spot of green around here right now, JoAnne, but I’m told it’s back to decent temps around here in March. I’d like nothing better than a visit from my Irish rose. Just what do you mean by serious?”

“That’s the wrong word. Sorry. Change that to important. Mister Kato says I ought to get a good look at your, uh, work site.” They were both watchful about using the name Site Green over open phone lines.

`“Not easy getting here. We’re sort of isolated.”

“Kato will arrange my ride. He suggested there may be a way we can run both projects from there if you agree.”

Joe went speechless. There should be plenty of room and ample power at Site Green to bring in her staff and any specialized equipment. This was the answer to what he’d agonized over since the night JoAnne accepted his proposal. Both of their teams could work under the security they needed and they could start making firm plans for their wedding.

“You already know my answer to that,” Joe said. “If I can find a broom, I’ll be ready to play host before sunset.”

“Just clear me a space by March fifteenth. I’m looking forward to seeing your house . . .”

“*Our* house, JoAnne,” he corrected, “and soon I hope.”

"I love the sound of that, Joe. And the sooner I can get the escorted tour of *the other place* the better we'll be able to decide about collocating."

* * *

Hundreds of miles away, an urgent meeting took place in a hotel room in a suburb outside Washington, DC. Two men sat at a small table sipping tea, sheltered from the biting February cold outside. They were wrestling with a thorny problem.

"And you're telling me you've exhausted all leads?" the swarthy young man asked in his Middle Eastern accent. "That is not acceptable! These EnzAm people are a serious threat to our interests. You put me in a very awkward position with my superiors. I want results!" He pounded the table top.

The slightly graying middle-aged man recoiled at the force of his companion's sudden move. He set down his cup with a trembling hand. "Their site has been abandoned. They have disappeared. We had multiple leads on where they were relocating, but we've scoured all over two states without finding their new home. Amos and his people simply vanished without a trail. The people I have working on finding them are the best in the business. Short of kidnapping families and friends, we've done everything possible to run them down."

"Let me remind you, Mister Foster," came Abdul's reply. He waved a forefinger under Foster's nose. "There's still the matter of a certain October day when EnzAm was breached and our problem should have been solved. Poor planning by you prevented that. The press would feast on your bones if we revealed your part in that debacle."

"Give me until after the election, Abdul. You know how much this election means. I need some breathing room. I won't let them go public with their energy scheme. EnzAm and its biomass nonsense won't pose an immediate threat to you as long as I have a role in energy regulation."

"Must I repeat that whether you remain in your position depends upon the substantial contributions we make to your expenses? You are not indispensable, and your people at home would not take kindly to learning how much you owe us."

Abdul produced a fat envelope and relented for the moment. “This is your last chance, Foster. You hand me EnzAm or your career is at an end. Unless we shut them down, there will be no more of these.”

Foster riffled the thick stack of green bills and nodded.

Chapter 46

The nearest airport that could handle the K-Tronics jet was a two-hour drive down off the mile-high mountain into the flatlands. JoAnne's flight landed within minutes of the estimate she'd given Joe. He waited in the small air terminal for her.

She seemed a tad flustered when he swept her off her feet, twirled her around and kissed her. Probably not what one would expect to see from two adults with PhD appended to their names. But Joe could care less. No one in this town knew them, and when she was near him, nobody else entered his orbit of attention, anyway.

"Whew! I was going to say hello, but I guess we already did!" JoAnne caught her breath.

The ride back to Site Green was a big improvement over his lonesome trip to the airport. A clear March day promised high temperatures in the low seventies.

"I expected a winter day with wind and snow," She told him. "You haven't pictured this as a garden spot."

"Remember this is my first season out here. Locals warn me I'll be wishing for cold soon when the temps go into the nineties and it's dry enough to spit fur balls."

"You don't think much of your new home, do you? I thought you'd be giving me a sales pitch by now."

"Oh, don't let me turn you off. The folks here are neighborly and down home helpful. There's plenty to do for outdoors lovers. The scenery's beautiful. I just don't seem to find the time to get out and enjoy it."

"Tell me how you and your team are doing in the lab. Kato said he and George thought it was time we brought each other fully up to date. Are you close to the conversion you've been looking for?"

"Long, slow road, but we're encouraged. I know this is doable, JoAnne, with time and patience. If we can just get an energy release, the rest is downhill. I hope we can work out setting up your nano project at Site Green so you can see first hand what our efforts are about."

"I'm looking forward to meeting your people, Joe. Are we going there now?"

"Everybody's at the site today, this being Friday. We'll get the introductions and tour out of the way before I show you our humble home in Alpine. After that we have some serious planning to do, my love."

* * *

Each of Joe's team members met JoAnne and talked about his or her part in the biomass research. She, Joe and Gary Harper, the facility manager, then set out in a golf cart for a complete Site Green tour. "I love to brag about this place," Gary told her. "It's my baby. I'm proud of what we've built. We have an abundant supply of sunshine to run our power plant and plenty of fresh water from the nearby mountaintop lake. Green could keep perking through a major disaster. Ask me anything you want, Doctor Donovan."

"Oh, I won't pull any punches, Gary," she said. He looked over at Joe and got a confirming nod he read as 'you can for sure believe that'.

Two hours later JoAnne had seen every nook and cranny of Green, even an outside view of the spectacular vista from atop the mountain ridge. "I'm impressed, gentlemen. It's much more than I imagined." She turned to Joe and said, "I can see my team fitting in well, and the site is definitely the answer to our security needs. We need to talk about the details."

"Lots of time for that," Joe told her. "Our work week is almost over. Then you're all mine for the weekend."

Saturday Joe introduced JoAnne to his new home town and showed off the house he'd bought there under the name Joe Zale. She took it all in, but he couldn't tell whether she was enthused or just being agreeable. Joe mused, *what did that look mean? Was it an approving comment or a so-so response? Come on, JoAnne, give me a clue. I want to start our family here.*

She kept instead coming back to the plans for collocating at Site Green. They had a site floor plan spread out on the kitchen table. She was pointing at a large unused area. "So you think my team of sixteen would fit into the unoccupied space? I estimate our equipment needs maybe eight hundred square feet of floor space. Maybe this area over here will work." She tapped the layout.

"Map out your best idea and we'll get to work on it. Gary is a wizard with construction projects. Be sure you've computed all your power requirements. He hires craftsmen that know how to keep their activities unnoticed outside the complex. Can we break for dinner?"

"I believe this is going to work, Joe. Can we order carry out dinner? I want to stay at this till the plan is done."

"Fine by me, baby. I'll go down to Maria's and have them whip up some of the finest TexMex you ever tasted."

She waved a hand at him and turned her attention back to the diagram. Joe gave her a peck on the cheek and left her alone. *Two days from now she'll fly home,* he thought to himself. *We have important plans to make. Tomorrow is about* us, *not work.*

Chapter 47

Sunday, Joe resolved, was for setting personal plans for the future. He'd asked JoAnne to go with him on his morning run to start the day on the right note. When she came to the kitchen in her running togs, he marveled at the fresh beauty of this amazing woman, the lady he planned to spend a lifetime cherishing. Joe handed her a cup of hot coffee and greeted her with a cheery, "Morning, sunshine. Ready to roll?"

She took a couple of short sips from the cup and challenged, "Jo's my name and running's my game. See if you can keep up." They were off as the sun rose over the desert.

* * *

They made a brisk three-mile jog, showered, and had breakfast. Joe was ready to talk. "As important as it is, the plan for moving your team is number two on my priority list. We need to discuss our wedding and settling down."

She averted her eyes, stood and reached for the coffee pot. A tingling sensation traveled up his spine and planted a note of warning in his brain. Was she having second thoughts?

"I want us to be together, Joe—really together, finally. Will you let me put everything in place first? Then I can concentrate on us."

"Can you be a little more specific? The site should be ready by the end of June. I want us to start building a life together. What am I missing?"

JoAnne's eyes widened as if his words had turned on a light. "You thought … Joe, I'm not waffling. I'm as committed as ever to be your wife, but so much depends on our relocation. This move is not for industrial security reasons. Our lives may depend on disappearing from view. My team is about to make breakthroughs that would be dangerous in the wrong hands."

"Then you have the same problem we've been dealing with. I had no idea. I just want you as my bride as soon as possible. The wait is killing me."

She did a bit of calculating out loud. "Hmmm. Construction done in June. Equipment running by July. Full operation in August. Can we agree on an August wedding?"

Joe reached into his pocket and pulled out a small box. He opened it and took out a sparkling diamond solitaire. "Yes. It's time you wore this."

He slipped the ring onto her finger.

She caught her breath and gave a long sigh. "It's beautiful, Joe. I love you."

* * *

A blustery early April day was ending as the sun went down over Rock Creek Park near Washington. Abdul, shivering in the brisk wind, walked up the footpath toward three waiting men. One of them, a small man in a heavy black wool coat, stepped forward and motioned for him to follow. They proceeded out of earshot of Wooly Coat's companions.

"You have found the people we seek?"

"Not yet, eminence. Our man on the hill is on notice to produce them by June. The elections are a distraction, but I have made it clear his first priority is to pinpoint their location."

"Perhaps both you and the infidel dog contact are, as the Americans say, in over your heads. I grow weary of waiting for results. These people at EnzAm present a threat to our continued prosperity. This scheme for making fuelfrom garbage must be stopped, destroyed. I want them all disposed of as if they were the garbage they so treasure. Must I find someone else who will deliver results?"

Abdul trembled noticeably, this time not from the swirling winds. “I will redouble my pressure on Foster, eminence. The foul project will be found and shut down. All knowledge they have gained will be seized for your eyes only, and they will be terminated. You have my word.”

“Then the last day of June is your deadline, Abdul. Do not force me to dispatch you in disgrace. I want you to see that your Congressman Foster understands clearly—his position does not insulate him from my justice. If he fails, at best I will see that his voters abandon him. At worst, his career, as well as all his earthly worries, will come to a sudden end.”

Wooly Coat turned toward his two associates. They quickly approached. “An object lesson in discipline is in order for our friend, Abdul,” the slight man told them. Then, in a calm, even voice he said to Abdul, “You will remember this day when next you prompt Mister F for action. Both of your lives depend on his success.”

Abdul’s outcries began as screams and subsided to whimpers before his abusers left him stunned and broken and drove away with their master.

Chapter 48

JoAnne's move from California took place discreetly. Her team disappeared from the labs of K-Tronics one by one and relocated to small towns within a fifty-mile radius of the Davis Mountains. In the early weeks they resided at Site Green and commuted to homes down in the valley.

Joe Amos was delighted to finally have his fiancée near at hand. They delighted in their time together daily at Site Green. Most nights they spent in separate assigned quarters on location. But at least once each week Joe and JoAnne drove to their comfortable home in the little town of Alpine. The wait was tense, but they were both determined to somehow get through to October and the wedding without giving in to their hormones.

On one of their evenings at Green they sat talking in the common area.

"You've seen enough by now, Joe, to understand how vital our nano work is. The last thing I want is to keep anything from you. Are there questions I can answer?"

"Why don't you give me the gold plated tutorial on using nanos in medicine? From my biology background, I obviously understand the basics. I've read Eric Drexler's "Engines of Creation." but it was more like fiction than science. Let me be your student and make me smart."

"Kind of interesting how our two fields merge, isn't it, Joe? Your biochem and my engineering have led us both to proteins as the key to human cell activity. We're just trying to use them to reach different outcomes."

"But that's one of the myriad of things that brought us together," Joe said and smiled.

"So listen up." She launched into her explanation. "We're here because our findings, in the wrong hands, could wreak disaster. Nanotechnology involves building microscopic machines from individual atoms, tiny devices we call nanites that measure on the scale of billionths of an inch. Our goal is to inject nanites into a patient's blood stream to sample and test human fluids for abnormalities. Where a deviation is found, we'll send another a batch of nanites loaded with targeted microdoses of medicine to treat specific abnormal cells."

"And once the cells are repaired," Joe posed, "I take it they resume sending out the correct amino acids that interact with the body's proteins. That results in instructions to the patient's body to correctly perform its functions."

"Exactly," she confirmed.

Well, I know it's a believable theory, but most researchers think we could be decades away from making it happen."

JoAnne gave him her knowing grin and corrected, "Till recently I would have agreed with them. But the science has accelerated. My team could be producing functional nanites within the next year."

"That's great news! Why would anybody not want that to happen?"

"Maybe you should also read Michael Crichton's book "Prey." He projected the eventual creation of self-reproducing nanites capable of disassembling molecules and reforming them into totally new structures. You know, like break down dirt and remake it into food."

"That's a good thing," Joe quipped.

"But Crichton also posed a bigger problem. Self-replicating nanites might eventually multiply exponentially, take over and disassemble all matter on earth to build more and more nanites. Unscrupulous rulers could also employ the devices as a military weapon. A horde of them turned loose on an enemy could leave a country totally devoid of human life and ready for occupation. That's why we're here now, to conceal our progress from prying eyes. We can't afford to have anyone get their hands on our processes and turn loose something they can't stop."

Chapter 49

Site Green was a busy place now that both the biomass team and the nano research team shared its facilities. The on-site solar plant was proving to be up to the demand placed on it for power. The only downside in Joe's life, and it was a major one, was his promise to wait until JoAnne gave the word for their wedding.

"October sure seems a long way off," Joe told her. "Want to reconsider? I could snatch you away to a justice of the peace and make it official."

They were in the midst of another wonderful weekend in what they referred to as their 'prairie home'. The weather outdoors was warming up and, to tell the truth, so was Joe. His eyes devoured JoAnne, drank in the statuesque beauty of his dream come true. Her aura filled his head until he had to stand and walk across to the piano to break the spell. Joe sat down and fiddled with the keys, picking a made-up tune.

The nights at the site I can take, he pondered. *We both work till late hours and all those other people are around. It's the weekends here at home that work a number on me. I want this woman so much it hurts. Three months of having her close is tying me in knots.*

She'd told him over and over, "I know it's been a long wait for both of us. Only a few weeks now, Joe, and we'll belong to each other for life."

She brushed her lips across his ear and said, "Soon now, Joe." He nearly exploded. Once again he grasped at the only thing that seemed to bring him down off highs like he was feeling now—talk about work.

It's either that or sweep her away and ravish her, he thought. *Get it together, Amos, or you'll go skittering around the room like a punctured balloon.*

The two teams coexisted well at Site Green. They each had their intense moments, their triumphs and disappointments, but these were people who understood how difficult scientific exploration could be. Joe worked to calm down and force himself to revert to his professional side. He swallowed hard and asked, "Anything new on the nano front?"

JoAnne beamed that sly little smile that seemed to say 'Thanks for giving us an out'. She walked to the kitchen and announced over her shoulder, "I found some of those big onions you like and the Stoli's chilled. How about a relaxer?"

With the tension relieved they settled down to talk shop. She handed him his drink and said, "You first. How goes the biomass world?"

"We knew at the outset this was no trivial undertaking, JoAnne. I'm convinced we're concentrating on the right enzyme as our medium to break down our raw materials. After that we have to fabricate a reasonable laboratory facsimile of the enzyme for large scale processing to produce quality energy cake. The energy release will come in time."

"Then how will you go commercial?" she asked. "That would seem to be the biggest hurdle to making biomass a success."

"George Adams and Carlos Estrada have that covered. They've started building a test town in east Texas to prove biomass is viable as a long-term energy solution. Think of it, JoAnne, a whole city that depends on garbage as its single source of raw energy! Carlos and his Carl's Foods markets will supply the inputs and George's GMed will produce the enzyme medium in bulk. I'm a major shareholder in EnzAm, so you and I could be sitting on top of the world when this industry takes off."

"Sounds exciting but isn't it long term and expensive?

Joe sipped the last of his martini, set down the glass and told her, "That was just what I needed, baby, and your timing was perfect. To answer your question, George has nearly unlimited assets to spend on biomass. Joe Whitley left him an immense fortune to use as he saw fit. Our research is an integral part of Project WAKE, Whitley's biggest dream. We have as long as it takes and the bucks to back it up My goal is to go commercial before the people who control oil production strangle us with their monopoly on energy sources."

"Refill?" Jo Anne asked, taking his glass.

"One's my limit tonight. Just make it whatever you're having."

"Mine's a Diet Coke."

"Okay. Now what's new in the world of nanos?"

They talked on late into the evening about the progress her group had made since settling in at Site Green. That move had proven to be exactly what they needed to leap ahead with their developing nanometer scale electronic devices. Their lab animal tests were proving they could steer medical dosages to precise locations within patients' bodies. She explained how the microscopic machines were maneuvered to find precise internal destinations to target problem spots in vital organs.

Joe interrupted her. "I remember you told me the little machines could home in on body fluids to find trouble spots. Does that mean they can key on, say, a predetermined enzyme to do their work?"

"Not a problem," she answered. "They can seek out enzymes, body secretions, foreign bodies or infections. Whatever we preprogram into their circuits they find so that minute dosages can be delivered directly to the trouble area."

"And if I wanted these nanites to sense a specific substance emitted by the body and issue an alarm, would that be possible?"

"Without more to go on, I'd have to say it's entirely feasible. You have something specific in mind?"

"Well," Joe said, "in our diabetes project we uncovered a protein the human body produces when the subject tries to practice deception. Lab tests on my own team members proved infallibly consistent. When they attempted to lie for test purposes, this enzyme invariably presented itself and was chemically detected."

"Whoa! Wait a minute, Joe. You're telling me you discovered a foolproof lie detection test and kept it to yourselves? That could be a landmark find."

"It was strictly by chance. I put it behind me in the rush to whip biomass reduction, but I guess you're right. If we could clinically prove that an enzyme test can detect lies, it would be a big help to law enforcement. Getting a guilty party to agree to an invasive test might be problematic, though."

JoAnne was a step ahead of him. "But if a medically accepted regimen was used, say injecting nanos once we get federal approval … I'd like to work on this idea, Joe, and see if we can make it real. The implications are enormous."

"Wow! Now I know how to turn you on, lady. Talk about snagging liars and you go all hot on me. I love it when you get excited."

"Just rein back, podner. You're pushing your luck. What I meant was law enforcement isn't the only place a reliable lie detector could be used. Think about the impact this could have in all sorts of situations including politics.

"Joe looked at his watch. "Hey, it's after midnight already. This is fascinating, but we'd better call it a night. There's a long trip up the mountain and a heavy day tomorrow. I have a warm bed I'll gladly share."

"Sorry, cowboy," she said with a smile that melted him. "Not as long now as it has been."

She kissed her fingertips and touched them to his lips. "Good night, sweet prince."

Chapter 50

The big day was finally almost upon them. Joe and JoAnne sat in the Odessa-Midland air terminal with her parents waiting for his folks to arrive for the ceremony day after tomorrow.

"Hope this roundabout trip wasn't too tiring," Joe told the Donovans. "You understand our need to conceal your destination."

Sean Donovan rubbed his growing stubble and answered, "Not that far here from Georgia unless you go by way of Minneapolis and Oklahoma City like we did. That does get tiring."

Joe said a bit sheepishly, "My parents are gonna be beat, too, by the time they get here. Their first stop was in Mexico two days ago. This industrial security thing can be a bear. But then it tells us some people consider our work pretty important."

And, he thought to himself, *some others would do whatever it takes, including commit murder, to stop us. We don't need to bring down another attack on EnzAm with our parents standing in the crossfire. Better they think it's all in the name of 'protecting trade secrets'.*

Two hours later they delivered four exhausted but anxious parents to their house in Alpine. In two days the wedding would take place in a local church. That gave the Donovans and Amoses a few precious hours to meet their offspring's betrothed and the in-laws. By the time those with criminal intentions could track down their parents, they would be back home after 'vacation' trips with stand-ins playing their parts.

* * *

On Saturday Fred Vinson rousted Joe to start him preparing for his wedding day.

"Last chance for a bachelor pad breakfast, buddy," Fred threw out when Joe stumbled to the coffee pot. "Bacon's done and I know two ways with eggs, grease fried or hard boiled."

"Maybe I'll stick to bacon and toast," Joe countered.

Yesterday he and JoAnne had thoroughly enjoyed time with their parents and a chance to unwind from their normal routines. Staying overnight with his best man got him out of the house for tradition's sake and the bride's privacy, but he'd much rather be jogging through desert country this morning with his soon to be bride. They'd observed decorum and conquered their raging hormones, even under the temptation of being in the same house weekends for the past four months. But in a few hours he'd whisk her away to a Mexican holiday where the newlyweds, under the pseudonym 'Mr. and Mrs. Zale', could hide away and gloriously seal their bond.

The morning was painfully slow. Fred managed to get Joe organized and to the church on time. The gathering would be small, only parents and team members and a few staffers from the site. George Adams, Hiro Kato and Carlos Estrada had all called in their best wishes via satellite phone to the prospective bride and groom. None of them dared come to Alpine for fear of destroying the careful veil of secrecy over their connection to Joe and JoAnne.

Joe confided, "Told myself I'd be cool and collected today, Fred, but the way I'm shaking, you'd think it was twenty degrees in here. I may lose my breakfast."

"All I ask of you is you manage to walk into that church on your own and watch your bride come down the aisle. It's a big step, but you two are as good a match as I've ever seen."

The ceremony proceeded without a hitch. Fred Vinson and Bonnie Hepler from JoAnne's team stood up with them. Only the select group of attendees, the preacher and town registrar knew the bride and groom's real names. To everyone else in and around Alpine, they were Joseph and Joan Zale. After a joyful reception, Joe and JoAnne said their goodbyes and hurried to their flight south.

* * *

What George and Hiro hadn't told the newly joined couple was that they and Carlos had planned a lively reception for some uninvited guests at a remote Nebraska site.

Jim Bledsoe, Estrada's security chief, waited and watched the concrete blockhouse that would soon be the target of an all-out assault. It sat nearly obscured by tall corn fields on all sides.

"Be sure you throw those switches as soon as I give the signal," he instructed his two sentries at the front and back of the blockhouse. "You men on the perimeter—if there are stragglers left behind for cover, make sure they are no danger then let them leave. In sequence, give me a check off."

Crisp, ordered responses came back to Jim from each of his men. They settled down to wait for the sighting of unfriendlies. If Jim's sources were accurate, fun time was about to begin beyond the corn rows. The attack came shortly after sunset. Six dark clad commandos silently slipped past the empty blockhouse parking lot. Another six men approached the rear entrance. They all carried automatic weapons, side arms and, as near as Jim and his observers could tell, two also lugged explosive devices.

Bledsoe watched as the men disappeared into the building. They were about to find a totally deserted maze of what looked like laboratory equipped rooms and a vault. Jim waited five minutes and lifted his radio. He gave a one word command, "Now!" Switches were activated and metal covers slid down over the few windows in the structure's exterior walls. Ventilation ducts clamped shut. A debilitating, non-lethal gas poured from multiple portals to fill the building's interior.

Jim listened to the sporadic bursts of gunfire from inside and imagined the scene taking place. "Dance, you rats! Fight it or give in—either way you'll be in la la land soon."

The cleanup was quick and efficient. Federal agents and Jim's crew rounded up twelve sedated invaders inside. A loud explosion followed. Two other bad guys lurking outside managed to flee. This time, unlike the incident in Virginia, not all of them were home-grown troublemakers. Four illegals, three of them guilty of overstaying their visas, were taken into custody. The other, a transplanted Saudi named Abdul, appeared to be the lead instigator.

Secured calls went out from Jim Bledsoe once all the facts were known. His report to his boss, Carlos Estrada, mirrored what he later told the other two WAKE sponsors.

"Couldn't have been smoother, Carlos. This Abdul character is singing like a canary with a hot foot. They gathered up the dummy materials from the vault before they realized the rat trap we'd set. Abdul wants to make a deal to turn in a certain US Congressman who ordered the hit. Says this Foster guy was living on borrowed time on orders to find and destroy EnzAm. Word is he also named a high official at one of the Washington embassies who's been paying off the Congressman."

"Good show, Jim," Carlos commended.

Jim laughed. "Yeah, boss, they bought our diversion. The blockhouse was a work of art; looked like the real thing."

"But the question is," Carlos posed, "did we convince them they'd shut us down?"

"Well," said Jim, "we gave those two stragglers a good fireworks show before they snuck away. Soon as we hauled their sleeping buddies out the back door, we used rigged explosives to send that place up in a big ole ball of smoke and fire. I'm bettin' these stragglers'll report back one o' their fellers screwed up and blew the place away with all his buddies."

"Yow! Tough way to go, huh, Jim? I guess that oughta keep the real site safe for a while."

Jim furrowed his brow. "Safe?" That's a word I rarely use, boss. Gotta believe we're far from bein' able to fergit about those oil dudes. They're persistent."

PART THREE

JoAnne (Donovan) Amos

"Joe Number Three"

Chapter 51

Site Green remained a bustle of activity. JoAnne's researchers made great strides in treating lab animals with micro medicines. Work proceeded on the application to the government for strictly controlled dosing of human subjects using nanites introduced into their blood streams. When approved, that work would take place in California under a joint venture between K-Tronics and GMed.

JoAnne remained at Site Green and continued to perfect and refine nano devices for other uses. She and her husband Joe lived quietly in the town of Alpine. But for one troubling fact, their life together was idyllic.

"I know this has been frustrating for you, Joe. We've tried everything and nothing's working. I want a family desperately, and my clock is running, but the doctors tell us I can't … too many candles on my last birthday cake. Maybe we should think about adopting."

Joe held her close and said, "You're more than I could have ever wished for, JoAnne. And you have lots of time yet. Women considerably older conceive all the time. But it's your call, baby. We'll do whatever you decide."

Their one shared goal persisted while they struggled for a solution. JoAnne tried hard to believe she could be happy with Joe alone, but a little one to love and share with him would be such an added blessing. Now Joe had made it clear it was her decision to make.

*   *   *

In October, Joe was already teasing JoAnne about what her Christmas present would be. They were staring into the fireplace when she jabbed him and asked, "So how close was my last guess?"

"No way I'm telling you what you're getting for Christmas," he replied.

"I'll tell you first," she teased. "But yours is on order; so it will be a little late."

"Let's see. Is it coming mail order?"

"Not exactly." She stood and smoothed her skirt. "You'll have a while to preview this present." The corners of her mouth slowly turned up when she gave him her 'I've got a secret' look.

Joe was normally quick on the uptake, but somehow her clue had escaped him this time.

She wiggled her hips playfully and broke into a broad smile. "How many hints do I have to give you, Daddy?"

That did it. Joe leaped to his feet and grabbed her. He backed up a step and said, "Maybe you better sit down. When, JoAnne?"

She laughed out loud. "In July, God willing, we'll be parents."

* * *

The winter and spring passed slowly. JoAnne kept her busy work schedule, though she gradually added pounds to her tall frame that slowed her pace. Joe found multiple excuses daily to stop by her lab and check on the mommy to be. Her team members poked fun at JoAnne about how her husband kept tabs on her. She began to wonder whether he wasn't even more anxious for the wait to be over than she was.

One morning in June, she felt something a lot more intense than the baby's usual kicking. She turned to Bonnie Hepler and said, "This could be the day, Bon." Her assistant took one look into her eyes and nodded.

"The boss and I are going to the clinic," Bonnie told the nearest team member as she hurried off with JoAnne in tow.

Joe Amos had his head buried in pages of chemical process formulas when something dropped on the book in front of him. He looked at the pacifier with its two ribbons, one blue and one pink, then up to see Bonnie in front of his desk.

An extra benefit of their remote location and mandated privacy was their own on-site doctor. JoAnne had been under Doc Thomas's prenatal care from the start of her pregnancy. Bonnie's words energized Joe in a flash. The pink and blue reminder of the event to come never left JoAnne's office, so he knew instantly. He kicked his chair against the wall and charged around the desk cradling the pacifier as if it were the baby.

"I took her to the doc's office ten minutes ago, Joe. He says it won't be long."

Joe was a couple steps ahead of her.

"Slow down," Bonnie cautioned. "We have to get you there in one piece."

All he knew was that his first child was on the way. They had purposely delayed knowing whether JoAnne was having a boy or a girl. Joe just wanted a healthy baby and the precious mother to hold. He would swear his feet didn't touch the floor all the way to the medical area. A nurse and orderly were wheeling JoAnne into delivery.

"Love you, lady," he whispered, kissed her and squeezed her hand.

Later the nurse took Joe to the recovery room and handed his beautiful baby gerl to him. "Your wife didn't waste any time," she said.

Joe chuckled. "She ran track, you know. Always has been a fast gal. And she does great work, too. Just look at this charmer." He looked down into the face of his angel, his own tiny copy of her mother. Joe kissed her brow and watched her blue eyes flutter.

JoAnne managed a smile. "Emily Kathryn Amos, meet your Daddy."

"She's perfect, JoAnne."

The new mom closed her eyes to rest.

Chapter 52

"She's a beautiful child," Bonnie Hepler said to JoAnne. They were sitting in the Site Green nano lab with little Emily Kathryn.

JoAnne beamed. "She's growing like crazy and Daddy Joe adores his little girl. We decided to have a whole day with her for a change. The morning is mine then Joe gets her this afternoon. Both of us can enjoy her tonight."

"That cutie's bound to be a lab dweller when she can walk," Bonnie told her. "You may have a second-generation scientist on your hands. After all, she's the daughter of mister biomass and missus nano medicine. It's in her DNA."

"Emmy can be anything she wants. Whatever Joe and I manage to make happen in our work, she'll always be the best thing we've ever produced."

"Speaking of the mister, how are those energy folks doing these days? I haven't heard any loud explosions."

"Joe's been hyper for weeks. They've gotten-past the waste reduction stage and produced fuel cake; been testing small samples trying to get an energy discharge. He believes they're close to success." JoAnne paused, looked at her watch and said, "Woops! Time Miss Em and I headed over there so Joe can play babysitter."

When the Amos girls arrived at the biomass lab there seemed to be an unusual level of activity. JoAnne found the entire team gathered up outside what Joe had identified to her earlier as the Reaction Chamber. She peered through the large window and saw Joe inside the enclosure setting dials and checking readings. He turned toward her and the baby, gave the thumbs up sign, and said into his microphone, "This one's for my ladies."

Joe pushed a button. After a few seconds delay the meter dials jumped. He threw both arms above his head in a gesture simulating 'touchdown" and danced around. JoAnne laughed out loud thinking that if he were Irish she'd describe his movements as a jig. His moment of childish glee past, he snatched up a pen and clipboard and recorded the meter readings.

When Joe emerged from the Reaction Chamber, JoAnne shared his triumph. A new source of usable energy had been realized. The hard-working biomass team surrounded him while JoAnne waited patiently to add her congratulations.

Joe managed to wade through the well wishers and come to the two women who meant the world to him. JoAnne hadn't seen him this emotional since the day he first held his new daughter. She put one arm around him as he kissed the baby then her, Then she whispered to him, "We're so proud of you, Daddy Joe."

"Well, the easy part is behind us now. We can commence the real work of making this process repeatable and practical for commercial use."

"This is a red letter day for the Amoses," JoAnne said.

Chapter 53

JoAnne stirred from a fitful sleep confused and terrified. She had tossed for hours with bits of a recurring nightmare haunting her. The unresolved remnants of her disturbing dream and the cloying stench of her soaked skin made her nauseous.

She looked at Joe sleeping peacefully beside her, eased out of bed and stumbled to the nursery. Her baby Emily, now a perpetual motion machine, was sound asleep in her crib. JoAnne plodded into the kitchen as the cobwebs of sleep slowly began to dissipate. She peered at the wall clock's hands showing five AM and decided against trying to return to bed. Putting on a pot of coffee, JoAnne sat down at the small kitchen table and tried to fathom the torment that had plagued her sleep and abruptly jarred her into a groggy half-consciousness. Oddly, there was a sense of guilt attached to her lingering uneasiness.

"Why on earth would I feel guilty?" she questioned the empty early morning air. She thought to herself, *Sure, I owe thanks for all the good things that have come to me. I'm a lucky woman—fully sponsored and paid education, a wonderful, caring husband and the most precious daughter I could ever want. But I've worked hard to pay back for my good fortune. Our nanomedicine work holds great promise for relieving the suffering of millions of people. Still I can't shake this overpowering weight of failing, a sense of embarrassment for not having done nearly enough.*

JoAnne poured a steaming cup and inhaled the aroma, attempting to awaken her senses. She walked to the living room. There on an end table was the prized brown leather copy of the US Constitution she and Joe kept for their lively discussions. The thoughts between the covers of that wonderfully concise, eloquent document had brought Joe and her together on a sunny day in West Virginia. Their meeting had completely changed her life, though it took many months for her to fully acknowledge her attraction to him. Now, as she ran her fingers lightly across the book's soft cover, her uneasy feeling intensified. The agitation that gnawed at her became an aching grumble in her stomach. It was as if in some strange way her discomfort and the little book had a strong undefined connection.

Walking back to the kitchen, JoAnne thumbed through the volume and sat staring at its pages. Her mind raced to process the hollow sensation in her gut, the disturbing roar that would not go away. Flipping through the pages she paused to reread key passages. Article I, Section 5 read: *Each House shall be the judge of the Elections, Returns and Qualifications of its own Members ... Each House may determine the Rules of Proceedings, punish its Members for disorderly Behaviour, and, with the Concurrence of two thirds, expel a Member.'*

She laughed and mumbled to herself, "*So only Congress can decide when a member is a scuzz ball. Sounds like the wolf guarding the hen house, doesn't it?*"

JoAnne sipped her coffee and read on. There in Article VI were the words, *The Senators and Representatives before mentioned ... shall be bound by Oath or Affirmation, to support this Constitution.* She jabbed at the silence with her words. "And then ignore that oath if it interferes with their own greedy personal interests," she said aloud and shook her head in disgust. Her clenched fist pounded the table top.

The challenging mental debate began to sap her strength. She laid her head on the table and tried to organize her thoughts, but she was still only half awake. The effort was too much. Her eye lids closed and she drifted off. The frightening nightmare vividly returned in the cold light of pre-dawn. JoAnne was running, trying to hide from a hulking, furry monster with dripping fangs and sharp claws pursuing her. In a tiny, squeaky voice, she protested over and over, *"I did my part,"* knowing full well that was only half true. Each time she repeated her defense a sharp pain rocketed through her body. *"I'm a scientist, not a politician,"* she begged. *"Leave me alone and let me do my work."* But her outcries echoed in that same timid voice. The monster ignored her pleas and drew nearer with each swing of its talons. Nowhere to hide. Walls closing in. Monster roaring. Huge claws swiping. Her skin burning and clothes ripping away.

A suddenly stubborn resolve came over her. *She had the answer to face down this fraud.* JoAnne stopped running, turned to face the snarling creature and defiantly challenged him. *"I refuse to let you win. We number in the millions and you* work for us. *I know how to fight you."* The creature stopped and tilted its head to one side, staring quizzically at her from its large eyes.

"Wake up, JoAnne! Who are you talking to?" a distant voice asked.

Her eyes snapped open. Joe had his arms around her. She held onto him as if she were in mortal danger; nestled her head to his chest while he dabbed at her wet brow. "It's me, baby, and you're safe. You must have had a monumental nightmare. But you're fine now." He tilted her chin and kissed her softly on the lips.

Gradually JoAnne found a chilling awareness sinking in. She knew what had been gnawing at her gut to the point of physical pain. For all the good she and her research team may have done for medicine, there was something missing. There was a potential crossover between her nano work and Joe's enzyme research that could shake the world!

She nestled close to Joe. Her pulse slowly returned to normal and the shuddering ceased. Looking up into his eyes she said, "It was awful, Joe. I was trapped, cornered. He was trying his best to . . ."

"Hush," he urged her and buried his face in her soft blonde curls. "Put it out of your mind, sweetheart."

"No! I can't Joe. I know exactly what my dream is telling me to do. We've had the answer all along. It's up to us now."

He looked into her eyes, at a loss over her odd words. "You need to calm down and forget whatever it was that woke you up."

"I can't. I just experienced a revelation, Joe. We need to talk now, while my idea is crystal clear to me."

Chapter 54

"We can talk about this later, JoAnne. Let me scare up some breakfast and bring you back to the real world. You'll feel better. We have to get ready for the babysitter and our trip up the mountain. Tonight, we'll talk about anything you want."

JoAnne seldom argued with Joe. He always had her best interests at heart. But this time she was right and he had to listen. The intensity of her nightmare made it urgent she put the ugly vision behind her and act on its message. Just once they could be late for work. They needed to explore something the two of them had talked about years earlier. Her instincts told her the idea she hatched moments ago would work.

"No, Joe, damnit! This *is* the real world. We need to talk now while my idea is fresh. This time I'm insisting."

She watched his expression and knew her own eyes must be firing daggers. She'd gotten beyond the paralyzing fear her terrifying dream had brought on. The time was ripe to work out a plan to permanently foil the evil monster who had menaced her. The beast had cowered in the face of her defiance. JoAnne now knew who that apparition represented. It was the face of the privileged class her fellow citizens had installed as their elected leaders. *Enough is enough.* she decided. *I'm ready to fight back*

Joe said, "You take the bathroom first while I start our meal. I can see how important it is to you to hash this out now."

"Thank you," she said, gave him a quick peck and left the kitchen.

JoAnne went through her normal early morning routine to get ready for work. As she came fully awake under the shower spray, she was even more convinced the horrible experience she'd come through could give her a new purpose. The nano work was going well so she could devote her time to this new challenge. With Joe as her partner, they could help the common folk recapture control of their country. As excited as she was when the nano work started, she sensed this undertaking could be even more exhilarating. She hurried through her morning ritual and arrived in the kitchen refreshed and prepared to tackle an exciting new project.

Joe told her, "I called Fred and Bonnie and told them we'd be noon or after getting to the site. They'll keep things humming. Whenever you're ready, I'm prepared to spend as long as you want talking our way through this epiphany."

JoAnne joined him at the small breakfast table and Joe set down juice and coffee for starters. "I can't wait to share my idea, Joe. I know it'll work."

"I'm listening," he answered.

She stared across the table, hesitated and sipped at herorange juice. Then she straightened up and began.

"Remember soon after I moved to Texas we talked about how our chosen fields surprisingly seemed to mesh in a number of exciting ways?"

Joe searched his memory and remembered how on that same day in their house in Alpine he had pressed her to set a wedding date only to have her deflect his probing with talk about work. That was when she made the connection that her nano devices could be programmed to detect human enzymes his research had discovered. She saw promise that those body fluids might be altered and used to treat diseases. Why was she bringing that up now?

"Remember you told me," she went on, "that you'd uncovered a specific enzyme that could be used as a fool proof lie detector? I predicted that finding may be more significant than you realized." She waited for her words to register on him.

"But what does this have to do with the fright I found you in a while ago?" he asked.

"Maybe nothing and maybe everything. That gruesome horrible monster that was chasing me was wearing a red, white and blue vest. Bad dreams don't often make their meanings obvious. I agonized over that sight and finally realized what it was chasing me. For lack of a better name, that beast was the figure of big, bloated, self-centered government. It was all the self-important public officials rolled into one star-spangled abomination. The government politicians were trying to rip away my last vestige of privacy and consume me in their collective hungry mouth."

Joe took her hand. "Calm down, JoAnne."

"Oh, I'm fine now that I've thought it through. Those lying pols aren't nearly as secure as they may think. We're about to gang up on them and set things right. This is my chance to pay back Project WAKE for all it's done for me. Don't you see, Joe, we can build a foolproof lie detection process. That will expose the dishonest members of the government and send them packing."

Joe broke into a broad grin. JoAnne might be a hundred percent right on. Maybe both of them were harboring the same hollow, unresolved spot where WAKE was concerned. After all this time she could have found the key to how they'd begin directly repaying their debt to Joe Whitley and his friends. George Adams had said that first day at GMed that *the new national revolution has begun and you're a part of it, Doctor Amos.* With JoAnne as his partner, they may finally fulfill that destiny.

"I understand," he told her. "The Constitution created a privileged class due to a very human oversight. Sadly, when men are left to power long enough they become far removed from the people and the power corrupts them."

"Exactly. And the system sets up Congress as the one and only control on wayward members. They fear sanctioning each other since they all have something to hide. Time and public apathy make installed politicians almost unmovable. But what if we see to it that the worst of them are publicly confronted by their own lies and deceit? It may well lead to a wave of replacements at election time, perhaps even much sooner in the face of outcries from their constituents. Applying a proven lie detector test and electing WAKE-sponsored citizen politicians could mark the end of politics as usual."

Once Emily's babysitter arrived Joe and JoAnne closeted themselves together in their library/office to work out the preliminary details of what they quickly dubbed 'Truth Time'. Their teams were perfectly capable of continuing both the biomass and nano projects without the full-time attention of the Amoses. Truth Time would be their contribution to the peaceful revolution.

Chapter 55

George Adams had enjoyed a private pastime for as long as he could remember. He loved going alone to minor league baseball games.

It began as a quirky lark to escape the pressures of business. Adams needed the relief from recognition as a wealthy industrialist; wanted an occasional opportunity to be just plain George. He could wind down from the daily grind, lose himself in the action on the field, and reenergize. A baseball fan since his stickball days on the streets of New York City, he discovered a whole new appreciation for the game played by eager rookies hustling to move up to the majors. And as the years went by he found his recurring trips to local ball parks also brought him into contact with some interesting people.

On this particularly hot, sunny day George drove down to Leesburg to enjoy another lively Commonwealth League game. He took up a place behind home plate in the limited shade provided by a tin roof. 'Grandstand' seemed a bit pretentious for where he sat; nevertheless, he gleefully settled down with a hot dog, super size soda and large bag of in the shell peanuts. He panned around the noisy crowd and genuinely relaxed for the first time in a week. This was his element!

"Nuthin' like a ball park hot dog, huh?" he heard and turned as an elderly white guy wearing a Leesburg ball cap and dark shades sat down beside him. The man finished off the last bite of his own dog and removed his sun glasses. George looked at the newcomer's slightly graying hair and took him to be a few years younger than himself, so that put him maybe close to sixty.

"Special treat," George answered. That was a total understatement. The way his GMed diabetes team monitored him, this dive off the diet wagon was a heavenly, if guilt-ridden, forbidden delight. If he dared, dessert would be the Moon Pie he'd stuffed in his pocket.

"I have to have two hot dogs every game," the newcomer said, "one before the first pitch and a second at seventh innin' stretch. Hey, you a Yankees fan?" He'd changed gears without a pause and pointed at the broken down Yankees cap George wore as part of his ball park garb.

"Watched 'em when I was growin' up," George said. "It was sort of a natural progression for city kids—goin' from stoop ball to stickball with a spaldeen to chasin' home run balls at Yankee Stadium. These youngsters remind me a of the kind o' scramble ball the old Yanks played in the day. Haven't seen you out here before."

"Name's Don Shupe." He stuck out his hand and George enveloped it with his oversized paw. "Been makin' the rounds of the local fields this season lookin' for a team I could latch onto."

"I'm George Parker, Don. Pleased to meetcha," He'd made up a name just in case.

The new arrival certainly knew his baseball. By mid-game the two of them had rehashed fond childhood memories of the sights and sounds of ball parks. Don and his dad had followed the local Boston Red Sox farm club down in Roanoke and watched Sox players climb to the majors. That made George and Don natural rivals but good-natured ones. They became so engrossed in conversation that they completely missed the seventh-inning snack break. When the game ended, George threw out an invitation.

""You got a spot for a hamburger, Don? There's a little place close by serves a mean burger and first-class milk shake."

They drove to the Virginia Diner with Don following George's green pickup in his shiny Buick sedan. Over burgers and shakes they continued to get to know each other. George made a silent vow to atone later for his tumble from dietary grace then proceeded to ravish his juicy burger and vanilla shake.

"What do you do for a living, George?"

"I'm into drugs," Adams answered before he realized how that must sound. "Legitimate drugs, that is," he amended. "Operate a pharmacy outlet up the road." *As natural as their initial meeting seemed to be going, he was far from comfortable. Why spoil the easy geniality with his new friend by telling him that the 'outlet' was GMed, a multibillion dollar company?* "How 'bout you, Don?"

"On my second career. Retired from the Air Force and went to work in northern Virginia as an electrical engineer. Live up over the mountain in West Virginia. The missus and I are lookin' for the ideal place to retire again soon."

A sudden inspiration hit George. He tested the water.

"Ever think about diving into politics?"

"At *my* age? Beyond some time on town council and a regional planning board, I never thought about being anything more than a decent EE. I was a young Republican in college, but the past twenty years I wouldn't have thrown in with either one of the parties. They picked their symbols well. Dems settled on a donkey and set out to act like a bunch of brayin' asses. GOP chose an elephant and lately they've been doing a bad impression of a herd of bumbling pachyderms. I'd have to be an independent."

Adams went silent and looked like his mind was a thousand miles away.

"You okay?" Don set down his chocolate shake with a puzzled frown.

George caught himself and came back to the present. "Oh, I was just mulling over sumpin'." He looked at his watch and said, "Gotta get on up the road, friend. Are you planning to watch any more Leesburg games soon?"

"I plan to make it to the Wednesday night game with Winchester. That one should be a zinger. Starts at seven, but I'll be in the stands before that chompin' on a hot dog. Can I save you a place behind the plate, George?"

"Can't think of anything I'd rather do. How about six thirty? You grab two cushions and I'll pick up the snacks at the hot dog stand."

Hmmm, George thought. *Don's a regular Joe, loads of experience, not hooked up with a political party. Sounds like a model citizen politician to me. This just might be worth exploring.*

Chapter 56

The WAKE founders convened in May 2017 on the north shore of Oahu. An estate on the water there had passed to George Adams in Joe Whitley's will. It was the perfect spot for Adams, Kato and Estrada to meet away from prying eyes. They were there to hear Raymond Crane's report on Project WAKE.

`George tilted his wicker chair back, propped his feet against the porch railing, and looked out at the incredibly blue waters beyond Hawaii's shoreline. Trade winds rippled through his aloha shirt and cooled his sandal-clad feet. "What's yer take on de election?" he asked Hiro. "T'ink the voters got it right this time?"

Hiro shuffled his bare feet under him and stood at the top of the porch stairs. "Hard to say, George. This new guy says he wants to bring people together. That's a tall order. He's gonna need a hell of a lot more than charisma to pull it off."

Carlos was just coming out the front door. "Whatcha sayin', Hiro?" he asked, handing each of them a freshly made mai tai.

Hiro took a sip of his drink, watched the surf break fifty yards away, and sighed. "This really is the good life, isn't it?" He leaned back against the porch railing and said, "To answer your question, for the country's good, I wish the new administration success, But the hate campaign being run by the losers is downright sickening."

Hiro continued, "Neither party had its act together in this election. One talked about all the hope and change her predecessor brought us and campaigned like a wet noodle. Thought she had it wrapped up. All I saw was a crippled economy, more giveaways, and massive new regulations. The other guy gave them a big surprise and rode in on lots of promises. Now we need to see if he can follow through.

"Lot o' truth in that," George piped in. "But instead of getting to work, the losers dug in their heels and determined they'd oppose any and all changes to what their hero had put in place. Hell, the real change we needed was to swap out the guys in both parties on Capitol Hill that got us into this mess. Last time I looked most of them are still up there mucking up the works. Sure, the new Prez is not an insider, but that's a good thing. I say, get on board with him and give him a chance."

"How do you feel about the new crowd, Carlos?"

"Listen, the three of us can survive whatever they throw at us. It's the average Joes I worry about, the hard-workin' stiffs. I'm much afraid we're in for some hard sleddin', fellers.

Carlos was raring to go. "It's time those high an' mighties on Capitol Hill got their act together. Before long some of our proteges will be there bringing about the real fixes we need. But we need action now."

George gave the time out signal. "All this venting may be good for the soul, gents, but it plays hell with the ol' blood pressure. Let's tone it down and wait for Ray's report tomorrow. I have a feeling we'll all have a better outlook when we hear how WAKE is woikin' towards toinin' things around."

* * *

Once again Ray Crane stood before the three remaining WAKE founders to tell them how their grand experiment was faring. Since their last update the country had been recovering at a steady pace from its economic doldrum. Employment was rising and regulations were being overturned to the benefit of most of the public. But the more successes the new chief executive produced, the louder the shrill voices of opposition rang out on the streets.

Hiro and Carlos continued to be prosperous with their firms experiencing new profit levels. They nervously awaited Ray's words on how WAKE was working to make things better.

"Good morning, gentlemen." Ray looked alert and enthusiastic as usual, though his hair was beginning to show tinges of gray. "I'm pleased to report that, in contrast to the uncertain times, Project WAKE is alive and well on its way to bringing the reason and stability you've all worked so hard to promote."

Ray paused to let his words sink in. He stared out at the founders over his reading glasses and waited for their reaction. To a man they wore expressions that told him his good news was not only welcome, it was a huge relief. With all that was going on they needed to hear that their unwavering support continued to pay dividends.

"This chart shows the current enrollment in WAKE," Ray said. "Eighteen classes of WAKE since its inception in 2000 have produced over 500 committed, continuing members. These young folks have gone on to fill important positions in industry, science, education, and politics. They're responsible for a multitude of inventions, new scientific breakthroughs and innovative business practices. The most recent class of 40 candidates, financed by your annual pledges, is now at campuses around the country. Your protégés to date have over 30 patents, dozens of national scientific honors, and three Nobel prize nominations. On the education front, WAKE members are becoming a strong force for truth in classrooms at all levels. They're helping cull out revisionist history and seeing that text books full of politically correct language are exposed and discredited."

George, Hiro and Carlos learned that there were currently more than 100 of their protégés serving in elected positions from town council to national level. One governor and eight sitting members of the U.S. House of Representatives were what George delighted in calling

WAKERS. Ray was quick to point out that most of the national WAKER electees had run as members of the two major parties but owed their primary allegiance to furthering Constitutional principles.

When the briefing ended, the three men smoked their Havanas to honor the memory of Joe Whitley. George motioned for attention and made a pronouncement.

"Hell of an idear old Joe came up with, fellers. I'm glad he brought us in on it. Could be WAKE turns out to be what keeps this country afloat."

Hiro gave a "Hear, hear." Carlos chimed in with, "Reminds me of when I was a rodeo kid. Feel like I'm about to straddle a big, mean ol' bull. This ride's gonna be one hell of a lot longer than six seconds, but we got us some smart young folks on our side. Hang on and ride hard. Yippeee!"

Chapter 57

This would be a tumultuous but encouraging year. JoAnne Amos was a scientist, not a political person, but what she saw brought home the lessons from her summer sessions. The government's bumbling contribution to a downward spiral and a prolonged recovery began to turn around.

The new President had set about making good on his promises. Regulations were cut, employment boomed and America announced to the world that we would no longer be the world's keeper or its dumping ground. We would be willing partners but the free ride was over.

Joe and JoAnne took a break from the grind to mull over what all this meant to their respective projects.

"Our teams are carrying on with the medical research, biomass, and nanomedicine," JoAnne said. "We're spending most of our time pursuing answers to further the Truth Time effort. The colocation at this covert site seems to have been the right move. One of these days we need to talk seriously about doing our bit in elected office. The WAKE founders put a lot of effort into getting us here and we owe them to take our turns."

I understand what you're saying, hon," Joe replied, "But we can't think about that till we can come out from under our secure cover. We can make a big difference by going full throttle on Truth Time to help expose some of the worst Hill dwellers. That may even convince a lot of the hangers-on to do the right thing—stand down and go home."

"So why do I feel so sick about Emily future, Joe? With all you and I have been able to accomplish, I'm beginning to feel helpless against forces we can't control. Tell me I'm wrong."

"Wish I could, hon. It's discouraging to watch people who hold our trust sell us down the river. Despite the warnings to keep their hands off and let the markets correct themselves, our social architects fumble forward, convinced only *they* know the answers. We have to hold on tight and try to turn around the bad decisions that got the country into this mess. Makes me want to jump into the solution but what we're doing now is too important to slow down. Just be patient and let it all play out as the WAKERS plan."

"I hope the founders' first step to loosen up security was the correct call, Joe. Sounded like a fair swap to me. We let them in on where you're testing medical delivery nano devices and they directly monitor your work. I understand the government has approved letting willing critically ill civilians take advantage of the tests. Along with the results you've had with your own volunteers, the improvements in those patients should convince the feds. They can help speed up approval of using injected medical nanos to target diseased cells. Could cut a couple years off the approval process," she told him. "And I see you've had a few visitors of your own."

Joe confirmed the attention being paid to his biomass project. "It made sense to brief the fed on the other work we were doing at Green and swear them to secrecy. The people from the Energy Department actually see the potential our energy cake has for producing commercial electricity. We're keeping them up to date on the progress at Bio City, too. Our best estimate is that we'll have the town of 3,000 in east Texas operational before the year ends."

"Fantastic!" she yelled. "Once Bio City proves it can provide biomass power to run a whole town, we can go public with Site Green. The cat will be out of the bag and it'll be too late for the bad guys to sabotage your new technology. Finally, we'll be able to tell the world their worries about dependence on fossil fuels are coming to an end."

"That will be an important day for my team, JoAnne. They've worked hard to reach this milestone. It could be a milestone day for us personally, too. How would you feel about moving to Bio City once it's up and running?"

"Just uproot from the home I love in Alpine?"

"Why not? Our teams can continue their work at Site Green, or somewhere else for that matter, after we go public with both projects. Fred and Bonnie are both doing well as team leaders since we started putting the bulk of our efforts on Truth Time. You and I can relocate from that big hole and start concentrating a hundred percent on the lie detection tests."

JoAnne thought about that. She balanced a forkful of fluffy scrambled eggs halfway to her mouth and stared at him. Leaving their very first home simply had not occurred to her. No more long drives up the mountain or evasive answers about what she did for a living or where. Emily Jo was happy and thriving here, but one day JoAnne would need to concern herself with school and a normal life for their baby.

"I'd consider moving, but there are some conditions," she answered.

"Spell them out and we'll make them happen."

"Offer the teams a chance to transition to a less remote work site."

"They can move to Bio City, too," he said, "over a span of several months. I'm sure George would agree to arrange for homes and lab space for them."

"Emily has to have the best pre-school and grade school available."

Joe flashed a big smile. "Bio City is planned as much more than just a place to test a new energy platform. The founders want it to be a location where technology thrives and young minds are stimulated to the maximum. Some of the best educators available are being offered homes and jobs there. Its location between Dallas and Austin is choice for growing families."

"And when would I have to expect to move?"

"Say the word, hon, and I'll start the ball rolling on our new home and project site. You design both of them and we'll put the builders to work. In six to eight months we can be there looking forward to a milder winter and a whole new style of living without looking over our shoulders. The nano and bio teams can follow as soon as their homes and work sites are ready."

"Then let's commit to the move, Joe. And let's get on with Truth Time. I can't wait to see some of the biggest liars of our time get their comeuppance."

"Best of all," Joe said, "we can drop our cover and live as JoAnne and Joe Amos."

Chapter 58

Three Middle Eastern oil men met at a posh seaside resort. Their agenda contained a single, all-important item—what to do about the serious threat to their energy monopoly. Mahmoud, a gray-bearded man in a flowing robe, spoke to his companions.

"This company of American fools must be stopped. It is clear that the man we bought and paid for in Washington was not as capable as he professed. Now we must take matters into our own hands."

Faraz, a bulky, robed man, shook his head. "I would caution that our earlier attempts to shut down their research ended in disasters. We were nearly compromised by the Virginia attack, and it is unclear whether the destruction of the Nebraska warehouse shut them down. We believe they could still be operating somewhere at a reduced scale. All of our efforts to confirm our suspicion have been unsuccessful. So I say it is time for aggressive action. Why do we rely upon Americans who offer results and fail to deliver? Congressman Foster was given our funding and patience and he fell sorely short. The solution is our responsibility."

The elder statesman Mahmoud stared at the others and slowly sipped his coffee. Ahmed, a younger man in a Western style suit, took the opportunity to be heard.

"Eminence—if I may suggest—I would caution that a measured approach is most likely to succeed. I have carefully cultivated strong ties with other important men in positions of authority in Washington. They can bring about the results you desire. The infidels will be able to inject their new fuel technology only insofar as these men allow. Already I have indications that, wherever they are, the EnzAm people have asked for Government assistance. The American system is fraught with delays and governing regulations that can indefinitely postpone the use of their garbage conversion for fuel production. Soon my contacts will determine whether this Doctor Amos still lives. If so, we will find his hiding place and capture him, his records and the people who devised the process. The records *and* the people will permanently disappear."

Mahmoud silently weighed their inputs as the others patiently awaited his decision. At length he made his pronouncement. "We will let your plan play out, Ahmed. I will expect frequent updates on your progress. I want the names and complete files on these contacts you value so highly. If I sense that the bio fuels madness is near to surfacing, your departure from this world will be in disgrace. Every one of the enablers you identify will be tracked down, regardless of their station in life, and they will meet a fate akin to our Mister Foster. This time they will not appear to be suicides as he was. My instructions will be to defile them so that those who understand such matters will know the jihad has reached their shores."

The three men went their separate ways. Ahmed boarded his flight to New York with Mahmoud's decree indelibly embossed in his mind and a new sense of urgency filling his every fiber. How matters played out during the coming months would determine whether he could aspire to greatness as a jihadist and a glorious future in paradise. Failure would mean the ignominious fate of being torn asunder, his body defiled in some nondescript place on hated American infidel soil.

Amos and his associates had precipitated the crisis. They insisted upon threatening the delicate balance his masters maintained in the world's energy supply. This heathen scientist and his troupe had begun the end battle, and it was Ahmed's responsibility to assure a final glorious outcome for the Islamic revolution.

Chapter 59

Adams, Kato and Estrada rendezvoused on their satellite telephones during June 2017.

George said to his compatriots, "We have us a whole new problem in dear ol' DC. For eight years we struggled along with a community organizer that thought he knew how to run a country. Then we got a whole new kind of Prez, one that knows how to negotiate, not apologize, and how to run things like a business.

I still can't get excited about goin' partisan, and I won't, but he's one big improvement. The Dems go on playing politics like it's a blood sport and to hell with what's good for the people. The GOP takes over both houses of Congress and the White House. Then they can't work together to make things happen. So one party screws it up and the other can't get organized to fix it. Still looks to me like the WAKE 'stand up day' is our one remaining chance to save the country from the numb nuts we've elected,"

"Not a pretty scene," Hiro agreed. "I had hoped the 'yes we can' gang had a plan, but they turned out to be a bunch of dyslexics who couldn't read the history books. Now they can't get organized to set things right."

"I worry," Carlos offered, "my workers were takin' hits and bein' jacked around so bad they may never recover. It was like a bad comedy, an' we got smacked with a new pie in the face ever' day. Then they told us it was un-patriotic to ask our elected reps to explain and stand behind what they're pushing. But when the new leader tries to remedy that, the hate cult calls him everything but a milk cow and stubbornly blocks progress.

"We're lucky," George reminded them. "Our own businesses are strong and they weathered the downturn. But what about the millions of average Bobs, Bills and Marys out there?"

Hiro asked, "What was it Jonas Whitley said about American dictators? If I recall he berated what he called the 'imperial executive'. Well, now we have another chance."

George gave a hearty laugh. "Old Joe had a way of blowin' away all the smoke and getting down to the nubbin, didn't he? I'll never forgot the warnin' he gave us. Said we'd had three dictators in America. Abraham Lincoln was one of the most hated men of his time for the controls and government reprisals he put in place durin' the Civil War. Woodrow Wilson glorified power and had the gall to say he was the right hand of God! To stand against him was to fight the divine will. What kind of horse manure was that? Good ol' Woody even called the Constitution's checks and balances 'artificial barriers' to progress. But the king of the hill was Franklin Daddy Roosevelt. Man used made up powers woulda made the founding fathers upchuck. After all these years, students of history are beginning to agree FDR stretched out the Great Depression by years with his one-man band style. Then the voters bought Mister Hope and Change's pitch and he turned into number four on the list."

"Damn, George," Hiro blurted, "you have that pitch written down somewhere?"

"It's imprinted on my brain, George retorted with a note of pride. When a fellow's right, he's right. Joe nailed it. And then too many folks bought into a forth big talker. But they may have finally woke up this go around. Time for doing not talking."

"But we need to put all that aside and think of how WAKE can help change the future. We have to hang in and let these young folks we've groomed take charge. Our projects in Site Green are a start, but it's citizen politicians from among our proteges that will take us where we need to go."

Chapter 60

"Damn it!" Joe blurted out and threw his pencil across the room.

JoAnne pushed away from her computer, looked over at Emily then stared at her husband. "You haven't been yourself lately, Joe. Emily and I are worried about you."

"It's frustration, hon, pure frustration. We've put Bio City on line and the results are even better than we hoped. You and I know first-hand the power provided to our home is reliable and certainly affordable. The raw materials we use are helping clean up landfills. This technology is a boon to breaking our fossil fuel dependence. Why is our own government doing everything possible to delay its use?"

"I know," she said. "The roadblocks some of these pompous officials throw up are unbelievable. First they tried to exhume the old issue of EnzAm using 'commonly produced refuse' to make a profit. Then they demanded costly, extensive environmental testing at every turn that nearly brought the biomass project to a standstill. Insisting on a conversion tax to reuse garbage took the prize for bureaucratic hogwash. Whose side are these people on?"

The Amoses had been busy in their new lab when Joe's uncharacteristic outburst occurred. They spent most of their waking hours these days striving to bring Truth Time, as they called the new regime for lie detection, to reality. JoAnne was well aware of how impatient and irritable Joe had become the past several weeks. Bio City, their new home town in east Texas, was humming along. Its quiet, efficient and non-polluting power plant furnished affordable electric power for 3,000 residents. Organic waste from Carl's Foods outlets was trucked in by Estrada's transport fleet. Were it not for the foot dragging and nay saying of Congressional oversight, work could be underway on the first wave of new power plants throughout the country. Yes, she could see why Joe was frustrated.

"What I need least right now," he said, "Is a hearing on Capitol Hill to explain what the biomass effort is about. One of the staffers keeps hinting they could call me to testify. You'd think the concept was simple enough for anybody to understand. Clean up a prime pollution mess by recycling municipal solid waste into reusable energy. Perform a clean conversion by breaking down cellular input material using a product resembling a natural human enzyme. Produce a transportable energy cake that can be activated to yield clean, efficient power for electric turbines."

JoAnne shook her head and frowned. "Realize I sound like a WAKER, but I just don't see the down side. Must be hard for politicians to accept that all we need from them is their sanction and non-interference. Bonnie is getting about as frustrated as you are with the endless procession of Congressional staffers and their bosses trooping through Site Green asking the same questions over and over about nanomedicine. Guess there's no avoiding your going to Washington to help them show off on television."

"Well, both the nano team and Fred's biomass people will be down here at Bio soon. Then we can fully disclose what's been going on inside that mountain at Green. The increased security the feds have here to protect a strategically important facility should keep the *real* bad folks at arm's length. Maybe I should just go ahead and log out a few days to satisfy the folks on the Hill and keep them out of the real workers' hair."

JoAnne made a face and let a nervous laugh escape. "I'm not so sure who the *real* bad folks are, Joe. Once we go public with your biomass technology, the big oil and Middle East interests will be stymied. The success of Bio City will knock their monopoly in the head. And the people that want to sabotage our nano work will soon be stumped, too, if we can only get approval to put our nanites to work for the general public. Maybe the best way to cope with politicians tampering with success is to give them their time in the public eye and keep pushing."

* * *

As a new year began the Site Green people planned their move to Bio City to occupy updated state of the art facilities. The federal government provided security and observers at Site Green and both vital projects flourished. JoAnne divided her efforts between Truth Time and the nanomedicine task and helped refine microdose delivery techniques. However, not a day went by without some member of the government contingent trying to erect a new barrier to progress for both teams. The Amoses accepted full responsibility for fending off these distractions.

"You won't believe what happened today, Joe." JoAnne's expression told her husband the news wasn't good. But her jaw was set in that determined manner that told him she was spoiling for a fight.

"I'm almost afraid to ask," he said. Joe was careful not to grin for fear he'd merely pique her rage.

"Henry Marcus, the Congressional staffer I described to you as having a nose like a hawk and the brain of an insect, struck again. He delivered this to me." She handed Joe an official looking letter with the letterhead of the US House of Representatives. The subject line read: "Presentation to Congressional Hearing."

Having received a similar summons only days ago, Joe emitted an audible grunt. "Must be something in the water in DC. Their summonses are multiplying."

“I’ve decided to go and let Bonnie stay here,” she told him. “We’re at a critical stage in perfecting the delivery procedures. This Congressional committee wants a full description of the nanomedicine project to, as they put it, ‘consider the benefits and attendant risks of government approval for general use.’ That sounds suspiciously similar to the verbiage in your invitation to testify on biomass energy generation.”

Joe laughed out loud. “I just saw the dates. You and I are going to be on Capitol Hill on the griddle at almost the same time. Need I say it? … two committees, one purpose: stop these pesky Amoses before they mess up our playhouse.”

He went away thinking *We’ve had more than our share of harassment from the oil sheiks and their flunkies. Matter of fact, I look over my shoulder every day wondering when they’ll show up again. Now we’re taking on the politicians. If those folks knew about WAKE they’d be on our case big time. Life was worlds simpler when all I had to worry about was being a low-profile scientist!*

Chapter 61

Joe called it a day, locked up the Truth Time space in Bio City and swung home to be with his ladies. JoAnne had spent the day with Emily while Joe pored over their latest Truth Time experiments. The lie detection work was moving along well now that they were at arm's length from the contingent of federal observers back on Site Green. Its implications were too explosive to trust to the feds. JoAnne's enthusiasm and perpetual smile always cheered him up after a long work day. Today she had a special glow about her.

She beamed that sunny look and told him, "You look like the tabby cat that swallowed the singing canary, Joe. Make my day. What put that grin on your face?"

JoAnne walked him to the family room. She sat waiting for his explanation.

"This was a milestone day," Joe answered. "I had quiet time to read over the results of our lie detection tests on our three latest volunteers. The outcomes are identical and repeatable. Enzyme A21 is the key to flagging deception. No matter how hard a test subject tries to cover up or misdirect with an answer, A21 is produced, detected by the nanites and signals a lie. Even practiced liars who convince themselves they're telling the truth can't fool their bodies. A21 is automatically released when they fib. We've proven to my satisfaction that the major reason lies produce electrical readings and muscle movement that traditional lie detectors pick up is the sudden presence of A21."

"I hope nobody realized what you were studying," she said.

"As much as I trust the EnzAm folks, we're not ready to draw premature attention to Truth Time."

"Don't worry," he told her. "All they know is that I was holed up with a stack of papers that could have been about anything. This is the breakthrough we've been looking for, lady. As soon as we get through these hearings with Congress, we need to bring in some trusted help and go full out on Truth Time. When we've gathered enough repeated results, we'll be ready to get the procedure certified. The best lie detector machines in use can't match our 100 percent reliability."

Joe gave his wife a hug. "I never doubted we'd prove our theory, JoAnne. Glad you insisted we push the envelope. Enzyme A21 nails even the most practiced liars. We'll be able to show by recorded electrical readings when somebody's trying to deceive."

"So you see that proper programming was the key all along. We calculate the proper algorithm for matching the enzyme secreted by the palatid gland for salivation. Then we inject nanos that are programmed to find and bond with that enzyme and introduce them into the subject's blood stream. They hunt down the A21 and alter its reaction. What would be even better is if we can visually display when nanites have detected the liar's body producing A21. Maybe we could have some kind of bells or whistles go off but more sophisticated and with instant visible impact."

Joe lit up and laughed out loud.

She gave him a sour look. "I'm serious, Joe. Why is that funny?"

"Oh, I totally agree with you, sweets. A totally mischievous thought popped into my head. What if the tip-off was a visual reaction that could be seen by anybody looking at the liar? Let's say we get nanites into a subject's blood stream and pose a pointed question. The subject lies and the nanites detect A21. We've electrically pre-tuned the detector nanites to react by lighting up.

The liar turns all blotchy and it's a dead giveaway."

Now it was JoAnne's turn to chuckle. She jotted hurried notes on a pad, studied them and broke into a wide smile.

"I believe you've hit on an important point, Joe. If we wanted to show a reaction taking place in the blood stream, where would be the most logical place on the body to do that?"

Joe mulled that over. "Near the skin's surface, I guess—maybe in a major artery?"

"Precisely," she agreed. The most conspicuous place would be in an artery or vein just under the skin." She ran a fingertip lightly down her neck. I believe we can do that with the carotid and jugular veins. The nanites can be preset to not only home in on A21 but also produce a visual display on the skin of the face and neck. Gives off a visual response when they find A21."

At this point she let go with a hearty guffaw. "What color would you like the liars to glow?"

Chapter 62

"How's the K-Tronics gig working out for you, Don?" George Adams asked. "Still thinking about retiring?" They were driving down to Leesburg together for another rookie league game.

"Working my butt off, George, but enjoying every minute of it," Don Shupe replied.

That had been the outcome of George and Don's chance meeting at the Leesburg ball park. They'd become fast friends and drinking buddies, if you could count diet sodas and an occasional milk shake as 'drinking'. They kept in contact year around and often met for a meal and chat at out of the way eateries. George had even introduced Don to a couple New York style delis.

Soon after they started sharing the baseball games, George asked him if he was interested in changing jobs to a nanoelectronics plant in western Maryland that belonged to Hiro's company. Said he had a friend that was looking for a seasoned EE with imagination and he could hook him up. Don went for an interview, took the job and he and his wife moved to Frederick within a few miles of George's estate. But the Shupes still had no idea exactly where George lived or who he really was.

"You likin' those summer classes I put you onto?" Not only had George managed to talk Don into moving into his own home district; he'd worked him into the summer Constitutional government sessions, two classes each summer for the past two years. Don gladly accepted the opportunity without questioning how George even knew the classes existed.

"Always wanted to learn more about how government *should* work," Shupe answered. "Met a lotta smart young people. Most of them took to calling me Pappy, since I was the only fellow over forty in the room. Now that I know more about how our government began, it makes me sick to see how Congress and the courts have botched their jobs. Congress passes bills thicker than the whole damned encyclopedia and so obtuse I defy any normal person to read and understand 'em. Nine frocked eggheads self-appoint themselves to interpret what the Constitution *really* says. If I hear somebody say precedence or stare decisis one more time as a cop-out I'm gonna barf all over 'em."

"What if I told you there are people workin' hard to change all that, Don? Folks that have a genuine shot at shockin' us back to actually followin' the Constitution."

"I'd say it sounds like a daydream or wishful thinking. The old timers are burrowed in so deep they've got the system permanently fritzed. With their connections and big money backing we couldn't throw the rascals out no matter how they screwed us over. Still, I'd love to have a decent chance to try."

"You and I have always been honest with each other, pal," George said with a hesitation in his voice. "I need to tell you sumpin' you din't know 'bout me. This lilttle tidbit might knock your hat off, Shupster."

"Whoa! That sounds downright weird, George. You gonna tell me there's some deep dark secret you been holding back from me?"

"You wouldn't be likely to see my picture show up anywhere. It's time I 'fessed up to somebody I consider a true pal. My real name is George Adams, Don. I own GMed, the pharmaceutical firm that's one of this area's biggest employers. I'm truly sorry I withheld this information from you. Didn't want to horse up what's turned into a genuine friendship. Now I'll be totally honest wit' you. Let me explain."

"This better be mighty good," Shupe told him. "I've advertised you to my wife as about the most up front guy I've ever run into. Don't disappoint me, George."

"When you hear the whole story, you'll understand why I have to be careful an' keep it close hold. It started way back in 2000."

George went on to give Don the whole dump—how WAKE began and grew, slowly at first, then at an excitingly growing pace. He revealed that some of the students Don had been in class with in the summer could soon be taking their places in Congress in future elections. George gave a thumbnail of the long-term goals of WAKE and said he was firmly convinced, after years of waiting, that they were reachable soon. Don sat in shocked silence soaking up every word of his friend's almost surreal narrative. Except for occasional glances to gauge Don's facial expressions, George attended to his driving and storytelling. The pickup rumbled on across the state line into Virginia.

"So now you see why I've been so tight lipped," George concluded. "I really am sorry I waited this long, but I had to be sure I could completely trust you. This info in the wrong hands could literally get me killed."

Don thought that over for a long time. The silence was broken only by the low roar of the pickup's droning engine. George looked over to see his pal struggling with the information overload he'd just been given. Shupe's eyes bored ahead down the road and gave no indication what he was thinking. George pulled to the shoulder of the road, shut off the engine and waited.

Finally, Don turned to face George and asked, "So what's all this got to do with me?"

"I believe you'd make a fine Congressman, Don," George answered. "Folks around here t'ink the world of you the way you took hold as a county planner. You can be a part of our plan."

"Boy, that was from clear out in left field," Shupe marveled. "Politics? Hell, George, I'll soon be sixty-two."

"I can name two dozen windbags on Capitol Hill who're that old and more. Worse, there are a lot of younger Congressmen that are, as my granny woulda said, worthless as tits on a boar hog. 'em, then go back home. You'll convince the locals you're their man. After that it's a question of organization and financial backin'. I have a lot of influence in this district.

We could do a lot worse than you. As you've loined in the summer groups, one of the original principles of the founding fathers was short term citizen politicians, people that give their neighbors a couple terms in Congress and do right by George restarted the truck and drove toward Leesburg. Don didn't say a word, but his silence didn't keep George from noticing his serious expression. The wheels were obviously grinding in his head.

After several long minutes, Don spoke up. "How long have you been working on this idea?" he asked. "Ever think maybe you oughta bring me in on the planning sooner?"

"I apologize for holdin' back, Don. Couldn't be sure whether you were ready to hear my idea. But today I decided it was time you either came on board or told me to buzz off. We're talkin' about a grass roots peaceful transition to men and women that believe in Constitutional government. You and others like you can be a big part of that. It's your decision."

"Man, you know how to put a fellow into overload, don't you? First I find out you're far from being plain old George; more like Mister Gotrocks. Then you spring this 'you ought to serve' argument on me. Got any other surprises?"

"That's about it, Shupe. Guess I shot the whole wad. The next move is up to you. You either decide to expose our plan, pretend you didn't hear me or join up with us."

A weighty silence followed as they drew near the ball field. George noted Don stared straight ahead out the windshield deep in thought. He wheeled the truck into a parking space and killed the engine.

Shupe touched his arm and said, "Hell of a plan, George. Count me in."

Chapter 63

Congressman James Grady, ranking member of the energy committee of the House of Representatives, strode to a bank of microphones set up in the U.S. Capitol hallway.

"Is it true, sir," a newsman asked while the network cameras whirred, "that you've called a hearing on some new process for producing energy from solid waste?"

Grady stood ramrod straight to extend his short frame. He proudly announced, "In the public interest I have asked that we investigate this new technology. The developers working on conversion of municipal solid waste to energy have been asked to explain to my committee its benefits and any potential environmental dangers it may pose."

"Is the process on line or merely a laboratory theory at this point, Congressman?" another reporter asked.

My understanding is that the conversion of biomass is in its infancy. We want to be certain there are no unidentified risks to the environment."

"Rumors have circulated," the second newsman persisted, "about a place somewhere out west, Congressman. We've been led to believe that Government observers are closely monitoring biomass energy experiments in progress. Is that true?"

Grady appeared ill at ease with this line of questioning. He turned to an aide and carried on a brief whispered conversation. Then he faced the mike again and stated, "I suggest you tune in and watch the hearing that will begin five days from today." He coughed and his aide handed him a bottled water. After a pause to swallow the liquid, Grady cleared his throat and pointed toward one of the correspondents.

"How do the oil companies feel about this new technology?" the lady reporter posed. "Some in the other party speculate that oil interests may be pushing for this investigation."

"Not true, madam. My one and only interest," Grady retorted, "is to see that the public is protected. What the oil people want is of no interest to me." He took another draw on the water.

His neck above the collar line oddly began to show a streak of color as he spoke. Grady worked to maintain his composure as an aide tugged at his arm.

"Congressman Phlegar also has an announcement he wants to make at this time," he said.

He yielded the podium to his fellow party member and retreated to the background amid a flood of shouted questions he chose to disregard. There was now a recurring, rapidly pulsing brightness about Grady's neck and cheek, an orange streak, as if he had developed a moving rash. A surprised gasp rippled through the newsmen. Ralph Phlegar from Missouri took over.

"Thank you, Jim. As my friend from Illinois indicated, Congress is sensitive to the need for oversight of new schemes proposed for general use. My committee has called for testimony by the proponents of another experimental new technology. Their idea would treat internal diseases by delivering medications via tiny electronic carriers in the blood stream. The leader of this exploratory research effort will testify before the health committee next week."

"Can you give us more information before the hearing, sir? Do you mean patients would be inoculated with some electronic device ? Are you saying … ?"

Phlegar waved a hand and interrupted the question. "I'm not a scientist, so I don't want to mislead you. The hearings will be televised and there will be ample opportunity for the public to hear the details of this proposed procedure."

A newsman who had been frantically attempting to attract attention shouted once more and was recognized by Congressman Phlegar. He spoke into the mike offered to him on a long boom. "Doctor Radke at Johns Hopkins has said this hearing is a witch hunt by the large pharmaceutical companies to discredit an effective new means of treatment. Have the drug companies exerted pressure to conduct this investigation?"

The Congressman moved uncomfortably under the klieg lights and appeared to measure his answer. "That's … it's not a matter of …" His voice trembled slightly before he regained control. "This session is being held strictly in the interest of the general public. Congress has a duty to protect citizens from well-meaning ventures that may have unanticipated side effects." His voice, despite his efforts, had a strange note of anger.

* * *

In their home in east Texas Joe and JoAnne Amos had been casually surfing the television channels when she ran onto the scene in the Capitol. She got Joe's attention and asked, "Aren't those the two rankling members of the 'inquisitions' we're facing in Washington?" They watched intently as the questions were asked and Grady put on his impromptu rainbow demonstration.

` Joe looked at his wife, who was grinning now, and said, "You knew this was going to happen, didn't you?"

"Oh, I have my sources, Joe."

"How in the world did you manage to feed a diet of nanites to the Co0ngressman?"

"The little buggers are tiny and safely transported. Food, drink, routine medical inoculations, all sorts of innocent substances can be packed with dozens of them. Besides, who says I had anything to do with those politicians ingesting nanites? I can produce documentation to show that two batches totaling about a hundred devices are missing from our inventory. Who knows where the thief may have taken them? Maybe you could have downed some of those babies in a coke or a bowl of soup, so don't try telling me any fibs, buster."

"You wouldn't."

"I trust you, Joe. But members of Congress, on the other hand . . ."

Joe gave her a high five and followed that with a long kiss.

"Wow!" she gasped. "I don't know whether you're pleased or turned on."

"Both, you gorgeous genius. Truth Time works and we just witnessed the first nationally televised proof. I hope whoever it was placed those teensies understands the favor he's done us. Once we break the story of our confirmed tests, every lying bum in the country will have to worry that he may have been 'nanited'. Not a one of them will feel safe from a questioning public."

JoAnne laughed till tears ran down her cheeks. When she finally got herself together, she looked him in the eye and asked, "Did you like the color, Doctor Amos?"

He considered his answer for an instant then asked, "Can you do plaid?"

JoAnne gave him a sour smirk. "I'm waiting, wise guy."

Joe straightened up and said with conviction, "I thought the bright green was an artistic touch. Why don't we go with that?"

"Actually," she said, "it seems to depend on the individual. Hard to tell what color may appear."

Chapter 64

"Well, they finally have us exactly where they want us," JoAnne told her husband with a sarcastic smirk. "Wonder why I don't feel intimidated?"

Joe Amos was busy unpacking his bag in their downtown Washington hotel room. He looked up and issued an exaggerated grimace. "Lady, I don't think you've *ever* been intimidated. Something tells me a bunch of pompous potentates are waiting to dig their claws into you but the joke's on them. They don't know what they're in for."

"Am I really that dangerous, Joe?" She clawed the air with her fingernails.

"No. You're a lovable little kitten, but you're also bull headed when you're in the right. I'll be watching every second of this shootout on TV and keeping score. Give me some good pointers on handling their counterparts when it's my turn."

She and Joe spent a relaxing evening entertaining little Emily Kathryn and sharing a leisurely dinner. JoAnne was pleasantly surprised that she was about to go into a den of wolves on the Hill tomorrow but felt none of the misgivings or nerves she had expected. There was truth in what Joe said. *Damn it*, she thought, *I* am *in the right here. Diagnosing with nanites is the best solution medicine has ever offered to detect and cure early stage diseases. It can save millions of people from suffering pain or radical surgery. I refuse to let these self-appointed experts derail the saving of lives.*

* * *

At precisely 10 AM the next morning, Chairman Henry Thomas gaveled his health subcommittee into session. Two people sat at a single witness table facing the chairman. Doctor JoAnne Amos, a striking, statuesque blonde, looked each of the committee members directly in the eye in turn. She appeared confident and at ease. Beside her sat Steven Pender, an experienced attorney provided by K-Tronics owner Hiroshi Kato.

In a hotel room a few blocks away two observers were riveted to the television set. Doctor Joe Amos and his year-old daughter, equipped with juice boxes and cheese sticks, settled in to watch. Emmy pointed at the screen and shouted, "Mommy!"

"Yes, that's your pretty mommy," Joe answered and joined the youngster's applause. "She's in a building not far away. When she's through talking to the men and ladies, we'll have dinner with her." He added his own prompt under his breath. *Give them both barrels, Jo. Kick ass, baby.*

* * *

Chairman Thomas gave his opening statement, "Doctor Amos, we are all anxious to hear about this groundbreaking work you are doing. We will try to keep this discussion at a level the non-engineer can understand." He went on to state his layman's take on what was briefed she and her people were bringing about. Said hde congratulated her and sincerely hoped she would succeed. Then the chairman turned to rankling member Phlegar for his comments.

Phlegar began with a particularly transparent accusation.

"I understand there are physical dangers to patients ingesting these devices. I hope you will address that. We also want to know your opinion of what many people would regard as invasion of patients' privacy in the act of inserting foreign objects into their blood streams."

Joe watched as his wife silently did a slow burn while Phlegar flung more verbal darts and arrows. When the camera briefly panned to her during the ranking member's comments, he took note of her determined look and firmly set jaw.

"Keep it together, JoAnne, Joe mumbled. *Your turn is coming. Don't let them rattle you."*

JoAnne was asked for her opening remarks. Her attornery Steven Pender placed a hand on her forearm and leaned in to whisper something before she began. She nodded and the corners of her mouth lifted visibly in a grin. JoAnne, exuding an impressive combination of beauty and composure, sat up straight, took a long, deep breath, cleared her throat and addressed the committee.

"This is an opportunity I have patiently anticipated for years. Our work to treat disease using tiny electronic devices called nanites in patient blood streams is ready for general application. We have compiled voluminous statistics confirming that nanomedicine is safe and effective. We selected more than thirty critically ill volunteers and they sanctioned the use of nanites as a last resort regimen. Fifteen of the subjects, within a matter of days of our commencing treatment, showed significant improvement. Another ten are now in remission and on the road to recovery."

Phlegar interrupted. "You quote short term results. How do we know these success rates are sustainable?"

JoAnne stared him down and calmly stated, "With all due respect, mister chairman, I would like the opportunity to complete my introductory comments before I respond to your specific questions. I believe most of the answers you want will be covered in my presentation."

An audible exhale by Phlegar was followed by muffled conversations among several of the committee members and their staffers. An air of restless anticipation seemed to ripple through the small assembly of observers. JoAnne Amos resolutely arranged her notes and waited. The chairman motioned for her to proceed.

In their hotel room, Joe Amos, normally a model of decorum, blew her a kiss and urged her on. "That's my girl!" He rubbed the small black device in his right hand and thought, *I told you security types we'd be fine here in DC. She's at the top of her game and next week it's my turn to tell it straight.*

Chapter 65

"So, Doctor Amos, can you assure the public that no physical harm will come to them if they submit to having these electrical devices injected into them?" JoAnne nearly laughed out loud when Congressman Smithers punctuated his statement with a contrived shudder. She started to speak but was cut off by the questioner.

"And should we consider placing legal constraints on the invasive procedure of intentionally placing foreign objects into human bodies?" His tone had turned decidedly hostile. It seemed to JoAnne to mimic the insulting onslaught the ranking member had begun. She took a deep breath and resolved to keep her composure.

"We have exercised special care," she began, "to assess any effects the nanites may have on patients' internal organs, cell functions, or normal body processes. We've found no adverse indications— zero. I can substantiate that a safe and efficient treatment for critically ill patients is to agree to be nanited. These devices hold promise for monitoring and early treatment of abnormalities before they reach the critical stage. Our detailed records document a number of project volunteers who have retained nanites for up to two weeks. We then have the option of continuing treatment with a follow-on dosage of identical nanites.

The next inquisitor asked for a capsule version of the theory and outcome of tests to date. JoAnne explained in layman's terms the concept of sending what she termed pathfinder nanites to seek out and collect readings on abnormal body cells and mark their locations. After studying the data and formulating a dosing regimen, the attending doctor then would order transport nanites with targeted microdoses of medicine injected to ho,e im on and treat specific cells. Results to date clearly indicated that this cell repair not only forestalled radically invasive surgery, it healed the damage in individual cells.

When she completed her riveting response, the room went silent for a full minute. Then conversation commenced among the podium sitters and whispers and note writing rippled through the audience of political and scientific observers. JoAnne surveyed the activity and made no attempt to suppress a smile.

Chairman Thomas gaveled for attention and a minority party member returned to his offensive. "So you can't guarantee your patients won't at some future date experience debilitating effects from these little machines."

"Our instrumentation allows us to detect any malfunction and extract individual nanites from the patient's body on demand. Experience shows this process to be relatively rapid and completely painless. Their small size permits easy flushing in body waste. A nanite is so small it is invisible to the naked eye. I vouch that the patient's well-being is at all times guarded in our regimen. If you found it necessary to be nanited for treatment, you would at no time feel discomfort, experience pain or suffer any long term effects from the procedure."

Phlegar twisted and turned in his seat and gave the impression of being repulsed by the mere idea of tiny transponders in his body. He fired back, "In no case can I imagine myself agreeing to such a procedure."

"Not even if the alternative was steady, eventually fatal debilitation without the repair nano dosage can offer?" JoAnne posed. I believe that life can be improved for every human being using pathfinder nanites to detect and promptly treat cell level abnormalities. Now, before I make my next statement, let me issue an apology to my husband, Doctor Joe Amos. As I speak to you today, I have fifty of the tiny electronic circuits in my blood stream monitoring my body's activities. This is going on without affecting me in the least. I would like to demonstrate with a test using the nanites I ingested only minutes ago. They will detect a specific enzyme the moment it appears in my body."

At the hotel Joe went into momentary shock. He stared down at his daughter and noted thankfully that she was focused on filling in a picture in her coloring book. He shook his head and tried to accept that his amazing wife would decide on her own to, in her coined phrase, nanite herself.

In the hearing room the ranking member showed a heightened level of irritation and stammered out a reply. "Please spare us the theatrics … I want to get on with …"

She ignored him and continued without missing a beat. "The nanites in my system are pre-calibrated to detect the secretion of a certain enzymatic protein we have named A21 by my body. Let me begin by assuring you I am honored to appear before you today. Your fair-minded approach is readily evident. I know you will give my testimony thoughtful consideration. Now for the test—excuse me." She paused and made an obvious effort to rearrange her notes.

After perhaps twenty seconds of apparent confusion ensued, the chairman reached for his gavel but hesitated. Before he could complete the motion, a bright green pulse of color moved up one side of JoAnne's neck. Seconds later, the other side of her neck showed a moving glow.

An audible gasp rippled through the room.

JoAnne pointed to the alternating chartreuse flashes in her neck and said, "I just told you what my body recognized as three untruths. The operative words I knew to be lies on my part were 'honored', 'fair-minded' and 'thoughtful consideration'. My body automatically responded to my dishonesty and secreted enzyme A21. The nanites in my blood stream detected A21 presence by distinct electrical impulses and emitted the bright green glow."

"A blood particle requires about one minute to complete a single transit of the human body. My jugular vein," she traced it with a fingertip, "showed one flash of color for each nanite passing through it from my heart. Likewise, the carotid artery over here," again the fingertip, "presented the same color as that nanite proceeded back to my heart.

Simply put, I intentionally lied to you and you saw a color glow for each nanite coursing through my blood. No matter how hard I may try to suppress this involuntary act, my body *will produce A21* with accompanying electrical pulses when I lie. If I had been hooked to a recording device, you would have seen spikes in the readings that occurred within seconds of each lie. If I had spoken an untruth at any other time in my remarks, you would have seen a glow then."

Phlegar interrupted and the chairman struggled to regain control. The gavel sounded repeatedly. "I object to this parlor trick demonstration, Doctor Amos. We convened this session specifically to give your research a fair hearing and you've made a mockery of the proceeding. You have tainted an impartial, objective investigation. I'm tempted to . . ." His tirade was cut short when an uproar and finger pointing broke out in the audience. All fingers were directed at Congressman Phlegar.

His neck was pulsing a well-defined purple hue.

Chapter 66

A knock sounded at the hotel room door and Joe heard, in a voice with a slight accent, “Room Service.”

“That’s our food, princess,” Joe told Emily and walked to the door. Emily alighted from the sofa and began clearing her toys and coloring books from the table top.

Joe opened the door to greet a young Middle Eastern man in a white coat pushing a service cart. The man smiled and said, “I am Ahmed. I have your lunch.” He rolled the cart in, looked at Emily and remarked, “Such a lovely young lady.” She thanked him.

While the waiter spread a tablecloth and arranged their meal, Joe took Emily’s hand and guided her toward the lavatory so they could wash their hands.

A surprise awaited them when they returned to the dining area. Ahmed stood holding a handgun fitted with a silencer. “You will follow my instructions precisely and without comment, Doctor Amos. I do not wish to harm you or your beautiful daughter. Take her hand and walk ahead of me into the hall as if you were taking a casual stroll.” He wrapped a towel over the weapon in his hand.

“Who are you?” Joe asked.

“I am your benefactor or your worst nightmare. The choice is up to you. There are people who will grant you a life of luxury in exchange for the technology you hold. If they can not have that knowledge, your life is without value to them.”

Joe did exactly as he was told. He swept Emily up and wrapped his left arm around her. Thrust his right hand into his trouser pocket and preceded Ahmed into the hallway. A house maid in an apron and cap stood by an open door down the hallway. She clutched a supply cart and rolled it slowly in their direction.

Amos turned toward the elevators and urged Emily along. With her lip trembling, she asked, "Why is the man …?" Joe answered, "We have to go somewhere, baby. It's okay."

They'd gone only a few steps when a low thud sounded behind them. Then all went quiet. Joe kept walking with Emily until a female voice called out, "It's okay, Doctor Amos. All clear."

He turned to see Sally Givens, one of Jim Bledsoe's security people, with her leg firmly implanted in Ahmed's back. Her maid uniform's apron was stuffed in Ahmed's mouth. She held a gun to his head while she worked to cuff him with her free hand.

"You were right after all, Sally." Joe pulled the little black device with the large button from his pocket. "Handy little item. By the way, you must have been in rodeo the way you bulldogged Ahmed."

Within minutes, while Joe and Emily calmed down and picked at their lunch, Mary and her partner had Ahmed in another room begging them for protection. He pled that his ruthless master could have him dismembered no matter where they held him. His life was worthless. He had only launched the one-man attack as a last resort. Sally told Joe they expected some major arrests before Ahmed stopped talking. He wanted to trade witness protection for damning information on Americans involved in the scheme to shut down EnzAm and the biomass project.

He spiced the offer by saying he could implicate an elected official on Capitol Hill who was taking bribes to assist.

Chapter 67

JoAnne, fresh from her stunning testimony on the Hill, coaxed Emily into a nap before dinner. She sat in their hotel suite with husband Joe as he activated the secure satellite telephone and rang up George Adams.

"Great show, JoAnne," George complemented. "Truth Time is about to shake hell outta politics as usual."

"Thanks, George. Joe has something urgent to discuss with you."

Joe took over and opened his update with, "I had a close encounter with one of the guys you've been worrying about, boss. He tried to kidnap my daughter and me. Luckily, Bledsoe's folks stepped in and subdued him without incident."

"You sure know how to lay down attention grabbers, Joe. Take it slow and tell me 'zackly what the hell happened."

Joe proceeded to explain how Ahmed had tried to walk off with them in tow until Sally responded to Joe's signal and lassoed the young Arab. Then he made his case.

"We've talked about the best time to explain Bio City to the public and make a clean breast of the information we've been holding back. My request involves outing EnzAm once and for all. I admit it also has an element of selfishness in it, George."

"Hang it on me, Joe. You're a major shareholder. Maybe the world is ready to hear what you've accomplished."

"From the song this Ahmed is singing, I believe JoAnne and I are under constant threat of being kidnapped and held captive or worse. As long as EnzAm and the knowledge in my head pose a threat to the Middle East oil cartel, we're in danger. That also includes some special oil interests in this country and their enablers and lackeys on Capitol Hill."

"So what's yer plan?" George asked.

"I've asked Fred to make copies of the full documentation on biomass conversion. We can turn over one copy to trusted agents in the federal government for secure safekeeping. Another copy gets locked away in a GMed facility you designate. We keep the original secured in our safe. I can issue the order from here and Fred will have it done by early tomorrow. Then I spill the complete EnzAm story on national television next week. JoAnne and I cease to be a threat to the oil folks. Unless our adversaries can manage to steal and destroy three widely dispersed information caches, they have no way to stop biomass from becoming a new fuel supply. That's our signal to press on with development of efficient liquid biomass automotive fuels. Checkmate for the oil potentates."

Total, tense silence set Joe's nervous knee to bobbing. He wondered if George had been disconnected. At last his boss answered. "Let it rip, Joe. I'll be watchin' you, hangin' on every word. Give 'em bot' barrels."

* * *

The following week JoAnne took Emily along to the Hill and they sat in the first row for Joe's appearance. The energy committee was behind schedule convening. Joe waited and mentally reviewed the sequence of events since their arrival in Washington.

She came off well, he ruminated. *Jo Anne more than held her own with a ravenous crowd that was itching to embarrass her. The TV and newspaper reports almost universally took her side and pictured her as the heroine of this episode. Sure, I overreacted when I heard she'd swallowed pathfinder nanites without telling me. But I couldn't stay mad at her. She believes in Truth Time and would do anything to have it succeed. Best of all, the media is widely speculating that Phlegar was, on two separate occasions, caught in outright lies. That is, if they can believe what JoAnne said about how nanites make liars glow. Her demo made that credible. One writer even remarked that the Congressman apparently had been 'nanited', a fate that could turn out to be nearly as destructive to him as being 'nuked.'*

Joe's daydreams were brought to an abrupt halt by the tap tap of a gavel and the chairman's silky smooth voice announcing, "The committee will come to order." Joe turned to give JoAnne a reassuring wink and telegraph a kiss to Emily. Then he sat up and waited for the assault to commence.

The chairman assured that he intended to see he was not subjected to the kind of indie criticism his wife had endured only days ago. He delivered his remarks before yielding the floor to the ranking member.

"Mister Chairman, Joe said, "I assure you every word of my testimony will be truthful, sincere and appropriate. And I wish to respectfully state that my wife's comments, in my opinion, were also entirely proper and necessary." But despite his intentions, Joe was under no delusion. He steeled himself to be harshly and personally attacked.

Challenge issued and rebuffed, JoAnne noted.

Ranking member Carl Rollins opened the formal exchange with an impassioned plea for considering the wishes and well-being of the public in developing biomass conversion. He expressed his own finding that the technology, while potentially beneficial, was unproven and still must pass muster as a safe, lawful and non-polluting process. Rollins admitted in closing his remarks that government energy personnel had been monitoring Amos's progress but were so far unconvinced. As he yielded the floor for Joe's initial remarks, Grady's neck momentarily flushed a shade of blue several times.

"I appreciate the opportunity to appear today," Joe started. "And I want to preface my comments about biomass energy conversion with a public announcement. The observation by government representatives referred to by the chairman includes continuing surveillance by a member of his own office staff. The observers have, in fact, been most complimentary. The oversight has taken place at a location known to us as Bio City. Most of the government observers are as enthusiastic as I am about the future of biomass conversion for energy production. By mutual agreement with the government's trusted agents, we've kept the real purpose of that town cloaked until now. That ends today."

Rollins halted Joe's statement with a warning. "Are you making a mockery of this hearing, Doctor Amos? We were told nothing of a planned announcement."

"If you will allow me to proceed, I'll show that my announcement is crucial to the testimony I am about to present. Or do I understand you would rather terminate the hearing than have it depart from a safe, scripted format?

"Rollins lunged toward his microphone to respond. The chairman urged, "Let him speak.. Most of us are interested in hearing the facts."

Oops! Joe thought. *Did I precipitate a minor mutiny?"*

Rollins put his hand over his mike and he and the chairman bantered back and forth in whispers. Fleming shook his head vigorously and pointed at his own microphone. A threat? Finally, the chairman gave Joe a wave of his hand to continue.

"Thank you," Joe said without specifying to whom his gratitude was directed. "The Bio City of which I spoke is my own current residence along with my wife, Doctor JoAnne Amos, and our daughter. What has never been revealed is that this town of 1,000 residents in east Texas is supplied by a single source of reliable, inexpensive and non-polluting energy produced by converting common industrial and residential waste into turbine power. The town has no refuse dump because all waste produced is promptly recycled as input material for our biomass conversion. Ladies and gentlemen, we have simultaneously addressed the solid waste problem and provided a clean, reusable form of non-fossil derivative fuel." At that point the hearing became the Joe Amos show.

Ninety minutes later Joe had succeeded in holding a national television audience spellbound for perhaps the most riveting afternoon of broadcasting the House of Representatives channel had ever hosted. He related the discovery of the enzyme that keyed the successful cellular breakdown of biomass waste. Joe detailed the long and arduous pursuit of energy discharges and how control of the releases was achieved in a safe environment.

He provided statistics on the amount of energy routinely produced on a daily basis to run Bio City businesses and residences. Energy plant emissions throughout the process were approximately fifteen percent of those in a coal-powered plant. Costs to the consumers were found to be significantly lower than those of fossil fuel-generated electricity.

Before the hearing ended, three of the committee's members had enthusiastically proposed a House floor vote to accelerate federal approval of biomass energy.
Repeated pointed questions from committee members prompted calm, straightforward replies by Doctor Amos. In most instances he offered specific documented proof to back up his answers. Each response provided a clear, uncomplicated and easy to understand reply addressing each aspect of multiple part queries.

Rollins not only became less vocal; he turned noticeably meek in his rebuttals.

Joe Amos insisted on making a closing statement. The chairman motioned and Joe began.

"Before the hearing is concluded, I wish to address those fossil fuel interests, both foreign and domestic, who may harbor thoughts of retaliation. Documentation of the complete biomass conversion process is now in the hands of trusted government agents. These details are also replicated at multiple secure storage locations. The world is now aware that biomass fuel is a reality and your oil monopoly is history. Non-polluting biomass power is functional and available to all who want it, and a new fully-tested bio fuel for automobiles will soon be on the market. Your leverage to affect or control biomass distribution has dramatically diminished. Prepare for the new energy revolution."

He looked directly into the camera and smiled. "My message to you, king oil, is: ***Move over. Biomass energy has arrived***."

Chapter 68

Joe and JoAnne worked hard to avoid public attention and get on with their critically important initiatives. This turned out to be no easy chore given the notoriety both of them had acquired from the Congressional hearings. Well wishers bombarded them urging them to run for political office, lend their credibility to various off-the-wall projects, sit on scientific and medical boards, or invest in dozens of money-making schemes. But they only wanted to see biomass and nanomedicine through to full implementation.

JoAnne confided during lunch, "Some days I wish I could just snatch you and Emily Jo away from this hubbub, Joe, and run away to some remote and peaceful place. I feel like we have to sneak around just to have a quiet meal together. This hastily arranged brown bag lunch in a corner of the Bio City labs complex almost has the feel of a tryst."

"It's the price we pay for taking on the big boys," he told her. "They forced the showdown. I never asked or this fight. Just wanted viewers to know how important biomass conversion is to them and prod Congress to get moving so it can spread."

"I confess I went to the Hill with a burr under my saddle," JoAnne admitted. "But it was only because the feds insisted on bleeding nanomedicine use to death with a thousand cuts. If Phlegar hadn't been so one-sided at the hearing, he wouldn't have prompted a blow up with millions of people watching."

"But you have to admit, hon, it was a priceless moment when the old boy turned purple right there in front of God and millions of viewers." Joe pretended to gag on his toast, grabbed at his neck and squealed, "I've been nanited!"

"So, mister comedian, what happens now? Do we give up and run back to Site Green, burrow into the ground and avoid people? I want to get on with my work and let somebody else handle the politics and rhetoric."

"Now that we've gone public with both projects, I'd say all we can do is get a firm grip and hold on for a frantic ride. With the approval channels speeding up in response to public pressure, we'll have all we can do to keep up with requests for biomass plants and enzyme fuel cakes soon. EnzAm already has dozens of inquiries and several tentative offers from state and local governments to build power plants. You and I are about to be a very rich couple. If we chose we could sit back, watch and let the money roll in."

"Not interested, Joe. Give it to charity. I spent a lot of years becoming an engineer, and I want to practice my trade. Besides, we have Truth Time to think about."

"That's one goal we can certainly agree on. The sooner we expose a bunch of lying SOBs and get the ranks of the elected cleaned up, the better off our whole country will be. And you and I will be on our way to paying back the WAKE founders for the trust they showed in us."

* * *

Many miles east of Bio City a gathering of wealthy, powerful men met in the palace of one of their number.

The acknowledged leader of this august group, a round man in ornate robes, spoke to his companions with a heavy tone of bitterness and scolded them for their failures. '

Our efforts have been misguided and poorly executed," Abdul-Alim chastised. "We sought to bury the technology, drown it in its infancy before it could compete with oil. The Americans we enlisted proved to be miserable failures. Our own people disappointed us."

He glanced over at Mahmoud, whose future remained fragile in light of his and Ahmed's disastrous performances. Ahmed had already paid a price. "Now the infidels have announced to the world their initial success and are hastening to fire up new biomass power plants. The entire outlook on fuel supplies has been distorted."

"If I may remind you, eminence," Umaru posed, "they have not yet marketed biomass fuel for automobiles. That market remains ours."

"My Nigerian friend has not been privy to the information my operatives have gathered. The EnzAm researchers may be near to introducing a liquid form of biomass fuel that could further cut our market. We would be financially devastated."

Hugo, the Venezuelan envoy, spoke up. "The leader speaks wisely. My own market will be virtually destroyed."

"Our path is clear, my friends. We have lost the initiative to this EnzAm scientist, Jordan Amos. He was almost in our hands along with his data, but now we must ensure we regain the upper hand. I propose he be offered a price beyond refusal for a share of his technology. We will grow that share with funds and pressure until we own the biomass market. Then we will again control fuel supplies and set the rules."

"But what shall we do if this man refuses our offer?"

"Our task is to determine his price. We can surely meet any demand he makes. The stakes are too high to fail."

Chapter 69

JoAnne's appearance before Congress created such a stir surrounding her that the media stalked her. They wanted to know everything about the lie detection routine she had revealed. She and Joe played along until mid-summer when a cable network channel pled for a television interview in prime time. The major broadcast networks, not willing to be scooped, asked for immediate equal access to the surprisingly popular lady PhD. Each of them insisted on being the first to interview her. The one she chose was a strategic decision.

"I'm pleased to discuss Truth Time with you," she told the lead news personality on a network that had been particularly hostile to her testimony. "This lie detection regimen is an important advance for law enforcement. I would suggest that this same procedure could give a few politicians pause to think before speaking."

Jo Anne's questioner, Christopher Madison, soon showed his bias with diversionary, misleading, and inaccurate statements. On each occasion, JoAnne merely let him have his say. Then she proceeded with polite finesse to shred his statement and counter the underlying bias with hard scientific facts. When the commentator's irritation peaked, he went on an all-out attack. She answered with a pointed question. "Have we covered all your prearranged talking points now, Mister Madison? If so I'd like to move on to discussing proven facts."

The show host flushed and blurted something about a 'low blow' from his guest. He was offended that she would, as he accused, '*Imply I have any agenda other than getting the truth in front of the public*'. Unfortunately, Madison was unaware what JoAnne had done when she diverted his attention earlier in the green room. She'd generously laced his coffee with a special batch of nanites.

Within seconds after his blustery outburst, Chris Madison's neck emitted a vivid purple glow on its right side then, moments later, on the left.

"I believe one of us has a problem," JoAnne calmly remarked and pointed to his neck. By now the studio crew was frantically signaling for camera angle changes, a commercial break, anything they could manage to divert viewers' attention. Madison glanced over at the live monitor and took on a flustered expression.

An impromptu station break was inserted and Madison charged off stage. A heated discussion ensued in the wings before a lady newsperson was thrust forward as a replacement for the disoriented host.

Back on camera, the replacement host told her audience, "We apologize for the interruption. Mister Madison has suddenly taken ill. I'm Sarah Hester. I will continue the interview with our guest Doctor JoAnne Amos." She turned to continue the questioning, but JoAnne preempted her.

"I think the viewers understand what just happened, Miss Hester. The results of enzymatic lie detection I call Truth Time colorfully displayed itself in Mister Madison's purple neck. He attempted to lie to me and your viewers about having mandatory talking points. His deception enzyme A21 kicked in and betrayed him."

The new host looked completely befuddled. She made repeated attempts to reply only to have her words sound hopelessly garbled. Finally, she managed to croak out, "As I said, Christopher is ill. We're rushing him to medical aid."

JoAnne snapped her fingers. "Oh, I'm so sorry. My bad. I should have invited you to join Chris and me for coffee before the show. You'd be flashing like a billboard right now."

* * *

The remaining broadcast networks cancelled their interview plans. Despite protestations from confident lead anchors that they could stare down the impudent lady engineer, their organizations did not choose hazard the risk. One discredited associate was plenty for them.

The cable channel that had issued the initial invitation seized on the golden opportunity. They set aside ninety minutes one week later to air the Truth Time controversy. A forty-five minute segment was allocated to Doctor Amos to explain the intricacies of her project, detail the scientific proof already accumulated, and answer questions posed by the host. The last half of their air time would be for free-wheeling questions from a panel of distinguished experts who had been given access to Truth Time project data. Repeated on-air and newsprint advertisement of the upcoming event attracted one of the largest audiences in television history.

JoAnne began by presenting her husband and fellow researcher, Doctor Jordan Amos, and stated he would also respond to questions. The host, David Painter, made a brief introduction to explain the lady doctor would give her uninterrupted explanation of Truth Time followed by his questions as both a newsperson and a voter. Both a world-renowned panel and viewers would then question her. The host finished with, “Before we went on I asked Doctor Amos to administer a dose of nanites to me. I have a circulating fleet of those tiny electronic circuits swimming in my blood, and I’m ready to face Truth Time myself.”

She beamed her approval and gave him an energetic handshake.

“Now the first segment is yours, Doctor JoAnne Amos. In language non-scientific people like I am can understand, what is Truth Time?”

For the next twenty minutes, JoAnne and Joe alternated in providing a layman’s version of how their project had been born from an enzyme discovery, nurtured through exhaustive tests, and adapted to apply universally for positively identifying a subject’s intent to deceive. They emphasized the role volunteer subjects had played and how many times the attempt had been made to intentionally skew the results with contrived deception without success.

"The bottom line is," JoAnne stated, "enzyme A21 can not be fooled. Even the most practiced pathological liar who thinks he truly believes what he's saying can not lie without detection. The body automatically produces A21 in every single case of attempted untruth."

"Conventional lie detectors," Joe Amos added, "monitor blood pressure, pulse, respiration and arm movement, but they are thought to be at best 90 percent reliable. In hundreds of repetitive tests of Truth Time using nanites to detect A21, we have yet to find a false reading."

JoAnne took over and continued. "I want to remind your viewers that we have administered nanites to dozens of willing volunteers over a period of several years with no adverse health results to the test subjects. Moreover, these recipients have enjoyed the benefit of constant diagnosis by the devices to detect any abnormal cell activity in their bodies. In dozens of cases, this continuous monitoring has resulted in successful treatment by nano medicine dosing to repair early cell damage."

"There has been much speculation," Joe interjected, "about certain political figures who displayed sudden bursts of color in their neck. Let me say that we are constantly aware of where each nanite has been used. However, two small batches of the devices, one programmed to produce an orange glow and one to emit chartreuse, were misplaced some time ago. Our security measures since that time preclude any further losses."

"And anticipating your question," JoAnne posed with a wry smile, "the recent episode on that other network was entirely my doing. I doctored the host's coffee with nanites having a response to A21 electrical impulses and he told a blatant untruth.

Then JoAnne fielded questions from David Painter and an intense interrogation by four imminently qualified scientific and medical experts and from call-ins. For more than an hour she endeavored to provide responses to every query including a few that came with the odor of extreme bias. In every instance, she took great care to ask whether the answer had fully addressed the specifics of the question posed.

Within hours of the broadcast, listeners flooded their congressmen with calls and letters demanding prompt action to certify the administering of nanites for internal health monitoring.

Chapter 70

JoAnne cuddled her daughter and basked in the welcome relief of a day off from work. Daddy Joe had long since left for their office/lab on the EnzAm campus. Emily snuggled close to her mother and slept peacefully. She barely stirred when JoAnne raised herself onto one elbow to check the time.

Eight twenty! *I haven't been in bed this late since ...when? ...eight years ago before I moved from California to Site Green. Seems like the distant past now. I've been so blessed. Have my sweet Joe and our precious little Emmy Jo, a beautiful home here in Bio City, fulfilling work. Our share of the advances EnzAm has collected to build power plants makes us richer than I could have ever dreamed. Our baby's future is secure. You are one lucky girl, JoAnne!*

She fluffed her pillow and scrunched down under the covers, closed her eyes and decided to enjoy the luxury of one more hour of peace and quiet. But minutes later little fingers touching her cheek brought that plan to a hasty halt. "Mommy? Are you awake?"

JoAnne opened one eye halfway to see Emily beaming up at her.

"It's our fun day, Mommy. I don't want to miss a minute of it."

Christmas was only a few weeks away. Emily said she had Mommy's present stashed away but wanted her help finding just the right gift for Daddy. This would be a day for the Amos girls to hang out, shop the mall, and have lunch at Emmy's favorite eatery with clown waiters and yummy ice cream creations.

* * *

Joe Amos took a solitary lunch break in his cluttered lab office. He munched away on a sandwich as he perused some very interesting news releases. With the mid-term election campaigns in full swing, rejection of incumbents had grown from a dull roar to a political tornado with increasing momentum. He paid particular attention to the names of some of the first timers being touted as possible winners. Joe's favored status with George Adams afforded him the closely held knowledge that several of these newcomers were, in fact, WAKE protégés.

"Carrie, Karl, Leonard, Judith—the list grows," he mumbled into his ham and cheese, then quickly checked again to be certain no one was within hearing distance. He pondered: *Add these new trends to those of our group who are already on the Hill temporarily posing as loyal members of the two major parties. As George has told me often, that's not the way the founders prefer to operate, but it gets the right people past the closed doors of the Congressional ranks.*

What had begun as a minor leaning after the last general election was rapidly becoming the little engine that could. The new President marched on eliminating regulations, improving employment. Even enacting a tax cut. But with every success there came a new call for impeachment of the 'maniac' in the White House. Hate and vilification ran amok in the streets.

But, in spite of the protests, Joe mulled, things are definitely looking up. The Republicans had actually won both houses of Congress and the Presidency, Unfortunately, they couldn't rise above internal jousting to exert their new-found power.

What did encourage Joe was that Truth Time had exposed a host of elected politicians as lairs.

Their constituents showed little patience or monetary support for their discredited representatives. \ spouted off and turned green in public. The voters showed little patience with them.

Yes, the future did look brighter now. The proof would be in getting the right combination of lawmakers elected to overturn the bad decisions over a span of several years.

Joe stared at his reflection in the small swivel mirror on his desk. *Don't look so smug, Amos,* he chastised the face that stared back at him. *Maybe it's finally* your *turn to step up. The House seat from this district is wide open.*

* * *

JoAnne and Emily arrived at the mall and took delight in shopping until noon. By then Emily had narrowed down her present for Daddy to a manageable list and was working on a final decision. She led the way to the Clown Town and laughed her way through a Big Smiley burger and a Circus sundae.

"I've made up my mind, Mommy," she announced after her last spoonful of ice cream had disappeared. "I think Daddy wants …" and whispered her choice to JoAnne, who nodded her enthusiastic agreement.

They gathered up their shopping loot and set out for the men's store to complete their important chore. Emily took JoAnne's open hand and skipped along.

An intense young man sitting across the room had been keeping a watchful eye on the Amos ladies. He rose, followed the two females out onto the mall concourse, and nodded to another male standing by the mall fountain. The second man fell into line and they both drew closer behind JoAnne and Emily.

Chapter 71

"Doctor Amos here," Joe said into the phone.

The voice on the line said in a raspy voice with a distinctly British accent, "I have an important message for you. Your wife and daughter are with me. If you ever want to see them again, you will come to the address I am about to give you. For their safety, you must do this within the hour."

`"What? Who?" Joe tried to form words, but he suddenly went mute. A delighted chortle from Raspy Voice struck a nerve.

"Who the hell are you?" Joe demanded.

"Just call me Bill," said Raspy. "Now listen very carefully."

"First hear this, Bill. If you do have them and you harm either one of my ladies, I make a solemn promise. You'll live just long enough to regret it."

"Oh, the women will be quite safe, Joe Amos … *if you comply*."

There were sounds of movement in the background then Joe heard JoAnne's voice. "They took us from the mall, Joe. I'm mad as hell and Emmy's frightened. Talk to him."

"Now, mister doctor," Bill cautioned, "do *not* enrage me or I *will* make them suffer. Do exactly as I say. Come to the Starlight Motel on Prairie Street. Be there by 2 PM. Find Room 201. Come alone or you will not like what you find. The conditions for the females' release are extremely simple. Do what I ask and they can leave here with you. However, if you refuse, the entire Amos family will be judged unworthy of existing."

Joe gritted his teeth and stifled the insult that nearly passed his lips. Then JoAnne cried out as if she'd been struck.

"You sorry … He swallowed hard. "I'll do whatever you want. Just don't harm them."

"A wise decision, Doctor," Raspy Voice counseled.

As soon as he heard the click on the line, Joe speed dialed the number for Jim Bledsoe. The security chief was in Bio City on the EnzAm campus for a periodic evaluation of physical security arrangements.

"Jim, it's Joe Amos. I need you in the Truth Time lab now! We have an emergency."

* * *

Within minutes Joe and Jim were on their way to the appointed meeting place. Joe had briefed Bledsoe on the fly and received his explicit instructions on what to do once they reached the motel. Jim rode along, talked to his people by radio and coached Joe as he drove. Amos rarely let his temper out, but he was seething with rage at this disgusting insult visited on his family. He wanted to take a bite out of something, preferably the ferret who seemed to be enjoying the despicable kidnapping.

"Keep your cool, Joe," Jim reminded him again. "They'll be fine if you follow our plan."

Two blocks away from the Starlight Joe brought his closed convertible to the curb, gripped the wheel and stared straight ahead.

Jim Bledsoe cautioned him, "Deep breath, Joe. Remember, it's Bill's game. Play along and let me choose the time to take him down. We'll have him surrounded. There's no way he can slip out of our grasp."

Jim left the car to gather and deploy his team.

Yeah, right, Joe agonized, *that's* my *family in there.*

He pulled into the motel parking lot. The Starlight, a two-story building of maybe twenty units, stuck out like a gaudy pimpmobile in a Ford truck kind of neighborhood. Its exterior flashed a canary yellow with maroon trim. He swept the building looking for room numbers.

"Upstairs front left corner, Jim, Room 201," he said into his watch transceiver. Bledsoe replied, "Got it. Slow and calm now, Joe."

Amos pulled beneath the overhang and walked toward the outside stairs. He stroked a small cylinder in his front trouser pocket to soothe his nerves and started the climb. Two men, one on either end of the open-air walkway upstairs, looked to be overly casual. Even to Joe's untrained eye, they were suspect. He concluded they were helpers for 'Bill'.

He rapped lightly on the door to 201 and waited. A window curtain moved then the door opened slightly. "I'm Joe Amos," he said and the door swung open just wide enough to admit him.

The young man pointing what appeared to be a compact automatic weapon registered on him as mid-twenties, Middle-eastern but with a cultivated British look. He was well-dressed and noticeably edgy.

"Bill?" Joe asked. "Where are they?"

'Bill' stepped aside and motioned for Joe to walk toward the bathroom. A pudgy young man of indeterminate ethnicity sat on the closed toilet in the small, crowded room. He held a handgun. Joe's heart dropped when he saw JoAnne and Emily huddled together in the bathtub. Their hands were bound behind them and they had gags over their mouths. He couldn't decipher their muffled pleadings, but when he read JoAnne's eyes his first impulse was to strike out at the captors. Only Jim Bledsoe's calm warning deterred him from committing a foolish act.

The man with the handgun cupped a hand to his ear and listened. He nodded toward Bill and said, "All is clear." Bill nudged Joe with his weapon and snapped, "We have confirmed you came alone. Now we will talk."

Joe raised a hand toward his own right ear and answered, bringing the tiny transceiver taped to the underside of his watch band closer to his mouth. "It took both of you cowards to put a woman and a child in the bathtub and tie them up?"

Bill struck Joe's head a sharp blow with his gun butt. Joe staggered before righting himself. Bill seized Joe's elbow, steered him into the bedroom, kicked the bathroom door shut, and led him toward a small table. He barked, "Sit. Do not make this more difficult."

When Joe plopped down, Bill opened a folder on the table and withdrew papers with a letterhead and seal. "Now, Doctor Amos, you will sign this document assigning your interest in EnzAm for the handsome sum indicated. I have the down payment. The remainder will be deposited in a foreign account. Then you will be a rich man who forgets what happened today." He opened a brown vinyl case containing stacks of hundreds.

Joe read the words that relinquished his interest in the company to one Sheikh Abdul-Alim Mahdani for the sum of three hundred million American dollars. The absolute gall of this outlandish event instantly overpowered Joe's carefully nurtured restraint. He thought *Those damned oil Arabs again. How many times do I have to put up with their harassment? If I don't stand up to them now, I'll never be able to live without looking over my shoulder. Besides, if Jim breaks in here, JoAnne and Emily could be hurt. I can't see this Bill letting the girls or me out of here alive if he has a choice.*

His mind whirred as he calculated the odds of a totally illogical, really hare-brained scheme. Maybe Arab radicals weren't the only crazed characters who could flip out and go into a rage. Could be exactly the distraction Jim needed.

Joe dug down into his pocket for the small silver cylinder. He palmed it then debated for an instant before putting his hand atop the table with a forefinger on the cylinder's aerosol button.

Before the young kidnapper could pick up his handgun, He called out, "Poison," and sprayed a stream of vapor directly into Bill's face.

The gun started upward but stopped. Bill jumped out of his chair, rocked back on his heels, and his eyes filled with terror.

Joe watched his captor freeze in place.

Chapter 72

"What did you do, you psychotic idiot?"

Joe quickly went into his best impersonation of Jack Nicholson in "The Shining" complete with an evilly twisted grin. "You left me no choice, Ahmed or whatever your real name may be. Those two women are all I care about in this world, so I'll trade my life for theirs."

Joe tapped his watch and announced, "Your life expectancy as of now is about thirty minutes, mine slightly longer. The people in the bathroom will be unaffected."

"That is totally deranged," the younger man said, swiping at his eyes and staring down at his own watch.

"Yeah. How's it feel, Billy? A genuine American jihadist. *My* cause is two ladies I adore. Let them go and I can save you. Without them free I don't care to live. Psychotic? Maybe. But it sort of limits *your* options. Either you and I die or you let them go."

"This is unreal, you crazy man. Sign the paper or I will shoot you!"

"Go ahead. Without my family I have nothing to live for. Shoot me and you're doomed to a slow, suffocating death. I have the antidote in my car, but you'll never find it in time. Release my family now and you can still survive that face full of virulent nerve toxin."

Bill stood there fidgeting, calculating his options. All the color had drained from his face and his brow furrowed with imagined pain. Joe nearly laughed when he realized the kidnapper was so scared he had wet his pants. "Mustaf! Quickly," Bill bellowed. "Unbind the females and bring them out here. Now!"

Joe prompted, "Cover your faces with wet towels before you come out."

A minute later Mustaf pushed the two women into the bedroom. Emily tried to be brave but she was sobbing softly into the towel over her face. Joe gave JoAnne a reassuring wink then clawed at his disheveled hair and returned to his grotesque, spaced-out look.

"Hurry, Bill. Time's running out. You and I can't stand indecision." The giggle of insanity he brought forth frightened even his own child.

"Take them outside. We will follow you," Bill ordered. He turned to Joe and said, in a tone bordering on pleading, "I have done what you asked. Now produce the antidote."

"I won't take you to it as long as you're holding that gun on me and Mustaf has my ladies."

"Then we will both die. Is that what you want?"

"Try me and see. Put the gun down and tell your buddy out there to release the girls," Joe answered. "Otherwise, you and I are dead meat."

Joe put both hands to his head, coughed and grimaced as if in pain. *I'm really getting into this shtick,* he thought with amusement. *Old Bill actually thinks he's about to die from a spritz of mouth freshener.*

The kidnapper clicked on the gun's safety and tossed it onto the bed. "Free the women, Mustaf," Bill ordered.

Seconds later Joe heard a commotion outside the door and knew instantly what was happening. He put all the momentum he could muster into a roundhouse right to the jaw of the young Arab and felled him.

As Jim Bledsoe rushed into the room, Joe straddled his downed harasser and pounded him unmercifully. Bill sputtered and begged, "The antidote. Please. You're crazy. We'll both die."

Jim dragged Joe off the young Arab and assured him, "JoAnne and Emily are safe. We rounded up the other three. Let it go, Joe. You made your point."

Amos reluctantly came to his feet and grinned at Jim. "Lord help me, that felt good."

"I told you to let me set the flow here, Joe. When I realized what you were pulling, it scared the crap out of me. We took down the two sentinels and fat boy, but you could have gotten yourself killed. His helper wasn't about to hurt the girls unless he was ordered to by this character you were pounding on. Gotta say something you did scared him big time; he was so spooked he'd soaked his own britches." Jim snickered in spite of his manufactured anger at Joe.

"Damn it, Jim, it was time I did something for myself and my family. Check that paper I was supposed to sign. The chief instigator's name is on page one."

Joe knew he'd launched a rash and very foolish act that could have ended with him shot and the girls still in danger. But he hadn't felt this good, this fulfilled, in a long time. They were all three free, and he had been the prime mover in the take down. He'd wreaked his revenge on the people who were making his entire world a shamble. The icing on the cake was that Joe had made his own opportunity to release his frustrations on the one that had frightened and insulted JoAnne and Emily.

"Just what the hell *did* you pull on him, Joe?"

Amos showed Jim the breath freshener and laughed. "I sprayed him with this and told him it was poison."

Jim tried his best to keep his composure and be firm.

"How the hell do I protect you if you pull goof ball stunts like that? This is twice you've stuck your neck out."

Yes, Joe remembered well the first time he'd let his instincts do the talking. That time in the Loudoun farmhouse he'd saved not only himself but Jim as well.

"Sorry I fritzed your plan, Jim. It was my responsibility to take charge and stand up for my family. I believe it actually worked." He rubbed his sore knuckles.

Bledsoe frowned and shook his head, doing his best to cover a growing grin.

Quietly in the weeks that followed, the government put together a case against the oil magnates who set in motion the outrage against the Amoses. The unsigned papers, as well as the money and young kidnapper, whose real name was Nadeem Zubaida, were all traced back to Sheikh Abdul-Alim Mahdani and his cabal of oil potentates. Three of the instigators, including Mahdani himself, were arrested when they entered the US on visits. They were charged and stowed away in jail pending trial.

Chapter 73

The result of the 2018 off-year elections was more or less a status quo event. The 'great red tide' predicted by the Dems was a grand fizzle, largely due to the electorate's disgust with their tactics of hate and violence.

But the message was somehow lost on members of Congress. The Republicans kept their majority in the Senate and most of their edge in the House. But the log jam was far from being over. GOP factions persisted in dissenting on hard core issues. The Dems threw up a solid wall against anything smacking of change.

But change was the byword outside the halls of Congress. Before appellate courts and in classrooms around the country, vibrant young lawyers and teachers insisted on quoting and adhering to the Constitution.

Voters demonstrated their distrust of politicians who were proven insincere or downright deceitful in statements to their constituents. An epidemic of dishonest public servants with flashing cheeks and necks aroused public outrage and demands for resignations. The election results gave testament to a new atmosphere. The tide that was rolling along now was the popular groundswell that announced change was inevitable.

A great orchestrated counteroffensive arose in support of the besieged politicians. Their defenders argued that, despite unproven charges of their deceit, only Congress had the power to sanction its members. That defense lasted only as long as it took for a veritable Coxey's army of irate citizens to descend on the capital riding tractors, motorcycles and semis and on foot to demand satisfaction. Many of them carried wooden and cardboard pitchforks with protest signs speared on their simulated tines. The chanting echoed across the Potomac basin and up the Capitol steps until dark: *YOU WORK FOR US! WE DEMAND THE TRUTH.*

When Congress balked and stalled any action to discipline the ranks, ten state legislatures called public referenda on the issue of term limits and recalls. Five states passed laws holding that citizens within their jurisdiction would be allowed to serve no more than six two-year terms as a US Representative or two terms as a US Senator. Law suits contesting the new statutes promised to be long-running sideshows.

Seven state legislatures passed laws demanded by public referendum to provide constraints on local candidates for national office. These measures basically stated that no candidate would be certified to run for national office unless he or she underwent and passed what was now being referred to as an enzymatic lie detection test. Pointed questions in these tests were aimed at determining if a candidate had ever violated his or her oath under Article VI of the Constitution or was inclined to do so if elected.

The Article at issue specifies that … 'Senators and Representatives … shall be bound by Oath or Affirmation to support this Constitution.' A positive indication on a nano lie detector test would be deemed a disqualification to run. The judicial system was swamped with civil libertarian challenges to these new statutes, but the states steadfastly refused to budge. As the Governor of one state eloquently stated, "*The people of this sovereign state have the right to insist they be fairly and truthfully represented. We have the right to peaceful dissent and the right to secede from the union if necessary. We will tolerate neither a deceitful person elected to speak for us nor a federal government that condones untruthful Congressmen.*"

George Adams made contact with Hiro Kato and Carlos Estrada on their secure satellite link. "Feel that hot breeze blowin' down out o' Washin'ton, fellows?" George asked.

Hiro answered, "Warmed my heart. It had the smell of alarm in it, George. What was it Thomas Jefferson said? *—when the people fear their government, there is tyranny; when the government fears the people, there is liberty*. I believe your assessment that this country has endured three dictators in its time—Lincoln, Wilson and Roosevelt. The fourth pretender played out his string but the new fellow is correcting a lot of those missteps.

Carlos broke in. "You two know how antsy I've been for WAKE to come this far. Took more patience than I thought I had. Now, I swan, it's time to finally kick some backsides."

George allowed, "It's a tasty stew but it's not done yet, Carlos. " George reminded him. "We have miles to go. Got our foundation firmly laid.

"That's why I'm calling. Mark down June 15th on your calendars. That's when we gather in the Georgia foothills. Ray Crane has great news for us. I want to propose a special twist this time around. You both said you want to know more about what the Amoses are up to. Joe and JoAnne Amos are a big part of our stage one success. I vote we invite 'em down there. And I want your take on lettin' 'em become permanent WAKE sponsors. Think about it."

"Don't need to," Carlos replied. "Those two kids are everything we hoped for in WAKERS. They've also made more money than they could burn in a lifetime. I say bring 'em on board, let 'em chip in, and let's boost the size of the next class of youngsters."

Hiro spoke up. "You have my yes, George. Let's take part of our time in Georgia to have the Amoses educate us on the ins and outs of their projects, particularly this Truth Time."

"To borrow one of Carlos's expressions," George said, "I'll issue their invite pronto."

Chapter 74

The Amoses left Bio City in June for what they billed as a much-needed vacation. Their flight departed Dallas bound for Atlanta and a connecting hop to Myrtle Beach. Two carefully chosen look-alikes boarded the second flight leg. Joe and JoAnne swapped identities with the newcomers and drove the short distance into the Georgia hills for their rendezvous with the WAKE founders.

George Adams greeted them at the rustic but well-appointed enclave near Lookout Mountain. "

Hiro and Carlos will be here shortly," he explained. "Let's have a drink and I'll clue you in on what goes on at our annual gatherings. Sorry about the roundabout travel. As you can see, we're still hyper about guardin' the identity of our meetin' place. Wouldn't do for some folks to know any of us are connected to WAKE. We'll save that shocker for after WAKE phase four is complete. You'll understan' later."

Adams and the Amoses walked through the expansive lodge front room that overlooked the Georgia foothills that were covered with bright fall foliage. One entire wall of the big room consisted of floor-to-ceiling windows with a southern exposure toward the city of Atlanta. Massive cedar beams crisscrossed the twenty-foot ceiling. A stone fireplace rose to the room's full height at one end. Flames danced and licked on its hearth, and the sweet smell of crackling oak and cedar wafted through the room.

"This is a big day for my partners and me," George said when they were seated. "We've been readin' in the WAKE protégés one at a time on the end plan. Joe, you met Ryan Bolger. He, a young lady lawyer WAKER and a key WAKER politician were sworn to secrecy by Carlos. Hiro clued you in some time ago, JoAnne. He's also laid out our plan to other protégés you'll meet soon. The insiders include five elected officials."

"Are they coming to the meeting?" JoAnne inquired.

"No, just you and Joe have been added this time. It's our chance to say thanks for bein' our superstars. As I've already told you, my partners want a full rundown on your three projects in diabetes research, biomass conversion and nanomedicine. Then we want to understand the ins and outs of your latest success, Truth Time."

"It's an honor to be here," Joe told him. JoAnne raised her tumbler high in a salute.

* * *

The first session of the founders' annual meeting convened early the next morning. Raymond Crane, WAKE's hard-working chief of operations, was upbeat as usual. Ray took center stage for his report. His precisely trimmed beard showed a growing tint of gray, but his steely eyes were as full of enthusiasm as they'd been at the project's beginning.

"Greetings, lady and gents. I'm especially pleased to deliver your annual update. The events during the months since last year's election clearly confirm that your phase three WAKE goal is well underway. There are over 700 proteges currently working in a host of professions. They're active in classrooms, courts, and scientific facilities across the country. More than 200 WAKERS hold political offices from town council to the state house to Congress. A significant number of those elected are viewed by people around them as being members of the two major parties. That cover will remain until the day they collectively announce their independence."

Ray went on to break down the current force of WAKERS by career specialty and geographic distribution. He reviewed some of their impressive scientific advances, educational improvements, and contributions to the return to Constitutional conformance at multiple levels. Crane acknowledged the Amoses and their groundbreaking achievements.

"You outlined the four phases several years ago that Wake Up America would go through to reach its end goal of a reenergized and reawakened America." He projected on the screen a visual aid that read:

Phase I – Directly Impact Science, Education, Equal Opportunity
Phase II – Set the Pace for Professional Ethics
Phase III– Regain Control of Politics by the Public
Phase IV– Return America to Constitutional Federalism

"Your patient mentoring of 20 classes of WAKERS has produced a group of achievers who excel in all of the Phase I areas of expertise." Ray placed a checkmark by that entry.

"The members of the first eighteen classes have set high ethical and performance standards. The four classes now in college show promise to strengthen that record." Another check mark went up.

"Thanks to Doctors Joe and JoAnne Amos," Ray continued, and gave a head nod in their direction, "Phase III is well on its way to being realized. The number of politicians who discredited themselves under questioning precipitated a purging of the ranks. Dishonesty and deceit in elected officials aren't dead, but they're clearly on the run. Government has a new respect for the voting public—perhaps even a healthy fear."

Ray tapped his marker on the entry 'Phase IV'. "WAKE is moving toward returning the country to universal respect for our Constitutional principles. After decades of erosion of federalism as defined by that document, you benefactors and, rest his soul, Joe hitleys are on the path to righting the ship of state."

JoAnne listened in absolute awe. She was finally beginning to comprehend the enormity of what these men had undertaken and patiently piloted to the brink of victory. To be invited into their inner circle was indeed a trust to be treasured.

George's concluding comment before they adjourned for the day both puzzled and intrigued her.

"Tonight is for enjoying each other's company. No more business till tomorrow. Then Hiro, Carlos and I have an important proposal we want to put to Joe and JoAnne."

Chapter 75

On the second day of their rendezvous in Georgia, the WAKE founders listened to JoAnne and Joe. Their two prized protégés told how their initiatives had been conducted. Joe explained the way George nurtured his work that led to approval of his diabetes treatment. All medical and governmental approvals were at last in place, and GMed would be allowed to put the treatment regimen into general use within the next ninety days.

George felt compelled to add a personal note of satisfaction. "Before Joe agreed to let me be his lab rat test case, I was overweight and in miserable health. Today you're lookin' at the updated model of George Adams, seventy-three years young, slimmer and fit. Before long diabetics everywhere will be sharin' my good fortune and beginnin' to toin their lives around'."

Joe answered the founders' technical questions. Then he moved on to a detailed history of EnzAm's success. He concluded that with, "As of today, there are twenty biomass conversion plants in various states of construction throughout the US and another twelve are planned overseas."

He executed a bow in Carlos's direction and said, "Mr. Estrada has played a key role. Waste dumps have been virtually eliminated in the locales of the plants as ninety percent of the municipal solid waste domestic goes directly into producing energy. EnzAm is negotiating fifteen more near term orders for conversion plant construction. Requests and queries from foreign countries number in the dozens and grow daily. Biomass is the new international fuel. Soon a reliable liquid biomass fuel will be ready to distribute to service stations for use in automobiles worldwide"

Carlos said with great pride, "And my markets have cut their pollution down to near zero. It's a win win, Joe."

JoAnne followed with a synopsis of the nanomedicine development she and K- Tronics brought to reality with Hiro's sponsorship. The long, arduous approval process, thanks to heavy public pressure, had during the past year concluded with full accreditation. Manufacture of medical nanites at three regional K-Tronics factories went on twenty-four hours a day to keep pace with demand and a fourth factory would soon be on line. GMed facilities formulated precise medical nanodoses for loading into the transport nanites. Original objections to placing the devices in patient blood streams were set aside by a landmark high court decision. Millions of people could now enjoy the benefits of continuous health monitoring and prompt, targeted treatment.

Hiro quickly explained, "The Amoses came up with the idea for applying nanites to the lie detection scheme. Except for a K-Tronics royalty on nanite use, they own the whole Truth Time business outright."

"Which brings us to your crownin' success from the WAKE standpoint," George crowed. "Tell us about the best cleanup of political doubletalk in US history."

Joe nodded to his wife and she took the lead. "This grew out of a couple discussions Joe and I had in Alpine shortly after I moved there," JoAnne began. "Joe mentioned that his team had discovered an enzyme we later named A21. They found this enzymatic protein is automatically manufactured by a person's body if he or she makes any attempt to lie. I reminded Joe that reliable lie detection could be a boon to law enforcement.

A long time later a sleepless night and a revelation reopened our conversation about detecting lies. We did extensive testing and the A21 enzyme proved to be a 100 percent accurate indicator of intent to lie. We decided it was time liars were exposed and that politicians may be an important part of that effort. Truth Time was set in motion. We used calibrated nano devices to sense the presence of the enzyme and give off a glow.

The road to getting nanite sensing of A21 approved for trials was long and frustrating. Some people may remember I literally stuck my neck out more than once for shock effect before folks started believing us."

George quipped, "Oh, yeah. And a rash of politicians with flashin' necks was a big convincer, too."

"Yes. I wonder how those two Congressional chairmen managed to swallow nanites?" She rolled her eyes and smirked.

"Once we attracted a national audience, the public clamored for nanite use to be approved for both medical analysis and seeking the truth, particularly from accused law breakers and public figures."

She asked Joe to distill the basics of the process and to give an up to date status on the use of nanites for both legal and ethical purposes. He recapped the spate of law suits lodged by civil liberties spokespersons, defense lawyers and a multitude of special interests.

"The collective panic by prevaricators and their vocal defenders fell on deaf ears," Joe told them. "At last the voting masses were once again in charge and the elite class of manipulators developed a healthy fear for the power of John Q. Public. Now that I've seen your Phase III goal, Regain Control of Politics by the Public, I suggest that Truth Time has helped pave the way."

Hiro had been ill at ease ever since today's session began. "I need to get something off my chest," he said and took the floor. "Nobody is prouder of this pair than I am, and I wholeheartedly agree they've been instrumental in the turnaround we're seeing. But let's not lose sight of the most encouraging fact of all. For this and other reasons the people are finally speaking out."

George signaled for attention and stood. “This has been a fascinatin’ day. Joe and JoAnne, you’ve warmed this ol’ heart. My partners and I waited a long time to get to where you’ve brought WAKE today. I’ll make a prediction. The next election is about to bring a groundswell in the rebirth of federalism as the framers saw it. Soon after will come what Hiro, Carlos and I privately refer to as ‘stand up day’. At that moment in this country’s history, the American voters begin to reassert their control of the federal government. To prepare for that event, we have a question for Joe and JoAnne.”

Hiro and Carlos both gave George the go-ahead with their affirmative head nods.

He continued. “We believe you have earned the right to join us as sponsors of WAKE. I don’t plan to leave your midst for quite a while t’anks to Joe’s life-saving treatment. But we’re getting older and it’s time to t’ink about all the good WAKE can do for years to come. There are new protégés every year to be steered toward the sort of greatness Joe, JoAnne and others are showing. The road’s been bumpy at times. No one knows better than the Amoses the mental and physical threats we’ve had, and our toughest foes are still out there—imbedded power brokers who’ll fight our every step. WAKE needs all the vision and vitality we can muster to reach our goals. We’d like for the two of youze to agree to permanently join us as sponsors.”

JoAnne’s momentary blank stare registered her shock. Then she looked at Joe and their beaming smiles warmed the room. An unspoken communication passed between them. Joe stood and addressed the three men who had extended to JoAnne and him the ultimate compliment.

“George … Hiro … Carlos … Jo Anne and I are delighted and honored to accept your gracious invitation. I can think of no better way to assist in restoring America’s glory than to devote our energies and resources to Wake Up America.”

Chapter 76

Joe and JoAnne turned over the biomass and nano technical efforts to their capable assistants Fred Vinson and Bonnie Hepler. EnzAm and the new NanoMed were both mushrooming enterprises that could afford to bring in accomplished managers and administrators. The Amoses settled for serving as board members for their respective companies, stood back and let the profits roll in. Their financial future was secure; in fact, they would soon be billionaires in their own right. Emily had turned three. Tending to her and keeping Wake Up America vibrant and aggressive gave them all the fulfillment they needed.

George and Evaline Adams came to visit in Bio City. The four adults packed a picnic basket and went to the pond behind the house bon a clear, hot east Texas summer day. George sipped at his welcome tumbler of iced tea and chuckled.

"Reminds me of when Carlton and Jenetta were tykes about her size. They loved playing with a kick ball of any size. Car went on to p[lay soccer in high school and college. Look at that. Once Emily gets the ball she's bound to keep it."

"She gets that from her Mom, George," Joe replied. "She's a lovable little gal, but don't get in her way. Wait till she takes on JoAnne's height. I can see her now kicking up dust around a track." Jo Anne prodded him with an elbow and beamed with pride.

Later, with the picnic dispatched and the women relaxing in the shade, Joe and George went for a stroll along the lake's edge.

George saw the pensive look on Joe's face and decided to give him a verbal nudge. "Might's well come out with it, Joe. I can see you're frettin' about sumpin'."

"I've been itching to get your take on this, boss," Joe said tentatively. "Some folks have been urging me to run for the US House. This is as good a time as any to take my turn in the barrel. What do you think?"

"I think you'd make a damn fine rep, Joe. My advice is to let the companies run on their own hook and go do your civic duty. We'd have a hard time findin' anybody better rooted in what government's all about. Besides, you're well known and admired for helpin' clean up the political act in Washin'ton with Truth Time. How could folks not want you speakin' for 'em?"

"Understand I don't want to do this as a career. Two terms, maybe three, is plenty."

"Exactly what I'd expect you to say. You understand the title *citizen* politician, Joe. You've loined well. Jump in and give it your best then hand off to another non-career politician to take his turn."

My main reservation," Joe said, "is being away from JoAnne and Emmy. We want to see our child has the best possible schooling we can give her. I know the elementary school in Bio City is top-notch."

"No problem," George assured him and placed a hand on his shoulder. "Don't forget about Serenity, the new biomass town in northern Virginia. Between Bio City and Serenity, your daughter can have the very best schoolin' on whatever schedule you choose. You lived in Maryland before. Why not let JoAnne and Emily spend part of the year wit' you back near your old stomping grounds?"

Joe lit up. "Should have known the best place to get good advice was 'Ask George.' If my ladies agree, we'll maintain residence here in Texas, I'll fly back and forth, and they can come to Virginia for the last half of Emmy's school year. That way I can stay in touch with my constituents and have the girls close by at least part time."

"Hell of a lot better than most politicians do now, son. It's been so long since some of those Hill dwellers spent quality time back in their home districts, they have zero idea what's goin' on outside their little enclave in DC."

"My hope is, George, if enough newcomers, including me, win their way into Congress, that's one of many things we can start to change."

They stopped at a high point on the lakeside trail, and George stared out across the calm waters. "You've seen the figgers, Joe. WAKERS are making big inroads and there'll be even more of 'em sitting in the Capitol in January. Change is coming, and this time that's not just an empty slogan.

"And this time they may even start to get it right, boss. Instead of change for the sake of change, we need real progress.

George admitted, "That's why we turned our proteges loose and vowed not to steer them or make them feel obligated in any way to us. It's why we had to hide our identities from, you WAKERS. All we insisted on was that you get schooled on the Constitution and then followed your hearts."

Joe said, "I'm ready to join the other WAKERS and turn things around. I'll run as an independent."

"Sic 'em, Joe."

Chapter 77

`The campaigns heated up. Most veteran politicians, even those exposed by Truth Time as recurring liars, declined to step down. Energetic new rivals emerged inside both parties and as independents, and they welcomed being put to the test on their honesty. Special interest groups began to cut back on their funding of incumbent campaigns and gave more attention to newcomers and independents. The Supreme Court refused to hear arguments that the new lie detection regimen infringed on civil rights. Fifteen state legislatures promptly enacted strong resolutions urging Congress to recognize Truth Time results as valid in court.

Joe Amos continued his whirlwind schedule as a candidate for Congress from his home Texas district. He hosted a town meeting in a local auditorium in May.

"I pledge to be truthful to you. I will work to see you receive the full benefits of open, honest government that is compliant with the Constitution. Friends, I owe no debt to a political party and will incur none." Joe confidently faced them with George Adams's assurance he would never come between Joe and the people he represented. As George had put it, *"You have one and only one commitment to Project WAKE—to do the best job you can for the people who gave you their trust and their vote. Anything less is unfair to them."*

"How do we know you're being straight up with us, Amos? We've seen too many of our so-called leaders exposed as liars," someone shouted from the assembled crowd.

"Fair question," Joe acknowledged. "Some of you know my background as a biochemist. In particular, my wife and I developed the recently approved nanite method of lie detection called Truth Time. My blood system currently contains a generous dose of the tiny devices as attested to by this certificate issued by the Department of Health."

Joe projected the document on a large screen. The government had insisted upon documenting each application of nanites to any citizen. Included was a verification that the devices had demonstrated their health monitoring and lie detection functions in Joe's system. The certification qualified a nanite recipient for reduced health insurance premiums since the devices were an important disease diagnostic and corrective tool.

"Please feel free to ask me about any issue. If I attempt to deceive you or evade your question in any manner, my neck will pulse in color. Fact is, my wife has tested me. When I lie, my cheeks and neck pulse pink."

Joe went on to repeat how honored he would be to represent the voters of the district. He stressed that it was essential for lawmakers sent to Washington to respect and conform to Constitutional principles.

"I believe that every dollar the federal government spends is money that rightfully belongs to you, not to those who dole it out. My agenda in Congress will be to express your views and your mandates, not to go off on my own path. I *will* alert you that I am a strong proponent of term limits because I believe in non-career lawmakers, people who understand what is important to *you,* and are best equipped to work for *you.* My goal is to take my turn in Washington then come home to be a better educated voter. I will serve you well and energetically then step aside so the next citizen lawmaker of your choice can offer his or her service. And I will accept no pay for that service either during or after my time in office."

"Okay, folks. Now it's Truth Time for me. Take your best shots. Ask me anything you like and we'll see if my answers are truthful. Don't pull your punches, please."

`The audience bombarded Joe with a barrage of pointed questions about his intentions in Washington, his background, political beliefs, ideology, any partisan leaning, even queries about acutely personal topics. He fielded their interrogation with unequivocal answers, including good natured responses to clearly barbed questions. Joe thought, *I wonder how many plants my opponents have sent here to embarrass me?* His recurring smile was accompanied by a conclusion. *No matter. Bring it on. I have nothing to hide.*

* * *

Back in Maryland a new kind of campaigner hit the trail. The wide wake Don Shupe left behind him proved impossible for stale, self-important incumbents to counter. George's friend and protégé waged a no holds barred battle for a seat in the US House.

"I bring two goals to my quest for this seat," Don told his audience at the local park. "First, I am one of you, an ordinary citizen who has acquired a lifetime of practical experience outside politics. That experience tells me without a doubt that my neighbors and I are in need of more responsive representation on Capitol Hill. We need someone on our side who understands why we sent him there in the first place. Friends, I humbly offer that I can be that person, the one who will be able to look you squarely in the eye and say, 'I stood up for *you*, protected *your* interests."

Don looked out over the audience and picked out familiar faces. "Yes, Jake, yes, Mary—Jamal and Grace—I want to be your voice and insist that Congress listens for a change. And the other goal I have is to see that we bring *our* government back to legislating by the Constitution, not by some made up set of rules. I will insist on true openness, not just the unkept promise of transparency. Join me in returning America to sanity. For years, most of our representatives in Congress have concerned themselves more with perpetuating their power than with passing laws you want and demand.

* * *

The polls began to trend toward Joe, Don and other independent candidates. Joe was acutely aware he was in the most important scrambling foot race of his life. He read and watched with interest news accounts of voter discontent with incumbents.

"The backlash is in full force, JoAnne," he related as he pored over the newspaper. "Even the judiciary is not exempt. Those two ninth circuit court judges have been dismissed for breaching the 'good behavior' clause of the Constitution in Article III, Section 1. Seems the judges somehow swallowed nanites and a few pointed questions lit them up like billboards. The peaceful revolution has arrived."

"I'm confident you're on your way to winning a seat, Joe," she said. "Even the liberal media has finally gotten the word to line up on the people's side or see their audience dry up. And did you see the latest college case at that Ivy League campus? It was another victory for impartiality in the classroom. That avowed Marxist professor was issued his walking papers under the school's revised tenure rules. No more spouting hate and bile at the students then punishing them for not agreeing with him."

"Not that I'm keeping count," Joe chuckled, "but I believe the new tenure rules have canned close to fifty of the most radical campus voices. Put them all out to pasture. Maybe they can preach their doctrine to the cows, but students' minds won't continue to be poisoned."

She told him, "I'm looking forward to our get together with our fellow WAKER sponsors. "Should be interesting."

"Wouldn't miss it for the world, hon. Ray Crane's report this year has to be a head turner. Did you work out our flight reservations to New Mexico?"

"All set," she said. "We're flying from Austin over to Albuquerque by way of Kansas City and Omaha."

"Stand up day can't come too soon to suit me, JoAnne. I want to stop having to sneak around to cover the fact we're WAKERS. Most of all I want to come clean with folks about

WAKE and let them see where a lot of hard work and the best instincts of the voters have brought America these past twenty years."

Chapter 78

Three months remained before Election Day in 2020. A handful of critically important people wound their way toward Albuquerque and the New Mexico high country. A critical gathering awaited their arrival. Joe and JoAnne left the air terminal, stowed their bags in the four-wheel drive rental vehicle and rechecked their route on a map.

"Appears to be a considerable upward climb from here," JoAnne told her husband. "Remind you of somewhere we've been before?"

"Feels kind of like being back in west Texas, doesn't it?" Joe answered and swung onto the hilly road. "Difference is we're already in high country before we get to the mountain. Maybe soon we can put all this undercover maneuvering behind us and let people see the plan George, Hiro and Carlos have embraced for so long."

"Sounds as if we're in for some surprises this time," she said as she opened a cold can of soda for him. "Any idea who these special folks could be that we're to meet?"

"You heard as much as I did, JoAnne. They're all WAKE protégés just like us. I gathered they could play a key role in the return to honest government. We should learn more when we meet with the founders today."

* * *

Joe and JoAnne unpacked and went to meet the other WAKE sponsors in the front room of the impressive rambling mountain cabin. Tomorrow morning formal sessions would begin with Raymond Crane's annual report.

Others were coming for that meeting.

Tonight was for George, Hiro, Carlos, Joe and JoAnne to talk about WAKE's future, something they had all invested in heavily with both time and money.

George hailed the Amoses and hurried across the cavernous space hung with hunting trophies. He shook Joe's hand and gave JoAnne a hug. "Hiro and Carlos are stowin' their bags. They'll be in here shortly. Tino here's a great drink wizard. What's your pleasure?" A small Hispanic man offered a large smile and waited for their answers.

"Just some iced tea for me, thanks," JoAnne said. Joe glanced at his watch. "It's a bit early, but I think I'd like a Stoli martini straight up. One time." He turned toward JoAnne and held up one finger. She indicated understanding.

"He likes big onions," George added. "Got any whoppers over dere?" Tino gave a nod and made an O with his thumb and forefinger.

"By the way, congrats," George said. "I just heard the appellate court agreed with the lower court decision. Truth Time's gonna be law by next year. I can picture the politicians standin' on line nervously swallowin' their nanites and dreadin' a green glow the next time somebody asks a tough question. Wonder how long those crooks can avoid their voters?"

"Not long if they expect to hold onto their seats," Joe declared. "I haven't known any invisible candidates to survive. Just wish the test was in effect for this election round."

"I t'ink you will get a special kick out of the roundup this year," George said and grinned. "We axed a select group of your fellow protégés to join us tomorrow. You'll meet 'em at breakfast."

Hiro and Carlos, chatting and laughing, arrived from their suites down the hall. Hiro was happy to see his long-time protégé and kissed her cheek. "Lovely as always, my dear," he said, "and you're obviously taking good care of this fellow. He looks ready to clock a few laps."

"Oh, I'm in a lively foot race already, Hiro," Joe said. "It's one that keeps me on the move much more than I'd like." Tino took their orders and the five of them settled on two massive sofas.

"Well," Carlos chipped in, "from what I hear tell, we better get ready to call you *Congressman* Doctor Amos."

George said, "I was just reminding' 'em we have some special attendees due in later. Why don't we spill what that's about now? Carlos, you wanta do the honors?"

"This is the time I've been looking forward to," Carlos began, "since long before I met Joe down in Dallas. George keeps telling me I'm the impatient one in our group, and there's some truth to that. But this promises to be a big year if we can believe the projections. In November we 'spect to have more WAKERS in both houses of Congress and in governors' mansions, if our indicators are accurate, and Ray Crane makes a habit of seein' they are. We're bringin' in five of your cohorts you need ta meet and get to know. One's a governor, three are in the US House and the other one's a Senator. These folks and you, Joe, are gonna play important parts in finishin' up Phases III and IV of Wake Up America."

JoAnne's mind snapped back to the meeting in Georgia and the goals Ray Crane had checked off. Phase III, regain control of politics by the public, was reported as being well along even then. The final goal, Phase IV, read 'Return America to Constitutional Federalism'. A rush surged through her. *Could WAKE be that near to fulfillment?* She looked at Joe's reaction and her pulse rate noticeably quickened.

"That's right," Hiro said. "This election cycle can bring WAKE into its own. One of the decisions our group of ten should make this week is when to announce WAKE to all the people. We've lived in the shadows long enough. It's time George, Carlos and I turned matters over to the next generation and watched our dream come true."

“That’s what I wanta put to a vote at the end of our meetings,” George insisted. “We got the bucks to keep toinin’ out WAKERS, but what youze young folks do wit’ our head start is your affair. Once the voters know what you’ve set out to do, they’ll be more than happy to help. We’re on our way to succeedin’. But don’t think for a minute the job’s gonna be easy. We thought we’d put away the oil peddlers more than once and they kept comin’ back to bite us. Now we’ve picked a fight to the end with the meanest, most detoimined crowd ever assembled—politicians. They’re powerful and they fight dirty. We can’t let our guard slip for an instant.”

Chapter 79

Joe and JoAnne went to breakfast the following morning to find five new faces around the table. George made the introductions.

"Friends, let me present to you a couple we're proud to call WAKERS. Doctor JoAnne Amos, as you know, developed the nanomedicine regimen that's revolutionized medical diagnosis an' treatment. Doctor Joe Amos is the brains behind the biomass conversion that's freeing us from dependence on fossil fuels. And together they put nanites and enzyme A21 together for lie detection."

"And had much to do with more of us being on Capitol Hill," said a handsome Hispanic man who looked a few years younger than the Amoses.

"Joe and JoAnne," George continued, "this is US Representative Jose Carillo from New Mexico. The young lady is Congresswoman Mary Kay Grant and this is Senator Tom Battle. Bot' youze have met Ryan Bolger, now a Congressman, and the gent who looks like a football player was All-America. He's Ken Parker, Gov'nor of Oklahoma.

They're all WAKE protégés and members of our new planning group."

Handshakes all around were followed by JoAnne's nearly breathless comment. "Joe has told me repeatedly that our fellow protégés were making inroads into politics. Now I see just how far reaching some of those successes have been."

The WAKE core group was joined by Raymond Crane and his assistants. By the time breakfast was over, JoAnne felt she knew and was impressed by her four new acquaintances. As she and Joe walked to the conference room, she kissed his cheek and whispered in her best Oliver Hardy voice, "Well, Stanley, this is another fine kettle of fish you've gotten us into. First the terrorists, and now we're fighting the revisionists to save our country. Thank you, Joe. It will be a wild, beautiful ride."

* * *

The annual report was even more optimistic than the one JoAnne had heard at her first WAKE founders' meeting. With the added funds she and Joe had pledged, the current class of protégés was at an all -time high of 60. Altogether, nearly 700 of their number were now active in the professions. A review of WAKER achievements sounded like a who's who of science, education, and law. She found the scope almost overwhelming and definitely felt a sense of pride in being part of the movement.

Ray put up the goals chart she'd first seen at the Georgia get together. Blue check marks highlighted the first two phases of WAKE's plan for success:

√ Phase I – Directly Impact Science, Education, and Equal Opportunity

√ Phase II – Set the Pace for Professional Ethics

"I believe we can finally safely check off the Phase III goal," Ray said. "WAKE members currently occupy ten seats in the US House and that number, if the polls are correct, will go up when the November election results are in. We also expect to have our second elected Senator to join Senator Battle." He nodded toward Tom. "And another WAKER could join Governor Parker as head of his state.

Ray went to the chart and placed a sweeping blue check by Phase III – Regain Control of Politics by the Public. "That leaves the final goal to be reached."

He drew a circle around Phase IV – Return America to Constitutional Federalism. "The staff stands ready and anxious to assist in bringing that end goal to completion. We await your instructions."

When the staff left and only the ten WAKE planners remained in the room, George moved to the head of the conference table. "Now the rest is up to us. Tom, Mary Kay, Ryan and Ken are already painfully aware of the truth in what I'm about to say next. Jose's running as an independent, but the other four had to t'row in with the two parties just to get on the ballot with a chance to win. A number of other WAKERS now in office took the same road. A decision we need to make here this week is when they can finally announce they're independents, not partisans."

"That's the one gut-wrenching concession each of us made early on," Mary Kay said. "We ran as loyal party members because to campaign as independents was a non-starter in our states. None of us set out to do our adopted party harm, but from the outset we voted on the side of our constituents not the party machine. Back then I didn't even know I *was* a WAKER."

Tom Battle picked up where Mary Ann left off. "Me either. Then Hiro sat me down and explained how I'd been sponsored through school by WAKE, not the Liberty Bell Council. He told me I was on my own to do as I wished, but there were others and we could be a real force if we chose. From that day on I've wanted to be part of the solution."

Ryan explained, "I got to know Tom and Mary Kay as WAKERS about a year ago; already recognized Ken and Jose from the summer sessions. We put our heads together and individually sought out the other House members Carlos and Hiro told us were WAKE protégés. As a group we all vowed to put together a coalition for Constitutional government that could speak with one voice on the floor of the House."

Tom said, "I gladly joined the effort as our insider at the Senate. Feel like my own man now that I know there's a higher purpose to my time on the Hill. Might make reelection as an independent tougher, but I'm ready to give it a go. Right now there's only me in the Senate. We're looking to change that this election. Now that Truth Time will be enacted into law, the rules tighten up for everybody. More voters will insist their district or state candidates volunteer for tests. I expect we'll see a good number of candidates chased away once they're nanited and exposed. The other WAKERS running on party tickets will be our responsibility after the new Congress convenes. I think we can make a good case for them throwing in with us."

George stood. "If you'd indulge me a moment, I have sumpin' very personal to say." JoAnne had never seen George Adams at a loss for words, but he was clearly struggling.

"I used to remind Joe Whitley that I was proud to be a black American and I still am. The 2012 election should have made me even prouder to look at the occupant of the White House and see, at long last, a face more like my own. But after eight years of his brand of revisionism, I'm ashamed, ashamed of the discredit he's brought on my race. Man had more ideas than I got hair and most of 'em were inane. Took a while for folks to admit their buyer's remorse for being taken in by him, but I always knew the public was too smart to fool for long. It was a long eight years. Saw a big turnaround in '16 and this time it's gonna be even better. The future belongs to John Q. Public, and WAKE has played a big part in getting America where it is today. At last we're on the verge of a return to order and decency. I pray our hearts and our minds show us how to finish the job we've started."

Hiro wanted a last word before they broke up. "We've had a terrific get together and the future's looking downright rosy.

Before we get carried away with enthusiasm, a word of caution is in order. Never let your guard down for a minute. It only takes one turncoat or an inadvertent slip of the tongue to give away our cover. Too much is riding on our efforts to let them be compromised now. Let's each one of us here vow to keep our bond of secrecy till the time is ripe."

* * *

JoAnne left the New Mexico roundup with a new appreciation for where WAKE was going. A peaceful revolution, a re-founding by modern day patriots, was unfolding before her eyes. She tossed that exciting thought around in her head as she and Joe drove toward the airport. A distinct feeling of warmth spread through her limbs and her stomach started to twitch nervously. She put one hand to her abdomen to quiet the rumble.

Joe looked over at her, saw her gesture and said, "Lady, you are positively aglow. Not about to spring another big surprise on me, are you?"

She considered his puzzling question, stared at his sly grin, and realized what he was asking.

"No way, Joe. Emily is our one and only miracle baby. I was just thinking how beautifully WAKE's efforts have finally come together. Exciting times are coming!"

"Well, our trip was a total success. I just hope Hiro's words don't come back to bite us."

"Oh, I don't expect smooth sailing, Joe. Lord knows, you and I have taken our lumps along the way. But if we succeed, it'll be worth every minute we've devoted to WAKE."

PART FOUR

Jose Carillo

“Joe Number Four”

Chapter 80

Jose Carillo and Joe Amos bonded quickly at the meeting in New Mexico. They had enlightening after-hours conversations about where WAKE was headed with its quiet revolution and how they could play a part in that movement.

"You're an odds-on favorite, Joe, to join us on the Hill," Jose told him. "I'd be happy to help you get adjusted to what can be a confusing and frustrating time. The rules, both the written ones and the subtle dos and don'ts, gave me a lot of long days my first term."

"I hope you're right, Jose, that I can win, but the votes aren't in yet. If I survive this pre-election treadmill I'm on and end up in DC with you, I'll need all the inside info and advice you can give me."

Joe hoped he could get to know Carillo better and work with him. There was a quality about this fellow that set him apart from most of the politicians he'd ever met. Jose fit the description of 'a man of the people' better than anyone he'd run across. There was no pomp or arrogance about him, which was seldom the case with the officious asses Joe had put up with during the biomass approval process. For Amos the political scene was a temporary gig, something he owed his all for two or three terms at most. Then he would go back to doing what he knew best, being a scientist. But Jose Carillo was different in some undefined way. There was an air of destiny about him, a sense that he could be a genuine leader.

* * *

They stayed in touch now that Jose had a sat phone provided by WAKE. Each of them initiated phone calls to talk about issues Jose was wrestling with as a lawmaker, questions that may soon be concerns for Joe as well. In one of their late-night long-distance conversations a week before election day, Jose made a bold prediction.

"Joe, I'll go out on a limb here. I believe we'll have a whole new situation in town by the time you settle in. Folks are fed up and ready to dump more of the lying SOBs—excuse me—more of my distinguished friends on both sides of the aisle. You have to learn the lingo to get along."

"How *do* you survive in that environment, Jose? I mean, it's one thing to work up front and in the open with the partisans, but how do you look some of those liars in the eye every day and not hurl?"

Jose made a series of non-descript hand and foot movements imitating the martial arts then bowed. "You must master the art of political posturing, butterfly. One can endure the stench of horse excrement when he knows he will ultimately kick the ass from which it issues."

"Hope I can learn to hold my temper, Sensei Jose," Joe said through his laughing.

"You will. I watch them constantly electioneer instead of working and wonder how they put it over on the voters. My mouth stays sore from biting my tongue. But the weeding process is underway and, with patience, we'll get the revisionists plucked out and dispatched."

"Seems I heard George Adams use that term—revisionist," Joe said.

"He had it right, too. You'd be surprised how obvious they are, friend. The rot goes all the way to the top. Our fearless changer-in-chief was a revisionist of the first order. Think about it: Saul Alinsky, Reverend Wright, William Ayers, Frank Marshal Davis. Hell, his whole background smelled of socialists, rabble rousers and domestic terrorists. They took him by the heels and dipped him in their ideological slime. Every effort to uncover the records of his past was stone walled. Talk about taking somebody purely on faith—ridiculous. That and a generous helping of narcissism and our boy president thought he was the promised messiah. And the media worked hard to perpetuate the myth. Well, those days are behind us. Fixing the wheels he and his crowd ran off the government won't be easy, but it's doable. We're already seeing prosperity."

"You're on a roll, Jose. What did I do to set you off? Sure you haven't had a few pulls on the stuff that comes in the bottle with a worm?"

"No tequila today, compadre. Had a long session on the Hill. Talking to a sane person is therapeutic after one of those sessions. But, believe me, our time is coming. The days of government-run businesses, union takeovers and a small army of czars running amok are old news. Now the people can get the attention they deserve."

Joe offered, "What you're telling me makes me wonder if I want to wallow in that mud pit for the next two years, friend. What am I getting myself into?

"The most fun you've ever had, amigo. You and I and a damned fine crew of WAKERS are about to stand that place on its head and set the train back on the track. Got a lot of short-sighted mistakes to undo to get the country headed right again. This time we'll do it by the rules and follow the Constitution."

Chapter 81

Jose Carillo counted himself an extremely fortunate man. Thirty two years ago he was born to middle class parents near Las Cruces, New Mexico. They were natural-born Americans. Jose vividly remembered sitting on the river bank listening to Grandpa Juan's tales of his own childhood in old Mexico. A trained doctor, the old man he adored had spent the last thirty years of his life attending to Hispanic patients in his adopted country.

"They paid what they could," Grandpa told him

"Sometimes money, but more often they gave me food or did chores for me. Your papa ate a lot of fried chicken and roasting ears growing up that paid for bones I set or babies I delivered. Some of my patients kept a garden for us since I had little time to tend one. Life wasn't easy for those folks, Jose, but many of them were determined to someday be Americans. Never forget, my boy, you have what millions of others all over the world want—American citizenship. Always treasure that and make the most of it."

Jose was a hard worker and a good student. He blossomed into a lean, muscular teen who excelled both in the classroom and on the playing fields. By age sixteen he stood an inch under six feet, head and shoulders taller than his father. His dark hair and eyes, handsome features and winning smile set him apart. He rose to election as president of his student body. Still, young Jose considered college an unreachable dream until scholarship search committees came looking for him. College and law school followed.

His six years as a successful trial lawyer taught him valuable lessons about human nature and the sanctity of the law. Jose managed to find time to serve as first a councilman then the mayor of one of the state's most forward-looking cities. Soon he found friends and associates urging him to run for national office. He agreed on the condition that they back him as an independent, someone who answered only to his constituents, not a political party. Two years ago, Jose went off to Washington as a newly elected Congressman, and soon he expected a second term.

Carillo sat alone now in his Congressional office in a rare moment of quiet introspection. *This past year has been a real whirlwind,* he reflected. *Here I am back for a second term, finally with some good committee assignments, and ready to plow new ground. Who knew when the Constitution Foundation gave me that first scholarship that I'd be sitting here today?*

A grin lit his face and prompted him to look around to see no one was watching. He unlocked the privacy drawer of his desk and withdrew a leather-bound notebook with a single word embossed across its cover. WAKE. *How long has it been?* he questioned. *When did Carlos finally clue me in about WAKE?*

His mind did a rewind back to the day when the man from Dallas, Carlos Estrada, first urged him to seek office. Estrada also took him into confidence about who had financed his education. In fact, he said, the same four men had arranged the yearly Constitutional government training Jose learned to value so highly, Carlos told him, "The founders of Project WAKE took a long-term chance on you, son. We made you one of our protégés. You've returned that investment many times over with your success as a lawyer and local politician. Now your fellow citizens want you to speak for them in Washington. We felt it only fair to lay our cards on the table as you wrestle with this decision. Whatever you decide will be fine with us. We want no personal power or influence, only the chance to help inject bright young folks into society and see you excel to America's long-term benefit."

Once Jose recovered from his shock he understood Carlos and his friends were offering to back him for a bid for Congress. Estrada made it crystal clear from the outset that Jose could walk away and the WAKE people would be satisfied their investment was well spent on a young lawyer who was a credit to his profession.

"If you choose to run, " Carlos had encouraged, "we believe you have an excellent chance of winning as an independent. I will alert you that protégés are running in other districts as members of the two major parties. That's their only viable option for being elected. Whether party backed or not, they remain committed to govern with the Constitution as their foremost guideline."

Jose had been reluctant to join what at first sounded like a political conspiracy. Carlos patiently explained the WAKE founders were not seeking authority and would shun publicity. They insisted on remaining within campaign laws in their support efforts. Only by remaining in the shadows and promoting bright young minds could they help bring the return of a truly Constitutional federal government. Whatever WAKE achieved would ultimately be determined not by the founders but by the protégés themselves.

* * *

The intercom interrupted Jose's reverie. "Mister Carillo, Mister Amos is calling on line two."

He returned the notebook to its place and answered the phone. "Chicano Joe here," he said. He and Joe Amos had quickly become close friends since their first meeting in Albuquerque. Amos liked to say they were just two regular Joes who'd far outdistanced their own high ambitions. Jose's comeback was that must make him the 'Chicano Joe' and Amos the 'Gringo Joe'. The names stuck.

Now Amos was about to sweep into office on the crest of a strong wave of voter discontent with incumbents. Jose, Joe and their fellow WAKERS could help set the pace.

"Howzit, Gringo?" Jose asked.

"Thanks to you, it's going quite well. Reason I'm calling is I had a call from George Adams last night, I wondering if you were up to a little private conflab off site. Maybe lunch at Ginovelli's?"

Jose checked the time, glanced at his daily schedule and replied. "Your timing is perfect. Swing by here by eleven. I can taste the lobster ravioli already."

He took care of signing several letters then sat back and thought about how his new friend Joe Amos would adapt rapidly to the heady atmosphere of the House. Jose remembered personally going through a long, painful transition when he was elected to his first term. But Joe could take it all in stride. The 'new kid' was a natural. For all his credentials as a serious scientist, Amos never came off as stuffy or egg-headed. Being an independent wasn't all that bad when a close vote was at hand, either.

If George Adams had called, could their lunch have something to do with WAKE?

Chapter 82

Joe and Jose slipped away to the quiet surroundings of their favorite dining spot off the Beltway. Ginovelli's offered some of the area's most authentic and tasty Italian food. Equally important, it was not frequented by their fellow legislators. They could talk freely here without fear of being noticed. Of all the inconveniences political life had dumped on Jose, lack of privacy was the one he most disliked.

"So what did George have to say?" he asked Joe.

Even at this back-corner table of the little hideaway, Joe couldn't shake the habit of being on guard when he spoke. He leaned across the table and answered cautiously.

"You know Carlos Estrada, but I don't think you've met his security man Jim Bledsoe. Jim and I go back quite a way. He saved my skin from terrorists on at least two occasions."

Jose dangled his tequila sunrise in midair and telegraphed a nonplussed expression. "Whoa, Gringo! Must be a lot about you I don't know yet."

"Those stories will keep for another time, my friend. For now, just let me say Jim is networked with everybody. He has sources in corners of intelligence I never knew existed. Anyway, Bledsoe and Estrada filled in George on some of the undertow Jim has picked up from his contacts. There's a stir on the Hill with our independent ways. A couple of our protégé friends have also attracted attention from their supposed party cohorts for not toeing the line."

"Interesting," Jose said. "Not that we didn't expect this sooner or later. After the last election stirred things up, both sides of the aisle were shaking in their boots. Who ever thought four years ago voters would get so torqued over the feds' power grab they'd put the GOP in charge? Now they may reelect this president twice. Despite the Dems throwing mud at him, calling him a mental midget and other assorted things, he took hold and returned the good times. Now it's time he had some independent help." "

We still have a Congress with too many stale old career hangers-on," Joe said. "They want to do just enough to buy another term, and another, and another."

"Yeah," Jose snickered. "I think my little dissertation during morning business yesterday actually snapped a few of them out of their nap time."

Joe lifted his martini in a salute. "I thought you did a masterful job of firing a shot across the bow. Guess they didn't like the fact a couple million people saw you on TV calling for an honest debate on term limits. That makes you a rebel smart mouth to the old crowd.. But they're gonna hear the same demands from me and some others—again and again."

"Well, Joe, you said George called. What words of wisdom did he pass along?"

"He just wanted to caution that the rumblings are getting louder and more disturbing. Said we may want to soft pedal for a while. I believe his exact words were, '*Youze guys might wanta go easy fer a spell.*' I told him you and I had talked about gathering up all of our, uh, group to do some serious planning. The time could be ripe to choose our stand up day and give all the House members the shock of their lives. We agree you're our unofficial leader in the House, Jose. When and where should we have our meeting? I could open my lodge down on the Shenandoah River for a weekend get together. As far as I know the media vultures haven't homed in on it yet."

"Perfect, Joe. We have a lot of fellow protégés here in the metro area. I suggest we keep it to the lawmakers for now. The judges, professors and others we can bring in later. Why don't we divide up the list and invite them by word of mouth. We can do this as an all-day event and everybody will be back home before anybody sniffs out the fact they're out of town."

"Sounds like a plan, Chicano," Joe concurred. He took out a small blue schedule book and flipped the pages.

Hmmm. How does Saturday the twenty fifth sound to you?"

Jose was already consulting his own daily guidebook. He gave him a thumbs up. "Let's settle on that date and ask them to clear their schedules.

You sure you can handle that many folks at the lodge?"

"We can have breakfast on the porch then meet in the lodge great room. It's an hour drive for most of our cohorts. That gives us maybe ten hours of meeting time. I'll get the place set up. Long as everybody comes casual and drives routine looking wheels, nobody'll pay attention. Folks on that river are too busy boating and fishing to care who's next door."

"Then let's round 'em up, Gringo Joe."

Chapter 83

The WAKE protégés received their verbal invitations from Jose and Joe during the next two days. Quick encounters in the hallways, lunch room, parking lots and common areas of the Capitol building served to pass the word and hand over brief written driving directions. All of the WAKERS in the House and Senate, most of them serving under the 'Democrat' label, but a small number as 'Republicans', agreed to commit a day at Joe Amos's lodge downriver from Front Royal, Virginia.

Soon after sunrise on the designated day, the first arrivals sat down at picnic tables under the trees for a bountiful breakfast prepared by Joe's cook. They had come in small groups in pickups and SUVs loaded with camping gear none of them would use today. Dress was casual and the patter stayed light and cheerful, but a day of serious business was about to begin.

Jose Carillo asked a fellow House member, Clay Richards, who was an ordained minister, to set the tone for their deliberations. Richards invoked the Good Book's directive to go forth into the world, multiply and serve their fellow man. He prompted a few snickers when he said, "We've gone forth into the very belly of the beast and, thanks to an awakened electorate, we are still multiplying. Now please guide us to serve those good people to the best of our abilities."

As soon as breakfast was over, Jose rose and issued the call to order. "There is much to accomplish today. I suggest we get started in the great room."

All of the furniture in the lodge's rambling parlor had been moved to storage and replaced by conference tables to accommodate their numbers. Jose checked off the attendees in his head as they took their seats. They were a diverse group that included seven women and multiple races. WAKE had been instrumental in continuing the encouraging trend of diversity in the people's representatives. Bill, Delinda, Terrell, Kwame, Letisha, Jerry—he knew most of their success stories in detail. And this was only the first wave of a crop of young politicians that were about to alter the landscape.

Jose said, "I think we owe Joe Amos, as one of the creators of Truth Time, an explanation about the number of major party pretenders in the room. Ryan, you want to take a crack at that?"

"Sure, compadre," answered Ryan Bolger, the point man who'd been Joe's liaison with Carlos Estrada on the biomass project. "As you know, I was a business major. Tried my hand at local politics and liked it, so I explored running for Congress. Turned out the Dems had my district bought and paid for, so the only way I could get nominated was to run as one of them."

"I'll ask the obvious question, Ryan," Joe posed. "How will you pass the Truth Time screening test for candidacy next cycle?"

"I make a practice of telling the truth. Besides, I never set out to do harm to the party that thinks they own me. As long as I can cast my vote with my constituents' welfare in mind, regardless of what position the party takes, I'm satisfied. That's what I was sent here for—to represent my people. If I run for another term and Truth Time is the law by then, I'll simply answer questions as honestly as I can and let the chips fall where they may. If I'm asked why I don't join the party's bloc vote on this or that issue, my answer will be, *I'm with you when it's right for my folks at home.*"

"So you've never been a strong party man," Joe concluded. "And unlike the habitual liar who falsely convinces himself he's being honest but knows deep down he's pulling a fast one, A21 isn't an issue with you since you're being truthful. But didn't all of you expect to break away from the party in time?"

"Remember," Ryan reminded him, "I was read in on WAKE Up America by Carlos a long time ago. I already knew I was a WAKER when you and I got together down in Dallas. Most of the others didn't even know they were WAKERS until about half the people in this room got together a couple years ago. Jose and I leveled with them and they realized the potential we had if we joined hands. I'd prefer we announce as independents before the next campaign. Get it all out in the open. How does the old saying go? The truth shall set you free."

Jose let Ryan's words sink in with the group and watched the gestures around the room. Their get together was about to kick into overdrive. He said, "I believe our numbers show we can wield influence on the House floor now as a coordinated group. The number one question is when do we make our solidarity known?"

Mary Kay Grant stood and asked, "Can I take a swing at that?" Jose motioned and sat.

"Like Jose and Ryan," Mary Kay said, "I've had time now to scope things out and sniff the air. Change is coming, and this time it's positive change, not just another dose of snake oil. What I fear most is making our move prematurely and fritzing a lot of work that's gone before. I say we bite our lips awhile longer. There's a critical mass we have to reach to be taken seriously, and I don't know what the magic figure is. Let's give ourselves another chance to boost our numbers."

Joe took his turn. "If my calculations prove true, the final numbers will show we've achieved that critical mass. I believe the time to announce is in the opening session of the new Congress in January. Might as well lay it out and get on with it."

After a lively debate, the first order of business was passed by a voice vote. Mary Kay was in the minority but she signed on.

Stand up day, the moment when WAKERS in the House would announce they were coming together as a unified front of Constitutional Independents, was set. It would take place as soon as the gavel fell to open the 117th Congress.

Jose had one more issue he wanted to cover during the opening session. He looked across the table at a slender, slightly gray-haired man who appeared a bit out of place with all these under-forty attendees. "In case any of you have missed it, Don Shupe is not an original WAKER. He's an important addition made to our rolls by one of WAKE's founders. I'll go through the entire WAKE story shortly. Don is a first termer in the House with a unique perspective on our work." He motioned toward Shupe, who stood to address his counterparts.

Don started, "We've worked together in the House without discussing our WAKE backgrounds. I'm a late comer, sort of an adoptee of one of the four men Jose will be talking about today as our founders. I know there are others in the room who were recruits outside the standard WAKER route. Bur we're just as devoted to Constitutional Federalist government as anybody. Since I came on board at George's urging, I've doubled up on the summer classes and met some of you there. This is the most fun I've had in my life, and the bonus is we're slowly changing the way people view the Congress. Little by little we're helping folks see who the party wimps are and what they've been doing to our rights. My real job as part of this group is to find candidates like me, people with life experience to share without being stifled by party allegiance. Soon you'll see more guys and gals who just want to take their turn helping bring government back to the people. If we get the chance to 'tell it like it is' and expose some of the egotistical dunderheads the two parties have pushed onto the voters, well, that's a big extra."

Mary Kay interrupted him to say, "We all love it when you give 'em hell on the floor, Don. That's what we need, more straight talk and less smoke."

"Thanks, Mary. I intend to keep tellin' 'em, too, till they get it right. Always thought I'd like to stand on the floor of the House and remind the poobahs who it was sent them there. We're the *people's* House and we better not forget it. The *citizens* hired us and they can fire us, too. I'll keep grooming new independents 'til we bring about the real change that's needed."

Jose prompted, "I think the group would be interested in knowing how much success you've had in enlisting solid candidates to run for office, Don."

Shupe's smile filled the room. "That's been the best thing about the small part I've played. We've found that there are people, *good* people, everywhere that want to serve and truly represent their neighbors—men and women that *understand* what has to be done and are willing to serve for the right reasons. Our target was to have a minimum of three independent candidates for Congress from 'off the street' so to speak, new non-politician voices that would help return government to the people."

"Wanta give us a progress report, Don?" Mary Kay asked.

"So far we have potentially double that number who are potential winners of House seats next month. WAKE opened the flood gates. Now *real* people are stepping forward to unseat the phonies we've tolerated far too long. Finally, average people with the smarts to govern are saying, "Go home! This is *our* country and we're taking charge."

Shupe took his seat and Jose gaveled the group to order.

"Let's roll, WAKERS," Carillo said.

Chapter 84

Jose's agenda for the riverside meeting was optimistic. They must all be off site by sundown on their way back to DC. The last thing anyone here wanted was to be chased down by a reporter and questioned where he or she had been this weekend. The time for disclosure would come, but for the present, the WAKERS still needed confidentiality on their side. A few extra pickup trucks cruising back from the suburbs shouldn't draw undue attention.

"Before we go any farther," Jose said, "I want to be certain everyone in the room feels he or she is a full and equal participant in what we've all come to know as Project WAKE. Some of us were read in individually by the WAKE sponsors. Several of us have since briefed the rest of you one at a time. Our benefactors have asked me to address everyone here and level the playing field so we're all armed with the complete story. After you hear the evolution of the project, you'll see how vital it is that we succeed. Then we can set our long term action goals."

He proceeded to tell the story of the four founders, whom he fully identified by name and background. He explained how they began the initiative twenty years back with a dream and a considerable amount of money and organization. Jose related that those men wanted the country returned to Constitutional federalism based on the original document and its careful amendment as provided for when it was written. A series of numbers tracked the steady growth of the group now referred to as WAKERS. He showed the names and career fields of the accumulated cast of successful WAKERS now actively performing services in law, education, and the sciences. Jose watched audience reactions and could almost hear the gears meshing in a couple dozen fertile minds. Their training in the formal summer sessions took on added meaning. An aura of increased comradeship hung in the air.

"So you see," Jose continued, "the WAKE founders' goal is a peaceful, lawful transition back to the original intent of the Constitution. Extreme care has been exercised to stay within the bounds of law in all respects and concerted lawful effort has built our numbers. Those of us here today are the catalyst for reaching the end goal of Constitutional federalism. You need to know that the founders who finance the continuing project have added two of our fellow protégés to their number as financial sponsors. Our colleague Doctor Joe Amos and his wife JoAnne are also now sponsoring new protégés with their generosity. As of today, there are 700 WAKERS."

Nearly an hour and many questions later, Jose concluded his narrative. "Now that we know who we are and how it all came about, we can talk about the future."

For the next three hours the assembly vigorously debated and settled on a six-point course of action to be introduced in Congress incrementally between now and the next election. By the time stand up day arrived, these items would be aggressively presented. Once the position of this sizeable group was made known to their fellow Representatives, energetic pursuit for enactment would follow. Discussion in the great room was lively, even contentious at times. As the sun began to sink toward the peaks of the Blue Ridge, Jose put the finishing touches on documenting the results and stood to summarize.

"Our goals are ambitious, fellow WAKERS, but we can reach them if we each keep them always in sight. The debate over whether we should form a third political party was an eye-opener. I am convinced more than ever that we have to cling to our independence. Otherwise we risk becoming a carbon copy of what we seek to change. Constitutional independents can be the one strong voice in the wilderness that says *the people rule* and we serve them. If we ever let ourselves be co-opted into a bunch of hungry partisans more focused on reelection than on doing the people's business, we might as well be Republicans or Democrats."

Joe Amos, until now a bystander more than a participant, decided it was time he spoke up. Now that Jose had revealed the Amoses were two of WAKE's five sponsors, Joe was being careful to avoid being perceived as steering the group's discussion. George, Hiro and Carlos adamantly insisted the future was for the protégés to determine, not the founders. Joe keenly felt the burden of having one foot in each group. Finally, he could hold back no longer.

"For what it's worth, I'm sick over how the two-party system has gummed up the works," he said. "Not because parties are all bad, but because they tend to naturally, over time, breed clannish politicians focused on winning elections and retaining power. Why would a three-party system be any better? I want to be free to cast my votes based on what's good for my people back home, not what responds to narrow special interests and keeps a party in the majority. I hope our debate put that to rest. And now I believe we're on the verge of coming to important decisions. Please continue, Jose."

"So," Jose said, turning to a hand-written flip chart, "these are the issues we've agreed to work toward beginning today. We'll pound on these points and get them before the public. No matter how much pressure we have to withstand from the Dems and the GOP, we keep these targets in mind and go forward."

The page read:

WAKER AGENDA

1, Enact ethics rules rules lie detector tests to certify candidates.
2, Pass Congressional term limits by legislation or amendment.
3. Set maximum terms for judges by Constitutional amendment.
4. Establish strict lobbying rules and enforce them.
5. Enact campaign finance laws with teeth.
6. Institute mandatory Congressional cost cutting.

"As time passes we will build our concerted plan for a coordinated campaign to reach all of our goals," Jose told them. He underlined goal number one. "Truth Time is well on its way to becoming law. Congressmen talk about voter mandates, and this is one they won't be able to ignore. We need to see that the voters come to expect us to purge our own ranks. Those who try to ignore the Constitution and sidestep their constituents' wishes will be defeated at the polls."

Placing a check mark by the number two, he emphasized, "This goal is the most revealing of all to voters. If we're willing to limit our own power by setting term limits on ourselves, the original intent of citizen-run government will be on the way to being realized. By agreement here today, our initial recommendation will be two terms for Senators and six terms for House members—twelve years maximum for each elected official."

"Goal three acknowledges an amendment is required to establish maximum judicial terms. The Constitutional phrase 'shall hold their Offices during good Behaviour' needs to be expanded and clarified to include a statutory limit on years in office. We need fresh minds periodically and renewed focus on the proper role of the courts, including rededication to Constitutional principles. A fifteen-year term limit at all court levels has been proposed here."

He drew attention to goal number four. "Tough lobby laws are sorely needed. The voters must not be insulated from their elected officials. But they must have reasonable restrictions to prevent the blatant bribing and influence peddling that now occur. Lobbyists should be lawfully limited in their numbers, size of support contributions, and extent of access to lawmakers. Meaningful financial and criminal penalties must be established and enforced when violated."

"Number five—campaign finance," Jose indicated with a large green circle, "means no more placating the power brokers with toothless gap fillers like McCain-Feingold. It's time greedy billionaires who attempt to buy candidates through illegal bundling of financial support face hard time in jail for their deceit. Our own WAKE founders have proven elections can be won by complying with the law."

Number six goal Jose traced letter by letter with a bright red marker. "This is where the BS hits the fan, my friends. If we in Congress are willing to suck it up and operate more efficiently, Sam Jones and Sally Smith back home can begin to believe we mean what we're saying. Among the suggestions we've recorded here are a voluntary ten percent pay cut for all members, trimming supporting staff size by thirty percent, mandatory limits on free franked mail, travel expense cuts and payment of expenses for only verified non-political travel incident to assigned duties. Voters are tired of hearing us say we feel their pain. They want to see us tighten our belts and *share their pain* to bolster the economy. Performing public service should revolve around looking after the people's rights, not getting rich off of them."

Joe gave a final word of encouragement before the session broke up. "This has been a productive day. For the first time since the inception of Project WAKE, all of the protégés who are serving as elected officials are on the same sheet of music. The future is fraught with danger. Our patience and commitment will be severely tested, but the prize is well worth the discomfort. You, you and I, all of us, are the answer to reclaiming '*government of, by, and for the people.*' WAKERS, our bond is strong and we *will* succeed!"

Every member stood applauding and sought out hands to shake.

Chapter 85

Jose Carillo took the call from the Minority Whip, Dennis Young. The new Congress would be in session less than two months from now. Was this the Whip's chanced to lay down the rules to Jose? The past session had been marked by a number of contentious moments between Joe and both parties. He picked up the phone and answered tentatively, "What can I do for you, Denny?"

"Got some time to stop by my office and chat before the midday call to order?" the Whip asked him.

"Sure. I can come over now if you like. Anything in particular you want to talk about?"

"Just good order and decorum, Jose. That's my job. Come on over."

Carillo confirmed he was on his way and suppressed a chuckle. Denny prided himself on being a peacemaker, but he was like an open book to a close observer.

Jose reflected as he walked down the Capitol hallway: *That floor time I used for morning business yesterday obviously rubbed the Whip the wrong way. No mystery there. My remarks on term limits were aimed directly at Denny's Demo pals as well as the TV viewers. This will be another cloaked warning coming from the Majority's bulldog. Maybe I should have put in my ear plugs.*

"Thanks for the prompt response, Jose," Denny said when Carillo was ushered into the Whip's private office. Young motioned for his secretary to close the door and asked Jose to sit down. "We need to talk more often. I genuinely value your opinion. Hope we can work more closely to get some important measures passed this session."

"I'm open to discussion," Jose replied. "When it's best for my constituents, you can always count on my vote." He thought to himself, *and when you're wrong I'll fight you to a standstill, you phony.*

"We want the same thing, friend," Denny said in his practiced oily voice. "You can be a beneficial ally. I also believe you'd be a valued addition to the intelligence committee."

Well, Jose mused, *we got the carrot out of the way up front—a choice committee slot. Wonder what it is he wants from me in return?*

Denny looked at his watch. "We only have a few minutes till we leave for the floor. I wanted to say to you that some of the folks on my side of the aisle were a bit concerned about your comments on term limits. I assured them you weren't trying to pick an argument, but a few of them don't agree."

"I meant every word I said," Jose stated and stared down the grinning Whip. "Sooner or later, we're going to have to address the issue at voter demand. We'd be well advised to make the first move and show we're sensitive to their wishes."

"You sound like a man determined to shoot himself in the foot," Denny said and telegraphed his annoying artificial smile. "I plan to be in this building for a long time, and that sort of rules out self-inflicting a term limit. Where's *your* sense of duty, Jose? Or, for that matter, where's your ambition?"

"They're both right where they should be, with the folks who sent me here. If they want limits on how long we can serve, so be it. I don't plan to spend a lifetime here, anyway. This is a temporary job for me, so I don't feel threatened if I lose an election. Unlike a lot of people in this building, I'm a trained, competent lawyer. It wouldn't scare me in the least to go back to making an honest living on the outside. Remember, Denny, back in 1994, the voters came within three states of mandating a vote on a Constitutional amendment to set mandatory term limits. There's a strong surge out there to force our hand. If we sit around and wait for the tidal wave, a whole bunch of us just might get swept away next election for failure to act."

Young exhibited a rare moment of anger. "Wake up, young man and extract your head! You have a bright future on the Hill. Don't let one issue ruin it for you. We want to work with you and invite you into the fold, so defying us is the last thing you want to do."

Jose bit his lip. Today was not the time to incite a showdown. *Keep your cool*, he counseled. *The moment will come.* To the gray-haired man with fire in his eyes, he responded as calmly as he could manage, "I'm not looking for a battle, Denny, but I believe passionately in the term limits issue and I'll continue to press for action."

"Then I guess our conversation is over. Sorry we can't agree. Believe me, it's your loss." He stared daggers at Jose; said nothing more, but his expression spoke volumes. Fifteen minutes later Carillo hurried toward the House chamber with a warming sense of accomplishment. Without being overtly combative, he'd delivered the message to the Minority Whip that Jose Carillo was his own man, not vulnerable to cheap attempts to bribe him, loyal to no one but his own constituents.

Wonder how long it'll take him to get the word back to the Leader? he pondered. *If they want to drive home their point, my next summons will be to the big office. Bring it on. So far, they've only seen the tip of the iceberg.*

As he reached his seat he noticed the Minority Leader and Young were in a whispered discussion near the front of the chamber. Leader Samuels listened intently then looked in Jose's direction. *Didn't take long at all*, he thought with some amusement. *Denny's calling in the heavy artillery. Folks thought the queen from California was hell on wheels when she was running the show. Samuels almost makes her look good. He's stumping for intimidator-in-chief. Well, I have the same message for him. I'm not for sale.*

Joe Amos's message at the river lodge echoed in Jose's head. *Our patience and commitment will be severely tested*, he'd said. How many times Jose had reverted to the impulses of his hard scrabble youth when some pompous House elder tried to dictate to him, So often he'd thought *just this once let me punch out this popinjay's lights.* But the WAKERS were in the fray for the long haul, and they needed to present a united, determined, but patient front.

Chapter 86

A large contingent of school teachers convened in Washington during the first week of December. Jose took a call from Lori Wong on Wednesday morning. She was one of his fellow WAKERS who'd made a real mark as an educator. He had met Lori at the long-ago awards ceremony in St. Louis and kept an eye on her impressive career as a university professor. She had become Project WAKE's leading insider in the education profession.

"Lori! It's great to hear from you. When can we get together?"

"I need to have a short off-line talk with you ASAP, Jose."

"That urgent, huh? Can you come by my office this morning?"

"Give me directions, Congressman, and I'll catch a taxi now."

When Lori called from the entrance to his Capitol office building, Jose responded to escort her. Petite and well beyond cute, she possessed a quiet demeanor that belied her considerable underlying enthusiasm and fire. Hiro Kato, her WAKE sponsor, once described her to Jose as 'a compact little tsunami waiting to happen'. She stood an inch over five feet. Lori had the dark, silken tresses, flashing eyes, flawless skin of an Asian beauty though she had lived all her life in southern California.

Even unflappable Martha, Jose's administrative assistant, registered a rare moment of surprise with a visibly raised eyebrow when Lori entered the office. Carillo introduced her as a long time friend and asked that Martha hold his calls while they visited.

Lori wasted no time getting to the point. "We have an opportunity we should exploit this week, Jose. The teachers are meeting at the convention center through the weekend. I've been in touch with every like-minded person in the assembly—there are twenty including me—and suggested we use our downtime to talk about near term plans."

"As one of the insiders," Jose told her, "you know we're in the countdown to an important event, Lori. It's important I meet with them, and Joe Amos can be there, too. By the way, I thought you were non-union. How'd you wangle a seat at this teachers' convention?"

"Oh, that clan works hard to make us 'right to workers' feel like scabs, but we tolerate their discrimination knowing the tide will eventually turn. I insisted on attending knowing I'd have to put up with heavy snubbing. Then it occurred to me this was a golden opportunity to bring some more of our other associates up to speed. Lots of good things are happening in the education field as well as here on the Hill. We need to mobilize our fellow . . ."

Jose stopped her in mid-sentence. "Best we defer that subject till later, Lori." He made a wide sweeping motion with one arm then pushed his ear lobes forward with both hands. Lori looked momentarily lost before letting a smile light her face. She had read his charade-like antics to mean 'the walls have ears.'

After a pleasant visit and catching up on a purely personal level, they concluded with an agreement to meet with the other WAKER teachers the next night at an address Jose wrote down for her. "Tell your friends I vouch for this place. It's not fancy, strictly informal, but it's private and the food is fantastic."

He returned with her to the Longworth Building guard station entrance where he took both of her hands in his, bussed her cheek, and said, "You've made my day, Lori. See you soon."

* * *

The next afternoon Jose left his office and found Joe Amos and his driver Brent in the Capitol parking lot. Brent acknowledged the written note Jose handed him, punched it into the car's GPS, and backed out of the space.

Across the Potomac in Arlington Brent dropped off the two men in front of a drab, inconspicuous building. A red and blue striped canopy angled over the sidewalk and a neon sign in the window read 'Bubba's'. The two Congressmen left their coats and ties in the vehicle and were in shirtsleeves when they walked into the eatery.

A big, muscular black man with a cordial grin and a red apron greeted them. "Hey, partner. Hope you and the doc are hungry." Bubba shook with his sizable hand then turned to lead them to the kitchen. The smoky pungent smell of barbecuing pork and aroma of sizzling fish filled the galley. The sweet promise of fresh greens steaming with ham hocks lingered in the air. A row of pecan pies cooled on a kitchen counter.

"Better get me out of here, Bubba, before I eat up the dessert," Jose said.

Bubba grinned and waggled a chubby forefinger. They followed him up the staircase.

The single, softly lit upstairs room held five six-place tables set with red tablecloths. A bouquet of wild flowers decorated each table centered by a hurricane lamp holding a lit candle. A long buffet table held heated food trays, garnish platters and an assortment of breads. Two white- clad servers including Bubba's son Jamal stood at the buffet making sure the offerings were just right. Jose turned to their host and said, "Bubba, once again you outdid yourself."

"Wait'll your crowd tastes tonight's ribs." He rubbed his ample front. "As the official food taster of this 'stablishment, I certufy this batch as super fine." Joe Amos took a long look at the talented cook and flashed back to another formerly large man he much admired. Two of that gentleman's favorite activities were sponsoring young people and devouring soul food. He catalogued a mental reminder to never, ever reveal this home of fattening heavenly eats to the now nearly svelte George Adams.

Jose began setting up for his after dinner briefing to their fellow WAKERS. Lori Wong arrived with Carrie Zeitler, a tall, red-headed DC lawyer, in tow. Both Jose and Joe had worked with and appreciated the two women for actively furthering the WAKE crusade toward ethical reform. Lori had played a major role in purging textbooks of their revisionist historical errors. Carrie regularly punched holes in the long-established liberal monopoly of the teaching profession and was a Constitutional law expert.

"How's the court test of the revised college tenure rules coming?" Jose asked Carrie.

"Got them on the run, Jose. Had a close vote by the SCOTUS on hearing our case, but sanity won out. We're doing preps for presenting to the Supremes next month."

"You make it sound like an audience with Dianna Ross and her group," he teased.

"Trying to reel me in?" Carrie poked in return. "I refuse to say anything derogatory about the regal nine. My case will win on its merits. Enough states have dismissed whack job profs since they loosened their tenure shackles to make this an irresistible national trend. I expect the high court to rule those actions Constitutional. That opens the door for more states to join the bandwagon. Maybe soon teachers can concentrate on teaching instead of spewing radical left doctrine and slavishly following union rules." Lori gave that the thumbs up sign.

Others began arriving with Bubba's daughter showing them the way. Jose seated them and began to feel a nervous surge.

Chapter 87

The tables in Bubba's loft filled up to near capacity before the meal began. When Jamal sounded the dinner bell the invitees moved through the serving line and Amos and Carillo followed. Then the evening hit a distinctly high note when two unexpected visitors made their appearance at the top of the stairs.

Luckily Joe hadn't yet started to fill his plate. The sudden adrenaline surge he experienced would have sent food flying. Everything else around him instantly disappeared. Standing in the doorway were the loves of his life, JoAnne and Emily. His body surged forward; he hoped his feet would somehow follow. Emily was already running toward him with the angelic smile she'd inherited from her mother.

"Emmy honey!" He swept her up and nuzzled her.

"Are you surprised, Daddy?"

"I am, baby, and it's wonderful!"

She whispered in his ear as JoAnne crossed the room to them. "Mommy said to tell you a little bird named Joe Chicago invited us." JoAnne caught up and Joe planted a long, hungry smooch on his dazzling wife. Then he backed up a step and broke out laughing.

"I'm not sure how to take that," JoAnne said, her expression a mixture of surprise and puzzlement.

"Honey, I just figured out Em meant *Chicano* Joe. Carillo lured you here, didn't he?"

She nodded. "Said it was an important gathering of WAKERS I'd want to be a part of, Joe. I already see some of the folks we've worked with before." She'd hardly finished her statement when both Lori and Carrie hurried over and exchanged hugs with her.

The barbecued beef ribs and fish Bubba served were a huge hit. Jose stood slowly after his hearty dinner and the best pecan pie he could remember.

He began, "Folks, I'm Jose Carillo, a member of the US House and a fellow WAKE protégé of yours. Much as I hate to break the spell with serious business, we have some important matters to talk about tonight. I want to say it's a pleasure getting reacquainted with those of you I know and meeting others for the first time. You've all previously been given some of the details about Project WAKE by Lori and Carrie. You understand that our project is about to bear fruit after a long maturing process—more than twenty years. We are on the verge, fellow WAKERS, of seeing this country returned to its rightful position of prominence with a federal government that honors and follows the Constitution."

A spontaneous burst of applause was followed by everyone in the room rising. Jose beamed when shouts of "Amen to that" and "Finally" bounced off the walls.

"Lori and Carrie have been in the front line fighting for your rights as teachers and seeing that the text books you use are at last purged of their poison and bias. You've all done your part, under continuing pressure and opposition, to promote the kind of education our children deserve. The new President recently dismissed several high-level holdover officials from the previous administration found to be knowingly aiding advocates of radical education revisionism. I can assure you when the smoke clears from the 2020 elections, we will be nearing the day when the federal legislature begins a sharp turn toward the center politically."

He waited for their animated response to subside then continued. "A landmark case brought by Carrie and others will be heard by the Supreme Court very soon on tenure rules at universities. Right to work is getting a new look, too. Those cases will be the first shots in a steady volley aimed at bringing teacher choice across the country to open employment and a return to good faith bargaining."

Someone shouted, "You go, girl." A rhythmic chant of "Carr-ie, Carr-ie" sounded.

Jose gladly paused and let the clamor play out. "I'm heartened by your enthusiasm," he finally said. "We're a little more than a year away from the elections that will stand the political system on its head. With a dedicated group like this and a couple thousand other WAKERS equally motivated, our objectives are in sight. I want to lay out the end plan for you here tonight so we're all equal partners in bringing it to completion. Then I ask that each of you consider this information an important trust to be kept close hold until the time is ripe."

Carillo launched into his polished presentation. He traced WAKE from its 2000 inception through twenty plus years of developing more than 700 patriots dedicated to saving their country from its downslide. He told them that Joe and JoAnne Amos, the champions of nanomedicine and diabetes treatment, developers of biomass energy production and Truth Time lie detection, were now two of the five WAKE sponsors. When the attendees acknowledged their huge contributions, Emily beamed and joined the applause for her parents.

Jose outlined the four phases of WAKE implementation to be certain everyone fully understood exactly what those objectives implied and how close they were to finally achieving Phase IV, Return America to Constitutional Federalism. Along the way WAKERS were responsible for far-reaching accomplishments in every field they'd entered. Throughout he was queried on numerous points. Penetrating questions led to enlightening dialogue about where WAKE was going and when.

He concluded with a detailed explanation of the six legislative agenda items he and other WAKER members of Congress were advancing on a daily basis. The slide he projected brought on an undertow of conversation, pointing and head nods. Jose concluded most of those in the room were for the first time grasping the earthshaking magnitude of their shared involvement.

"So you see, fellow WAKERS, we're in a battle for the survival of our country. Our nation's future rests squarely on our shoulders. We can't yet tell outsiders why we're so adamant about the actions we propose. But in time they'll all see this is a peaceful revolution, just like the surges of people on the mall in September 09 and spring 2012 that they ignored and then suffered for their inattention."

Jose paused and homed in on a gray-haired man at one of the front tables. "I want all of you to meet one of the most energized freshman members of the House of Representatives. He, more than anyone I know, is a shining example of the attitude that pervades the American voters. They realize political power is theirs to exercise and they're stepping up to the challenge. Ladies and gentlemen, Representative Don Shupe from Maryland."

Don came to his feet and walked to the podium. He methodically made eye contact with each person in the room and acknowledged their polite applause. He had already made the rounds before dinner speaking with every attendee. As usual, Don Shupe had made a hit with his common sense philosophy and down home good humor.

"I'll be brief, folks. Meeting you tonight has been a real kick for me. I'm heartened to see that people like you are doing everything you can to steer my grandchildren right. Lord knows they need the help countering all the distractions and bad influences they face every day. I'm very proud to be an adopted member of Project WAKE. My role has been to find and help seasoned citizens successfully compete for office with the assistance of talented WAKE staff. In the upcoming elections we expect to have at least fifteen candidates for the US House running for seats as proponents of Constitutional federalism. They are vying in districts from Virginia and West Virginia to Florida and Georgia, from Rhode Island to Indiana to Wyoming and California. The most exciting part of the awakening your efforts have brought about is a renewed desire by citizens to get involved. Friends, the day of the people is nearly upon us and we're all a part of it. A peaceful revolution that will transition America back to its roots is in full swing and it can not be stopped."

Shupe motioned toward Jose and returned to his seat.

"Let me conclude our discussion," Jose said, "by agreeing that a watershed day is approaching. On what some of us refer to as *stand up day* the entire country will be made aware of how far WAKE has come. That precise date is not yet set, but it will shock the world of politics. Then all Americans will hear from WAKE independents that we demand a return to Constitutional federalism. Until then we must meet like this and carefully guard one of the best kept secrets in our nation's history."

Chapter 88

The past year in Congress had been tumultuous from its opening days. Freshmen Congressmen from both parties, prompted by voter outrage, pushed for reform. This time there was no doubt the people were *demanding* change or they'd elect a whole new slate of legislators.

Since the new president took office in 2016, ill-advised programs put in place by the prior administration continued to fall. The new leader rescinded old executive orders. The markets rose. Employment reached new highs. Thirty-three state legislatures issued petitions for a Constitutional convention to consider issues including the amendment of Congressional term limits.

Jose continued to press for self-imposed action in the House. "We have a choice to make," he had stated on the House floor. "We can wait for one more state to step up and make a convention mandatory, or we can take responsibility and frame our own amendment now. I doubt either side of the aisle wants the uncertainty of an open convention that could enact multiple Constitutional amendments or destroy the integrity of that fine document. I propose we accept the spoken will of the people and start with the obvious issue—term limits. Congress must return to true public service by citizens, not career power seekers."

His remarks met attempts to shout him down. Derision and implied warnings from House colleagues were heaped upon him. Jose even received written and verbal anonymously-issued physical threats to his person. Far from discouraging him, these insults stoked his determination to show the voters they were being manipulated. Mary Kay Grant joined the battle, much to the disdain of 'her' Democratic leadership who instructed her to fall in line. She kept her WAKER connection secret and blithely ignored them. Joe Amos spoke out at every opportunity and became a surprisingly eloquent champion for term limits.

* * *

One week after the educators met with him and Joe, Jose booked the upstairs room at Bubba's grill once more and spread the word. Mary Kay and seven other House members filed in and gathered upstairs. Jose looked out across the room at anxious faces and issued a challenge. "The battle is on, my friends. We attack without let up till election day."

Mary Kay asked to be recognized and stood to speak. "I for one plan to make term limits the subject of the day every day. It's our pivotal issue, and they're gonna hear about it till they get off their dead humps and do the right thing. But I can't wait to strap on a whole menu of other changes. Health care, cap and trade, nationalization of corporations—I say don't stop till we undo all the excesses that brought us inflation followed by an even worse depression. Then we can weed out and rescind what they foisted on us under their guise of responding to trumped up crises."

Carillo applauded. "Thank you, Mary Kay. You've said what all of us are thinking. It's high time the public realized they haven't been foreclosed. It's our job to dispel the myth that once a government program is begun it can only grow. We have to take it as a personal mission to show that anything Congress can botch up it can damned well reverse. But that will come with time and strength in numbers. Our target for now has to be getting like-minded candidates elected in November so we can set about making the necessary changes. We must see to it that the voters understand electing a new slate is the only way their wishes will ever begin to be met."

Joe Amos joined in. "I second that. The one convincer that can decide this election is to identify to voters those House members who have stubbornly fought against term limits. In today's climate they're playing with defeat at the polling place. And if they try to weasel out, Truth Time will catch them lying. Just because they've already passed a qualifying lie detector test doesn't mean the right question asked in public can't show they're liars."

The group laid their plan of attack for the coming weeks on the House floor. Morning business and every other opportunity to speak would be filled with impassioned pleas for internal action on term limits. Jose would offer to co-sponsor a bill with either party to establish term limits in lieu of allowing a Constitutional convention to convene.

* * *

Carillo and Amos stayed late into the night after their associates left Bubba's. The big man ceded a corner near the kitchen to them and kept them supplied with cold beer.

Joe took a pull on his longneck and quipped, "Remember, Chicano, how those guys on TV used to talk about tingling all over when the last White House dweller spoke on the campaign trail?"

Jose, in mid-swallow, let out a laugh and nearly choked. "Yeah, Gringo. They didn't know the buzz they felt was more likely the cattle prod his handlers were using to goose them toward socialism. And the flaming revisionists damned near pulled off their plan: Get a majority of voters exempted from income tax and sucking up supposedly cheap health care to lock in a long-term dynasty at the ballot box. Mary Kay made some good points. If we don't get health care and cap and trade rescinded, we'll be strapped with burdens that break us. And we need the feds off the backs of businesses dictating how they operate. The new president wants to move to scrap all those bum decisions, but he needs our help."

"What I can't agree with, though," Joe said, "was the part about making the last bunch account for their actions. We had enough of that with the old Majority. Don't step up to doing the right thing, just waste time investigating everybody and trying to place blame. No more staring in the rearview mirror for me. Let's concentrate on the road ahead."

Chapter 89

December 20 arrived with blowing snow and biting cold in Washington. But the weather was no obstacle to the public. This winter day would also be marked as the day a massive rally took place on the Capitol Mall.

A convoluted approval process and autocratic attempts to halt the gathering placed big hurdles in its way. But George Adams and his people, with the able assistance of key lawmakers, most of them WAKE protégés, had finally successfully run the gauntlet of officialdom. Before this day ended, the organizers expected to witness a crowd approaching a million citizens covering the mall like a moving human canopy.

They came on foot, by air, bus and train, astride bicycles and motorcycles, by every imaginable form of conveyance. The mass of people assembled peacefully but with resolve. The scene was reminiscent of the massive rallies held on September 12, 2009 and again before the 2012 elections. Those earlier gatherings had been likened to the Coxey's army of 500 that marched on Washington in 1894 to protest unemployment and depression. But all of the earlier events paled in comparison with the size and sheer intensity of this great outpouring of irate citizens. An electric charge pervaded the scene.

Jose Carillo and Don Shupe stood on the balcony in front of the Lincoln Memorial and looked out over the seething ocean of humanity. The protest signs decried the wrong-headedness of a federal government gone wrong. Rhythmic chants of *'Give me back my country,'* and *'Work smart or go home'* filled the air.

"Nervous, Don?" Jose asked.

"Anxious," Shupe countered. "Those are my people out there. They're the folks who own this country and damned well ought to say how it's run. I've dreamed about a day like this with one chance to say what's in my heart. I wouldn't trade it for a billion dollars."

The formal speeches revved up the hundreds of thousands overflowing the mall. Their chorus of discontent grew more insistent. Each speaker, among them Jose Carillo, other lawmakers, a doctor, a sports figure, and a prominent businesswoman, all issued pleas for restraint and peaceful action at the polling places to gain voter redress.

One speaker, a Virginia housewife, emerged from the audience and handed off her sign before taking the podium. The sign read: *'Who stole my government?'* She pled for sanity and a return to carrying out the wishes of the people. At one point the man at the podium called for the entire throng to turn and face Capitol Hill with an invitation. Hundreds of amplifiers and thousands of voices chanted, "Come out and talk to us," but not one Capitol dweller accepted the challenge.

After four hours of addresses interspersed with musical entertainment, the crowd was becoming dangerously restive. Carillo concluded they were more than ready for the voice of reason to calm their anger. He strode to the microphones and asked for the crowd's attention. "I want you to hear now from a true patriot who has much in common with you. This man served his country in uniform as a career military man. Then he learned the workings of big business with years in industry. He also has the perspective of a small businessman, having been one himself. Above all he is a father and a grandfather who, in his sixties, rededicated himself to serving as a citizen politician. His experience from town council and county planner to regional planning board member to Congress gives him a rounded take on governing. Now he is embarking on a second term in the U.S. House where he is setting the standard for ethical and reasoned representation of his constituents. I have to tell you this man is making others in Congress sit up and pay attention. Ladies and gentlemen, meet my friend and fellow Independent Don Shupe."

Don stepped forward and scanned the crowd slowly, waiting for the rumbles and outcries to die away. Then he made a sweeping motion with his arm across the expanse facing him.

"Fellow Americans, this is *your* Capitol mall and your day. The numbers and enthusiasm are inspiring. You came to be heard by those who, once elected, often forget why they are up here and who it is that put them here. Well, today you've left no doubt about either of those questions. Your demands have been heard in that big building at the end of the mall. Today, in this hallowed place, the voters have demanded, '*Heed our voices or go home*.'"

Thunderous applause and cheering rolled across the basin for minutes while Shupe patiently waited for their fervor to play out. Finally, he continued. "But remember, ours is a peaceful revolution. More than that, it represents a transition back to where this country belongs—a re-founding of our republic. It is in many ways like the force that brought thirteen states together under a Constitution for the ages. True to the fears voiced by those founding fathers, greedy men have methodically set about weakening that wonderful document for their own selfish purposes. But we WILL have our government back. The voting public, you and you and I—we set the agenda and the politicians must either work for us or leave. When the throng had quieted again, Shupe pointed over their heads at the Capitol.

"I, an average Joe like most of you, have been granted the privilege of representing my friends and neighbors in the building on that hill. Along with my faith in God and my devotion to family, I consider this privilege a sacred trust. If I can not voice my constituents' wishes in Congress, then I don't belong here. Independent members of Congress are driving that point home, but the habits of career politicians are hard to change. In November, *they will listen* when you go to the ballot boxes and issue them one-way tickets home."

Protest signs bobbed and a chorus of voices boomed agreement.

"The power is yours. Exert your will and elect those men and women who will listen to instructions and return this country to a government *for* the people, a federal republic compliant with the Constitution. We Independents have tried to warn them, but sane voices are seldom heard in the halls of Congress. The two major parties control floor time and severely ration our chances to speak. Well, today we have our audience, and I say the time has come for *you, the voters* to tell them who's boss."

During the next election, you will witness the results of the new lie detection law when candidates attempt to deceive their way to victory. Make them answer the hard questions and sort out on your own which ones will truly serve your interests. See to it that the liars and connivers are exposed and disqualified. Demand that all who want to be elected listen to what you are telling them, not to the persuasions of lobbyists and special interests. Insist they pass reform, beginning with voluntary term limits and meaningful cost cutting. Support independent candidates and break the hold of the major party mechanisms.

There was a new awareness all across the country. The people who truly count, the vast electorate across fifty states, is speaking with one voice. Public servants have been put on notice: either you govern as we mandate or we'll replace you. No more privileged class telling us we're not smart enough to understand what's best for us. No more being ignored for the good of the party. The heyday of partisan politics is behind us and the time of citizen rule is here."

Don extended his arm and pointed toward the Capitol dome. "In a few short months, the people in that building will hear our voices through the ballots we cast. For many of them it will mark the end of their careers. Once again that edifice will become the people's house."

A great swell arose once again as the assembled masses turned and directed their outrage at the building on the hill. Shupe waited patiently for several minutes for the clamoring to die away before concluding.

"This election is your moment, my fellow citizens, your time in history. Take the initiative and make it a new mandate for a return to reason and Constitutional lawmaking.

As Thomas Jefferson said, '*When the people fear their government, there is tyranny, but when the government fears the people, there is liberty.*' Demand your rights!"

Chapter 90

The Minority Leaders of the Senate and House and their Whips assembled in the nearly deserted Capitol building. Only an emergency could have interrupted the Christmas break they all treasured so highly.

"Denny, we need to get tough on these pesky rebels. They're trying to spark a mutiny." House Minority Leader Greg Samuels was highly agitated. Dennis Young, the House Whip, squirmed uncomfortably in his seat.

"I still don't understand," complained the House Leader, "how you let those crazies get a permit to overrun the Mall. We bought a lot of misery wit that fumble. Now the independents won't shut up with their crowing and yapping about term limits. Some of our own freshmen are even in our face."

Just an angry mob," Denny countered, "and a bitter crowd working off steam. It will all settle down."

"Well, it damned well better. We have some fence mending to do. Took some hjts last month so this session won't be a cake walk. My reputation depends on us working around these young folks that think they know it all.

Denny proposed, "We can start by cutting off the worst troublemakers from floor time, but that'll take cooperation from the majority. Have to make sure they clamp down and enforce the rules with some ingenuity."

"And have the public jump all over us when the child prodigies complain we're stifling them? Try again, Denny."

I've dangled every carrot in my bag, Greg. Didn't get a nibble. Offered choice committee posts, campaign contributions, lobby pressure. They just tune me out. It's like they smell blood in the water and their teeth are bared."

Greg Samuels fired back, his voice rising another level. “The crossover votes are killing us. What the hell do you think your title whip means? High time you started cracking the whip harder. What really worries me is we don’t know how many wolverines in puppy dog clothing have been elected this time. I want them controlled!” He shook a finger at Denny.

Samuels was riled now. “Every day I look at the tallies and scratch my head. Some of our newbies may be faithful to the party just long enough to get their campaign financed and touted. He balled up both fists and his face turned red. Kicked at his wastebasket and sent it rattling across the floor.

“Denny, I look to you to drill some sense into these ankle-biters. They’ve already helped the other side push through that disastrous campaign finance change and our war chests are drying up. Two of our most reliable money sources are about to land in jail. The damnable lie detector issue shooed away our candidates like flies.

Young protested, Carillo and Amos, Bolger and Shupe—they all seem immune to anything I try.”

“Well, I’m through talking,” Samuels proclaimed. You’re my point man. The polls are already looking gloom and we haven’t even convened the new session. Take charge and deal with then. Do whatever it takes to stop this insurrection. Get tough, shake the upstarts, enlist outside help, whatever will work. Even if you have to . . . just do it!”

“Maybe we need to pick out one of the ringleaders and throw a real scare into him, boss,” Denny put forward.

Greg Samuels waved off his question. “Don’t involve me, Denny. I don’t want to know any details. Just get it done or I’ll find somebody that can. Now get out there and make it happen.”

Dennis Young has his marching orders. Samuels had left the details up to him. The two minority party figures from the Senate kept quiet. The needed no part of this. Young sat there shaking his head.

Chapter 91

"It's an idea whose time has come," Denny. I'm merely voicing the people's wishes. You'd do well to consider acting." House Whip Denny Young worked to regain his composure after the tongue-lashing he'd just finishing delivering to Jose Carillo.

After the meeting with the Leaders and his Whip counterpart yesterday his ears were still burning. The second-term Representative from New Mexico listened until Young completed the dump. His calm acceptance of his admonishment appeared to serve only to stoke the intensity of the Whip's diatribe.

"You really should calm down," Joe cautioned. Can't be good for your blood pressure."

"Are you purposely trying to be a smart ass, Carillo? Haven't learned much up here on the Hill, have you? He turned his back to look for something and mumbled one word, "Wetback!" when he faced Jose and rattled a sheet of paper in his direction, Jose stepped closer and cut of whatever Young was about to say.

"I heard that word, Greg. Believe you owe me an apology. My citizenship is by birth just like yours. My grandfather immigrated legally and my parents were born in this country."

Now Young was really steamed. He turned red, shook his finger inches from Carillo's nose, and bellowed. "I insist that you show me the respect due my position!"

Jose fought the impulse his street-smart youth begged him yo exercise. He unclenched his fist and retreated to take a seat facing the huge cherry desk. Jose took a deep breath and stared at Young thinking *If this had happened a few tears earlier, I would have . . . cool it, Joe.*

I'm listening, Greg. Let's talk this out calmly. Maybe it's just a misunderstanding we can put behind us."

Young took the cue and sat. His temper was cooling. "What I want, Jose, is your word these repeated attacks on the term limits issue will throttle back. We have a lot of business to conduct and the other side still has a majority. Your issue is a distraction. I value yourt independent voice but you're slowing down important work we need to debate this session. We have to shortcut the majority's attempts to undo the work of the last administration."

Young handed him the paper he had retrieved. "This is a record of the multiple times you and others have hammered on term limits the past several weeks. We both know that issue is going nowhere."

Jose scanned down the page. There were entries showing when he and seven other House members had come down hard for either passing voluntary term limits or framing a proposed Constitutional amendment for ratification by the states. Five of them, beginning with Mary Kay Grant, belonged to fellow WAKERS. The list also contained two non-WAKER partisans, one from each side of the aisle. The drumbeat was growing and had become a real irritation for the leaders of both parties.

"I can't speak for the others," Jose said, "but I still have a lot more to say on that subject, Denny. We're only three state petitions away from having a call for a mandatory Constitutional convention. The polls are showing that seventy percent of the people want term limits now."

Young sat there with his mouth turned down and his eyes shooting thunderbolts. His lips moved but no words came out. Jose seriously worried that the man, who was probably nearly twice his age, was about to have a stroke, He sprang out of his seat and hurried around the massive desk to the Whip's aid. Young emerged from hs catatonic state and pushed him away.

"I tried to do this the easy way, Carillo. You leave me no choice. As of now, reelected or not, your days in the House are numbered, young man. This could get very painful for you. I'll make you an example for many others who think they can defy the leadership. Your political career is about to be over. And that's not the worst that could happen."

Silence pervaded the room. The two men stood there staring each other down. Joe considered the words he'd just heard and the unnerving silent threat they implied. This self-important ass could have mayhem on his mind. The last thing Jose would have ever thought possible was a physical threat by a fellow member of Congress. But then politics can be an all-consuming business. Maybe he should set the record straight.

"I guess that says it all, Dennis. Hope you're through ranting, because now I have three things to say to *you.* He lifted a forefinger and began, "One, I don't work for you so you can't tell me what to do. Two, he added emphasis with a raised ring finger, "only the voters back home will decide whether I stay or go, and three, be careful what you start. If I spread the real truth about you, you may leave before I do."

At this point Jose accentuated his reply with a raised middle finger, turned and exited.

Chapter 92

The invitation had arrived from one of the television network's senior newsmen. Jose and Joe quickly accepted. It was weeks after Election Day and only days before Congress was to reconvene. Offered a timely national audience to hear their plea for political sanity and responsibility.

Vern Bennett introduced the two men to his viewers.

"I'm honored to have with me two of the newest bright lights in a US House that is too often a bit dull and disappointing. Jose Carillo is about to start his second term representing New Mexico. Joe Amos is a first term Congressman from Texas. Amos has garnered much publicity recently for his accomplishments in the energy industry. They both welcomed a chance to talk to viewers about term limits and other items on their agendas. Welcome, Congressmen."

Jose and Joe acknowledged his warm greeting and Jose tool the lead

"Vern, this is indeed a special opportunity to talk about a vital issue. What Joe and I are about to present is in no way partisan. If either party was seriously interested in the voters' desires, they would have done this long ago. We are both Constitutional independents interested solely in what we feel is good for the people we work for—citizens beyond the DC beltway. This year, more than at any other time in our history, every vote can be a petition to return the power of government to the voters. Joe Amos and I, along with other concerned House members, expect to be on the floor often i insisting we return to the ideals of government that were established by the founding fathers. We can do that by following the constitution as it was written and amending it legally through the states if required."

Bennett tried to remain aloof, but a smile crept across his face.

Jose continued. "A number of major actions unilaterally taken by the prior administration are now before appellate courts and the Supreme Court for rulings on their constitutionality. I believe the majority of them will be struck down. And if I'm wrong, Congress should meet its responsibility by vacating those unwise and illegal measures.

When one more state signs up, there will be a call for a convention to propose term limits. Wouldn't it be better if we in Congress stepped up and imposed them without a convention? We plan to push in that direction.

Vern cut into Jose's statement with a question. "Is that a realistic goal? Do you think Congress will act on its own?"

Joe Amos picked up that challenge.

"Vern, there's a false belief that needs to be dispelled here and now. It's within our power. All these court cases wouldn't even be necessary if the legislative branch would show the ba . . . the courage to act on its own. That's all we ask of our fellow lawmakers. Show the fortitude to take us back to the day of citizen legislators as the founders intended. Clean out the backlog of tottering old cronies. Let them go live on the fortunes they've amassed while in office."

Bennett by now was chafing at the bit. "Some of my fellow newsmen have likened your demands to sedition. How do you respond to them?"

Joe and Jose stared at each other and Joe made a sweeping motion toward his friend. "I defer to you."

"False and misleading," Jose replied. "There's nothing violent about demanding the people you elect protect your rights and govern by the Constitution. The only revolution we support is at the ballot box. Voters need to say to their representatives, 'Move over and go vegetate somewhere else. We want to be heard. 'There are strong independents who can bring government back to the people."

The program continued with Bennett asking hard questions and insisting on unequivocal answers. Joe and Jose welcomed that. They framed the term limits program in terms of getting rid of self-obsessed, special interest-driven legislators. That would be the linchpin in returning Congress to its proper role. Call-in questions from viewers, pro and con, brought up other issues including failed healthcare, energy debacles, corporate excesses, and union coups. Amos and Carillo took them on and left no doubt where they stood.

Bennett was asked by one listener how his network could justify providing air time for his guests. His reply was, "I want to hear both sides on the burning issues of the day. Perhaps there are members of the two major parties who want to comment on what these independents have to say. I stand ready to hear them as well."

* * *

In a large suburban home, a group of powerful men watched the TV interview with intensive interest. Throughout the broadcast the comments of Carillo and Amos had invoked verbal outbursts, grunts and harrumphs around the room, even an occasional punctuation of profanity. A call-in question one of them fed to an "interested viewer" was methodically dissected and politely shredded by Jose. The author of the query drained his scotch and turned ashen.

"Those two are slick," Dennis Young said.

"And very dangerous," the scotch drinker grumbled.

As the hour wound down, the Congressional switchboard was flooded with calls. Mister Ashen Face was seething with anger.

He turned to Young and gave him a nod. Then he conveyed a single word to Dennis—"wetback. Young excused himself and left with his cell phone.

"Wetback is on," he instructed.

Chapter 93

The two Joes shook hands and walked toward the TV station's elevator. They agreed the session with Bennett had gone well. Given the viewer audience Bennett usually drew, this appearance could be a plus for them.

"But the downside is obvious," Amos told Jose and expelled a long sigh into the chill air. "Life in the chamber will be tough for both of us. We'll be lucky if most of our 'colleagues' even speak to us."

"I never knew a little snub to discourage you, Chicano," Joe quipped. "Matter of fact, I think you'll enjoy the outrage as much as I will. If the truth hurts. I'd say we managed to chap close to four hundred Congressional backsides today. Want to drop by Bubba's and celebrate with a brew?"

"One round then I have to call it a night," Amos answered. He exited the elevator and walked to his car while Carillo rode up another level.

Jose stepped off seconds later and turned up his coat collar against the stiff wind blowing across the parking tower. *Hope we were level-handed with our pitch,* he thought to himself. *No doubt some of those call-ins were plants, but I was honest with them. They didn't need any more liars with glowing necks.*

He drove out into the busy street, never noticing the car that followed him. And he was not aware that a hooded man waited in a second car a block away.

"Got it," said hooded man. "Don't worry, I never miss." He raised his sniper rifle and peered through itss scope. A black Toyota sedan came into view. The gunman leveled on his target.

Jose Carillo hit his brakes to miss a stray dog. He heard a sharp crack and felt a burning sensation at the back of his neck. As soon as the car came to rest, an unexplained impulse told him to hit the accelerator. Tires screaming, the Toyota lurched forward. An instant later the rear driver side window shattered. Jose pressed his right hand against his neck and came away with blood. He pushed the gas pedal to the floor and sped away, trying to remember the way to the nearest emergency room.

* * *

"Thought you said Jose was coming, Joe." Bubba said as he placed a long neck bottle on the table. "I saw you on the boob tube tonight. You made a convincing pair."

"Thanks, Bubba. Jose is running kind of slow. The station's not far from here."

Joe's cell phone rang and he grabbed it. "Amos here. Oh, damn! Which one? Hang tight, Chicano. I'm on my way."

* * *

Joe ran to his Caddy and scratched away in the direction of Fairfax Hospital with a head full of questions. Emergency room? That's all he said. Car accident? Sudden illness? Him or somebody else?

He wheeled up just past the emergency room entrance, grabbed his car keys and dashed toward the door. An ambulance driver on standby shouted, "You can't park there!"

"Do me a favor," Joe returned. He tossed the keys to the driver and dashed inside.

The drive bent down and picked up the keys, looked at the Cadillac's US Congress license plates, and parked it. Went looking for the driver.

In Emergency Joe accosted the first nurse he saw and asked,

"Congressman Carillo. Where is he?"

"He's down the hall," she said, pointing. "but you can't go . . .

Amos was already past her and homing in on voices behind a green curtain. When he drew aside the drawer he saw four people.

"So how's *your* evening so far, Joe" Jose tossed at him. Jose was sitting upright and shirtless on a bid with a compress on his neck. "Sorry about making you wait. I had an unscheduled stop to make."

Joe looked around at the other three people in the small curtained cubicle. A doctor wrote on a clipboard sheet while a nurse prepared a bandage. The other occupant of the cramped space was a uniformed Fairfax County policeman who rushed over and clamped a firm grip on Joe's arm.

"He's okay, Officer Brown," Jose vouched. "That's one of the good guys." Brown released Joe's arm and stepped back.

"Just what in the devil . . . Joe began before Carillo cut him off with, "Looks like somebody took a pot shot at me, Gringo"

The nurse, an attractive, obviously Hispanic lady, blanched when she heard Jose use that term. Jose grinned and explained, "It's an inside joke, nurse. He's also a Congressman and he's my best friend."

She carefully checked the compress and replaced it with a bandage that was much less obvious The doctor left after giving his patient instructions and a caution to come back right away if he experienced discomfort or nausea. Officer Brown made no move to follow the medical personnel out.

"Brown's been told to stick like he was super glued to me, Joe. Guess he's staying the night at my place."

Joe turned t Brown and said, "Officer, if it's okay with you, I'd like for Mister Carillo to come back to my house. His wife is out of town. He lives in the District but my apartment is in your jurisdiction."

Brown nodded agreement and said. "Give me a minute." He stepped outside to get approval for the change in plans. Joe advised, "My Caddy's outside if I can find it. An ambulance driver has the keys.

A nurse appeared in the cubicle dangling keys. "You mean these? Driver says it's in the second reserved space near the entrance."

"Works for me," Jose said. "Brownie had my car picked up

by the forensics team. They're searching for a couple slugs."

That brings us to the rest of the explanation I've been waiting for, Chicano. And go slow, because I'm confused."

Jose detailed how he'd left the parking lot garage expecting to top off his evening with a quick brew at Bubba's. A stray dog saved him by making him brake.

"Thanks to Fido, a sniper missed by inches taking my head off. I made like Dale Jarrett after that smoking wheels and all. A second shot shattered my window.":

"Who." Why." Amos collected himself and tried again. "

"Did somebody follow us to the station and lie in wait? Why not try to take both of us out?"

"Oh, I have a pretty good idea who's behind this, Joe. And he made a major mistake. It's about to boomerang on him."

"Don't stop now," Joe prompted.

"Trust me, Gringo. You'll know when I turn on him."

Chapter 94

An interesting night continued at Joe's apartment in Fairfax. First a two-man FBI detail appeared at the door and relieved Fairfax Officer Brown.

Jose's Toyota had yielded a high velocity slug that passed through the rear driver side window and imbedded itself in the front passenger seat. The lab had die identified it as coming from a professional rifle of sniper caliber. Once the incident was confirmed as the attempted assassination of a federal official, the Bureau took over. All incoming calls were screened except the one Joe took in his bedroom on the satellite phone.

"Joe, this is Bledsoe. I know Jose is with you and that somebody tried to take him out. In fact, we have the shooter and he's passed on some interesting information."

"How did you get involved so soon?" Joe puzzled.

"Surely you didn't think the founders would let down their guard when you went to Washington. There are more buzzards doing slow circles around that town than anywhere I can think of. George and the others have a small army keeping track."

"The FBI is here, Jim. But with your connections, you probably already know that.

"Hey, what can I say? You two barnburners cut a wide swath but we got you covered. Anyway, the shooter was in our hands less than ten minutes after he took a pop at your pal. We know who the trail leads back to. Is Jose handy?"

"He may be asleep. I'll check."

"Don't bother now. I'll be in touch. Give us some time to get all the details. Call me around 9AM your time."

"Thanks, Jim."

* * *

At nine straight up in the morning, Joe and Jose were at the sat phone contacting Bledsoe.

"Go ahead, Jim We're both here." Joe prompted. "We convinced the agents we needed a quiet breakfast alone."

"Morning, Jose. You are one lucky dude. The kind of ammo this bad boy was flinging at you could have . . . well, just remember to say a little prayer o' thanks tonight."

"Anything new since you talked to Joe," Carillo asked.

"If you ain't awake by now, cowboy, this'll pry your eyes open for sure. My people tracked down the guy that shot at you. He's had an eventful night that set his tongue to waggin'.

"I'm awake. Go ahead."

"Does the name Dennis Young mean anything to you?"

Chapter 95

A bone-chilling winter snowfall covered the ground. On a mountain top an hour's drive from DC, there was movement. A van unloaded eight passengers by a large home. A Range Rover brought Joe and Jose.

Congressman Ryan Bolger lugged his bag into the former bed and breakfast recently restored for meetings the WAKERS needed to hold under wraps.

"Great idea," he said to Congressman Terrell Jenkins and Senator Tom Battle, his erstwhile housemates for the next two nights. "Pick a room, partners."

The remaining attendees flied ion and chose rooms in the big mansion. Then they gathered up in the large parlor downstairs. The snow-covered ground added a touch of isolation to this back-country trek. Important planning decisions demanded the attention of the group before Congress reconvened. The grand plan conceived by four wealthy patriots was, after twenty years, about to become a reality.

Jose Carillo, Joe Amos, Mary Kay Grant, and Delinda Lewis, all existing or about to be members of the US House and Senate, settled into the old house along with five other newly elected members.

Joe instructed the carefully chosen kitchen/wait staff of three. The five-bedroom relic mansion would host the crucial two-day meeting. Final preparations for Stand Up Day and the new legislative session would be finalized here. The new arrivals warmed by the fireplace in the inviting main room.

"Thank goodness," Jose told his companions, "we can stop sneaking around like this once we go public. Never been my nature to be so secretive. I'm more of the 'in your face, take me or leave me' type. Where I grew up you either had attitude or you spent a lot of time licking your wounds."

"Come on, a lovable guy like you?" Mary Kay chuckled. "I know you're scrappy, but I can't imagine you as a ruffian."

I had my moments." Jose flexed his right ear with a fingertip. "I used to tell folks a bear bit this notch out of my ear. Truth is it happened in a knife fight. Unfortunately, the other guy had the only knife. I whacked him with a baseball bat or I might have lost more than that."

"We saw some others showing up down the way as we came in," Delinda said. She glanced over at the table the staff was setting up. "How long before we convene?"

Jose consulted his signature timepiece, an old pocket watch Grandpa Juan brought from Mexico long ago. "Everyone should be here in the next hour. We'll meet in this room and take our meals here. Got four bathrooms. If that's not enough, There's lots of tree cover outside."

Mary Kay and Delinda looked at each other. "I'll be back. Have a chore to take care of before the crowd arrives."

Jose poked, "Don't slip in the snow, Mary" as she disappeared. Delinda blushed a bright red.

* * *

At a few minutes after ten AM Jose went to the head of the table, did a final head count and called the meeting to order.

"Good morning, WAKERS. Our numbers have grown since our last get together. Let me formally introduce the newest members of our group. He went through the list of the four more House members and one new Senator, all of them to be sworn in exactly five days from now.

"Our wait is almost over, friends," Jose continued. "This election cycle was the tipping point. Soon both houses of Congress will feel our presence and the public will be read in on the silent revolution WAKE has waged on their behalf. For the next two days our task is to set the agenda that will help return government to its rightful owners, the voters. Don Shupe wants to say a few words before we go on."

Don, newly reelected to the House from Maryland, swept the room with his gray eyes and let a mischievous grin curl his mouth. "You know I care for each and every one of you, so I apologize for how this may sound. I've read that the US has eight percent of the world's population and seventy percent of its lawyers. My job with WAKE was to find and help groom folks whose main qualifications for office are life experience and common sense. We may even manage to send some of those overdue career lawmakers back to looking for people to sue instead of weighing us down with new laws. It's time we and lots of others took our turn in the battle then went home with a lot better idea of what governing is all about."

For the rest of the day the group reviewed the WAKER agenda. Court rulings had found enzyme lie detector tests to be constitutional and they would proceed in a majority of the states before the next election. That took care of the first WAKER issue. The remaining five were Congressional term limits, judicial term limits, stringently enforced lobbying constraints, real campaign finance reform, and self-imposed cost cutting by Congress.

"We're staring at ambitious goals, fellow WAKERS. But consider how far we've come. And I'd like to add an urgent new item to our list," Joe Amos proposed. "We must press to wipe off the books the most revisionist disasters manufactured since 2009—universal health care as currently framed, cap and trade, government intervention in corporate operation—the abominations forced on us by the so-called 'progressive' crowd. It's time to help our business-oriented President right the ship of state."

* * *

Two long but satisfying days of hard work produced a detailed sequence of coordinated actions over the span of the next eight months. The WAKER legislators came to their feet on the second afternoon and cast a final voice vote to implement the plan.

Jose faced the assembly and announced, "We've had a productive meeting. Now I want you to share a special treat. I deem it a profound honor to present to you the Chairman of Project WAKE, George Adams."

A tall black man with a beaming smile appeared from the hallway. He was large and solid but fit looking. His dark skin presented a pleasant contrast to the curly white hair framing his brow. His smile warmed the room as he strode to Jose's side and pumped his hand. The WAKERS fell silent and awaited the founder's words.

"Today," George began, "I'm seeing a dream fulfilled. Joe Whitley, the man who generated the idea for WAKE, can look down at this gathering and be proud." He extended one hand high above his head, looked up, and came to attention. Then he came to rigid attention and saluted his departed friend. "Thank God we listened to you, Joe W."

He walked to Joe Amos, gave him a hug, and whispered. Turning back to the group he spoke.

"Seems a lifetime since 2000 when Joe Whitley, Hiro Kato, Carlos Estrada and I took an oath to return this country to the representative federalism the Constitution mandated. We gave our project the name WAKE for our last names and agreed that would stand for Wake Up America. In 2001 we launched a national leadership university. Bright young WAKERS started attending the summer classes on the Constitution you've all experienced. Now you number more than 700 and are making your marks in all segments of society including governing. I am so proud of you.

"You've achieved and excelled. WAKE belongs to you. Now it's your turn to set the course. The future is out there. I'm told you have set the schedule for Stand Up Day. I look forward to sharing that moment with you."

Adams took a red baseball cap from his pocket, put it on and walked to Don Shupe. The cap bore the initials DS. I'm your number one fan," George told him

Chapter 96

Jose Carillo and Joe Amos departed the woods and wound toward Route 7. An early sunset had passed and the hills were now shrouded in darkness. The two-day meeting had been a resounding success. The appearance by George Adams just before they left made it even more special.

Now they were the last two to depart the mountain retreat and wind down the country road.

Joe engaged the rented Land Rover's four-wheel drive and picked his way down the curving road now covered with a new snowfall. Visibility was drastically reduced as the snow increased its intensity.

He asked Jose, "Is everything okay, Chicano? Sure you've recovered from that neck wound?"

"I'm fine, Gringo. Just mulling over the past two days. He gingerly touched the scar he'd removed the bandage from when they arrived on site to forestall questions.

Joe steadied the vibrating steering wheel and blurted out, "Those ruts make this thing buck like a rodeo bull." They turned onto the main road down the mountain, but it wasn't much better. Joe relaxed a bit but still had trouble seeing past the snow. "You never did tell me what you intended to do about Denny Young," He told Jose.

"He's small potatoes now," was the answer. "I'll take care of that later."

There was a loud pop and the vehicle swerved to the right. Joe hung on and fought for control. "Bummer", he said. "Got a flat. Hang tight."

They hurtled toward the sheer drop on their right. Joe saw

the trees below and made his decision. He called out, "Wish us luck, Chicano," and spun the wheel. The Rover did a 180, shuddered and slid backward down the road. It gradually settled to a stop near the road's shoulder. Joe sat back and gave a sigh of relief.

"Way too close," he sputtered. Jose hadn't said a word, but his face was nearly as pale as the falling flakes.

The vehicle's rear was implanted into a snow bank that stopped their progress toward the drop. Both of them exited the Rover.

Jose called out, "Flat's on my side in front, Joe."

Joe circled around to look. "That tire is shattered. I believe somebody *shot* it out!" He heard a noise from the woods and peered over as two men emerged. One carried a rifle; the other had a pistol.

"Grab the back of your neck with both hands," the taller man with the handgun ordered. He waved his weapon. "Turn around, bend over the car and don't move a muscle."

Amos mumbled something under his breath and complied. He put his forehead on the icy car hood. Jose stared at the tall man in disbelief. *Does this never end*, he pondered. *Why do they get a kick out of taking turns drawing down on us?*

"You're about to regret being so slow, Carillo," the gunman barked. "I got a bead on your ear hole."

Carillo quickly drew two conclusions. First, these attackers knew exactly who they'd waylaid and two, he was about to be blown away. He grabbed his neck and winced with the pain in his neck.

Someone nearby cried out in pain. Joe tuned his head but Joe resisted the temptation. Then a female voice behind them ordered, "Drop the weapon, buster, or I'll cut you in two!" Both of the WAKERS stayed motionless listening to the rush of sounds but afraid to move.

Then a hand tapped Joe Amos on the shoulder and the same feminine voice said, "Relax, Congressman. The cavalry is here."

They both came out of their crouches. A black clad man who carried a menacing automatic weapon stood twenty feet away. A woman, also in black, was beside them. Joe recognized her as Sally Givens, the security agent who'd collared the terrorist that tried to kidnap him and Emily. One of the two ambushers was on the ground holding his arm and his rifle was in Sally's possession. The other bad guy lay trussed up a few feet away from the Rover.

"I was about to make a dumb remark, Sally, but I'll just say thanks."

"Yeah, mister Amos, I know. We *do* have to stop meeting like this."

"My good luck is holding," Joe said.

"No luck involved," she told him. "Didn't Bledsoe tell you we always have your backs? Now let's see what we can do about slipping on the spare."

Joe leaned over and asked Jose, "By the way, Chicano, what did you mumble at that tall guy?"

"I quoted an old saying we have about the cockroach. Good thing for me he doesn't speak Spanish.

He knew my name, though."

"Question is, how did they track us down? Could there be a rat in our group?" Amos posed. He peered over at Carillo and furrowed his brow. "A WAKER turncoat? Are we compromised?" They both agonized over that possibility while Sally's partner took care of the tire change

They were ready to remount and leave when Sally's cell rang. She listened then broke out in a broad grin.

"Good news. That was the security agent we placed on the kitchen and wait staff. He nabbed our rat. It was one of the two waiters. Caught him making two cell calls before you left the site. One call must have been to the chap that ambushed you. When we tracked the other call down, it was to a Dennis Young. The mole confirmed Young sent orders to tall and skinny over there."

That lifted a terrific weight off the two Joes. As well as the workers had been vetted and kept away from the assembly area during discussions, somehow one ringer had slipped through.

At least they didn't have a dirty insider.

Chapter 97

January second. Tomorrow the new session of Congress would begin. Minority Whip Dennis Young looked up from his desk as his inner office door burst open. "Judy, what . . . but there were two people standing in the doorway.

"I told him I would let you know he was here, Mister Young, but he ignored me."

"I'll close the door, Judy, Jose Carillo told her, "and I'll announce myself." He slammed the big oak door, turned and pointed a finger at the Whip. Young looked like the skittish squirrel trying to cross the road, but he tried to go on offense.

"Who do you think you are, coming in here like a madman?"

Jose noted with some amusement that Denny was so flustered he'd actually picked up an ornamental gavel and raised it in front of him.

"What do you plan to do with that thing before I feed it to you, Denny—rule me out of order?"

"You're mighty brave for somebody on the bottom of the food chain, Jose. I ought to have you barred from the opening. What do you plan to do, sic some of your buddies on me? I believe you have sealed the end of your short but interesting career. My first official act of the new year will be to offer a resolution for your sanctioning."

"Denny, my man, I've taken about all the flak I can tolerate from you and your cohorts. Fire your best shot. I've been threatened by better men than you. My opening shot will be to see you're exposed as the louse that hired a shooter to take me out at the TV station. Then you sent a second ambusher after both of us on the mountain. Your mole gave you up. I'd say conviction of collusion to murder two of your fellow House members should buy you a nice long trip. You can resign now or I'll turn you in. You have three hours to pull the plug. If I don't hear directly from you by then, I'll make my own public statement."

The blood totally drained from Dennis Young's face. His fingers went slack and the gavel tumbled to the floor. He clutched at his heart and slumped into his chair.

"Three hours," he repeated and strode out. "Judy," he flung out, "I believe your boss needs a doctor."

* * *

Three hours later the deadline had not been met. Jose dialed Lon Evans at WDMV TV. "Lon, I have an exclusive for you, but it has to go on the air today. If you can't handle it, tell me now, and the next network on my list gets the story."

Evans asked for details and verification. Jose gave him the gist and said, "If you don't trust me as a source, say it now. He had already stated that they had signed statements from two persons who were in their custody—one of the shooters and a co-conspirator who relayed the order to the other assassin. But Jose did not give Evans the name of the man behind the hits.

Evans thought it over, went over the details again and said, "Give me the details and watch the six o'clock news."

Jose replied, "Dennis Young, the Minority Whip."

There was an audible gasp from Evans.

Copies of the sworn statements were delivered to Evans by Sally Givens. He was convinced. The six o'clock news began with John Evans making an announcement.

"This is an exclusive news flash. I have been handed documentary evidence of a major scandal involving members of the US House of Representatives. We can report that two attempts have been made on the lives of elected Representatives. The signed statements of hired assassins are in our possession as I speak. Both statements incriminate a well-known figure as the instigator who ordered both of the attempts to kill two members of the House.

We are not revealing the name in these statements pending police investigation at their request. I have provided the signed statements to the authorities. We will report further details as they become available."

Across town Jose Carillo and Joe Amos watched history unfolding. The numbing late December cold wrapped its fingers around the row of buildings where the two men sat in Amos's upstairs apartment. The gas log flame in his fireplace warmed them and brought them back from a harrowing experience on a cold mountain.

Jose shook his head and remarked, "Quite a day, Gringo. Old Denny had no idea he was giving us the perfect lead-in to Stand Up Day."

Joe agreed. "We couldn't have written a better script ourselves, Chicano. That ambush was the fright of my life, but it was worth the agony. Get a good night's sleep. Tomorrow promises to be a red-letter day."

Chapter 98

Preparations for the opening session of the 117th Congress were complete. The capital buzzed with excitement and high expectations. A strong possibility existed that this time the voters had finally gotten it right. But it remained to be seen whether the two parties could put aside their differences and expand on the progress the new administration had begun.

Jose Carillo finished breakfast and tried to collect himself, His wife Theresa did her best to bring him back to earth. She had made it back from her trip late and found Jose worn out from the frantic activity of the past week.

He picked up his winter coat and briefcase and downed a last gulp of coffee. Theresa cautioned, “Relax and enjoy the day.”

“Sure. Relax. It’s only the second most important day of my life after our wedding day. And I don ‘t think I was this nervous waiting for you to come down the aisle.”

“A lot of people are depending on you, guapo. This is what you’ve worked for.”

“Years of waiting and millions of dollars spent by three of the finest men I know. Hundreds of WAKERS’ futures in the balance. No pressure.”

“Juano and I will be watching from the Adams house. As big as the moment may be, you’re up to it, Jose. Make us proud.” She kissed him and squeezed his hand.

* * *

Joe Amos had an important chore to tend to before reporting to the House floor. He asked for five minutes of the Speaker’s time. Speaker Carter Dean reluctantly acknowledged his request. Joe went to his office and waited for him to arrive.

Dean entered the outer office with a hasty gait. He was barking out last minutes instructions for the opening to an aide.

"Get in here, Amos and let's get this over with."

When the two of them were alone, Dean had only one question. "Why now? Like I didn't have the weight of the world on my back, you pull a shock like this?"

"Excuse me, Mister Speaker. I'm the one that took the brunt of this situation. Nearly rolled off a mountain!"

Dean collected himself, sat down and said, "Sorry, Joe. The timing just stinks. I have ten minutes to listen then I have to get the opening set."

"That's all I need. We know who tried to take out Jose and me. I can't believe the police would hold that back."

"Well, I don't know—and right now it wouldn't matter. The whole day is about convening the 117th."

Then consider this," Joe insisted. "Dennis Miller is about to be indicted on two counts of conspiracy to commit murder—and I was one of the targets."

The Speaker bolted upright.

"Their Whip did this?" He reached for the phone and summoned his chief staffer who came running.

Dean issued his demand. "Call the sheriff. Tell him if the name of the Congressman responsible for those two shootings is not released to the press, we're gonna . . . you fill he blank."

The House opening ceremony was on tap for 10 AM. Joe kept an ear to the ground.

Thirty minutes before the gavel was due to drop the Fairfax County Sheriff appeared across the TV channels and named Dennis Young, Minority Whip of the House, as a suspect named in attempts on House members' lives. He had been detained at his home.

Joe and Jose watched then headed to the House floor.

Chapter 99

Four hundred thirty-five representatives of the people assembled in the House chamber, hailing each other and glad-handing. They were in their glory basking in the limelight with the cameras rolling.

Forty-five newly elected members, the largest single turnover in decades, found their assigned seats and excitedly surveyed this inner sanctum of government. They had arrived! The old timers settled in at their familiar positions, being sure to pose in regal profile for the public.

But the public faces of this august body belied their true feelings. What the viewing audience did not hear was the shocking news echoing through the chamber. “Denny Young arrested? How far up does this go? How does it affect me?”

The WAKERS scattered throughout the chamber were buoyed by the news. Word had passed from Joe and Jose and from the other attendees at the B&B gathering that it was ‘game on’.

Before today’s opening session was over, the public would realize that a bloodless revolution for Constitutional federalism had arrived.

Stand Up Day was here!

The Clerk of the House called the 117th House session to order. After the chaplain's prayer and the Pledge of Allegiance, the Clerk asked for a roll call. Each member-elect registered his or her presence with an electronic vote.

The Speaker was elected, sworn in and escorted to the dais for the oath of office. Carter Dean, after his reelection as Speaker, administered the oath to all members in the chamber.

Joe and Jose were by this time nervously eyeing each other, wondering at what point the news of Young's plight would cast its shadow. Chatter increased among their fellow members.

The tension increased as all of the routine first-day formalities were adhered to. The party Leaders and Whips were announced and received the oath. Then the Clerk, Sergeant at Arms, Chief Administrative Officer and Chaplain were elected. The Speaker repeatedly gaveled for order as the undertow of off-line conversations became more obvious.

By the time the elected leaders had informed the President Congress was ready for business and rules of the House were adopted and a daily meeting time was established, the two Joes were ready to spring from their seats. But patience was the order after all these years of waiting. Joe Amos made a downward hand gesture to Jose Carillo that silently said 'simmer down.'

When at last all of the formalities had been dutifully observed, Jose rose and sought recognition. The chair acknowledged and he began, "I have a statement from the newly elected members. Request permission to address the chamber."

The Speaker noticeably hesitated but there was no reason Jose should be denied the right to address the house. He stated, "The gentleman from New Mexico is recognized for a period of five minutes."

Jose strode confidently to the podium and started to speak.

"My remarks will be brief. I am speaking on behalf of

the newest members of the new Congress. We have been duly elected to represent our constituents at home and are ready to go to work. But first we owe it to all of you to make known our common goal."

The Speaker reached for his gavel. Before he could swing the instrument, however, Jose faced him and stated, "I will only need three minutes of the time granted to me.

With great pride and hope for the future, I want to introduce the group of Congressmen and women who declare themselves independents for Constitutional federalism. As of this date they reject all allegiance to either political party."

"WAKERS, STAND UP!"

Seated members in nearly every row came to their feet. The reactions of those seated was a collective outcry of shock and anger. Some appeared to be counting heads as they stared in disbelief.

He swept an arm around the chamber. "By my count, a majority no longer exists as of this moment. There are thirty-five declared independents. That leaves exactly 205 Republicans and 200 Democrats. As of today, we are asserting our rights as duly elected legislators. Henceforth, unless the two parties can at last legislate in good faith with each other, no legislation can be passed without our concurrence. We look forward to working to make this body receptive to the wants and needs of the electorate."

With that Jose reclaimed his seat and the room went eerily silent.

* * *

At nearly the same time over in the Senate, Tom Battle made his statement. He recognized three new Senators and himself as independents and declared that the balance in that chamber would now stand at 48 Republicans, 48 Democrats and four Constitutional federalism independents. The days of blood sport in the Senate were history.

Chapter 100

George Adams, Hiro Kato and Carlos Estrada watched a split screen version of the House and Senate proceedings on a studio size television at George's rural Maryland home.

JoAnne Amos, Theresa Carillo and Evaline Adams had joined them. Little Emily, now three years old, had taken to the other ladies quickly and made quite a hit with them. Evaline remarked that Emmy had JoAnne's natural beauty and brains from two brilliant parents. The little one was in the kitchen with Carson and Jenetta working on a celebratory dinner that would welcome Joe and Jose later.

Emily asked if she now had three grandmas. Evaline's reply was that she would be thrilled to have her call her Auntie Evaline.

The group in the TV room intermittently groaned and chortled at the events on the screen that seemed to move at an agonizingly slow pace. George was particularly critical. "Hope the ladies are putting together a great dinner for those two Joes. Reckon they'll have plenty to tell us. Just hope they'll have taste buds left after some of their 'fellow ladies an' gents' drive away their sense o' smell."

Better them than me," Hiro jabbed. "Don't think I could hold my tongue in the midst of that bunch of blowhards. Are they really the best we can find?"

George turned to JoAnne and said, "Your guy must be in his glory today. Glad youze ladies could be wit' us to see it. I wouldn't miss the next hour for the world."

"Emily starts pre-school tomorrow and our house in Bio City will be ready next week," JoAnne told him. "Guess we're part of the DC beltway gang now."

Carlos, in his usual downhome style, put it all in perspective. "You young folks are in charge after today. The three of us plan to ride off crost the prairie an' enjoy a hard-won victory. Never 'magin'd way back in 2000 it'd feel like this. I'm gettin' plumb goose bumpy!"

George pointed toward the screen as Jose walked to the podium. "Sic 'em, Joe Four!"

"What's that about?" Hiro asked him.

"Did you ever stop to think how many Joes have been part of WAKE? Joe Whitley's idea, Joe Amos and JoAnne here as our superstars. Hell, wouldn't su'prise me if 'Joe' Carillo became our first Hispanic President."

ABOUT THE AUTHOR

Don Otey has been writing novels since 2004. He grew up in Virginia and was a career Air Force officer in the field of communications-electronics. He earned his first degree in Agriculture at Virginia Tech and now also holds a degree in Electrical Engineering and an MBA in Business Management. He served tours in Greenland, Hawaii and at various stateside bases. He was later an engineer and manager in the high-tech industry. Don and his wife now live in King George County, Virginia.